THE FORGOTTEN QUEEN

THE FORGOTTEN QUEEN

HALEY ELIZABETH GARWOOD

1998
THE WRITERS BLOCK
BRUCETON MILLS, WEST VIRGINIA

iv

THE FORGOTTEN QUEEN

The Writers Block/published by arrangement with the author

First Printing, March 1998

Cover concept by Mel Graham

Cover art by Tell Hicks

ISBN: 0-9659721-9-4
LCCN: 97-61552

THE WRITERS BLOCK
The Writers Block books are published by The Writers Block, Laurel Run, Route One, Box 254, Bruceton Mills, WV 26525-9748
Designed by Pioneer Press of WV, Inc., Terra Alta, WV

Publisher's Cataloging-in-Publication
(Provided by Quality Books, Inc.)

Garwood, Haley Elizabeth
    The forgotten queen / Haley Elizabeth Garwood. — 1st ed.
    p. cm.
    Preassigned LCCN: 97-61552
    ISBN: 0-9659721-9-4

    1. Matilda, Empress, consort of Henry V, Holy Roman Emperor, 1102-1167. 2. Princesses—Great Britain—Biography. 3. Great Britain—History—Henry I, 1100-1135. 4. Great Britain—History—Stephen, 1135-1154. 5. Great Britain—History—Henry II, 1154-1189. 6. Civilization, Medieval—12th century. I. Title.

DA198.6.G37 1998   942.02'4'092 [B]
                                QBI97-41247

Printed in the United States of America
10 9 8 7 6 5 4 3 2 1

DEDICATED TO

Charles, my husband,
for his fervent support

and

A. Haley Thomas, my mother,
a modern woman warrior

and

my family
for their faith in the novel.

ACKNOWLEDGMENTS

No author works alone, even though it seems lonely in the late hours. The first person I would like to thank is my mother, A. Haley Thomas, who taught me perseverance, strength, honesty, and humor.

I would like to thank my youngest son, David, who took time from his archaeological dig in England to haunt the London bookstores. He brought back invaluable information about Empress Matilda and the 12th century that gave the novel depth.

I want to thank my husband, Charles, who has been not only financially supportive, but had a belief in this project. I am lucky to have him beside me.

My brother-in-law, Ralph, was always at the other end of the telephone with a clever quip to keep me going when I needed it the most.

Thanks to Terry for his help with the computer, Paul for his enthusiasm and artistic advice, and Ellen who has always believed Matilda's story and encouraged me from the beginning.

The Cervilla clan was unequaled in their support through their marketing expertise, but mostly their emotional support is appreciated. They are a family of strong women who have made their mark on the world. Their influence has permeated my life.

Thanks to Mel Graham for cheerfully helping with the research, the map, and for talking me through the dark days.

Thanks to Trinette who edited the manuscript, dragged me kicking and screaming through the rewrites, and gave me advice about the early medieval period.

Without the encouragement of my agent, Cynthia Sterling of the Lee Shore Agency, I would have given up years ago. Thank you.

Lynda and Rich Hopkins of Pioneer Press deserve a huge thank you for their dedication to this project and their patience with the author.

Lastly, I cannot forget the hours that Catherine Cometti took from her own grueling writing schedule to read the manuscript and offer suggestions as well as moral support.

ABOUT
THE FORGOTTEN QUEEN

A chance remark by a friend of mine, Mel Graham, sent me on a trail for information about the heroine, Empress Matilda. It was like searching for a missing person because Empress Matilda was often mentioned in passing or as a footnote to history. However, she had no story of her own.

The more I discovered about Matilda, the more impressed I was by her accomplishments. She was an Empress by the age of twelve and a judge for the courts by the age of fifteen. She led the last land invasion of England on September 30, 1139, to reclaim the throne that was hers by birthright.

This remarkable woman has been forgotten by historians. It is my wish to write Empress Matilda back into history.

ABOUT THE AUTHOR

Haley Elizabeth Garwood was born in Lafayette, Indiana. She graduated from Purdue University with a degree in journalism/creative writing. After she moved to a farm in West Virginia, she received a master's degree in theatre and a doctorate in education from West Virginia University. She taught special education before becoming a high school principal.

Ms. Garwood's goal is to write women back into history with her Warrior Queen Series.

MAIN CHARACTERS

Empress Matilda, daughter of King Henry I of England, grand-daughter of William the Conqueror.

Adelicia, Matilda's step-mother, wife to King Henry I of England.

King Henry I, king of England and Normandy.

Stephen de Blois (King Stephen), nephew to King Henry I.

Maithilde, wife to Stephen de Blois.

Ella, lady-in-waiting and friend to Matilda.

Brian fitzCount, lifelong supporter and friend to Matilda.

Robert, Earl of Gloucester, King Henry's illegitimate son and half-brother to Matilda.

King David of Scotland, maternal uncle to Matilda.

Geoffrey, Count of Anjou, Matilda's second husband.

William of Ypes of Flanders, bastard son of a countess. Head of Stephen's army.

Roger, Bishop of Salisbury, regent to King Henry I.

Young Prince Henry known as Count of Anjou, Henry fitzEmpress, later Henry II of England.

Henry, Bishop of Winchester, brother to Stephen, cousin to Matilda.

Miles of Gloucester, constable to Henry I and supporter of Matilda.

Count John of Ludgershall, supporter of Matilda.

John Fitz Gilbert le Marechal, marshall of horses for King Henry I and a supporter of Matilda.

William, Count de Albini, Adelicia's second husband and a supporter of Matilda.

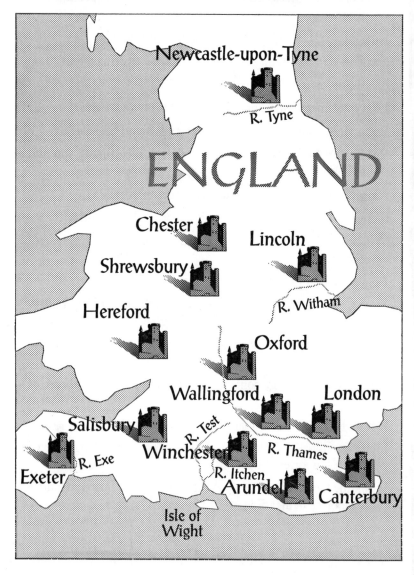

Maps Of Matilda's World

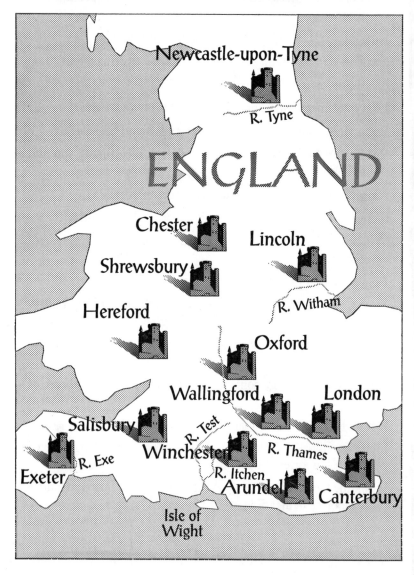

Newcastle-upon-Tyne

R. Tyne

ENGLAND

Chester

Lincoln

Shrewsbury

Hereford

R. Witham

Oxford

Wallingford

London

Salisbury

R. Test

Winchester

R. Thames

R. Exe

R. Itchen

Exeter

Arundel

Canterbury

Isle of Wight

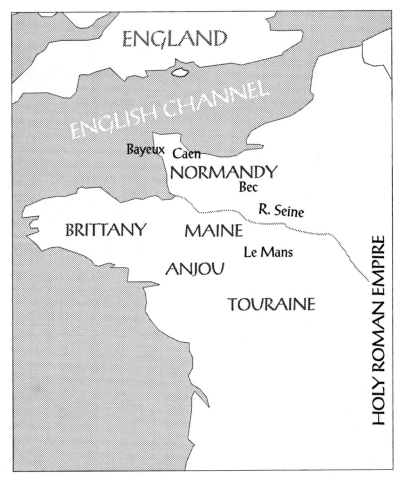

ENGLAND

ENGLISH CHANNEL

Bayeux Caen
NORMANDY
Bec

R. Seine

BRITTANY   MAINE

Le Mans

ANJOU

TOURAINE

HOLY ROMAN EMPIRE

Western Europe
in the 12th Century

English

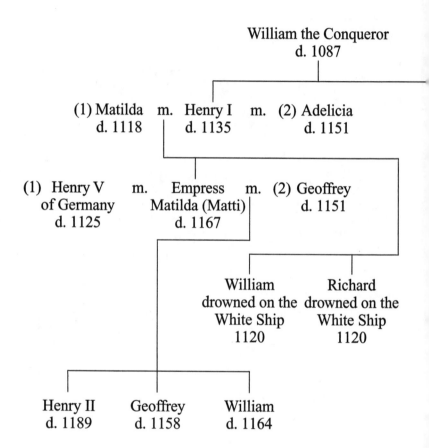

William the Conqueror
d. 1087

(1) Matilda   m.   Henry I   m.   (2) Adelicia
    d. 1118   d. 1135   d. 1151

(1) Henry V   m.   Empress   m.   (2) Geoffrey
of Germany   Matilda (Matti)   d. 1151
  d. 1125   d. 1167

William   Richard
drowned on the   drowned on the
White Ship   White Ship
  1120   1120

Henry II   Geoffrey   William
d. 1189   d. 1158   d. 1164

Royal Family

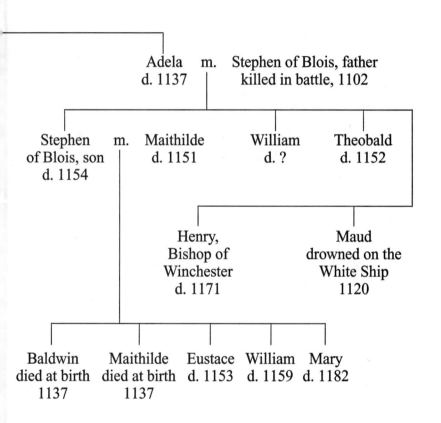

CHAPTER
I

ARRY THAT BARBARIAN! Has my father totally lost his senses? I am Matilda, daughter of that same Henry I, King of England, granddaughter of William the Conqueror, empress of most of the civilized world, and princess of this graceless island." She spun around. Her dark hair whipped across her face, and she stared at her step-mother. "I am not going to marry that . . . that childish half-wit who thinks nothing of hunting from dawn to dusk."

Matilda kicked a small stool across the floor where it hit the damp, stone wall with a cracking sound. Its carved wooden legs were left in splinters beneath the brocaded seat.

"Matilda, compose yourself. You are not behaving as an empress." Adelicia's voice was soothing in contrast with Matilda's ranting. The effect was an instant calming.

Matilda looked away from her step-mother because she knew that Adelicia was right, as usual. Matilda sat on a stool next to the fireplace, holding her back straight and her chin tilted upwards. She had been trained to be an empress from the day she had been betrothed to Henry V at the age of seven. Matilda liked being an empress. She believed it was ordained by God that she had been chosen to fulfill the role of wife to the Holy Roman Emperor, but since his death, she felt unsettled like a country without a king. Matilda had seen the sky the night before, and it had been without stars or moon. The sky had seemed to hold no pattern. It had been empty like she was now.

Matilda stared at her step-mother; her bright blue eyes snapped lightning. "It is not fair that my father thinks I can be married again at my age. I am far too old."

Adelicia's laughter was gentle, but Matilda winced. "Do not tease me. I am too old to be wed and bed. The year is 1128. I have seen twenty-four summers, and I am in the autumn of my life." Matilda kicked a piece of the broken stool and sent it flying into the fireplace. She watched the flames wrap around the wood changing it from an ornately carved leg to ashes. The only sounds in the apartment were the flames as they chewed the leg of the stool. Matilda imagined the flames were wolves and the leg was the boy Count of Anjou.

Adelicia leaned forward and peered at the tiny stitches she had placed on the silken material. "We are near to each other in age. Believe me, neither of us is too old to be wed." Adelicia's honey-colored hair rippled as it slid from beneath her cowl. "Do you trust me, Matilda?" She continued stitching.

"With my life, Adelicia. You know that." Matilda smiled as Adelicia swiped at the strand of hair from habit, and tried to contain it beneath her cowl. It gave Matilda a sense of security to see the familiar movement. She studied the queen. Adelicia had the deep brown eyes of a doe, which was fitting Matilda decided, for she was quiet, loving, and trusting. Sometimes Matilda felt her step-mother was too trusting and too loving.

Adelicia could be seen every Sunday after Mass walking through the poor section of town giving out coins to the destitute who crowded around her. Matilda shivered at the picture forever etched in her mind of the seemingly hundreds of dirty hands reaching, grabbing, clawing. The stench of unwashed people that had assaulted her the time she had mistakenly accompanied Adelicia from the cathedral was unforgettable. Matilda knew that it would be impossible for her to go with her step-mother again.

She admired Adelicia for her courage, while at the same time she thought the queen demented. The people adored Adelicia. At every public outing, the people chanted Adelicia's name much the same as they did the saints' names on their days. Matilda gave away large sums of money during the year to the poor, but she did it through a trusted servant. She gave money to the poor out of a sense of duty, but Adelicia gave out of sense of love. Matilda wished she could be as charitable.

Adelicia stopped sewing, and cutting a strand of thread with her teeth, glanced at Matilda. "Do you love your father as your father and as your king?"

"With all my heart."

"Then understand that we trust and love you, too. Your father and I would never do anything to harm you. Do you know that?"

"Yes, I do."

"Please believe that this marriage is not only good for you but for England as well. Your father explained it to me."

Matilda closed her eyes to shut out the calm demeanor of the queen. She felt her lower lip protrude, unbidden, and it dredged up memories of herself as a small child trying to get her way with her nurse. Matilda forced her eyes open and her lower lip in place. She could not act the child now. "Geoffrey of Anjou is only a boy. He is fourteen years old."

"He is an heir to extensive lands. Some day he will be as powerful as is his father. We need to form a partnership. It is better to be an ally than to be an enemy." Adelicia carefully knotted a silken thread and put her stitching aside.

"It is not fair that I have to marry a mere count! He and his father may have power, but they are my inferiors in so many ways. Why, his father is not much more than a barbarian from the forests of Europe. I am not going to give up my widow-hood for marriage. I realize that no one can live up to my expectations. I am accustomed to being an empress." Matilda looked at her step-mother to see if she had shocked her yet. She sighed. She had not.

Adelicia smiled and deftly threaded another needle with maroon thread. "Can you not forget your first husband?"

Matilda scuffed her suede shoe across the reeds. The crackling sound irritated her. "No, I can not. The emperor was exciting. In fact, he included me in everything he did. I was his representative when we went to Rome." Matilda twisted the ends of her girdle around her finger. "I was only fifteen when I sat in judgment in the domestic court. It was exhilarating to know that my decisions would be followed as law." She stood and paced back and forth in front of the fireplace. "It was an awesome responsibility, too, and I took it very seriously. When he died . . ." Her voice caught and she cleared her throat. "I was at his bedside when he died. One of his last acts was to place the royal insignia in my hands. His people begged me to stay in Germany, but . . ." Matilda waved her hand to dismiss the sad thoughts. She growled, "Intrigues! Always intrigues when a head of state dies."

She stopped pacing and watched her step-mother's delicate hand movements. It calmed her. "I think I did well. My husband complimented me on my judgment, and I still remember the pleased look in his eyes. He gave me everything I wanted. I had the best dressmakers, the most expensive materials, and the most beautiful gems." She held out her hand and wriggled her fingers. A blood-red jewel the size of a pebble rested on Matilda's slender finger. She studied the ring in the daylight that filtered through the window in the thick wall.

Oddly-shaped panes of clear glass were interspersed with bits of colored glass. Matilda knew that Adelicia had made certain there was at least one apartment at Cotton-Hall with colorful windows to block Westminster's grey winters. She had told Matilda that she loved the hues that streamed through. They matched her embroidery.

"May I ask how long you intend to stay with me?" Adelicia asked.

"As long as you will allow me." Matilda returned to the stool by the fireplace and sat. She reached down and massaged her foot. The pacing across the reeds had made it sore. She wished her shoemaker would invent sturdier soles for her slippers.

Adelicia studied her step-daughter. "I have always told you that my apartments are open to you. I have always loved you as a daughter, but I also love you as a friend. I am curious as to why you have decided to go into seclusion."

"I had to get away from my father and his matchmaking." Matilda tucked her foot under her kirtle. She wrinkled her nose. "I do not even want to think about marrying that silly young count. He is not even old enough to make a good lover." Matilda smiled at the shocked look she finally got from her step-mother.

"Really, dear. Your father has England's welfare foremost in his mind. He has to worry not only about these current years, but about generations to come. It is an awesome task."

"He is a great king, is he not?" Matilda picked up a corner of blue silk from Adelicia's lap. It felt as light as a spider's web. "I do not understand how you have the patience to make all those tiny stitches. You are an artist."

"Oh, Matilda." Adelicia shook her head in denial, but smiled. "If you must know, I am making a new kirtle for you. I want you to have something special from me." She spread the gown across her knees so that Matilda could see it. "You are so slender that I will probably have to take it in. See how the color changes within the folds? It should flow about you gracefully as you move."

"Are you trying to placate me?"

"Certainly not. I just like to do things for you. You are the child I may never have," Adelicia said.

Matilda leaned forward to look closer at Adelicia. Were there tears in her eyes? She hoped not. "You are hardly too old to have children. You told me that yourself just a moment ago. You look young enough to have dozens of children." Matilda was surprised to see red spots appear on Adelicia's cheeks.

"Your father and I have been married too long to count on an heir for him. It would be so much easier for you if I were to have a son to replace his son who drowned." Adelicia bent her head and let her hair fall forward. This time she did not try to put her hair back into place.

Matilda watched a tear slip down Adelicia's cheek. It made her even more beautiful, if that were possible. The tears always came when there was talk of unborn children. Unborn or born. Children had a way of making women cry. Matilda thought of her mother's tears when her twin brother had died. The pain her mother had felt affected Matilda. She had not shed tears for her brother, but had for her mother. His drowning on the White Ship had filled Matilda with more concern for England's future than remorse for a lost twin. She had tried to feel sadness for Prince William, but other than time spent in the womb together, they had hardly been in the same place. After their infancy, the twins, both black haired, intelligent and tenacious, Matilda remembered, had been reared differently. Prince William was to have been the next King of England. Matilda was to be the bond between differing political factions. She hated the thought of being the thread instead of the cloth.

Matilda got up from the stool and moved to the stained-glass window. She peered out through a yellow piece of glass, making sunshine of a gloomy December day. "If it were not for you, dear step-mother, I might not have done as well here. This country is much more barbaric than that to which I have become accustomed. The people in the courts of France and Germany know how to respect royalty. Here my own father entered and left the great hall with no more ceremony than a commoner. These people are unfamiliar with what is correct. England's lords and ladies are so peculiar to me, Adelicia. You were gracious to take time to teach me the ways of the English," Matilda said.

"I did what was needed to help you."

"You are much too modest. I was lost. You showed me tolerance."

"I have often wondered about your childhood," Adelicia said. "Was it difficult to be taken from your family and sent away to Germany as the betrothed of the Emperor?"

"I have memories of my mother telling me that I was destined for greatness and that meant sacrifices. I did not understand. I still do not, and I feel I have not achieved whatever I am supposed to." Matilda blew on the window, her breath making a light frost on the glass. She blew again to obliterate the world.

"That is why it is important for you to listen to your father. He understands that the future of England rests on your shoulders. I think your greatness will come in a way neither you nor anyone has imagined." Adelicia folded the kirtle aside and watched Matilda. "Please listen to your father and king, Matilda. He names your destiny."

"I have always been a pawn in the game of ruling England. In my second year, I was sent to the Abbey of Wilton to be educated. Although I did see Mother often, I hardly ever saw Father. The most difficult thing for me was leaving the abbey for Germany. I was not yet in my eighth year." Matilda looked out through a piece of clear glass blemished with bubbles. Snow was swirling down from the grey sky. "I went to a country completely different from that to which I had been accustomed. I could not even understand the language. I did not know the term 'betrothed.' I only knew that I missed my mother."

"You must have been very lonely," Adelicia said. "How did you ever do it?"

"I do not remember." Matilda pushed away the vision of a lonely little girl and turned toward Adelicia. "Let us not talk of the past."

"All right. Then, what shall we discuss? The handsome young men of your father's court?"

"You are teasing me." Matilda smiled at her step-mother.

There were shouts from the courtyard below, and Matilda heard the creaking of the heavy wooden gates being opened. She turned quickly and looked through the clear pane of glass again, trying to make sense of the distorted shapes in drab colors moving haphazardly about. Impatiently, Matilda pulled down on the latch and opened the window a crack. The snowflakes were sucked through the window and stuck to her eyelashes and hair as she leaned out. The wind swirled around the room and sent ashes dancing across the stone hearth. Matilda's intake of breath brought Adelicia to the window.

"It is the king!" Adelicia said. "Hurry, we must receive him."

"You receive him as his wife and his subject. I choose not to receive him at all," Matilda sniffed.

"You can not do that! You must accept him as your king, even if not your father." Adelicia tugged on her step-daughter's sleeve. "You have the same obstinate set to your jaw that I have seen so often in your father."

"Really?" Matilda chuckled.

Adelicia sighed. "He has been gone for many weeks, Matilda. He had to speak to the barons in the northern parts . . . for your sake, I might add."

"For my sake?" Matilda asked.

"I am not supposed to say anything. You will find out about your father's plan soon enough. I must go. Will you come with me?"

"No." Matilda closed the window and leaned against it. She felt the muscles in her jaw tighten as she clenched her teeth together. She looked down at Adelicia, who was shorter by half a head, and folded her arms. "No," Matilda said again. She enjoyed the perplexed look she had elicited from Adelicia.

"Can you not pretend to play the dutiful daughter?"

Matilda picked at the folds of her pale gold kirtle, adjusting them to fit evenly. She pulled at the girdle to straighten it and moaned inwardly. She always had trouble keeping herself neat and ladylike. Her untidiness made her feel like a wanton child. "I will not meet with my father. Tell him I am angry."

Adelicia sighed. "Very well. Your father will not be pleased."

Matilda adjusted the sleeve of her chemise. The blue color reminded her of the summer sky near the time of her birth date. "Good."

"Matilda!"

"Go and see him. I know you are anxious." She watched Adelicia turn and almost run from the apartment. "You will need your fur, Adelicia." Matilda laughed at her retreating step-mother. Mayhap Adelicia would not need her cape after all. Her cheeks were flushed with excitement.

Matilda turned, pulled open the window, and amused herself with the scene in the courtyard below. Horses and people were milling about. The grooms were sweeping out the stables and putting new hay in the mangers. Excitement made the horses dance about the grooms and paw at the hunting dogs. Matilda shook her head. "Now who let loose the dogs? We have no need to hunt, yet." She leaned further out the window, ignoring the blowing snow that swept past her and into the room. The blacksmith continued hammering, heedless of the activity going on around him, the steady pounding of metal against metal creating a calm rhythm of its own.

Matilda saw that the man was untouched by the cold and snow. His thick arms glistened with sweat. His leather apron deflected the sparks that flew about him, but Matilda noticed that even when a spark hit him on the face, he did not seem to feel it.

Across the courtyard and away from the ashes, the laundress and her apprentice, a scrawny child with nondescript hair and features, held a thick stick in her thin hands and pounded the linens in a trough. The laundress reached into the hot water with another stick and pulled out a table cloth. Matilda liked the contrast of light colored material against the dark water of wood ashes and caustic soda. She watched the laundress as she held the cloth out of the water to drip, then slung it expertly into a second trough to rinse.

It was easy to find her father, the king. He was the tallest, and sat straightest on his black stallion, the only horse that was not skittish. The snow whirled around him, as if gathering strength from its king. King Henry's black hair whipped around the edges of his fur wrap. Snow was clinging to his hair in spite of the wind, making it look salt and pepper.

Matilda watched her father smile as Adelicia ran toward him. He scooped her up effortlessly with one arm, kissed her, then deposited her back on the earth. Matilda could imagine her gentle step-mother's fragile laughter that would cover embarrassment.

Her father looked around, then spoke to Adelicia. When Adelicia shook her head, Matilda closed the rainbow-colored window. She crossed the room and sat by the fireplace and held out her hands toward the golden flames. Until that moment, she had not realized that she was chilly. Matilda watched the wood change to flames and ashes while she waited.

Her father would be arriving soon. She wanted to see him and yet she dreaded the argument that was certain to follow. They argued often. He was so stubborn.

The barking of dogs accompanied the tramping of feet up the stone steps. When the heavy timber door was pulled open, Matilda quickly stood and dipped low in a graceful curtsy to acknowledge her king.

"You may arise, my daughter." King Henry's voice reverberated off the stone walls, not softened by the many tapestries that hung around the room. It was the voice of a man used to hunting and to giving orders. Matilda stood and waited for her father to speak again, her gaze steady. She thought him to be the most handsome man in all England. His brown tunic came to his knees. Above his leather boots, strips of hide, darkened from use, criss-crossed his legs to hold the woolen leggings in place. The wrappings did not hide the strong legs of the warrior.

King Henry threw his fur cloak across a stool. "Have you and Adelicia decided to start a new style in lady's hair? Neither of you has it done in braids as is customary."

Matilda laughed. "It is so like you to know exactly what to say to amuse me. How can I remain angry when you do that to me?"

"Now, there is my darling! Come here, you stubborn daughter. Embrace me before we start our fight." King Henry held out his arms and Matilda ran into them. She loved the strength of him, the outdoor smell of him, and the rough feel of his tunic against her cheek. She buried her head into his strong chest, aware of the odor of the black stallion. The memories of her father always flashed through her mind like lightning whenever she smelled the fragrances of hay and horse. Matilda turned her ear to his chest and listened, a habit she had kept from childhood. She could hear his heartbeat. As long as it did, England would be safe.

Henry held her close. He cleared his throat, breaking the silence. "As your father I have loved you as much as I dared given the terrible survival rate of offspring. As England's king, I have plans for you as my only legitimate heir. I have prayed to God that you would continue to live in health."

"Father, your words are pretty and wind about my heart like ivy, but I can not agree to your latest scheme for me." Matilda pulled away from her father and moved back to the fireplace. She stood as straight as she could, trying to diminish the difference in height between her and her father. "I will not marry that low-born and low-bred count."

"Matilda, he is, from all reports, quite handsome." Henry said. "You have the same inflexible carriage of your shoulders that was your mother's. You remind me of her, for whom you were named."

"Do I?" Matilda smiled, for she knew it was a compliment.

King Henry ran his fingers through his hair. "Do you suppose the name foreordained your personality, or are you the mixture of your parents' two souls?" Henry frowned. "Ah, well, let the priests worry about that part. I have another problem. I have thought, briefly, about ordering you, as your king, but just as quickly decided I could not break the tenuous thread of our future with an outright disagreement. Matti, will you listen to me?"

Matilda winced. Why had he used the pet name for her she had not thought of since she had been a tiny girl? He had no way of knowing that her heart twisted at the memory of a parting long ago when he had waved and called to her as her ship sailed into the channel. What had he said to the child that had left her home? She could not remember. The silence became as viscid as the stones that formed the walls of the room. It threatened to separate father and daughter, king and subject.

When at last Matilda spoke, she saw that the king was visibly relieved. "I want to remain Empress, if only as a widow."

"You have a false idea of the importance of the title without the Emperor. It is far better to be the Countess of Anjou to a living count than empress to a dead man," her father said.

"It is far better to be the daughter of King Henry the First of England than wife to a boy who is still playing boy games." Matilda turned toward the fireplace, hoping she would irritate her father by her rudeness. "How long must I be a pawn to be played across the squares on a game board? Is it a game with you? Do men and kings never quit playing childhood games?" Matilda felt the heat from the immense fireplace burn her cheeks. She only felt the imitation fever on one side of her body, and she was conscious of the cold draft of air that crept into the apartment and chilled her back. She felt the air stir about her as her father moved toward her. She would not turn around to face him, and she sensed that he stopped.

"Matilda, as King of England, I need your help. Without powerful allies, I can never hope to secure my succession. It has been a problem ever since William died."

Matilda heard the snag in her father's voice before he covered it with a cough.

"Oh, my poor father. For whom do you weep? For England, or the son who will not be king?"

He reached out to touch her, but she was too far away. "I can not separate my sorrows, my daughter. If I weep for my son, I weep for England, but I smile for you."

She watched from the corner of her eye as her father moved toward her, but his feet seemed leaden. He stopped behind her, letting his arms drop to his side.

"Father, do you toy with my emotions?" Her voice was soft, but her back was as straight as the castle walls, her resolve just as formidable.

"I can place you in a position higher than a mere empress." He whispered, as one conspirator to another.

It was Matilda's turn to flinch. He knew her weakness, for it was his own. She turned her head toward him, but was unwilling to look at her king.

"You could become the most famous woman in our history. Mayhap more so than Boadicea, whose fame lives on in our stories."

"She was a queen who led her people in battle." Matilda looked at her father. "Are we going into battle? Do you need a female warrior?"

"I am strong enough and still able to lead my men into battle, but someday I will die. Where will England go with no male heir?" King Henry asked.

"I do not know."

"I can not let anyone other than the flesh of my loins rule England. I have mixed too much of my blood with the earth of England to give it up. I have a plan for the future; England's and yours."

The crackling of the logs in the fireplace was the only sound Matilda heard inside the room. She kept that silence. She felt as if she were on the edge of a deep woods with no path to follow through to the other side. She hoped her father did not intend to push her into the woods with an inappropriate marriage.

"Mayhap I ask too much of you," King Henry said.

"How do you ask too much of me? Most of the time, you do not bother to ask anything; you just order me. I know what you are doing. You have made a decision about me, again for the good of England, and I am the one who will have to suffer for it. You hope I will not notice the suffering if you involve me in the scheme to gain whatever it is you are trying to gain. I am certain that you told Adelicia to let me know that you were in the north on my behalf."

Matilda folded her arms and turned her back to her father. "You want me to think that you do this for me, but I know you plan for England. I am like the falcon who thinks he flies free, but has been trained to be controlled. I can no longer be fooled into thinking I am actually in control. That worked when I was a child, but I have been grown for some time, and I have been in control over men and their valuables, their very lives. Do not treat me as a mere woman. I have taken on the trappings of a man."

Matilda moved away from the fireplace toward the window. She put a slender finger on the sun-colored glass. It was cold to the touch. She scratched at the ice that had formed on the flower design, and waited for her father to speak. She would make him sorry if he made her marry that boy.

She had scraped ice from the roses and daisies and the green glass with a well-manicured nail before her father broke the silence.

"I am proud of all you have done. You have been more than a daughter to me. You have made me proud of you as a natural leader. That is why I want to talk with you."

"I am listening." Matilda stared through the bubbled and wrinkled clear glass to the court yard below and watched two sleek-haired dogs fight over an old animal skin. The younger dog was mud colored or muddy, Matilda could not tell which. The other dog was black with a white blaze and a long tail that ended in a point. Neither dog was particularly handsome, but Matilda liked them both. They were constant companions to one another and to her whenever she was outside.

The younger dog had the strength to win the tug-of-war, but the older dog knew the strategies and soon had dragged the skin to a corner.

"If you marry whomever I choose for you, then I will make you King of England and all its holdings."

Matilda whirled around, her black hair spinning from the force of the turn. The light through the window high-lighted the wisps of hair that would not conform to the new style. Her eyes were wide with shock. In her mind she quickly balanced the hated idea of marriage to a mere count with the possibility of ruling England. England was provincial, to be sure, but it was powerful and wealthy.

"How would you do that?" she asked.

"I am king."

"That is not enough. You have to have power and friends who will do your bidding." Matilda looked carefully at her father for signs of jesting.

"I have many friends who will do my bidding."

"You are planning the unthinkable," Matilda said.

"I am planning a secure future for my beloved England. I have already talked with your uncle, King David of Scotland, and he believes in you." King Henry watched his daughter's face closely.

Matilda pursed her lips, a habit she had when deep in thought and when in a tug-of-war with her father's will. "King David is not enough support. I need support closer to London."

King Henry threw back his head and laughed. "You are ever the manipulator, the politician. You are truly your father's daughter."

"I do not like it when you think you have won something from me." Matilda felt her heart beat faster. Now she felt she was in the middle of that woods with no path. She knew that her father had her trapped. To be King of England would be worth the sacrifice in marriage. It would only be a marriage of convenience anyway. She was strong enough to control one boy. After all, her father believed she could control his kingdom.

"My statement still stands. I need more support than my dearest Uncle David can give to me, so who else is there?"

"Your half-brother, Robert of Gloucester, your cousin Stephen, and, of course, the Church. The Archbishop of Canterbury, William, has agreed to support you. It will all be done publicly during Christmas court."

"Do you think Stephen's wife will allow him to give up his claim to the crown to support me? She is far too ambitious," Matilda said.

"I wonder if it is in the name," King Henry said.

"The name?"

"Stephen's wife and you share both the name and aspirations for control of England." King Henry looked at his daughter, but then let the philosophical thoughts give way to more practical ones. "I do not think she will give you much trouble."

"Do not underestimate the woman who bears my name," Matilda said. "She has a strong will and no fear. She can be difficult. I wish you had not arranged that particular match."

"I had thought to give Stephen some backbone from his rib bone," King Henry said.

"Father, this is no jesting matter."

"Stephen is my favorite nephew, son of my strong-willed sister, but he inherited much of his father's propensity for making poor decisions. I chose his wife to help him." King Henry frowned. "I hope I did not choose too well."

Matilda became bored discussing her cousin's wife, a woman that she remembered as being perpetually cross. She shifted to a subject more interesting to her. "Your scheme for making me a female king is tenuous, at best. Even with the barons and the Church behind you, if Stephen chooses to oppose me, it will be difficult for me to raise an army."

"I will take care of that."

"You will be dead."

The king physically recoiled from the thought. "Death has always been a noxious intrusion into my life, wrenching cavities in my plans. I have dreaded the thought of my own death even though it means being reunited with my sons and your mother. They were the radiance that guided my life through the ebony hours of acquiring this kingdom." The king sighed. "Yes, I will be dead. So, that is why I must plot and plan now, while I am still here to help you. It has been planned that at the forthcoming Christmas Feast, in the great hall at this self-same castle, we will ask the barons and bishops publicly to support me in my bid to have you declared the first female King of England."

"It is an intriguing thought, and one that must be planned to the last detail. The timing is important, and the atmosphere. We must have the best feast ever. The wine and ale should be very fine. I will have to appear capable, but not overpowering. I have to be more leader than woman, but not demanding." She felt excitement building within her. There was nothing she could not do. She knew she was more capable than most men.

Matilda raised one eyebrow, cocked her head, and looked at her father. "I will imitate King Henry and become a King Matilda." She held out her arm. "Ale!" she bellowed. "Give me some ale to put some life into these tired, old bones!"

King Henry looked at Matilda in disbelief, then laughed with an explosive sound that bounced off the stone walls. "Then you agree with my scheme, and you will marry Geoffrey of Anjou."

"No." Matilda did not wish to give in easily to her father's demands and his plans.

His laughter stopped abruptly. "What did you say?"

"No."

"You are more stubborn than your mother ever was. Why do you do that?" King Henry asked.

"Because I am granddaughter to William the Conqueror, daughter to King Henry I of England, and I am Empress Matilda. I do not wish to change."

"I thought you understood the political ramifications of this marriage I have arranged for you. You need an army. You need lands. Geoffrey of Anjou will have both."

"You said you could get me armies," Matilda said.

King Henry rolled his eyes toward the ceiling. "You need a stronger bond than just promises given at a Christmas Feast. You need the assurance that marriage will provide. You need strength behind you so that you can move forward and gather more strength."

"Do I have to live with him?"

"Certainly. I need a grandson to strengthen the ties that bind this country together."

"Ha! You will not get a grandson from a child. You should have me marry a man if you want grandchildren."

"I can wait. I am not dead yet."

"When will this illustrious wedding take place?"

King Henry grinned. "You agree to marry the count?"

Matilda reached up and held onto the mantle-piece with one hand to steady herself. She was about to embark down a path that had not been taken before. She tapped her fingers against the lime-stone mantel-piece. "No, I do not agree to marriage with the count, but I will have to do it anyway. Just give this child some time to grow up. I do not want to play mother to his crying and mewling."

Satisfied, but not capitulating, King Henry said, "I will put you in charge of the Christmas festivities, my daughter, since you stated that it must all be perfect. We will have more guests than usual. The future of England is to be sculpted to ensure the endurance of my bloodline. I am, mayhap, selfish, but I do not care. Survival is a natural animal instinct."

"How am I to survive?" Matilda asked.

"You will always survive, for your lineage includes rulers from both sides of your family. Your mother was sister to four kings," King Henry said. "You are only being asked to do what I know you can do. If ever God meant for a woman to rule, he meant for it to be you."

Matilda looked into his eyes to see if there were a hint of false-hood, but she could see none. "If you believe what you say to me, then I thank you for the confidence you have in my abilities. I will do as my father and my king asks. I do what my father asks first, for I love him deeply. I do what my king asks, for I respect his ingenu-ity." Matilda grasped her gown in both hands and curtsied.

"You will make a great lady," King Henry said.

Matilda smiled at the phrase, for the term 'lady' was only used for a queen.

The day before the feast was bitterly cold. Grey skies blended with grey stone, and even the ground was grey from all the extra ashes dumped outside from the fireplaces and cooking fires. Every available sleeping space was occupied by visitors; the barons and their wives, single knights, Church bishops and priests, plus the entourage of personal servants who always accompanied the mas-ters and mistresses.

The servants, of course, were housed in the great kitchens or the barracks above the stables along with the castle's servants. The master of the kitchen had a small, two room apartment he shared with his wife and four children. His four assistants slept in the barracks, but there had been little time for sleep in the past week.

Matilda left her apartment in the west tower and took the shortest route to the kitchen. She wrapped a fur cloak tighter around herself, pulled the hood over her hair, and stepped outside. A gust of wind swirled the ashes around her blue chemise, decorating it with grey streaks from her ankles upwards. Her leather shoes were dyed red to match the kirtle that fell gracefully to her knees. Today she had her hair plaited and the ends wrapped in red and gold embroidered casings. She had no need to braid in fake hair as other women did since she was blessed with the luxurious, black hair of her father's people, the Normans.

Matilda rushed past the dogs who were fighting over scraps of discarded food and wondered if the black one would be able to trick its companion out of its share today. She walked quickly past the children who were in charge of feeding the smaller domestic animals, not speaking to them because she never knew what to say to those solemn creatures. She noticed they were in need of a bath, but other than that, children were almost always non-entities to her.

Outside the kitchen door was a pit lined with flat stones. Above the pit, two older boys turned the handles of the rotisserie upon which a full-grown steer was being roasted to a rich, golden brown. She remembered as a child that she used to follow the herd of cattle as they wandered across the meadows. She liked listening to the crunching sound as they chewed. It was like music to her. When she was a child, a full grown cow seemed enormous to her even though they were no bigger than a large dog.

A third boy basted the slabs of meat with a long-handled brush. He looked up at Matilda and smiled. She could tell he wanted to speak to her, but custom prevented him from doing so. She smiled as she recognized his agitation at the adult rules forced upon him.

"What do you use for the basting?" Matilda asked.

His smile widened. "It's honey and spices, your highness. It is my father's secret recipe, handed down from his father's father. It is perfect for the feast tomorrow."

"I am positive it will be. I shall ask for this dish." Matilda liked this boy's manners. He bowed to her as she moved away from him.

The kitchen door was open, and it was like a blast of summer when Matilda stepped inside. She immediately loosened her fur and had started to remove it when a servant took it from her shoulders and hung it on a peg. She looked around at all the activity. At first it seemed purposeless. The master of the kitchen and his wife were moving from servant to servant overseeing the tasks they had been assigned.

Across from the door, two gigantic stone fireplaces were attended by three servants. Four pigs cooked on a rotisserie in one fireplace, and two lambs roasted in the second. Large kettles of sauces and stews had been placed directly onto the coals at the edges of the fireplace. Every so often, someone would carry a plate full of turnips, carrots, or meat to a kettle and add it to the mixture. Wooden pails were used to dip water from the stone sink where it was piped downward from a cistern two stories above. The water was used for cooking and washing dishes, as well as to put out the frequent small fires that started whenever the wind blew sparks on the reeds that covered the stone floor. No one seemed bothered by this problem. One servant seemed content to stand by with a pail of water and wait for an errant spark.

Matilda reached down and scratched the kitchen cat, ostensibly placed there to catch mice, but he was so fat and shiny Matilda was sure the only things he caught were scraps. He stood up slowly and rubbed against her legs, standing so high on his toes that he looked like a dancer. His loud purr matched his meow that grated out in a greeting to all visitors. He looked up at Matilda with gold eyes peering out from a white face edged by grey tabby fur. She laughed at the effect of a cat wearing a hat. He seemed to know he was the object of her laughter, and haughtily marched back to his favorite spot and sat down next to the buttery room where the butts of wine, mead, and ale were kept.

The wife of the master of the kitchen saw Matilda first and stopped to curtsy. The other servants followed her lead. Matilda was pleased to see they had learned this custom well. She had insisted that the servants be taught to respond to royalty as in the European courts, even though her father did not see the need for it. Matilda did notice, however, that he seemed pleased to have the servants pay him this courtesy. Adelicia was embarrassed by the custom and always waved her hand, which had come to mean that she wanted the servants to rise quickly and go about their business.

Matilda had given up trying to convince her that royalty deserved the consideration. "I came to see how the preparations are progressing," Matilda said. She heard her own voice. It was commanding, and she wondered why she could not speak that way to her father. Why, with him, did she always sound like a child?

She pushed those thoughts from her mind and turned her attention back to the kitchen. "How goes it?"

"Very well. We have many loaves of bread, a goodly number of lambs and goats to roast, salted fish and five wild boars as well as the usual rabbit and game birds." The wife of the cook wiped her hands on her apron. "The buttery holds some of the best barrels of ale and wine we have ever made. The mead is very good, too." The woman stopped, suddenly abashed by her enthusiasm.

Matilda noticed the embarrassment and smiled at her. "It pleases me to see you enjoy your work so much. You have much to do, so you may go. I see that the kitchen is in capable hands."

"My husband is a true master of the kitchen," the woman said, then her face reddened at her impropriety.

Matilda looked at the woman's husband and wondered what their life was like during private moments. Had they married for love — something she would never be able to do — or had their marriage been arranged, too? The woman loved her husband, that was obvious, but did she love him and then marry him, or learn to love him later? Matilda's heart constricted at the thought of someone who would love her, but she knew that could never be. It seemed peculiar to wish for something a servant had that she could never have. She turned from the busy kitchen, hesitating only to let a servant get her fur and follow her through the small door into the great hall.

She sighed. "Well, enough thoughts of love. There is too much to do to worry about the impossible."

Outside of her own apartment, the great hall was her favorite room. Matilda stopped in the doorway and looked up. Two stories above, ten huge beams arched upward from stone corbels set eight feet off the stone floor. The arches had been oiled and hand-rubbed, and they glistened in spite of the grey day. The sheer massiveness of the beams and the stone walls made Matilda feel secure, even though the hall was over one hundred feet long. A stone fireplace, one of three, held logs more than nine feet long. Matilda watched two servants work all three fireplaces to keep the room warm. Above her, just below the enormous end beam, daylight shone in through a recessed, elliptical window that took up at least a third of the two story end wall. More than sixty panes of clear glass had been fitted into lead frames to give the room a light and airy feeling that offset the heaviness of the walls.

Matilda also liked the three immense windows in the eastern wall of the great room. She crossed to the closest window and stepped into the recess in the wall to look out the glass. Each window formed the third wall of a small room six feet wide, its length matching the twelve foot width of the castle wall. Matilda wanted to sit on the stone bench built into the window-room, but the cushions were being filled with fresh down, and she knew the stone seats would be too cold. The glass in the window panes was still dusted with a sugar-like frost, and Matilda could see her life's breath escaping. She blew gently on the panes and watched more frost form, then scratched "*Veni, vidi, vici*" with her fingernail. She looked at the phrase. "I wonder," she said.

Matilda shivered and glanced across the great hall toward the fireplace on the west wall. The fire was leaping upward in sun-like colors toward the chimney, and Matilda could no longer resist its invitation of warmth. She moved between the long tables and benches; the fresh reeds snapped beneath her feet and pulled at the hem of her kirtle. She took a deep breath, inhaling the dried basil, fennel, and lavender that had been mixed in with the reeds. Matilda stood with her hands behind her back and her back to the fire. Soon the warmth of the fire on her one side forced her to turn around. The enormous fireplace was well designed.

She moved back and sat on a bench, going over everything she wanted to check. Matilda watched the flames wrap themselves around the logs, and whispered, "Well, my departed husband, you taught me to be methodical, and so I am. You taught me to check on everyone and everything, and so I will. I wish you were here so that I could thank you for teaching me the ways of your German court. I wish . . . no, I wonder, if we had love."

Matilda was surprised at the loneliness she felt. She did not want to forget her deceased husband, but each day he seemed to fade further into the past. He was a part of another world that she had to fight to remember.

The crackling of the reeds on the floor close to where she was seated startled Matilda, and she turned to see who was behind her.

"Can it be the beautiful Matilda?" The man was dressed in a scarlet over tunic trimmed with silver brocade that matched his suede boots. Even his hose matched the scarlet of his tunic, and Matilda was astonished to see that the lining of his boots matched the scarlet tunic as well.

He bowed low. "If you are not a king's daughter, then you should be."

"Just who are you?" Matilda forced herself to frown. He was too impertinent.

"I do not know. I have been bewitched."

"Bewitched! You fool, there are no such things as witches." Matilda no longer had to force herself to frown since his manner was irritating. She could not tell whether he was making fun of her or not. It did not matter.

"You have become a very beautiful woman." The man stood before her, hands clasped in front. His eyes were the deep brown of a forest animal's.

"Have become? What do you mean by that?" Matilda felt her neck and cheeks getting hot. She prayed he would not notice her discomfort.

"I have not seen you since you were a very small child. As a child, you were a solemn little girl." His smile was that of someone who knew how to create consternation among women.

"What do you know about my childhood?" Matilda was irritated that he knew who she was, but she could not place him. "My childhood is none of your business."

"I was a part of it."

"You? Who are you? And do not tell me a stupid story about being bewitched. If you really think you are bewitched I can arrange to have you put out of your misery." Matilda rose and walked away from the irritating man. The cracking of the reeds under her feet echoed off the walls, making her feel large and clumsy.

"Wait, please, your highness," he said. "I did not wish to insult you by my flippancy. I . . . I wanted to renew an old friendship, and I am afraid I have done rather badly."

Matilda stopped. He was the most interesting guest she had met so far. Most of the others were nearer her father's age, or older. She turned and waited for his approach. He did, and bowed again. His manners were good.

"If you will permit me, my name is Stephen of Blois."

"Stephen? Is my tormenter really my own cousin? The self-same cousin my father brought to his court and spoiled so badly?" Matilda could not help but smile, for although she had only been seven when sent to Germany, she still had wonderful memories of the cousin who had made her laugh, had taught her to ride and to hunt. He was a few years older than she. At the time, he had seemed so much wiser.

"I am that very cousin who was enchanted by the clever little girl of King Henry's court," Stephen said. "Can I convince you to stay and relive the past with me?"

"I have so much to do."

"I have so much to remember, and much time to make up. I have followed your life closely. Now that I have you here in the same castle, the same room, I can not let you leave so soon."

Matilda's eyebrows raised at his presumptuous behavior, even for a cousin, and when he laughed, she felt her face flush. "Why are you laughing?"

"I am overjoyed to be reunited with you. You are like a ghost from my childhood. You were the reason for my wanting to rise each day at dawn, the reason I tried to please your father in all that he required of me, and your existence gave meaning to mine. I had always believed that our paths were meant to do more than intersect. Our paths were meant to be intertwined. I know this. I feel it. And so now here we are, and I do not want to waste one moment."

Matilda stepped away from Stephen as he moved closer to her. She felt uneasy with his easy manner, and he made her lose control of her thoughts. "You are audacious. We are no longer children."

"I have missed our companionship. Even though we were only children, we had a strong attachment for one another." Stephen waited for her reply.

Matilda's eyebrows were still arched, and she was studying him with a detachment that a priest might use to study a confessor. He held his gaze steady. Matilda sat on the bench closest to the fire. He was right. They had been especially close as children. It would be wonderful to remember happier times. "Let us visit the past together. I have fond memories of you, cousin Stephen. I remember that you brought lightness to the dark court." She gestured toward the bench opposite her. "Please, sit down."

Stephen stepped forward, not too close, and sat on the bench. He accepted her scrutiny for a few seconds before he spoke. "You were a beautiful child, and I would not have thought it possible for you to be more beautiful now, but you are."

Blue eyes stared steadily at Stephen. "Are you trying to seduce me?"

"Your highness, I have forgotten that many years and many miles have separated us. I also have forgotten that you have risen to a higher station in life. I hope you will forgive my enthusiasm, which undoubtedly seems inappropriate, and remember that I am older. Mayhap my memories of our childhood together are stronger."

"Do you remember when you taught me to ride? You first taught me that in order to control the horse I had to convince it I was in control. You also taught me to be kind to the animal that walked through mud and dung so that I would not have to dirty my feet. I never thought those lessons from childhood would influence my adult life, but they have."

Matilda leaned over and took Stephen's hand. "I did not know how much I have missed you until this moment."

Stephen leaned forward, brought her hand to his lips, gently kissed the tips of her fingers, then let go.

Matilda felt a shock like a lightning bolt travel up her arm straight to her heart. Was it possible to love so quickly, so deeply, or was this a dormant love left from childhood? She could not continue, or all would be lost. She shivered from a picture of forbidden love and prayed for reason to guide her rather than her heart.

"You are cold. We should sit closer to the fire," Stephen said.

"I am not cold."

Stephen bowed his head. "I apologize for my behavior. I can not seem to act as a rational man when I am near you."

"Nor can I act as a rational woman. I am to be married again. I will be traded off to a boy for a piece of property. I am naught but a game-piece, a lowly scrap to be thrown to the fighting dogs."

"I heard." Stephen leaned toward Matilda. "Does anyone marry for love?"

"Only the peasants have that advantage, if their lord approves. Imagine how different life would be if love were the cornerstone of marriage instead of property gains."

Matilda did not move away, even though she was aware he was closer than propriety allowed. She looked past Stephen toward the far end of the room where two servants were putting more logs into the fireplace. They were too far away to hear what was transpiring between herself and Stephen. Just the same, she had lowered her voice when asking the question, which seemed conspiratorial. "Do you love your wife?"

"It was a planned marriage by your father, the greatest match-maker of all time. He gave me a Maithilde for a wife, but he gave me the wrong one."

"We both have been recipients of my father's meddling, but the deed is done. I have agreed to marry that boy, although I wanted a man." Matilda blushed at her brazen statement. She stood and walked quickly from Stephen to escape him. He seemed to bring out an intimacy in her that caused her to fear his closeness. She was out of control and being dragged into a whirlpool. She had to be careful so that she would not destroy what her father planned. She knew only that Stephen made her feel vibrant.

Christmas Day was bitterly cold. The snow was spit from the pewter sky in minute, translucent drops that pelted those who had to venture outside. Unlike usual snowflakes, these icy bits refused to melt quickly, even when the attacked person scurried inside to stand next to one of the stone fireplaces.

The kitchen and the dining hall were alive with streaks of color as servants rushed about to the shouts of their masters. In the center of the apparent chaos was Master Dafid, who hurried from the cooking pots to the trestle tables in the hall and back to the kitchen, shouting orders like a commanding general to an army, which certainly he was. He raced from the kitchen to the dining hall to check the laying of the tables. He had hired new servants from the village, and Master Dafid was worried about their performances. It was imperative that the king not be embarrassed in front of his guests.

"No, no, no!" Master Dafid said. "The cloth is not even. I told you this morning that the cowche is to be straight and even, so that the second and third coverings will be even as well. How dense are you? Can you not see straight?"

Master Dafid rushed through the great hall, stopping at each table, every one in a different state of readiness, his face getting redder, sausage fingers moving faster and faster as he adjusted salt cellars, finger bowls, and eating utensils to match a pattern only he could sense.

"Set the salt by the king's right hand! To the left of the salt, you will place the bread. The knife is placed left, all by itself and plain to see. The spoon is placed on a napkin next to the knife. Cover it all so that no dust or dirt is on the utensils. Hurry! We have so little time."

Master Dafid watched the servant lay out the spoons. For the moment, he seemed content. Suddenly Master Dafid squealed like an injured animal and snatched a spoon from one of the servants.

"Who is responsible for this? No unclean eating utensils shall disgrace this table. Who did this? You?" Master Dafid's thick fingers punctuated each word as he poked the servant in the chest. "You are to inspect the utensils."

Master Dafid carried the offensive spoon back to the kitchen where a young girl was washing dishes in steaming water. Her face was shiny with sweat, her kirtle glued to her body. She could not have been more than eight years old.

"Here. If any more unclean utensils come out of my kitchen you will be beaten. Is that understood?" The spoon was thrown into the hot water, which splashed onto the unfortunate child. She wiped her sweaty face with the sleeve of her kirtle. "Yes, Father." She leaned into the table that held the tub of hot water. Her lower lip stuck out and she scowled.

"He has gone already, running back to the great hall. He will not beat you. He always says that when there is a big banquet for the king."

The ragged clothes were the first thing the child noticed about the boy, then she noticed his pixie-like face. He was smiling at her while at the same time picking his teeth with a splinter of wood.

"I am going to run away. I do not care if he is master of the kitchen, I am no better than a Saxon slave."

"I have worked for your father for three years now. He always threatens us, but he never beats us."

The child looked at his sooty face. "What is your job?"

"I tend the fires and keep the wood supplied to the kitchen. Some day I hope to be in charge of the great hall."

"I want to get as far away from a kitchen as possible," the girl said.

"Do not be stupid. This is the best place to be. There is always something to eat for us, and in the winter it is warm. This is the choice part of the castle, other than the king's chamber, of course."

The young man glanced over to the fireplace, waved to the girl and pulled his shabby cape closer in preparation for the trip outside to the wood pile.

The girl felt a gust of bitterly cold wind sweep through the door a moment later. It picked up the edge of her kirtle and whipped it around her thin legs. She was grateful for the brief blast of cold air, although it did her no good. Sweat dripped down her face and tickled her nose. She hated holidays, especially Christmas.

CHAPTER

II

HE CREAKING OF SHUTTERS as they were moved back
against the walls awakened Matilda. She pushed
the muslin sheets and heavy, sable-lined wool cover
away from her and sat up. Curtains encased the massive bed. She pulled back the veils, and her breath
was visible as it plumed outward into the cold room.
Matilda noticed the wooden shutters were opened to an overcast
sky. Ella had already directed the build-up of the fire in the stone
fireplace. As soon as Matilda's feet were seen dangling over the side
of the bed, Ella rushed over to put on fur-lined slippers before
Matilda could reach the square of linen cloth that covered the reeds.
Matilda wondered why Ella had to watch her so carefully. It did
not matter to her whether she was properly dressed to ward off the
chill of winter.

Matilda looked down at the top of Ella's head as she knelt
before her. Ella was such a worrier that one would think that she
was an old woman when in fact she was only a few months older
than Matilda. Matilda could not remember when she had been
without Ella's companionship.

"You will catch your death of a cold if you place your feet on
these cold planks, even though I have made certain there are extra
reeds covering the floor," Ella said.

"I do not get ill." Matilda stretched her arms above her head
and yawned. It was always difficult for her to wake up on cold

mornings. Maybe some nourishment would help. She yawned again. "Where is my broth?"

"Here, your highness."

"Did you have your broth?"

"No, your highness. I have not had time."

"Then pour yourself a tankard full."

"I can not do that. It is not proper."

Matilda laughed. "You have always worried about my improprieties, have you not?"

"Oh, no, not yours, your highness. Just my own." Ella tied the rawhide cords gently around Matilda's slender ankles. "I have arranged for your bath to be done in here rather than in the bathing room. It is much too cold."

"I hope you found a better tub than that wooden thing I used the last time. Even the linen padding does not help soften the blow of bathing." Matilda stood and let Ella help her into a heavy wrap. She took her mug of steaming broth, but frowned. "If you do not take that pot of broth and pour some for yourself, I will roll in that snow out there and get a deadly cold."

"You are most difficult, your highness. You always have been." Ella poured hot broth into a pewter mug and held her hands above it to warm them.

Matilda nodded. "I know."

The banter, which had been a part of the morning ritual for years, was interrupted by a knock. Ella nodded to the servant who tended the fire, then smiled at Matilda as if she had a secret. The servant moved quickly to open the heavy plank door that led into the hallway. Two men carried a large metal tub that they placed in front of the fireplace. A series of servants came after them, each with two wooden buckets of steaming water. The tub was filled in a short time, and the servants bowed before leaving the apartment. The fire tender put several logs into the fireplace and departed.

"Ella, you darling!" It was lined with the same type of padding the wooden one had. "It is so shiny," Matilda said.

"I asked the blacksmith to scour it with sand and vinegar like he does the armor. He thought I was insane." Ella opened the lid of a gold box on the mantelpiece, took out dried rose petals, and sprinkled them into the bath water. She swirled her hand through the silver-rose liquid, then added more fragrance.

"Put in some of the spice Father got for me last summer." Matilda moved toward the tub of steaming water and shrugged off her heavy robe. She tugged at her sleeping kirtle until she had it over her head. She tossed it on the bed.

Matilda stepped out of her slippers into the steaming water and slipped down between the rose petals and cloves. Long strands of black hair floated around her, swirling in a whirlpool pattern as she gracefully moved her hands in the water. This was her favorite ritual of the day.

"I have the sponge, your highness."

Matilda stood, her eyes closed, while Ella gently washed her with a rough sponge. Ella filled a large ladle with clean water from a bucket and poured warm water over Matilda. After Matilda stepped from the tub, Ella dried her with large cotton cloths and wrapped her in a robe.

Matilda sat in front of the fireplace while Ella dried her hair and tried to untangle it with her fingers before using an ivory comb. Matilda hated to sit still while Ella did the required one hundred strokes. However Matilda sat still, for she had learned a long time ago that if she squirmed, it took Ella longer.

The chemise that Ella chose for Matilda was a beautiful, clear red. The material, a fine Egyptian cotton, was silky to the touch. Matilda loved the feel of it, and she remembered touching her mother's fine clothing. After her mother had died, Matilda had spent hours holding one of her mother's gowns. She had taken one of the gowns back to Germany with her, wearing it whenever she had felt particularly lonely. She wondered what had happened to the gown. She did not remember, and the thought made her feel guilty.

"Sit on the bench so that I can do your stockings and slippers," Ella said.

Matilda was startled from her reverie. "I do not want to wear those woolen things. They scratch horribly." She wrinkled her nose. "How can the English stand their wool?"

"I made these stockings myself." Ella held up the stockings. "I made them from cotton. They will fit your legs perfectly."

"You spoil me." Matilda let Ella slip on the soft white stockings and tie them to the knee garters. Her light blue kirtle was startling in its workmanship, and Matilda anxiously awaited for it to be placed over her head.

"Adelicia is truly an artist." Matilda traced the multi-colored embroidery that covered the entire front of the kirtle. With delicate stitches, Matilda's favorite Biblical stories had been stitched. Animals glided two by two through a sea of flowers toward a golden ark. An angel with a trumpet hovered over a garden.

While Matilda looked at her reflection in the mirror, Ella pulled the lacings as tight as she could on the kirtle. Matilda always refused to suck in her breath to emphasize a tiny waist much to Ella's annoyance. Finished with that task, Ella held out red leather shoes for her mistress, knelt in front of Matilda, and slipped the shoes on her feet.

Matilda held her foot out and twisted it from side to side. "These are my favorite shoes. I had them made in Germany just before I came."

"They are pretty." Ella stood behind Matilda and combed her hair. "Your hair gets thicker every year. It is beautiful."

Matilda shrugged. "I find it annoying to have to deal with it every day. Do you not wonder how much time is wasted with combing, brushing, and trying to be in style? I am happy to see that loose hair is the new fashion."

"I like braids much better, for it leaves ones hair wavy when the braids are taken out at night. It makes men weak with love to see their women with wavy hair."

Matilda giggled. "Why, Ella, for shame. Do you fancy my caring whether or not I make my boy bridegroom swoon for my wavy hair?" She heard Ella's embarrassed gasp.

Matilda was always surprised at the deftness of Ella's fingers, and soon Ella announced that Matilda was presentable. With hair plaited and hanging to the embroidered girdle that encircled her waist, and braids wrapped with the same bright red material as her chemise, Matilda was ready to make her entrance into the great hall.

Adelicia felt the hardened muscles of King Henry's arm as she rested her arm lightly across his while he held her hand. Her husband smiled at her as he led her into the great hall. They moved through the crowd of guests, Adelicia greeting each one in her genteel manner, smiling at their jovial faces, and happy for the festivities. Her normally shy manner was momentarily forgotten in the excitement. This was Adelicia's favorite holiday, but she was not certain which she liked more, the mass said in the private chapel, or the banquet that followed. She stopped and looked at the crowd trying to memorize the colors and the noise for her dreams. Adelicia sniffed the air. "Dear Henry, it all smells so delicious. I love the spices and the pine boughs. I think we have the entire forest in here."

King Henry smiled. "Your eyes are as bright as newly minted coins. The child has never left you, has it?"

"Not during the Christmas season. It is a time to have fun and to see friends."

King Henry leaned down and whispered, "Adelicia, there are Miles of Gloucester and John Fitz Gilbert le Marechal. My greatest advisors have returned from Scotland. Let us see what they can tell us of King David."

"Is King David a part of your plan for Matilda?" Adelicia asked.

"Indeed." King Henry nodded toward Sir Miles and Sir John, waiting for them to step to his side. "What news have you?"

Miles stepped close to the king. "Your brother-in-law follows me by only a few hours. He believes in your plan for your daughter. He says that he is willing and capable of supporting his late sister's daughter."

"That is good. Thank you, Miles." King Henry turned to Sir John. "What think you of my plan?"

"It is creative, but logical. I will be most happy to give all that I have to support you in this quest." Sir John knitted his thick eyebrows together. "Let no man stand in our way."

King Henry clapped Sir John on the shoulder. "I knew that I could count on the two of you."

Sir John nodded, then bowed to Adelicia. "My lady, you look happy tonight."

"I am. I love Christmas. Henry, look! There is one of my favorite people. Excuse me?" Adelicia waited for the smile from her husband that meant she could go. Receiving it, she moved away.

Adelicia stopped before a woman, small of stature, who was nearly as wide as she was tall. Her white hair was neatly covered by a widow's cowl. Adelicia noted that her eyes sparkled in spite of the milky-white color that encroached on the brown irises. "Lady Sarah, it is wonderful to see you. I have missed your charming little vignettes. You always make me laugh."

"I am honored to be invited to your Christmas Court, my lady." A small bow acknowledged the ranking of the queen, and a smile expressed gratitude for being recognized by Adelicia.

"You must come and tell me another story after our dinner." Adelicia glanced around for the king and saw that he was at the high table already, greeting Stephen's wife, the other Maithilde. She watched Maithilde laugh and knew that the king was in a fine humor, for he had obviously told her a joke. Adelicia saw that King Henry was looking for her, and she moved toward the high table.

"My queen looks lovely today." King Henry took Adelicia's hand and kissed her fingertips. "I have been blessed by a lovely wife."

Adelicia felt her cheeks burning, and she quickly took her place at the long table. A servant immediately poured warm water into a finger bowl from the lip of a pewter pitcher shaped like a wild boar. The tail formed the handle. It was not one of Adelicia's favorite pieces because the boar was ugly, but it was well crafted.

One servant waited on his knees with a clean linen cloth folded across his arm, while Adelicia washed her hands. She dried them on the cloth, looking up at a disturbance near the doorway to her left.

Adelicia could see Stephen standing with a group of barons next to the entrance of the hall. He and the others were laughing, drinking tankards of ale, and from their gestures, Adelicia guessed they were probably talking about the hunts last fall and teasing each other. The group's raucous behavior quieted, and Adelicia was puzzled, then smiled when she realized her step-daughter's arrival was the reason for the silence. Matilda's cousin Stephen had moved to her side, and three young barons had vied for position on her other side. In her mind, Adelicia compared them to children fighting over a new toy. She giggled at the confused look she saw on Matilda's face. It was obvious that her step-daughter did not realize how beautiful she was. Her beauty was not lost on the men of the court.

Matilda glanced from one baron to another as they pushed into each other, then whispered to Stephen. "What is this madness? Is it an English game?"

"Just the madness of the season coupled with your beauty," Stephen said.

Matilda whispered to him once more. "Young gentlemen in Germany did not act like this flock of peasants, but then this court is more lax than what I am used to."

"Are you suggesting we are not gentlemanly?" Stephen asked.

Matilda felt like stamping her foot at his impudence or igno-rance. She was not sure which was being displayed. "The European courts are much more civilized than this lowly island's. I am ap-palled at my father's court. The King of France insists on excellent behavior at his court."

Stephen chuckled. "The King of France has hardly enough ter-ritory to claim he has a court. An island in the Seine is not much of a country."

Matilda wanted to be angry with Stephen, but she could not. First, he was right about the King of France, and second, Stephen was charming. She did not want him to think he was too charming, so she turned toward the person next to her. The young man to her right was almost handsome. He was auburn-haired with a scatter-ing of freckles across his nose and cheeks. His grey eyes watched her, and when her glance caught his, he smiled. Matilda blinked quickly. She felt like a deer being stalked. Why were these men acting so blatant? She glanced toward her father, but he was still busy chatting with Stephen's wife.

Matilda took Stephen's outstretched hand, relieved that he was going to help. He escorted her to the high table and helped her to sit. She was thankful to be placed next to Adelicia. She glanced down at the other tables set below them laden with tremendous quantities of food. The odor from the food was wonderful, but Matilda was not hungry, for there was too much to see. She leaned toward her step-mother. "Are all my father's banquets like this?"

Adelicia patted her hand. "Oh, no. This one has been expertly planned. You have done a better job than I ever did."

"I hardly think so. You are being kind, as usual." Her father's voice boomed out, and Matilda leaned around Adelicia to hear the conversation between her father and Stephen's wife.

"Would you be interested in a good hunt?" King Henry asked. "I could arrange one as soon as the weather clears. There is nothing like a good winter hunt. It invigorates both the mind and the body."

"I would like nothing better than a good hunt," Maithilde said. An eyebrow raised, she watched Matilda. Turning to her husband, she said, "You are taking your cousinly duties a little too seriously, Stephen."

Stephen waited through the hand washing rituals before he answered. "King Henry, my wife questions me. Do you find that all women are thus endowed with curiosity?"

King Henry chuckled. "Whether they be mothers or wives, they all are as curious as the cat. What think you of a hunt?"

Stephen nodded. "A hunt would be a fine idea."

King Henry laughed. "We will need one to work off the lard we will carry from this banquet. My daughter has done well in the management of this feast." He leaned over to see around Adelicia, and held his pewter chalice of claret toward Matilda. He winked.

"Oh, Father, I do not deserve credit for this. It would be difficult not to do well with all the resources you have."

Matilda looked down the feast table. Even though it had been constructed of sturdy oak planks, it looked as if it should have bowed in the middle from the weight of the food. She had made certain there would be no shortages. Matilda took a quick inventory of the dishes and the crowd of laughing guests seated at the trestle tables. In addition to the roasted meats already on the twenty long tables, each held a variety of salted fish and vegetable dishes. Bowls of cooked eggs, every dish different because of the spices that had been used, sat between flagons of ale, mead, claret, metheglin, and Matilda's favorite, fermented mulberry juice.

Matilda closed her eyes and counted the number of game birds she had seen in the kitchen this morning. There would be enough. The deer were small, but plentiful. Satisfied, she opened her eyes. Now she was hungry.

A servant presented Matilda with a platter of fish, but she refused. She could not eat the creature that had been swimming so gracefully in the vivarium just this morning, its multi-colored scales reminiscent of stained glass windows. She took pleasure in finding bits of color in this grey England, but now the color had been replaced by brown; life had been replaced with death.

A platter with beef was placed before her, and Matilda smiled as she took a small portion. She did not mind eating a cow, mayhap because they were not pretty to her. The honey and spice sauce was hot and syrupy. Remembering the promise made to a young lad, she allowed the servant to pour it over the meat. Across the great hall by the kitchen door, she noticed the youngster watching her.

Matilda took a bite, carefully, for the sauce was quite hot, and smiled at the boy. The smile she received in return was tenfold to hers.

Matilda had learned long ago, at the urging of her German husband and her German servants, to eat sparingly. It kept one from the sin of gluttony. Although she scarcely touched her food, she immersed herself in the entertainment. She watched a juggler throw gleaming knives higher and higher until she was dizzy and feared that he would slice off his nose. The light from the fireplaces made the knives appear to be sharpened flames. The eerie gasps from the audience gave Matilda chills. The other entertainers, minstrels and bards, were not as exciting, but were just as fun to watch.

Matilda relaxed as the mood of the guests changed from awe to pleasure. The Christmas feast was perfect. She would remember this day with fondness, and she sighed with happiness.

The stained glass windows darkened as night crept over England. King Henry had sent for Matilda, and as she followed the servant's lighted torch down the darkened hallway toward the meeting room, her heart constricted. This would be the first of many confrontations with all the barons and lords of England. Would they think her father genius or mad? Would they protest and threaten war? What about Stephen's feelings? After all, he was assumed to be the natural heir to the throne since he was the only male in the line of succession. His lineage was as good as hers, flowing with the blood of William the Conqueror. There were other kings whose particles of life flowed within Stephen's veins. He had almost as much royal blood as she.

Matilda hesitated at the door to take several deep breaths. She forced her hands to relax, for she had noticed that people often betrayed their states of mind with their hands. She nodded to the servant, and he opened the heavy oak door. The massive, hammered-metal hinges groaned from the weight. This room had been built to house the royal family in case of enemy attack and a breach of the keep.

The first person she sought with her gaze was her father. He was where she expected him to be, sitting in a chair of carved wood and brocaded cloth. The others were seated in similar chairs, on stools, and a few even lounged on the floor near the fireplace. They arose, almost as a unit, and bowed. Matilda stopped in the doorway. She could go no further, even though she willed her feet to move.

"Come in, my daughter, my sweet immortality." King Henry waved his arm toward the chair next to his. "Sit here. This is an auspicious moment in the history of England, mayhap in the history of the world."

Matilda was so accustomed to obeying orders from her king that her feet moved automatically toward the chair. She saw nothing but King Henry's face in a grey swirl; she heard nothing in that room full of people but the king's words, and his breathing. She sat, waiting for guidance from him, while her blood stopped flowing and her heart surely had ceased.

Matilda shut her eyes for a fraction longer than a blink, and opened them when she had willed herself to see everything. Stephen stood near her, his eyes flaming from the reflection of firelight. His cheeks were flushed. Matilda wondered if he were angry, or merely had had too much to drink.

King Henry did not stand to speak. He did not have to. "I am a king with a country, but I am also a king without a direct male heir. When I die, my lineage, the lineage of my father, William the Conqueror, will no longer run straight like an arrow, but will fall useless to the ground.

"I was a broken and disillusioned man when my sons drowned on the White Ship. I could not understand what God wanted from me. Why did he take my sons? Why did he take my first wife before we could have more children? Why, when I married the angelic Adelicia, did we have no sons to continue what William the Conqueror began? Not until I learned of the abilities of Empress Matilda did I fully understand God's plan."

Matilda saw her father wait until he saw a light of recognition in Brian fitzCount's grey eyes, and the subsequent look of surprise that passed briefly across his face before the mask fell into place. King Henry looked at Stephen, his favored nephew who had the most to lose, and Matilda was pleased to see that the talks about what was to come that had been directed toward Stephen by her father the last few days had preserved her cousin's dignity.

"I wanted you, my friends and supporters, to be the first to know of my plans to follow God's will. I wanted you to have the chance to swear to support Matilda, at my death, as the first female king of this great land of ours." King Henry paused. The silence was thick. "I want Matilda to inherit the throne. I will go willingly to my death knowing that England and Matilda are in your care. I ask much, but England must be preserved, and our people saved from a civil war."

Stephen was the first to respond. He dropped to his knees in front of Matilda, his head bowed. "My king, I must do as you and God wish, that is understood, but I want my liege and Lady Matilda to know that I will be your faithful knight in all things. I swear upon the four Gospels of God that I will always be a faithful vassal to Matilda, and to her successors."

Matilda made herself look down at her cousin who bowed before her. It seemed peculiar to her. She swallowed the lump in her throat, and looked at her father. He was leaning back in his chair. He stared at her. Matilda knew that he waited for her to speak. She looked directly into her cousin's eyes. "Dear Stephen de Blois, arise, as your position in life dictates. You should not humble yourself before me in our family castle which has been your home more than mine."

"Your graciousness makes me all the more humble. I can not arise before one better than I," Stephen said.

Matilda sighed. "Please, Stephen. You make me feel uncomfortable."

"Do not think that I envy your hold on the future crown of England, my lady. I believe that God intended you to lead us."

A young count knelt before Matilda. "Brian fitzCount, at your service and God's. The quest is the same. I, too, believe that you were meant to lead England. I will follow you to the end of our island and to the European continent, if you desire, my lady."

The gentleman's freckled face was topped by a thick shock of auburn hair, and Matilda recognized him as the young man who had stood next to her in the great hall. She remembered him as the object of attention from several of the ladies at court.

Matilda thought about the intrigue of her late husband's court regardless of the precautions taken and knew it would be no different here. She glanced from one man to the other. Which of the barons who bowed before her and swore fealty would be faithful to King Henry's plan? Which of these barons who professed to support her would turn against her if they perceived her position to weaken?

Her eyes shifted to her half-brother. It pained her to see him kneeling before her. "Dear Robert of Gloucester, please do not bend your knees in my presence. Although circumstances dictate that you can not be heir to the throne, you are my brother in full spirit, if only half in blood. I love you as much as if you had been born of both my mother and father. I can not think of you as my father's bastard son, for I have wonderful memories of our childhood together." Matilda took Robert's large hand in her two small ones. She had always liked the roughness and warmth of his fleshy hands, and she basked in his nearness. As a young girl, Robert's strong hands had helped her off her horse, picked her up when she had fallen, and had smoothed her hair when her feelings had been hurt. In Robert she found the duplicated strength of King Henry. If ever her brother would deceive her, all would be lost for England.

Robert of Gloucester squeezed Matilda's hand gently, giving her the secret signal from her childhood that she had all but forgotten. She felt her heart would burst with the love she had for her brother. Matilda looked into his eyes and saw the same loyalty for her that he had for their father.

Robert leaned closer to Matilda. "I was your protector when you were a child, Lady Matilda, and I wish to continue in that role. By the grace of God, I not only claim King Henry as my father, but you as my sister. I am doubly privileged."

"Oh, Robert, thank you." Matilda smiled at him, but his figure in front of her wavered until she pushed back tears that threatened to spill from her eyes. It would never do for these barons to see her thus, so she forced the tears to dissipate.

Matilda's attention was diverted by another gentleman who came forward and knelt before her. She looked down at sand colored hair. "Please arise, sir." The man stood, and looked at her with eyes the color of the sky beneath heavy brows. He was the age of her brother and was just as straight and strong as Robert. Matilda recognized him immediately. "John Fitz Gilbert le Marechal!" She forced herself to assume a calmer tone. "It is good to have you with us. A family friend is most welcome."

"Thank you, my lady. My father served your father and I would be honored to serve you, if you please."

Matilda liked him immediately. The boy had become a man. She felt that he was strong and the most sincere of them all, save for

Robert. "You honor me with your presence, Sir Marechal." She smiled for him and was rewarded with a look of admiration.

A movement caught Matilda's eye, and she nodded to acknowledge the Archbishop of Canterbury. He was always a bit pompous.

"Lady Matilda, the Catholic Church sees the wisdom of King Henry's only legitimate heir continuing his lineage, and the Church understands God's will in this. Please allow me to give you the spiritual assistance you will need." The Archbishop of Canterbury, William, stood before Matilda. He did not acknowledge that anyone was above him, except God, and he only knelt to God in his cathedrals.

Matilda forced herself to be civil. "I accept your spiritual assistance, but I would not turn away your army if they were needed."

Matilda kept a smile from her face as she watched King Henry. His facial features contorted while he tried to control his laughter. Matilda winced when he gave up and let his thunderous voice rattle the eardrums of everyone present. She noticed that the others could not contain their own laughter except for the Archbishop who, she imagined, saw no humor in the situation.

King Henry winked as he whispered to her. "I should say something to you to correct your irreverence, but I can not decide what that might be." He shook his head. "Matilda, my daughter, you are a priceless jewel." King Henry looked out at the assemblage of men before him. "I thank all of you for the support you have shown the empress and me."

The screeching sound of metal scraping metal interrupted King Henry, and he looked toward the huge door as it opened. A large fur-and snow-covered bulk moved into the room with flailing arms and stamping feet. A shaggy head of hair was white with snow, as well as with age. David, King of Scotland, shook himself, removed the fur cape, and handed it to a servant in one flurry of movement that included giant strides toward King Henry, whom he pulled from a chair and grabbed in a bone-crunching bear hug.

"You old bruin!" King Henry said. "Where has my brother-in-law been? You missed the Christmas Festivities, but I do not think it hurt you at all." King Henry patted the large belly of his latest guest.

"The weather was so bad north of here that we had to stop several times. Our normal road markers were gone, spirited away, I think, by snowflakes. I did not think we would get here at all. We had to walk and drag our horses with us. The ladies were sent back to Scotland, for I feared for their safety. However, I could not stay away from your feast." King David turned and looked at Matilda. "You are as beautiful as was my sister. You are truly her daughter. I am pleased." He looked at King Henry, then back to Matilda. "I have braved the weather, and I would have braved all the spirits in Hell to be with you tonight, my lady, for I have received a communique from your great father. I am here to pledge my support in your quest for the throne of England."

Matilda could play the calm politician no longer. She threw herself at her uncle and wrapped her arms about his huge neck, her hands barely touching as she pulled him to her. She loved the smell of the outdoors that was mingled with the odor of wet wool and fur. A piece of ice melted against her cheek as she leaned against him. "Uncle, this does me more good than a thousand angels carrying me to Heaven." Matilda tried to keep her voice from cracking with emotion. She was conscious of King David's return hug that was as gentle as a mother's, for he always seemed to be aware of his bulk. Matilda felt his strong chin as it rubbed against the top of her head, and that movement brought back poignant memories of her early childhood.

King David pulled away from her and held her at arm's length. "You were meant to be King, for you are every inch a ruler like your father. On your mother's grave I swear to protect you."

Matilda felt the need to touch her uncle's face as she often had done when a child, but resisted since it would not seem appropriate in the company of the others. She could not keep a lump from forming in her throat, and it was with great difficulty that she spoke.

"I thank you from the depths of my being for your support. My heart is filled with joy and love, but I have no words to describe my deepest gratitude."

After forcing herself to gain control so that she would not appear weak, Matilda turned toward the barons and earls who stood before her. They watched her closely, and she knew how the cornered hare must feel at the moment of truth. The thoughts raced through her mind as to what would be best to say. She could not think of any words except those that formed the truth. She took a deep breath and spoke slowly, trying to feign calmness.

"I am so happy with your support that words seem to have failed me. Do not let my stunned brain and voiceless voice be taken as a sign of my taking you for granted. On the contrary, I am pleased, but amazed that the course of history will be changed by your words on my behalf."

Stephen stepped forward. "It is the will of God, my lady, and it is also my will. I will die, if need be, for you and my country. Please accept my offer of help."

Matilda did not hesitate, although a fleeting thought reminded her that Stephen could be king when her father died if she were not strong enough to keep the throne. "I accept your offer, Stephen, for I will need you." Matilda was relieved that he voiced his support, not once, but several times. She smiled at him with eyes that shone in excited reflection of the last few minutes.

"A toast to our future female King of England." King Henry raised a tankard of claret toward his daughter. The barons and earls held their glasses raised toward Matilda.

Matilda smiled to repress a frown. She knew that in all probability one or more traitors to her cause toasted her at this moment. There was no way to guess who they would be. If she knew who would plot against her, she would send them all to Hell. Politics were unpredictable. She would have to plan for the unexpected.

She looked from one supporter to another. Some of them would defy her father, seeing her as a weak vessel because she was born a woman. Never mind that she had more education than most of them and more experience in affairs of state than everyone in the room except her father and her uncle. Where would the traitors be? She glanced from one man to the other. Matilda looked into the eyes of Brian fitzCount. The light from the fireplace was reflected in them, or was it the light of Hell? There was no one to trust, in truth.

Matilda was closest to Stephen, and she was aware that her heart beat quicker in his presence. Matilda remembered their childhood together, what little there had been of it. They would have been perfect together, but fate was an uncaring controller. Matilda forgot that it was her own father who had found spouses for each of them, and that her marriage to the Holy Roman Emperor had kept them apart.

She sighed, resigned to the trick that fate had played on her. What was done could not be undone. Marriages were political, and neither of her marriages would be different, whether it was the one in the past or the one in the future.

Matilda awoke to the kind of winter day in which the sun shone through translucent air and reflected off crystal snowflakes. Colors were brighter, the air was biting, and she needed to be outside. Matilda listened, wondering what sound had awakened her so early, then heard running feet. It was only a moment before the door to her room opened, and her father's valet stepped inside.

"Miss Ella, please tell her highness that the King wishes her to join him on a hunt. He will leave in one hour and will wait no later for any gentleman or any lady."

The servant took a deep breath to replace lost air, bowed and almost ran from the apartment.

Matilda was on her knees and peered from between the heavy curtains that surrounded the bed. She shivered, not from the cold, but from the anticipation of the hunt. It had been a long time since she had been on a hunt with her father. She knew which horse she would use. He was full of life and pranced around the stables with impatience at being penned in. Matilda had watched the groom work with the sorrel horse until he was perfectly trained. This horse belonged to no one, but was part of the stable collection. Maybe her father would let her have him.

She was dressed in woolen tunics and the hated woolen hose had replaced the fine cotton ones that Ella had made for her. She did take time to place silken and cotton undergarments next to her skin for protection. She wiggled her toes deep into soft, fleece lined boots as she waited impatiently for Ella to tug them into place and tie the leather lacings. The boots had been an early Christmas gift to her from Adelicia. It was so typical of her step-mother to combine the necessities of life with comfort and beauty.

Matilda held out her dainty foot and inspected the boots. She loved the vermilion suede and smiled at the memory of the argument she had had with Adelicia. It was only through Matilda's own skill at begging had Adelicia given in to her and let her have the boots before Christmas Day.

"But I shall be so cold, and I know you have something to keep me warm. You told me so yourself only yesterday," Matilda had said. She remembered the crackling of the fire that had not quite warmed Adelicia's chambers. "Look, at the frost that covers your colored windows. The cold weakens the color just as it weakens me."

"It is a special gift and meant to be given on the day of the Christ child's birth."

"I am not used to these ferocious winters. I am probably going to suffer a great deal and get a disease and die and you will feel guilty. I am trying to preserve not only my life, but your sanity. Look, I am on my knees at your feet, begging you like a common servant."

"All right, Matilda. I can no longer resist you." Adelicia had laughed, lightly like the sound of distant bells.

The sounds of horses and men brought Matilda from the recent past and into the present. She jumped up and walked swiftly to the door, grabbing her fur wrap from the ready hands of Ella.

"Please be careful," Ella said. "Let me tie the straps on the cape for you."

"No, I do not have time." Matilda opened the door and a swoosh of cold air from the hallway rushed past her and tried to kill the fire in the huge stone fireplace. "It's going to be a wonderful day. I can feel it."

"Do not get a careless horse like you are so inclined to do."

Matilda put her hands on her hips and pretended to frown. "Why, Ella, you of all people should know that I ride as one with any horse I have ever been on. For shame to think such thoughts!" Matilda watched Ella smile and push the door almost shut. Matilda waved as she turned and hastened down the stone staircase barely aware of the hinges complaining about the weight of the door.

The sun was so bright that it took a minute for Matilda to adjust to the light after the semi-darkness of the castle. She heard rather than saw her father across the courtyard and turned toward the laughter. He was testing the balance and tension on a bow, specially built for his immense strength. Matilda watched her father and remembered the same scene that had been played over and over for her before she was robbed of her childhood and sent abroad to be married. She was still staring at him when he seemed to sense her watching him. Matilda always wondered about his uncanny knack of knowing when he was being watched.

"Daughter, come over here and select your bow. Hurry, the sun is already up and time is wasting."

Matilda pushed through the pack of hunting dogs, causing one to yelp as she stepped on its toes. She wrinkled her nose at their smell, barely tolerating her father's favorite, a huge black thing with a long, wet tongue that sat next to him. King Henry put his arm around Matilda and squeezed her. She folded against him, comforted by his presence. England would always be personified for her in the aura of King Henry.

"Come, let us select some good arrows." King Henry licked a finger and held it up. "There is very little wind today, so a feather that is not as stiff will be fine." He walked with Matilda to a tall, woven basket filled with arrows.

Matilda looked into the basket. The servants had been busy. She reached in, being careful not to let the goose feathers scratch her hands, grasped an arrow by its shaft, and pulled it from the basket. It felt smooth to the touch and silky. She bounced it lightly in her hands. It balanced easily. She liked arrows made of ash as much for the light color as for the feel. She believed, as did her father, that the best arrows were made from ash. Matilda ran the ball of her thumb down the white feather. It was not too stiff and not too soft. Twirling the arrow around in her hand, she saw that the twine had been neatly wrapped around the arrowhead and the split shaft. It was an excellent job.

She spent at least fifteen minutes choosing two dozen arrows, fighting often with her father over a particular one. She had to smile at him, for he always let her win. It was not until after she had chosen a bow with perfect balance that fit her and a gut string with just the right tension that she realized she was being watched by the young man with the auburn hair. She could not place him. She ran his face through her memory from the time she saw him at the banquet to the oath of fealty he had given her as the next ruler of England. It took her a moment to remember that he was Brian fitzCount. He smiled at her. The thought that he might betray her flared through her mind and burned out just as quickly. She liked him, so she smiled back.

"Let me get your horse, my lady," Brian fitzCount said. "I know there is a gentle mare that should be to your liking."

Matilda's anger flared at the suggestion that she was not as good a rider as any man on the hunt, but she calmed herself immediately. It would not be prudent to alienate supporters over a horse. She would be tactful. She looked Brian fitzCount in the eye. "Do not underestimate me. I have already chosen the sorrel stallion over there." Matilda almost laughed at the look on Brian's face when he saw the restless animal dancing around as the groom tried to saddle him.

"I do not think that you should take a chance with a horse that is not well trained."

"He is well trained. Watch." Matilda strode across the court yard and placed her hand on the sorrel's glistening neck. He settled down, not completely, but long enough for Matilda to slip her foot into the stirrup and swing her right leg gracefully over his back. Her hunting skirt billowed out like the sail of a ship and settled across the back of the stallion. She reached out with a gloved hand and patted the horse again.

She almost giggled at the startled looks on the faces of the men as the stallion responded quickly to her touch. Long ago Matilda had found that she could ride faster on a stallion, and consequently, she could hunt better. She did not care what anyone thought or said about her peculiar habits. As Empress Matilda, she had learned that she could do almost anything she wanted without reproach. Her husband had merely laughed and indulged her.

Matilda scratched the horse's neck. "What is his name?" The groom handed her the reins. "I call him Dancer, but if you want to change his name. . . ."

"You know him best. Dancer is a good name," Matilda said. She leaned forward and whispered into Dancer's ear. He twitched one ear backward and pawed the ground, then stood patiently while the drawbars were pushed back into the walls to allow the two gates to open toward the inner court.

The outer gate was drawn upward and even though it looked like lattice work, it was much more formidable having been made from huge oak beams. The bottom of each vertical piece was sharpened to a point and encased in metal. Matilda shuddered at the thought of anyone getting caught as the gate came down.

Matilda held Dancer with a firm hand as he became more impatient with each gate opening. As soon as the all clear signal was given, the entourage flowed out of the castle in a river of color and moved as a unit toward the woods. The huntsman with the hounds walked behind her father. The dogs yelped and strained at their leashes. The bowmen were between Matilda and the king. The falconers followed closely behind.

It was a perfect winter day for hunting, and Matilda did not care to be cautious. In fact, she wanted to be alone in order to think about her future, and she welcomed the solitude. Whenever she felt that her life was becoming difficult and almost more than she could bear, she would go hunting. It was a good excuse to be outdoors. To her, God was in nature and to see his creation, to be a part of it, made her feel that nothing would defeat her.

The sun was high in the sky when Matilda realized that she was far ahead of the rest of the hunters, even outrunning the dogs, for which she was thankful. Her father would not have let her ride off alone if he had not been busy chasing down a stag. She had already let fly three arrows and had two rabbits for her trouble. The rabbits bounced against the horse where Matilda had tied them together and had slung them in front of her. The smell of blood had Dancer more skittish than usual, or mayhap the large wolf tracks she had seen were fresher than she thought. If she had been honest with herself, she would have admitted that wolf tracks made her nervous as well.

Matilda let Dancer run across the open fields to expend his extra energy and distance herself from any wolf that might be lurking about. When she looked back, she could not see any sign of the hunting party. She frowned and looked at the sky. The sun was nearly overhead so she could not tell which direction to ride.

"How stupid I am. I think I am quite mad for getting myself into this mess. I could freeze out here." She shivered more with the thought of the cold that would come than the way she felt now.

Dancer snorted, tossed his head and pawed at the ground. Matilda looked toward the edge of the woods. She shuddered at the dark grey shadows that flowed around the trees like fog. "Of course, there are the wolves. Always the wolves."

Matilda leaned over and patted Dancer on the neck. She pulled on the reins and turned Dancer in wider and wider circles until she found her tracks that led back toward a low hill. She was relieved when she remembered that she had ridden around two low hills just after leaving the woods, and the camp was not too far away. She nudged Dancer in the ribs with her heels and settled in for a quick ride back to the edge of the woods where the daytime encampment was located. A piece of freshly roasted meat would taste very good right now. Better yet would be the fire, tales of the hunt, and good company.

The snow covered hill shimmered like crushed diamonds beneath a sapphire sky, and Matilda followed her tracks around its base. She heard the swishing sound an instant before she was knocked off Dancer. She landed with a thump, and her pain was not from the fall. She knew that an arrow bit into her skin and muscle an inch below her collar bone before she opened her eyes to look. She forced herself to watch ruby red blood flow down the front of her breast, roll off her fur cape and splash onto the spotless snow. The blood steamed as it hit the cold snow.

Matilda acted quickly, pulling at the arrow. The survival instinct was bred into her from before William had conquered the island, and she refused to let an arrow stop her from living. She nearly fainted from the pain. She sucked in great quantities of air and pulled the arrow again. Matilda prayed silently to her protector. Once, through the pain, she became angry with God.

"This is not the time or the place to test my mettle. Have I not proven myself, yet?" Immediately, she apologized like a petulant child. For some period of time, she knew not how long, Matilda vacillated between anger, fear, and hot flashes of pain. She nearly fainted a second time. The snow covered hill on which she lay swirled into the blue sky and both became black. She screamed to arouse herself from what she feared would be the last sleep.

Again she grasped the arrow, but this time she looked to see the angle of penetration. She held her breath, grasped the shaft tightly, and quickly pulled it out at the same angle it had gone in, slapping her hand over the opening. Blood flowed through her fingers turning the fur of her cape crimson.

"I will not let myself die in such an idiotic manner." An involuntary groan spit out through her clenched teeth. She shook her head to keep the blackness at bay and reached down for the bottom of her kirtle. It was too tough for her to tear. She could only wiggle around until the skirt was around her waist, and she could finally place the material beneath her cape against the gash in her chest. The blood flow was slower, but not stopped.

"Come here, Dancer. I will have to get back to the day camp because no one will find me here." Matilda reached toward the horse with her uninjured arm. The horse would not move, but stood out of reach and pawed at the ground. The smell of impending death made him more nervous than usual, and his nostrils flared out with interest and aversion.

"Dancer, please." Matilda groaned again as she forced herself to crawl toward the wild-eyed horse. "It is all right, boy. You are supposed to be trained as a hunter. The smell of blood is supposed to be part of it all." Matilda kept talking to the sorrel stud as she moved toward him an inch at a time until she had her hand on his front leg. She stroked the lower part of his leg and talked to him, then carefully pulled herself up by holding onto the stirrup. The activity of the past twenty minutes made her weak, and she almost fell back to the frozen ground.

"I am Empress Matilda, daughter of King Henry. I will not let death and pain conquer me." She pulled harder on the stirrup to get in an upright position, but this action startled the already jittery horse, and he bolted forward. Matilda decided in a lightning flash of pain that her only chance of survival was to hang onto the trotting horse. She closed her eyes and hoped he was following his instincts and heading back from whence he had come. She felt her legs bouncing over the uneven ground and her new fear was that she would end up crippled, so she released the stirrup. She heard Dancer's trot change into a gallop, and the sound faded as blackness surrounded her consciousness and squeezed it to oblivion.

A pile of brown fur and maroon wool in a pool of bright blood lay against the snowy ground. Stephen pulled the reins up tight and fast as his horse reared and twisted away from the strange apparition. It was Matilda. Everyone had been looking for her the entire afternoon, and now with the sun getting ready to set, it was lucky that he had found her. Shadows flitted in and out amongst the trees; ghost-like wolves looking for a kill. Their tracks attested to the fact that they had become braver, and the vortex of prints had come closer and closer to the fallen empress.

"Matilda! Speak to me. Wake up!" Stephen peeled back the woolen material that was stuck to her. Before it started bleeding again, he saw that the wound was deep. She would not awaken, and the others were looking for Matilda in another direction. There was nothing for him to do but carry her the two miles back to camp.

The gates to the castle opened as quickly as possible, but not quickly enough for King Henry. The sound of squeaking winches did not arouse Matilda as the litter was carried into the inner courtyard. Her dark lashes seemed darker against her white skin, and there seemed to be no life in her limbs. King Henry heard the murmuring of the servants from the castle as they crowded around to see Matilda, and he knew they were startled by the amount of dried blood encrusted on her cape. King Henry rode next to the litter, his eyes staring at the space in front of him, only seeing the picture of his daughter as she had been carried by Stephen into camp. King Henry remembered his heart had stopped because he thought his Matilda dead.

His mouth clenched shut, and the muscles along his jaw hurt. His mind raced at the possibilities of her accident, but he could only conclude that someone had tried to kill his only legitimate heir. It was his fault. If pride had not gotten in the way, no one would have tried to harm her. He let his horse pick its way across the inner courtyard toward the stable, the reins held loosely in his unfeeling hands. The animal, always sensitive to his master's moods, moped along with head hung low. The horse's groom took the bridle and halted him before the stable door.

"Your majesty, sir. You may dismount." The servant, old and grey haired, did the unthinkable and touched the King's arm to remind him of the task at hand. King Henry looked down and nodded in recognition of the gesture of one father to another, of one man who had suffered similar pain comforting a fellow being and knowing that shared pain transcended any class structure for the moment.

King Henry followed the litter as it was carried into Matilda's apartment. Adelicia was already standing by the bed holding the curtains back while Matilda was placed gingerly on the fur covers. The fire blazed and the room was hot, but King Henry barely noticed the beads of perspiration that peppered his hair line. He looked for the castle's physician summoned by Brian fitzCount who had raced ahead of the other hunters.

King Henry was relieved to see that the physician was waiting and had taken charge. King Henry felt out of place in a sick room. He was glad to see Adelicia sit next to Matilda to assist the physician. He watched as she deftly cut away the layers of clothing, her tears splashing down onto the clotted mess of blood mixed with material. When she finished cutting, Adelicia held the limp hand of her step-daughter and brushed the damp hair away from Matilda's forehead with her free hand.

That act alone caused King Henry to swallow hard to get rid of the lump that arose in his throat. King Henry moved to the window alcove where it was cooler and sat down. He was intrigued by his wife's skill as well as being worried about Matilda. He knew his daughter was strong, but nothing would save her if infection set in or if the tip of the arrow had been poisoned. He feared an assassination attempt more than a simple accident. This might be the first of many. Adelicia's voice was tremulous and King Henry focused on her.

"Ella, get me some cloths and a bucket of cool water. She has a terrible fever." Adelicia frowned and bit her lower lip.

King Henry had seen this action many a time. Adelicia did this to stop her lip from trembling whenever she was nervous. The thought of Matilda's death that he had repeatedly tried to push away burst forth. What would he do if he lost his daughter as he had his sons? A man of action, King Henry could not sit still any longer. Jumping up, he strode across the room to the fireplace and pulled out his dagger. He held the blade to the fire until it was red hot. The physician reached for the knife, and King Henry handed the dagger to him gingerly.

The physician lay the hot blade against Matilda's open wound. King Henry winced for his daughter as Matilda cried out through her unconsciousness as the hot dagger seared the edges of her injury. The odor of seared flesh filled the air.

"If I find out who tried to kill my daughter, his death will be slow and torturous." King Henry spoke through clenched teeth. "Stephen, you will find out who did this to her."

Stephen sucked in large gulp of air. "Mayhap it was an accident."

"I hardly think so. She was quite visible in the open and at the distance that the arrow had to have traveled, not only could someone tell it was a person on a horse, but they could also tell it was my daughter. It was an assassination attempt that, God willing, will not work. Find the person who did this. I want to see his face when I define his sentence for him. He will die piece by piece, and his parts will be scattered across England as dinner for the animals."

"I will do my best, sire." Stephen bowed low and backed toward the door, his eyes shifting from one person to another.

CHAPTER

III

HE VOICES WERE FAR AWAY and Matilda's shoulder burned. A sliver of light hurt her even through closed eyes. She willed them to open. She wanted to know if she were in heaven and if her mother were waiting for her. She had no strength, so she allowed herself to drop down into the grey ocean and soon the voices faded, then became clear. Matilda felt Adelicia's presence. She knew she had not gone to heaven, yet.

She opened her eyes. "I feel terrible."

"Oh, Matti. Are you back?" Tears slid down Adelicia's cheek.

"I am thirsty."

"Stephen, get Matti something to drink. Quickly."

Stephen had hastened closer to the bed and was already fulfilling the wishes of his cousin. He poured claret from a small jug into a chalice and held it to Matilda's mouth. Adelicia held her up so she could drink.

"Take this," Stephen said.

Dark red wine trickled down the corner of her mouth and dropped onto the white cloth of her night gown, mirroring the dark red blood that had seeped through white bandages on her other shoulder.

The wine burned Matilda's throat, and she pulled back. "I want water."

"You may have anything you want," Stephen said. "Ella, bring your mistress the coldest water you can find."

"Send down to the kitchen for some broth, too," Adelicia said. "She must get her strength back. And send for her father. He is in the great hall with the barons."

Matilda's father appeared before her floating like an apparition. She blinked her eyes several times, and King Henry became less ghost-like and more human.

"How is my daughter?"

Matilda did not know whether he spoke to her or not, but she felt compelled to answer. Her voice cracked. "I am not that good, Father."

"You have to fight, Matilda. Do not let anyone stop you from the mission that God has set before you." King Henry leaned down.

"I am not certain that God wants me to hunt rabbits anymore, Father."

A frown graced the King's face. He laughed; not the uproarious laughter of the hunt or the great hall, but the cautious laughter of a man who may have to bargain with the devil to keep his daughter alive.

"Someone shot me with my own arrow," Matilda said. "I could not find it after I missed the first rabbit, so I left it."

"You are certain it was your own?" Stephen asked.

"Yes, I will not soon forget that particular arrow." Matilda touched the bandage with her hand. "I hope I never have to see it again."

"I will search until I find the bastard who did this to you." Stephen leaned closer to Matilda. "Then, with the King's permission, I will have him hanged."

"You have my permission." King Henry's huge bushy eyebrows were drawn together. He turned and strode from the room.

"I wish you would not, Stephen," Matilda said.

"I have to protect you. If he tried it once, he will try again, for you are a symbol of England to come. People do not like change, Matti," Stephen said.

"I do not want you in danger."

"I will be. Do you not understand that I can not imagine life without you?" Stephen said.

"I do not want to hear this. Adelicia, make him go away." Matilda turned away from Stephen and closed her eyes.

"You heard her request. As a gentleman and a friend, please leave Matilda alone. She needs her rest. Do not argue. Take your leave quickly." Adelicia waved her hands at Stephen. "Go, go, go."

Stephen shook his head. "Adelicia, you have also been here for the same length of time. You go and get some rest. I will stay here."

Matilda glanced from Adelicia to Stephen, who looked like he had been run over by a hundred horses. If she had the strength, she would have laughed at him.

Adelicia leaned toward Stephen and whispered, "Do you really want Matti to see you in a disheveled state?"

"You are right. I will see her later. I promise you this, however. I will find the one who tried to kill her. I will protect her with my life, if necessary." Stephen bowed and left the room.

The next time Matilda woke, it was dark except for the fire that had been banked for the night. The pin feathers from the down mattress had pushed up through the sheets and were poking her in the back. Matilda moved to get more comfortable. She saw that Adelicia was asleep next to her, arms above her head. She looked across the room at the mound on the cot next to the inside wall. Ella was sleeping peacefully. The detail of the tapestry above Ella was not visible in the flickering light, but Matilda remembered the picture of a downed stag with an arrow buried in its withers and she shuddered.

Everything seemed to be normal within this room, and she felt good. She sat up, slowly, and realized she was thirsty and dizzy. She winced when she put weight on her left arm, but sucked in a large gulp of air and swung her feet down to the stool next to the bed. She wanted to step down, but again the dizziness dampened her will to move further.

A gentle hand was placed upon her back, and Adelicia spoke softly. "Matti, please lie down. I will get you whatever you want. Are you thirsty?"

"Very. What time is it?" Matilda asked.

"You should be asking what day it is, not the time. You have slept for three days more since the last time you were awake." Adelicia crawled across the bed and sat beside Matilda. "There were many times when I had to hold a polished metal mirror under your nostrils so that I could tell you still had life. I prayed as I did so." She placed her hand on Matilda's forehead. "I believe your fever has broken. A good sign from the angels."

"My lady!" Ella threw back the wool and fur covers on her cot and sprang across the distance that separated her from her mistress. "May I be so honored as to get you a cool cup of water?"

"Please." Instantly a cold pewter cup was placed in her good hand, and she raised it with trembling hand to her lips. She drained it and handed the cup to Ella who refilled it without being told.

"I want you to lie down and sleep," Ella said. "You need to rest. Mayhap tomorrow I will allow you to sit up for a longer time."

Matti smiled at Ella's impertinence, knowing that in this case, as usual, she would forgive her. "I agree. I feel dizzy, but so much better." With that, she allowed herself to be helped back to a prone position by her closest companion as Adelicia fluffed her pillows.

Adelicia propped her own pillows against the head board and leaned back. "Ella, I have something to tell Matti, and I want you to listen, too. I can not seem to make sense of anything that has happened the last week. Maybe talking will help."

"This sounds very interesting. Sit here, Ella." Matilda patted the bed.

Adelicia took Matilda's hand in hers. "I am not very intelligent when it comes to the intrigue that seems to surround you. Your father knows what is best for England, but I hope his dream does not end with the end of your life."

Ella gasped. "Do you think Matti is in more danger?"

Matilda snorted. "Do not be silly, Ella. I am not in danger." She wished she felt as confident as she tried to sound. The low flames from the fireplace cast shadows like black ghosts across the room, and Matilda shivered. She spoke again, more to convince herself than the other women. "I am not in danger."

"Do not be so sure." Adelicia squeezed Matilda's hand. "Over the last few days while you were ill, I had a chance to observe people who came around you. I was afraid that someone would harm you, so I slept very little. I tasted everything that was given you."

Matilda gasped. "Adelicia! That was not your place. You could have died!"

"That is my point. You could have died. Given my place in history and given yours, I made the decision that your life should be preserved, even at the cost of my own." Adelicia held up her hand to stop the flow of words from her step-daughter. "I do not want to dwell on that. I wanted to talk to you about Stephen de Blois and Brian fitzCount. I studied both of them closely as they came to see to your health."

Matilda did not want to appear curious, but she could not keep the words from tumbling out. She stared at her step-mother. "What did you see?"

"I was very suspicious of Stephen because with your ascension to the throne, begins his descent. He seemed to have a great interest in your health. He sat next to your bed by the hour. He often went to get the wine when you asked for it, and I feared for your safety. I believed his interest in you to be above what would be expected. I was also concerned because Brian fitzCount stayed by your side for long periods of time. Your father allowed him to do so because he is the son of one of his good friends."

Matilda pulled the covers up to her chin. "I do not understand which one you suspect."

"Brian fitzCount spent many hours sitting next to you, but then one day he failed to come. He has not been back since. I find the behavior of both Stephen and Brian rather odd, but I can not prove their ways wrong." Adelicia pursed her lips. "I suspect both, and I suspect neither."

Ella squirmed around until she was sitting cross-legged on the bed between the two women, facing them. "It will be my duty to make certain that you are safe. It is unseemly for Queen Adelicia to taste your food and drink, so I will do so from now on."

Matilda giggled. "You two are being so morbid. There is no need to worry about poison. My problems will come in a more direct way like the arrow. I will have to trust to God to see me through. Now, it is the middle of the night, and we need to sleep."

The days merged into endless periods of sleep, wakefulness, and more sleep for Matilda. Slowly, the periods of wakefulness lengthened until she was on a regular schedule once more. Matilda was happy when most of her strength returned. She laughed at Adelicia and Ella whose scoldings increased as her own restlessness got her in trouble with them. The bed was less and less inviting to Matilda as she ventured first about her apartment, then tried to sneak into the hall. Her pleas to be allowed to use the garderobe were finally listened to. However, for several weeks, Matilda was confined to the upper floors of the castle. She began to suspect she was being guarded against assassination rather than an injury. It was with some relief that she accepted her father's invitation to be involved in the trial of the assassin who had been captured by Stephen's army. On the other hand, she had a fear of facing the man.

Matilda had sat in judgment in many courts in Germany and Italy and had presided over more than she could remember. She suppressed a sigh. She hoped that this would not take long. She had spent so much time in her chambers that she was anxious to walk around the castle. Adelicia claimed it was still too chilly and would not allow her outdoors.

Matilda sat with her hands in her lap, trying to look interested in the proceedings. In her experiences, one court was the same as any other, and she supposed her father would preside over this one the same as she had done when asked to by her late husband. Matilda glanced at her father out of the corner of her eye. She had merely nodded when she had entered the great hall to acknowledge his motion that she sit next to him on the platform. Now, his scowl was still in place, and Matilda did not want to risk hearing his angry words. It would be soon enough to hear the booming voice as he pronounced sentence. She did not like sitting next to her father when he was in one of these moods. He seemed massive to her. He had towered above her as a child, and now that she was older other men she had known in her youth looked smaller, but not her father. He seemed as solid to her as the thick stone walls of the castle.

Matilda looked around the great room. The long tables had been pushed to the sides of the room creating an open space in the middle that was filled with the people of the castle. King Henry's knights were mixed with the servants from the castle and the kitchen as well as the blacksmith, the shoemaker, and other craftsmen and women. Her father always ordered everyone to come to any trial he held. He had told her it was a deterrent to others who might have forgotten that England was a land governed by laws enforced by the king.

Sunlight came through the tall windows and fell across the audience, making a pattern of light and dark bands. Matilda watched pieces of dust dance around as if they had been infused with life. She smiled at the memory of one of the servants from her childhood who had shown her the balls of dust under the bed and told her they were dust fairies that hid there during the day. When she had grown older, she still called the balls of dust by that name. Matilda had been disappointed to learn that there were no dust fairies, and now as an adult she felt foolish for still wishing there were such creatures.

The commotion of Stephen's guards under the direction of William of Ypes caused Matilda's heart to beat faster, and she gripped the arms of the chair in which she was sitting as her accused assailant was brought in. She immediately felt foolish at her fear of a man under guard and in chains, and forced herself to loosen her fingers from the wood. She tried to appear calm. Mayhap it was not fear of the man, but of the deed. Until she had been declared heir to King Henry's lands, her life had been safe. Usually women were merely pawns in a political game, and thus not worth killing. The physical part of Matilda healed well, but she was not certain about the mental part. Her mind felt like it was at the bottom of a river.

Matilda had been surprised to learn that it was Stephen who had returned with the man who had let fly the arrow that had almost killed her. She wanted to hate the man, but she did not want to be the reason for his demise. That peculiar sentiment did not seem to fit her normal personality, and she was perplexed by her uncustomary disposition. Matilda forced herself to look at the man who had been dragged in by Stephen's knights. She was taken aback to see that he was merely a peasant. It seemed ludicrous to her that she, an empress, would have an assassination attempt on her person by a mere peasant. The thought made her snort with scorn, and she felt herself flush at the insult.

Matilda focused on Stephen who had followed a few steps behind his knights. She watched as the prisoner prostrated himself before King Henry. Matilda saw the welts through the torn tunic that barely covered his back, and something tugged at the back of her mind. She concentrated on the feeling, but could not pull it to the front of her mind. She leaned forward with interest as her father glared at the man before him.

"Speak," King Henry bellowed.

"I beg you, great King Henry, to listen to this pitiful man who kneels before you. I have done nothing wrong. I know not of what is spoken by this stranger behind me." The man dropped his head almost to his knees and seemed to grow smaller.

"You have been accused of an assassination attempt on my daughter and heir, Empress Matilda. You have committed a crime against me, and that is treason." King Henry looked down from the chair that had been placed on a platform. His scowl was fierce.

"Please, your majesty, I have a family and three small children. I have been your faithful servant my entire life. I would do nothing to harm you. I know not what crime I have committed." The peasant was shaking, and when he looked up, there were salty tear tracks down his dirty, brown cheeks. Matilda looked at him. His left arm was in front of him, holding his trembling body in a semi-sitting position. His other arm was beneath his mud-covered cloak. He was weak from having been beaten, and he had a long, dark scab forming on the top of his head. Someone had clubbed him. Why had he fought so hard? Afraid of the gallows, no doubt.

The peasant spoke again. "Please, your majesty. I am not afraid to die, but if I die, then who will care for my wife and my babies? Without a man to work for them and feed them, they will die. Not only will you condemn me to death, but my innocent babes will die. Give me a moment to prove my innocence."

Matilda shook her head to dislodge the thought that continued to nag her. Her attention was drawn to Stephen as he knelt before King Henry. "My lord, may I speak?"

King Henry nodded. "Please do so."

"I find it difficult to feel compassion for this peasant. I found this man with the arrow that nearly killed our lady. It was found in his hut and was hidden under a dirty mattress. I also found a gold coin in the same place. He is the assassin."

"Then he shall die." King Henry rose from his chair.

"No!" Matilda was surprised at the strength of her own voice that rattled off the stone walls of the great room, and she was startled that she had spoken aloud.

King Henry looked at his pale daughter. "Why do you speak? Do you know something that will help this case?"

Matilda was aware that the room was silent. Her father waited. Stephen waited. The peasant looked up at her, and he waited. Matilda had reacted instinctively, and she was pushing the thoughts forward that had caused her to react. What was wrong? Why did she not believe this was her assassin? She arranged her thoughts, hoping the hidden ones would surge forward. She was not

particularly fond of executions and death, but she believed that punishment was a necessity of civilized life. So why did she feel this
man was innocent? The reasons burst forward so quickly that Matilda
barely had time to put them in order before she spoke.

"King Henry, this peasant had no cause to kill me. Only those
in attendance during the Christmas court knew that an oath had
been sworn to you to make me king of England. I hardly think that
a peasant would be hired for an attempt on my life." Matilda looked
down at Stephen. He was obviously puzzled by her reaction. She
hurried on, taking advantage of his momentary confusion. "This
peasant has worked for you, Father, all his life. He was not allowed
to hunt, for you have restricted all the lands around this castle. He
would not know how to draw a bow and aim an arrow."

"He is not only a field servant, but he works in the butcher
shop as well during season. Those who butcher usually do the hunting for the castle's kitchens," Stephen said. His eyes narrowed, and
he stared at King Henry. "Do not forget that I found the gold piece
under his pallet."

"Anyone can slip a piece of gold into someone's home. It would
not take a genius, just someone with the determination to protect
himself. I have difficulty believing this man would be part of an
intrigue." Matilda leaned forward and stared down at the accused.
Again, something struck her as peculiar about him.

"I do not understand why you want to protect a common peasant," Stephen said.

"Because I was taught in the courts of Germany, and by my dear
mother, that even if we are not equal in our stations in life, we are
equal in the eyes of God. She would go out into the streets of London and the peasant villages and wash the feet of the poor and tend
to the sick. I can not forget her teachings of so long ago. That was
her legacy to me, along with her name."

"Matilda." King Henry's voice was soft and velvety.

Matilda looked at her father. She did not know whether he was
speaking to her or to a memory. "Father, ask the peasant to stand.
Something is different about his posture."

Matilda noticed that it took a moment for King Henry to focus
on her. She waited.

"Do as my daughter asks. Stand."

"Have him remove his cloak," Matilda said.

"Remove your cloak."

Matilda watched the field-dirty cloak slide from the peasant's shoulder where it had partially covered his right side. His arm was withered.

"There is your answer, Stephen. He was chosen by someone to die, and you, in your impatience to seek revenge, did an ungodly deed and reacted without thinking. You could have cost this man his life." Matilda glowered at her cousin. Why did he not see the trap? Or was he the one who had tried to set it? Either way, Stephen did not seem very intelligent.

"I believe we owe this man his freedom." King Henry turned to Matilda. "I have learned a lesson from my daughter."

Matilda felt her father's hot breath on her as he leaned over and whispered to her. "You are so like your mother, Matti. She was always teaching me, too, and I was always in wonder of her. She will be alive for me as long as you are."

King Henry looked down at Stephen. "This peasant is to be released at once. The gold coin that was found under his pallet is his. His torn tunic is to be replaced, and he is to be given a poultice for the wounds on his back. He will not work until he is healed."

The peasant dropped to his knees and fresh tears rolled down his weathered face. "I will pray for you every night. I will pray for your judgment to remain as keen as it was today, and I will pray for Empress Matilda, for she is truly wise."

"She has the wisdom of the ages that most of us do not have. You may be dismissed," King Henry said.

Matilda watched the guards remove the peasant, helping him out the door nearest the kitchen. She saw Stephen hand him the gold coin as he passed by, and she wondered whose gold coin had passed back to the peasant. She was more shaken than she realized. Someone had tried to kill her. They, whoever they were, had absolutely no scruples, no conscience. The peasant was as expendable to them as she had been. A cloud passed over her life at that moment. No longer would she be free.

Matilda felt oppressed by the atmosphere of the great hall and stood. Today should have been a good day, for she felt almost healed, at least physically. She stepped down from the platform and moved across the room to the kitchen. A servant was sweeping the stone floor in the kitchen and a second servant followed the first placing fresh reeds on the floor. Matilda noticed that both of them watched her as she moved through the kitchen toward the outside door. She had chosen this way out so that Adelicia could not see her leave. She felt like a child again, and it reminded her of the times she had sneaked off to the orchard to eat green apples. She had never had the stomachaches that everyone had predicted she would get if she ate green apples.

A youngster pushed open the door for her and bowed as she moved through it. She pulled her fur wrap tighter even though the sun was out and there was no wind. Today was the first day since the assassination attempt that she had gone outside the protection of the castle. She walked past the servants who were preparing the mid-day meal outside on a spit for the guests who would remain in residence at the castle until spring. Matilda watched the youngster who turned the handle of the spit. Even in the cold, perspiration glistened on his forehead. One cheek was smudged with ashes. The grey color matched his dirty tunic and the material that he had wrapped around his feet. Matilda wondered if he had shoes under the rags. Probably not.

The wind shifted sending smoke into the boy's eyes. He could only close them since his job was to continue turning the meat without fail. The wind shifted again, and the boy took a moment to rub his eyes. Matilda grinned as he swore and kicked at a dog that had sneaked closer to the meat. An assortment of dogs sat out of range of the boy's reach. Further back, a black and white cat sat with her half-grown litter of kittens clambering around her. The cat licked her whiskers in anticipation of a scrap of meat, Matilda supposed, and she hoped the cat would be rewarded.

Matilda walked past the animals, stopped out of range of the smoke and shivered, but not from the cold. "I can not sit around and fear for my own safety." Matilda forced herself to cross the snow-covered courtyard to the stairs that led through the gate towers to the walk on the top of the wall. The stairs were steep, and she was breathing hard when she came out into the sunlight at the top. It was a good thing that Adelicia could not hear her ragged breathing or she would put Matilda right back to bed. Matilda leaned against the rough stones of the tower to rest. She did not like the feeling of weakness that she had for the first time in her life. She did not like the feeling of vulnerability that would be a part of her for the rest of her life. She would just have to push it to the back of her memories, but not so far back that she would become careless. She moved down the wall-walk that was wide enough for four abreast, and decided to complete the circuit back to this point no matter how long it took. She wanted to prove to herself that she could overcome her physical weakness and the fear that had changed her.

The sun was behind her, and she felt its warmth through her fur wrap. The sky was a light blue. She recalled that it was on such a day that she had been wounded. "That should not matter. I will continue to love sunny days more than rainy ones, for like a precious stone, they are rare."

Matilda was surprised that she had spoken aloud. Glancing around, she saw that the guards were not within hearing distance. She stopped walking and looked out between the embrasures, the lowest part above her waist. Rolling hills were white as far as she could see. The forest was to her right and the place where she was attacked was on the far side of that forest. "If I could find the person. . . ."

She shook her head. For every one who failed to kill her, there would be another to take his place.

A hand reached out for her and wrapped itself around her arm. She jumped and involuntarily screamed.

"Matilda! I am sorry. I thought you heard me walking up behind you."

Matilda pushed Stephen away. "Never do that again." She moved away from him and stopped by the next embrasure.

"I am sorry. I did not want you to be alone and unprotected." Stephen followed her.

"Do you have reason to believe the assassin is in the castle?" Matilda turned and looked into his eyes.

He did not look away. "I have been thinking about what you said in the great hall. You are right about there being someone who does not want you to be England's next ruler."

"Who?"

"If I had known that, I would have told King Henry immediately. I fear I do not know. I am to be your protector. I have spoken with your father, and he has asked me to do so."

Matilda frowned. "Why would he do that? He should be my protector, as my father and my king."

"I . . . I think that you need several protectors."

Matilda's thoughts went back to what Adelicia had told her about being suspicious of both Stephen and Brian fitzCount. Mayhap no one could be trusted. Mayhap the conspiracy against her might be the work of many. She glared at Stephen. "Then, who else will be my protector besides you? And who else will be close enough to kill me, to do the job correctly the next time? Who will protect me from my protectors?"

"Your assassin will not be me."

"How can I be certain of that? Let us be honest, Stephen. I can trust no one. If it had not been for my father's wish to place me on the throne as his heir, you would be the next king of England. I can not believe you do not want that title and the privilege that goes with it, including the treasury."

Stephen put his hand on Matilda's arm. "There are some things that are more important than a kingdom."

Matilda pulled away from than man who spoke such foolish thoughts. "Not to me. What is more important than a being king?"

"Love."

"Love?" Matilda's eyebrows raised and her eyes widened. Her cousin was obviously not in his right mind. Mayhap he was teasing her, playing a game. She frowned and shook her head. "I do not understand."

"I love you, Matilda, and I have always loved you. Ever since we were children I have loved you."

"I . . . I . . ." Matilda blinked rapidly then looked down at the packed pebbles and dirt at her feet. She did not know whether to be angry with him and quell the surge of feeling within her or to allow him to flatter her further.

Stephen stepped closer to her. "Do you find it difficult to believe that I love you? Do you find it abhorrent?"

"I do not know what to think. I never imagined that you felt this way. I do not think that we can ever be more than good friends. I am to be married. . . ." Matilda willed herself to step away from Stephen, but she could not make her feet move. All she could do was look toward the woods in the distance.

"Ha! To a boy. You were married to an old man. . . ."

"Stop that! My husband was not an old man. He was very kind to me, and I learned to love him deeply." Matilda turned away from the view of the woods and leaned against the merlon partly to get away from Stephen and partly to ward off the eerie feeling that she was about to get an arrow in her back.

"Yes, you learned to love, but you did not really have a choice, did you? And now you are to be given to a boy for the sake of a few hundred thousand acres. When are you going to learn to love?"

"Love, if there is such a thing, is for commoners, not for royalty. I have to think of England. I can not be selfish."

"I love you, Matilda, and I want to be selfish. I love everything about you. I love your intelligence, your beauty. Your existence is sacred to me. I love the very ground upon which you walk."

"The very ground upon which I walk? Oh, surely you can be a better poet than that." Matilda turned and faced Stephen. "You have forgotten your wife. What makes you think that I would be content sharing you with another woman? What makes you think I would stoop that low?"

Stephen started to grab her arm, but she stepped away from him, sliding to the next merlon, and his hand dropped to his side. He was silent as he stared at her.

"I can not blame you for doubting my love. I can understand that you think I am a rival for the throne. It is not I who wants to be king, but my dear wife, Maithilde, who wants to be queen. She can be ruthless in any of her chosen quests."

"She has to be strong, Stephen. It is her nature, just as yours is to be . . . to be . . ."

"Go on and say it, Matti. You think I am weak."

"I do not think that."

Stephen's voice was nearly a whisper. "I know that your father and others think that I am weak. For this reason, King Henry ordered that I marry, not the woman of my choice, but a woman who is domineering and hateful. She is filled with even more contempt because I spent so much time at your side while you were ill. Her tongue drips acid. She asked me if I had tried to kill you so that the kingdom would be ours. I find that her beautiful face is marred by the twisting of her mouth into a sneer. I have tried to love her, but I have found that love has been stolen from me piece by piece by her greed."

"She is hateful?" Matilda placed her slender hand against his face. She was startled to find that she had moved toward Stephen without realizing it, and she wondered whether her heart was in control instead of her mind. "Who could be hateful to someone so gentle?"

"So, now it is gentle, is it? A moment ago you said I was weak." Stephen's smile was bittersweet.

"Those were your words, not mine. I prefer someone who is confident enough to be tender and thoughtful," Matilda said.

"Am I good enough for the Empress Matilda?" Stephen looked toward the woods where the fateful hunt had taken place.

Matilda followed Stephen's gaze toward the trees that were stripped of their leaves. The woven pattern of branches reminded her of the twisted pattern of her life with Stephen. They had always managed to cross, to meet, to be together, but ultimately they had diverged.

"You are good enough for me, dear Stephen. I do not like to admit that I have also loved you since I was a child. You were always my knight. There, I have confessed. What are we to do? You are married forever, and I am to be married next year." Her life would have been better with Stephen by her side. Mayhap it was not too late. She looked across the lands that her father wanted her to rule. To love Stephen would mean the loss of the kingdom. Her father was right in that marriage to Geoffrey of Anjou would mean the preservation of England. Matilda looked from the land toward Stephen. She touched his cheek, then dropped her hand. She whirled around and hurried away from Stephen and his offer of love.

"Wait!" Stephen caught up with Matilda. "You can not leave me. We were meant to be together. Our paths have crossed many times, and to me that is a sign."

Matilda stopped, but did not look at Stephen. She stared at the land that surrounded the castle. She stared at all that was England. "I see no future for us, Stephen."

"I see no future without you, Matilda."

Matilda bit her lower lip. She felt herself wavering in her resolve to do what was necessary for England. "Will you stop making this so difficult for me?"

"No."

"It would be an unholy union. It would be adulterous."

Matilda opened the door to the tower stairs intending to pull it shut between them, but Stephen was quick to place his hand above hers and slip through behind her. "I do not believe that and neither do you. I have never seen you bow to convention. You have agreed to become the first female king of England, and you are worried about a liaison with someone who loves you?"

She walked away, more quickly this time, but Stephen followed her down the tower steps. Matilda could feel his breath on her neck, and she felt her face flush. She stopped at a curve in the stairwell where no one could see them and turned toward Stephen. He stepped down onto the same step, and Matilda kissed him. He kissed her in return, and the feeling of overwhelming desire coursed through every part of her body. She pulled away and put her head against his chest.

"I do not know why I did that, but I do not care," she said.

Stephen put his arms around her. "Send your lady-in-waiting away for the night."

Matilda listened to the sounds of night. Stephen's offer of love echoed in her thoughts, and she could not rid herself of them. Should she give in to him? He waited for her. He promised her love, and she wanted love above all else. Why should she not have what should have been hers? She could have both Stephen and England if she were careful.

Ella's quiet snoring drifted across the chamber in rhythm with her breathing. The logs in the fireplace snapped, then shifted as they burned. Matilda could hear nothing except the winds of winter as they swooped down the chimney or past her shuttered windows. She sat up and pulled the bed curtains aside. She shivered as the current of cool air that invaded the warmth of her bed swept past her, ruffling the curtains on the other side. The tallow candles, which were placed in a wrought iron tripod on either side of the door, had not burned down more than two hour's worth. Matilda swung her legs over the side of the bed and listened to Ella's snoring. She smiled at the contrast between Ella's easy rest and her own restlessness. Matilda slid to the floor, her night gown sticking to the linen sheets. She jerked the gown down impatiently and closed the bed curtains.

She hesitated. Could she really have Stephen and England? She thought of Stephen's dark eyes and the way he smiled at her. If they were found out, what then? Matilda's nerves tingled, and she liked the feeling. It was new to her, for Stephen had been right. As much as she had learned to care for her late husband, the truth was that he was much older than she and lovemaking had not been as exciting as she had been told it would be. Matilda wondered what it would be like to feel the tight flesh of a younger man that covered muscles still hardened from youth. She felt herself flush and knew it was not from embarrassment, but from anticipation. Matilda felt for the boots that she had hidden under the bed. Finding them, she pulled them out, being careful not to drag them across the reeds. She tiptoed around the bed, watching Ella as she slept. The crackling of the reeds sounded like thunder no matter how slowly she tried to move.

When Matilda reached the door, she found she had been holding her breath, and now she took a large gulp of air as she pulled her fur cape from the peg on the door. An image of her father flickered across her mind, and she hesitated. What would he do if he found that she were having an affair? What could he do or say? He had had several affairs and almost as many children. Even her favorite brother, Robert of Gloucester, born before she was, had been the issue of an affair with a nobleman's wife. If she were to be king, then the pleasures that went with the king should be hers as well. Tradition could be broken in more than one way.

With that thought to encourage her, Matilda opened the heavy door. She smiled to herself as she remembered complaining to Ella that the hinges squeaked so badly they unnerved her. As expected, Ella had made certain one of the servants used animal fat to grease the hinges, and the door opened quietly. Not pausing to look back at Ella as she closed the door, Matilda slipped into the darkened hall, and moved to a wooden bench. She sat, relieved at the stillness in the castle. She was also glad to have a rest from the crackling of the reeds underfoot. She had never noticed before how loud they were.

Matilda tied the straps to her boots and flexed her ankles to see if they were too tight. She was not used to putting on her own boots. The left one felt tight, but she did not want to waste time. Flinging her cape around her shoulders, Matilda eased down the tower's stone steps and made her way down a short passageway to the great hall. She hoped that the cape's dark color would hide her, or at least make her seem ghost-like. She stopped at the door and pushed it open. Matilda peered in and glanced around. Fortunately no one was sleeping by any of the three fireplaces. She took a deep breath, bit her lower lip, and crossed the room to the middle window alcove. The light from the fireplaces barely illuminated the room, making it difficult to see. It was even darker in the shuttered alcove, and Matilda did not see Stephen before he pulled her into his arms. She stifled a yelp and collapsed against him.

"Did I frighten you?"

Matilda could feel her heart thumping against her rib cage. "Yes!" she whispered.

"You knew I would be here."

"Yes, but I did not know it would be so difficult to get here. The next time I will take your advice and confide in Ella, so that she may leave my chambers."

Stephen chuckled. "Is that a promise that there will be a next time?"

"I can not deny my feelings for you. I will allow you to do what you want with me, for when I am around you, I have no will of my own." Matilda lifted her face to his and kissed him. "See? You do not even have to ask for my favors." She felt Stephen kiss her in return, and she was happier than she remembered ever having been.

Stephen took the cape from her shoulders. "What manner of clothing have we here? A cape and a night gown? There is not much here to hinder a romance."

Matilda took the cape and laid it on the alcove bench. She untied the first ribbon on her night gown, then the second. She did not notice the night's chill as she let the gown drop. A weakness engulfed her as she felt Stephen's hands on her, and she fell against him. "I have never felt like this before. Promise that you will come to me every night. I do not care what the future holds. I know that I can not live without you."

"Nor I without you, Matti. I have dreamed of this moment. Nothing shall stop us now."

"Stephen, in a year and a half I shall have to be wed. How can we stop that?" Matilda felt a sadness creep in to temper her happiness.

"Shhhh, we will think of something. Tonight is for us. Let us not think of anything else."

Matilda shivered. "Does love have to be so difficult?"

"Yes, or it would not be as sweet. Stolen moments are more precious than all the gems in your father's treasury."

"It seems that it is so. Enough talk." Matilda helped Stephen remove his tunic.

Matilda stretched her arms above her head as she looked out the window from her dressing table. The morning sounds of Ella's rituals were as comforting to her as the common rituals of the nights with Stephen. Matilda felt a familiar cramping in her abdomen and smiled. "I think it is the moon time for me. Where is the rag box?"

Ella stopped making the bed and looked at her mistress. "At least you are not pregnant with Stephen's baby. That would rush your marriage to Geoffrey by six months. It would not be the first time a baby has been born early and to the wrong man." Ella giggled. "Only the mother is known for certain at the birth of babies."

"Six months! Oh, Ella! Is my heaven going to end that soon? Can nothing be done?" Matilda leaned her elbows on the table and stared into the mirror. "Is this happy face going to disappear in only six months?"

"Yes. You have no choice, so you may as well get used to the idea of marrying the Count of Anjou. Maybe he can make your heart pound and your eyes glow."

"Do not be absurd. He is just a child. I have been loved by a man." Matilda whirled around at Ella's laughter and glared at her. "Just where do you go every night? Where do you spend your time? Is it not with your dear Edward?"

"He is my boundless love. Why, he makes love to me three or four times a night. It should make me tired to be deprived of my sleep so, but love gives me boundless energy. How often does your Stephen awaken you in the night?"

"Why, Ella! How crass you have become." Matilda grinned. "Stephen will not let me sleep at all. He loves me from dusk to dawn, and my energy surges to meet his."

Matilda started at the sound of a knock on the door. "Who could that be at this hour? It had better be important. Open the door, Ella."

Ella whispered across the room. "It is later than we thought. See the sun is halfway to its zenith."

"Send whoever it is away, unless it is my father or Adelicia." Matilda looked in the mirror and picked up a comb. She turned at the sound of Ella's voice as the door banged against the stone wall.

"You can not push your way in here!" Ella shouted. "I will call the guards and have you thrown out."

"Oh, you will?" Maithilde stepped around Ella and marched over to Matilda. "If you throw me out of here, I will tell King Henry what I know about my husband and you!"

Matilda's anger was coupled with dread. She remained seated to emphasize her higher position, and tried to appear indifferent. "It is all right, Ella. Maithilde is obviously not in her right mind. We can forgive her."

"Not in my right mind! I will tell you what is in my mind. I have been highly insulted by my husband. In a moment of weakness, I tried to kiss him. He pushed me away and said that I was no match for you." Maithilde paused to get her breath, then raged on. "I suspected that his bed had not been warmed for long whenever I went to his chambers in the mornings to see to his needs. For almost a year, he has paid little attention to me. With Stephen that means only one thing. You look at me with surprise? Do not think you are the first woman he has bedded while married to me. Do not think you will be the last."

"You are an impertinent and vulgar person. First, you burst in here, raging, and then you insult my intelligence with stories of Stephen's romances. I can understand why he might have had mistresses in the past if he had to contend with the likes of you." Matilda was glad for the gasp she had elicited from Maithilde. She had to undermine any effort by Stephen's wife to control her. Threats from Maithilde made her angry and with anger came strength. It had always been that way for her. Her mother had told her that she inherited that trait from her father. Matilda scrutinized Maithilde with a look that implied Stephen's wife was beneath her and hardly worth the effort of a reply. "Rest assured that whatever you decide to tell the rest of the castle will be confirmed by me. I have nothing to hide. I will make certain, however, that you will be made to look the fool."

"Do not fret. I have no intentions of revealing your affair with Stephen. It suits my purposes to keep everything hidden. The time will come when you will pay for this indiscretion." Maithilde whirled around and stomped across the room. She turned at the door. "I am not without my own admirers. Your liaison does me more good than it does you."

"So be it. You have told me nothing except that you know about Stephen and me. That is just an excuse to try to annoy me. What is the true reason for your visit?"

"Time will tell. I am with child and if the child is a boy, I will name him for his natural father, not the one who will give him a name." Maithilde laughed. "I will bear the child as proof of my own frivolity. Every day Stephen will have to pay for the feeding and care of the child that is not his. Every day that he looks on the child will be a day he is reminded of his own cuckolding."

"You make no sense. Go, and do not bother me again, or I will have you flogged in the castle yard." Matilda waved her hand to shoo away her adversary. She turned to the mirror and with shaking hands, tried to comb her hair. She did not like the pale face that stared back at her. She winced when the door slammed, then was relieved by the meaning of the sound. She glanced in the mirror into Ella's eyes. "She will not tell anyone."

Ella took the comb and began combing Matilda's hair. "She can not say anything for fear of being called a traitor to King Henry. He would not hesitate to stop her prattling mouth permanently."

Matilda sighed. "I wish I could ask him to do the deed." She closed her eyes and tried to forget the confrontation. It always relaxed her to have Ella comb her hair, and she was almost asleep when a knocking at the door pulled her back. "Ella, if it is Maithilde, do not let her in." Matilda sat very straight and still while Ella opened the door. This time the mirror showed Stephen as he burst into the room.

"What did she say to you? Are you all right?" Stephen dropped to his knees in front of Matilda and grasped her hands.

"She said nothing that was important. Do not worry about her." Matilda glanced toward the door that Ella had closed. "You should not be here. It seems our indiscretions have caused us some trouble, but that will pass."

Stephen stood. "You are right. Until tonight."

"No! Not tonight."

Stephen laughed softly. "Why not tonight? My wife has her own diversions. She only wishes to intimidate you. She needs a reminder that King Henry would not be amused by her harassment of you. I will explain to her that it could be construed as treason."

"Whatever you wish."

Stephen kissed Matilda's hand and walked quickly to the door. "I came to make certain that you were not upset. I should have known that your strength would carry you."

Matilda stared at Stephen as he retreated, closing the door behind him. She thought of her mother and knew that there would have been disapproval from her had she been alive to witness this passion for Stephen. Her mother had never complained about the King's philandering, once having explained it as a man's way. She had told Matilda, however, that her belief in God, the Church, and their Laws prevented her from considering lovers. Matilda remembered that her mother's pious beliefs were well-known throughout England, and no man would have dared approach her. Matilda sighed. She could never live up to her mother's expectations in love or in religion. Matilda was glad that her mother was not alive to see her fallen daughter. The power of love for Stephen blocked all resolutions from her mind. Her mother must have had a will of forged iron. What would happen when the few months she had left with Stephen were over? Matilda pushed that thought from her mind. She would live for today.

The moments with Stephen seemed like a dream. Time became the enemy as the days continued to flow together into months. Their love-making was as exciting to Matilda now as it had been in the beginning. She had thought, briefly, about giving up the quest for the throne. She almost wished she had never agreed to love Stephen, but would smile and try to hold onto the memories for the future.

The leaves were the dark green of summer, and Matilda was uncharacteristically saddened by that fact. It meant her marriage to Geoffrey of Anjou was only a few days away. She sat on the cushioned window seat in the alcove and plucked the ticking until a pin feather poked through. Matilda pulled the tiny feather out of the cushion. She placed it on the palm of her hand and blew it across the room toward Adelicia. It fluttered and twisted in the air currents with a life of its own until it came to a rest on the floor. Matilda turned away from the feather, leaned her elbows on the cool stone sill, and placed her chin in her hands. She stared through a section of red-stained glass. Even that cheerful color did not make her world seem happier. A sigh. She wished that Stephen could be with her for one last time.

"Matilda, you are too quiet." Adelicia laid her sewing aside and crossed the room. "I would rather that you be in a rage, or at least argue with your father. I know that you love Stephen, but it is an impossible romance."

"It is not fair. If I had never loved Stephen, I would not have this pain now." Matilda leaned back against the wooden shutter. "I wish a splinter would pierce my heart."

"You are not the first woman to love one man and marry another." Adelicia sat on the opposite bench and placed her hand on Matilda's arm. "When I found out about you and Stephen, I worried about you. I was right. Your love was torrid, but it has to be over. You will leave here in a few weeks with your husband and cross the Channel to start a new life. You will probably never see Stephen again."

"I thought that an eighteen month betrothal was a lifetime away, and yet the time is gone."

Adelicia dropped her hand from Matilda's arm. "It was a lifetime ago. You have another life now."

"I have never known such sorrow. Adelicia, when he touches me, I shiver. I spend hours watching his every move, and I marvel at how it never tires me. When he is away from me, I feel as barren and cold as the stones in this wall."

"You can not be so foolish. Stop this right now."

Matilda's eyes teared as she looked at Adelicia. "How can you say that? Not only do I have to leave the man I love, but I have to marry a mere boy, thanks to my father and his political ambitions."

"You understand better than I the ramifications of refusing to marry the Count of Anjou. His lands are vast. You know what could happen if you do not strengthen your power through this marriage. You have to ask yourself what you need to do to gain and keep the throne upon which you wish to sit." Adelicia frowned. "I hate these intrigues."

"No more than I, but you are correct. If I do not marry Geoffrey of Anjou, I may not have the money or power to maintain the throne. I can not have Stephen as my husband unless Maithilde were to die."

"I hope that you . . ."

"No, I can not commit murder as easily as I commit adultery. I can only break one commandment at a time." Matilda smiled at her step-mother and saw a frown returned to her.

"I do not want to hear about broken commandments. You frighten me with such talk."

"I frighten myself. I do not break a commandment easily. Do you think I will go to Hell?" Matilda asked.

"I do not think so. God has plans for you and England. Besides, I think you would have a lot of company in Hell."

Matilda laughed. "You have pagan views, Adelicia."

Adelicia nodded. "I have often been told that by your father. Compared to your mother, I must seem quite wicked."

"Do not be silly. I find that you are as virtuous as she was. You have the same quiet strength. You are different, though, in that you are strong enough to question the beliefs of the Church. Mother was strong in the beliefs of the Church, but she never questioned them." Matilda touched her step-mother's face. "You have been so wonderful to me. You have been strong for me."

"I do not feel strong, Matti. I know only that I do not believe some of the teachings of the Church, and it frightens me." Adelicia was quiet. "I have never confided this to anyone."

Matilda nodded. "It is better left unsaid."

Adelicia brushed her hair behind her ears and stared at Matilda. "Do you feel badly about taking Stephen from Maithilde?"

"Not at all. She is hateful to me. Stephen is too gentle for her. She pushes him toward something he can not have."

"What is that?" Adelicia asked.

"She wants to be Queen of England."

"That is preposterous. She can not marry your father unless I die, and I will not do that for a long time, according to the readings from the fortune teller."

"She wants Stephen to take the throne away from me when the time comes."

"Matilda! That is treason. She could be hanged for thoughts like that." Adelicia's eyes were wide with wonder and horror. "What are you going to do?"

"I have no desire to further complicate my life with the death of my lover's wife. I have caused her pain, and I do not wish to add to her problems. I would feel guilty if I used what information Stephen has given me to put her to death. I wish I could dispose of her without feeling guilty, but I can not. It may be a weakness I should strive to overcome."

"Do you not think she is dangerous?"

"Mayhap. Stephen loves me. He will not raise an army to stop me. Some day, if God permits, maybe we will rule together."

"You do want to be our sovereign, do you not?"

"I do. I believe it to be God's will," Matilda said.

"If God had wanted you to rule with Stephen, you would have been given a sign. Without that, you may as well resign yourself to a future without him."

"I have done so. I have not seen Stephen for three agonizing days. I feel that Hell is thrust upon me while I am still on this earth." Matilda looked at her step-mother with eyes she knew were parched from crying.

"Did Stephen agree to not seeing you?"

"He argued with me. I do not want to discuss this anymore. It wrenches my heart." Matilda stared out the window.

The banging of the door against the stone wall brought Matilda and Adelicia to standing positions instantly. Matilda searched the figure for a sign of an assassination weapon. She realized that in the depths of her mind where it did not show, was hidden the fear of annihilation that had been made stronger after the attempt on her life. It slipped into her mind during the dark hours as a nightmare, or it leaped into the brain as a response to sudden and unexplained noises. Every nerve in her body was ready for fight, and it took her a moment to realize the intruder into her chamber was Stephen.

Matilda had not recovered from the banging of the door before her heart pounded and blood surged through her body again at the sight of her Stephen.

"Please." The agony of the last few days, highlighted by the stress of the last minute, underscored her plea. Matilda noted the anguished look on Stephen's face. His hair looked unkempt, and he had not shaved.

Stephen strode across the floor and grasped Matilda's hands. "I can not stay away any longer."

Matilda jerked her hands away and stepped behind Adelicia. "Do not do this to me, Stephen. You torture me." Matilda turned away. She wanted to be strong, but she could not do it alone. "Adelicia, make him leave." She felt tears, and she blinked to stop them from flowing. Stephen must not see her like this.

Adelicia blocked his outstretched hands. "Stephen, you must go."

"Leave us alone, Adelicia. Just for a little while." Stephen's voice cracked.

Adelicia placed her hand on Matilda's shoulder and tried to force her to turn around, but she stood like a rock. "Stephen, you look as if you have not slept for days."

"That is true. I have come to you for help. Please let me talk with Matti."

Matilda felt panic at the thought of being left alone with Stephen and she called out, "No!"

"Matilda, you owe Stephen and yourself time. I will leave you here for only a few minutes while I go visit the kitchen to check on the food for the wedding. I will be gone for half of the hour."

Thoughts were racing so quickly through Matilda's mind that she did not hear the door close behind her step-mother. She refused to turn around. Stephen stepped into the alcove and slid his arms around her. Matilda could not resist the familiar form, and she folded into his body, pressing against him, assuming a familiar fit from habit.

"I love you, Matilda. I can not live without you. Can you not change destiny and leave with me? We can go to Germany. Your people would welcome you back. You were loved and respected there. You are still their Empress."

For a moment, the idea seemed to make sense, then Matilda rejected it. There were many reasons, one of which was that she wanted to control England. She wanted to be the person that every-one had to answer to, but instead of voicing these feelings to Stephen, she chose to give him a fact that he could understand. "I can not go back. The throne is in the hands of my enemies."

"I have never known you to worry about that before. The people love you. That should be all you need. We could live there together . . . forever." Stephen leaned down, moved her dark hair aside and kissed the back of her neck.

"You are asking me to walk away from all that my father has strived to give me. You are asking that I give up the throne."

"When the time comes, you can come back and take the throne. You can still rule England." Stephen kissed Matilda's ear and nuzzled her cheek.

"Stop!" Matilda jerked away and turned to face Stephen. "You do not have the common sense of a goose. How do you think England would react to a female king who lived overseas with a man to whom she was not married? How do you think they would react to our leaving Maithilde and Geoffrey behind? What would I use for power? Our love? Think about it, Stephen. I need the Count of Anjou because of his lands, or I can not keep the throne. It is inevitable that someone will try to seize the throne. I will have enough trouble convincing the barons that I am a capable ruler in spite of being female without giving them an excuse to work the people against me."

"Do I understand that you prefer the throne to me?" Stephen reached for her again, but when Matilda stepped back, she found further retreat cut off by the window in the alcove. She held up her hand. "Come no closer."

"Are you choosing me or the throne? A lifetime of love, or a lifetime of struggle?"

"I do not have a choice, Stephen. God has decided for me. Mayhap I failed the test, for I fell in love with you. I still love you, but I have to try to follow the path God has chosen."

"That path has no width," Stephen said.

"What do you mean?"

"There is no room for me."

Matilda looked down at her hands folded in front of her. "I wish it were not so." The tears came again, hotter than before. The pain of this moment would be etched in her memory, and she knew it would surface again and again. -

Stephen looked into Matilda's eyes. "My pain mirrors yours. My future has crumbled, and is washed away by your tears. I can take no more." Stephen walked away.

Matilda watched as he left the alcove and crossed the room. "Stephen!" She stretched her arms towards him.

Stephen whirled around. "Yes?"

"Do not leave me! I can not say farewell a second time. I can not do it." Matilda ran into Stephen's arms and gripped his tunic as if she were hanging onto her life. Stephen held her lightly, and she pushed against him, trying to get closer. "I need you too much."

Stephen stepped away from Matilda. "What about your marriage to Geoffrey of Anjou?"

"I have to do that for the crown."

"No! You do not have to prostitute yourself for England. I can help you gain the throne."

"If you continue to argue this with me, then I will be forced to leave you. I have to do what my father and king ask of me. It is only a political marriage. I will not love him. I promise that I will not let him touch me. He is only a boy, after all."

"Do not forget that the boy will grow into a man." Stephen gently kissed the palm of her hand. "What man could resist you?"

She shivered at the way his words touched her future. She closed her eyes. "I shall be his wife in name only, I promise you. How can I let anyone else caress my body after you have stolen every inch of it with your hands?"

"Let us not talk of what pains the two of us. We should spend these last few minutes in each other's arms. I want to remember the feel of you." Stephen pulled Matilda to him and wrapped his arms around her.

"I will savor this moment. There may not be more." Matilda put her head against Stephen's chest and listened to his heartbeat.

Matilda was still clinging to Stephen, the colored light shining on them from the window, when Adelicia returned.

Matilda let Stephen go as Adelicia led him to the door and closed it behind him softly. Adelicia spoke no words, and for that Matilda was glad. There would be no comfort in anything Adelicia could say.

The day of the wedding was cool and rainy. The chill from outside could not be stopped even by Ella's careful attention to the small fire in the fireplace, and Matilda thought she would never stop shivering. She was dressed and waiting for William, the Archbishop of Canterbury, to send his assistant for her. The chapel had been decorated with summer flowers, and Adelicia had insisted on braiding flowers into Matilda's hair. They looked stark white against her black hair and were out of place because of Matilda's frown. Her lavender chemise had been made especially for the occasion and fell in graceful folds to the floor. It hid the leather strapped shoes that had been made for her by the castle cobbler in pale blue, almost white, and they matched Matilda's kirtle that looked white except for the folds, which revealed its true color. Adelicia had embroidered the kirtle with pastel flowers of spring, making certain that the blue flowers matched Matilda's eyes with perfection. A girdle of blue silk had been braided and placed about Matilda's waist. The ends were tasseled and hung below her knees.

"Do not frown so," Ella said. "It will cause terrible wrinkles."

"I do not care." Matilda sighed, but she forced herself to smooth her forehead. She paced about the room, wincing once when a sharp reed on the floor stabbed her heel through the thin leather. The room had been aired and fresh reeds and spices had been placed on the floor for the bride and groom.

"This waiting is horrible. If I have to go through with this marriage then I wish to get it over with. I feel as a pig must when it is about to be slaughtered."

"Matilda! What disgusting thoughts you have," Adelicia said.

"I feel disgusted. I think I shall act the shrew. I want him to hate me."

Adelicia put her hands on her hips. "I do not think playing the shrew would be an intelligent thing to do for a lady."

"If being a lady forces one to marry a boy, then I will no longer be a lady. I will be so awful that dear Count Anjou will race away from here so fast that we will forget he was ever in England." Matilda marched toward the door and jerked it open. She had the strength born of anger, and the door banged against the stone wall. She hurried down the stone steps with Adelicia and Ella in tow, both of them calling to her to wait for the Archbishop's call. Matilda would not heed their pleas to act the lady. She swept into the tower chapel before the musicians could begin playing.

The lute player saw her first and began strumming. Matilda glared at him and he hit a sour note. She cringed at both the wronged note and the music he had undoubtedly written for the occasion. Matilda almost smiled when the other musicians looked at him, startled, then watched as she walked up the aisle. The archbishop stood by the altar and watched his assistant place the parchment scroll and seal next to the sacrament cups.

The stained glass windows were at the second story level, their colors subdued because of the greyness of the day. Ordinarily, this was one of Matilda's favorite places. She loved coming to Mass, sitting with her family in the second story alcove opposite the altar above the wooden floor where the other worshipers stood. She always felt at peace during Mass when everyone prayed. It was a great leveler for her. Only today there was no peace for Matilda. If there were to be no peace for her, then she would make certain that there would be no peace for anyone.

Matilda stopped in front of the archbishop. He looked dwarfed by the two story chapel as he turned toward her. "I did not call you, my lady."

"I know that. I am ready. Let us proceed."

"It would be difficult without the groom and the bride's father. They will be here shortly. I have sent for them."

The archbishop stared at Matilda. "Are you troubled about something, my lady?"

"Do not be ridiculous. I am very happy to be sold off like a piece of property." Matilda turned toward the back of the rounded room. "I will wait there."

Adelicia took Matilda's arm and steered her away from the altar. "Let me help you."

"I do not need help." Matilda growled like a she-wolf. "Why must you help me?"

"I do not want you to say something horrible that will make lightning strike you dead."

Ella stood on Matilda's other side and chewed on her lower lip. She held a hand out nearly touching Matilda's elbow as if ready to guide her through the ceremony if there were resistance. "We are both afraid of your temper. You seem to be in the best of form today."

Matilda waved her hand to dismiss those thoughts. She was staring at the stones that framed the windows when the sounds of people coming nearer intruded on her thoughts. She watched the small archway that led in from the hall. Her father was the first to step into the chapel, and Matilda started toward him. Then, she saw the young man behind him. She stared at him without wanting to. He was tall and muscular in spite of his youth. A shock of straw-colored hair fell over his forehead and green eyes stared across the chapel straight at Matilda. He tried to smile, but a tremor forced him to stop. Matilda was surprised to see that he was not happy about the forthcoming ceremony. She chuckled, deep and quiet, causing Adelicia to look at her.

Adelicia squeezed Matilda's arm in warning. "I do not like your laughter. You sound positively wicked. What are you going to do to that poor boy?"

"I do not know yet, but it will not be difficult to deal with him. I bet his knees are shaking."

"Matilda! You are the devil himself today," Ella said. "I think you are God's punishment for that poor soul."

"Thank you very much, Ella. I think I like being the devil. I will make the most of it," Matilda said. "Ah, the signal from the archbishop. I will see you in the great hall for the feast after the ceremony, and then you will see some wonderful antics."

"From the jugglers and that fool of your father's, I hope," Adelicia said.

"Mayhap." Matilda stepped away from her two guardians and walked down the aisle formed by family and guests. She hoped they would mistake her smile for that of an angel. It would serve her purpose better.

Matilda shut the massive door behind her, leaned against it, and glared at Geoffrey as he surveyed the room. She was irritated by the intrusion of her new husband into her domain, and she resented his inspection of this private part of her life. His things were nowhere in sight; she had made certain of it. Her things were everywhere. Kirtles and chemises hung on pegs, her cosmetics, comb, and mirrors were scattered across the only table in the room, and her precious books were locked in the armarium next to the great bed.

Matilda pointed toward the curtained bed. "This is where you are expected to bed me. Do you think you have reached manhood yet?"

"In some ways." Geoffrey walked across the room and stood before the armarium. "May I see your books? I understand that you are quite learned."

Matilda picked up a vase and turned it upside down. A gold key tumbled into her palm and she held it up. "My books are precious to me. Do you know how to care for them?" Not wanting to be any closer to Geoffrey than she had to, she tossed the key across the room. He caught it easily.

"I have a book or two of my own," he said. He put the key in the lock and turned it, then opened the door. Gently, Geoffrey removed a book.

Matilda watched him turn the vellum pages. She wanted to snatch it from his hands. "It is in Latin."

"I know. I have studied Latin all my life."

Matilda laughed. "All your life? All fifteen years of it? I am impressed. Do you read ancient Greek, as well?"

"I do. I also have learned the language of the Hebrews. I seem to have facility for languages although I find English almost as harsh and disturbing as German." Geoffrey replaced the book.

Matilda was taken aback at the depth of his education. Her chin tilted upward as she stared at her new husband. "Mayhap we should speak the language of love. I know you understand French."

"I hardly think we should waste such a beautiful language on this relationship. It would be hypocritical," Geoffrey said.

"Oh, my! A young gentleman with a barbed tongue. I think I shall weep." Matilda smiled instead.

"I want to explain something to you," Geoffrey said.

"Please do."

"I did not want to marry an old woman. . . ."

"An old woman? How dare you, you disgusting little boy!"

"I did not want to marry an old woman, but after seeing you, I want to say that I think you are beautiful." Geoffrey gazed at her with his green eyes and would not glance away.

Matilda felt as if all her anger had been swept away. She knew that he was just as much a pawn in this game as she was. She wanted to hate him, but that required emotion that she did not really feel for him and energy she did not want to waste. There was no point in continuing the sham. "I am sorry. I did not want to be married to a boy, either."

Geoffrey looked at her with narrowed eyes. "I have led an army into battle and won. I have made decisions that have affected my father's kingdom and thousands of his subjects. I have sat in judgment in our courts. I have fathered a bastard child. I am not a boy, Matilda. I am your husband, and you will treat me as such, with all the courtesies and respect due a husband. If I choose to bed you, I will do so. Is that understood?"

Matilda was aware her left eyebrow rose to its customary position when she was angered beyond words. The only sound she could utter emerged from her lips in an animal-like snarl as she lunged at Geoffrey. "I am Empress Matilda. Do not speak to me that way."

Geoffrey grabbed both her hands before she could get them to his face. He jerked them down. "You are the Countess of Anjou, wife of Geoffrey. Nothing more, nothing less."

Matilda tried to pull her arms from Geoffrey's grasp, but was unable to. She pulled harder, then winced when he held her tighter, causing her wrists to chafe and turn red. "Let go of me before I scream for my servants."

Geoffrey laughed. "Who would rescue a bride on her wedding night because of a little scream?"

Matilda stared at Geoffrey. He was handsome and more intelligent than she had expected. He had little finesse. However, like a fine, but gangling colt, this would be overcome. He was so unlike Stephen. With that thought, Matilda found that she no longer wanted conflict with Geoffrey. Her strength was gone. "You did not want to marry an old woman, and I did not want to marry a young boy, so let us agree that this is only a political marriage and go our separate ways. I will not ask what you do, and you will not ask about my activities. Can we make a pact, much as our fathers made for us?"

"Oh, I do not know. It seems that for certain manly needs a wife would be very convenient." Geoffrey still held her wrists.

Matilda stood still. "Do not be so disgusting."

"All right." Geoffrey released her. "I am sorry. I did not mean to hurt you, but you angered me. I see no future for us. Later, maybe we will have to have children to continue the line of my father and yours."

"I do not see that necessity. I have plans for the throne of England. After I acquire that, mayhap we shall discuss heirs. Until then, I would rather not think about sharing your bed." Matilda backed away and sat on a bench next to the fireplace. She stretched and yawned. "Where will you sleep?"

"Why, right here, of course. Next to my loving wife."

"What!"

"I do have some pride. I may have to pretend that I know nothing of your lover. . . ."

"What could you possibly know about my lover?" Matilda felt her cheeks getting hot.

"I will pretend not to know about dear cousin Stephen, and you will do me the courtesy of pretending to be my wife. I am feeling generous. Mayhap it was your father's fine claret, or mayhap it is your beauty. You are a rare woman, for you are intelligent and politically knowledgeable. I believe you will be an asset to me." Geoffrey sat on the bench opposite Matilda and removed one black suede boot, then the second. He placed them neatly, side-by-side, and slipped his outer tunic over his head.

Matilda frowned. "You really are going to stay here."

"I will not wound your pride by touching you, and you will not wound my pride by forcing me to sleep elsewhere. For all concerned, I will be your mate."

"I hope you have bathed."

Geoffrey threw back his head and laughed uproariously. Matilda eyes opened wide. She thought he was acting peculiar. "Why do you laugh?"

"I was hoping the same thing about you."

"You are terrible. I trust I do not have to put up with you for long. Maybe you will die," Matilda said.

"You are older. The chances are that you will die first." Geoffrey chuckled. "I shall enjoy irritating you. You are more interesting than the simple young girl who birthed my daughter."

"Humph!" With a swift movement, Matilda was off the bench and across the room. She stepped behind a large tapestry set up as a screen and changed to a long, blue night kirtle. She tried not to notice that Geoffrey was looking her direction. She knew that he could only see her head and the movements of her arms as the night chemise slid into place. Matilda was annoyed to find she enjoyed having him stare at her. She peered furtively at him. Her enjoyment escalated when Geoffrey stripped to his bare skin, except for his braies that came to his knees. Matilda found it interesting that the fine linen had been neatly embroidered with his family coat of arms near the waist in front. Matilda waited until Geoffrey had slipped into bed, then stepped from behind the tapestry and walked slowly toward the bed. She knew that her face showed her feelings as she stared at him with a mixture of contempt, curiosity, and humor.

Geoffrey laughed. "Good. This is better than I had hoped. You are not certain how to react to me."

"I will share my own bed with you, but if you touch me I will bash your head into a thousand bloody bits."

"It will be difficult, but I think I can resist your charms. Please have no fear of me." Geoffrey rolled over and turned his back to her. In moments, he was snoring softly.

Matilda stamped her foot. "Wake up, you common clod. I did not say you could go to sleep. Do you not have manners?" Her answer was a snore. She stood by the bed staring at the back of her new husband, then shrugged, and climbed quietly between the sheets, her anger replaced by relief that their pact would be kept.

CHAPTER
IV

TEPHEN PACED ACROSS THE FLOOR of his chambers. It had been more than three hours since the revelry had ended for Matilda and her groom. Stephen suppressed a groan that welled up within him unannounced. It was reflective of the pain that gripped him regularly. The room seemed to grow smaller as he paced from one end to the other. He tried to ignore his wife's scowl, but that, too, drove him from wall to wall. He wanted to kick the table that held her jars and pots. The subsequent rattling and banging would undoubtedly bring his wife's wrath down on him. She spent hours in front of the mirror that hung above the table, but she could not conceal the permanent frown line between her brows.

Stephen turned at the door and stomped by the tapestries that hung from ceiling to floor, separating one large room into two sleeping areas. Stephen hit one of the tapestries as he went past. The dust flew out in a small cloud and drifted toward the reed covered floor. He was glad that there had been no reason to share these quarters with anyone during the wedding. He felt a strong need for privacy. As it was, having Maithilde in the same chamber was annoying.

"You are a distracting force at the moment. What ails my dear husband?" Maithilde asked.

"Nothing."

"Do you see the kingdom slipping from your grasp?"

"I do not know." Stephen clenched his teeth together to keep from screaming at his wife. He turned his back to the woman who sat propped against large down pillows and looked out the window at the moon. It was bright and full and coolly beautiful, much like his wife.

"When the time comes, you will have your chance at the crown. Our dear cousin will be with her new husband across the Channel. When the king dies, we will be close by to take the throne. It will be simple if we work toward that end now." Maithilde smoothed the woolen cover that was needed even in June. "I have recovered quite nicely from the unfortunate miscarriage that I had. Come, let us talk about the kingdom that is supposed to be ours."

"I do not want to think about that," Stephen said. He glanced at Maithilde. She did have good color and seemed to be all right. He turned away. He had no concern about her health. Her problem was part of the woman's world, not his. He had almost felt sorry for her when she had miscarried. She was very ill, but then, he knew it was not his heir. "I am not going to think of the throne."

"You must think of the throne. You have to plan how to undercut the hold Matilda has on the barons and the Archbishop of Canterbury."

Stephen tried to keep the irritation from his voice. He preferred looking at the moon to looking at his wife. "You seem to have the answers. What do you suggest?"

"You will have to talk with the barons and ask them to imagine being led around by a woman. It is unholy. If God had wanted a woman to rule, he would have shown us a sign before this. You can plant a fear that she will be unable to lead a country as vast as this; that enemies could easily take over. Our dear Matilda was not even reared in this country, and she comes back to us a foreigner. She will not understand our needs."

"That is absurd." Stephen turned and faced his wife.

"Of course it is absurd. Just as absurd as the rumors that you and dear Matilda are lovers."

Stephen stopped breathing. He could feel perspiration along his hairline. He swallowed, then forced himself to face Maithilde. "Do not be stupid."

Maithilde smiled and held out her arms. "Now, come to me. Let us share our craving. I need you beside me. Mayhap it was the wedding that brought back pleasant memories of our youth and the passion that could not be abated."

"I have more need of sleep. The claret has affected me." Stephen turned back to stare at the moon.

"It never has affected you before."

"I am, mayhap, feeling the effects of age."

"You, Stephen?" Maithilde laughed quietly. "We both know why you do not fancy my affections. Do not worry, dear. I have resources of my own."

"I am aware of your resources." Stephen's voice revealed his anger even though he tried to hide it. He did not want Maithilde to know she could anger him so easily. She always seemed to know how. He turned to face his antagonist. "I hope you are discreet, for your sake."

"You are a peculiar one to talk of being discreet. You and your mistress were the talk of the castle. Of course, I presume that is over." Maithilde scooted down under the covers and closed her eyes.

Stephen clenched and unclenched his fists to keep from smashing Maithilde's face into a bloody mess. He and Matilda had been cautious. It must have been his wife who spread the gossip.

The air was warm. Matilda pulled up her hair from the back of her neck with both hands. The movement caused the sorrel stallion to dance beneath her and she squeezed her legs against his rib cage to settle him down. She felt her husband's eyes upon her, and she turned to face him, her blue eyes meeting his green.

"You look lovely today. I fear that I will miss your company. I had not wanted to miss you," Geoffrey said.

"The only thing you will miss is the target of your barbed comments. I will not miss you." Matilda let her hair fall. It rippled down her back.

"Then why are you here to see me off on my long and arduous journey?" Geoffrey asked.

"To make certain that you actually leave my homeland, like the unwanted invader you are." Matilda smiled.

"Have not the last two months meant anything to you?"

"Misery and pain, my dear Geoffrey."

"I am distressed to hear that."

"Really? How kind of you."

"Do you not remember any happy moments with me?"

Matilda started to laugh, but was stopped by the serious look on Geoffrey's face. "Do you mean to tell me that you care whether I was happy with you or not?"

"I know that we have many things against us, but I did hope that we could come to an understanding, mayhap a reciprocal respect. We are bound together, after all. I would like to part as mutual admirers rather than adversaries." Geoffrey reached across the space that separated their two horses and put his hand on Matilda's arm.

She started to pull away, but did not. He was serious. She liked the feeling of warmth that radiated from his hand. Impulsively, she leaned over and kissed him on the cheek. "I guess I am used to you, after all. I will miss you."

"Like the ache of a tooth, eh, Matilda?" Geoffrey laughed.

"Mayhap, but still missed when gone."

"Some day I hope that you will be over your love for Stephen, and you will let me be a proper husband. Until then, I bid you *adieu*, and may God be with you." Geoffrey kicked his horse and rode off with his entourage toward the Channel and his waiting ships.

Matilda waited for him to look back so that she could wave, but he never turned, and it unexpectedly saddened her. The emptiness surprised her. Did she love him after all? She was still watching the receding figure of Geoffrey when Stephen came up beside her. She looked away from Geoffrey to smile at him.

"Are you ready to return to the castle, my lady?" Stephen asked.

Matilda knew the truth of her love for the man whose eyes laughed with hers, and whose smile made her quiver. She loved Stephen. There were no doubts. "I prefer a ride through the countryside with my knight at my side."

"And a promise of romance?" Stephen asked.

Matilda glanced toward the direction that Geoffrey had taken. He had already disappeared and with him, any feelings that might have developed between them. "Yes, a promise of romance, for I love you more than I have ever loved anyone." Matilda looked down at her hands. Her unabashed passion embarrassed her.

"Wait here while I dismiss the others, and we will celebrate the leaving of Geoffrey."

Matilda looked up. "I do not think celebrate is the right word."

"What?"

"Nothing. Dismiss your men, then see if you can catch me." Matilda reined Dancer sharply to the left, kicked him to a gallop, and flew across the grasslands towards the forest. She could feel her black hair streaming out behind her like a dark standard.

"I will catch you, Matti!" Stephen pushed his horse forward and pounded across the earth toward her.

Matilda rode like she and Dancer were fused into one. She guided him around a hillock, and when she looked back, Stephen could not be seen. Matilda rode a short distance into the forest. When she came to their customary meeting place, she climbed down from Dancer and waited by a creek. It was not long until the muted clip-clop of Stephen's horse could be heard on the forest floor. As soon as Stephen appeared abreast of her hiding place behind a tree, Matilda reached out and pulled him off his horse. They both landed on the ground with a thud and rolled. Matilda's subdued laughter echoed in Stephen's ear. He put his arms around her and pulled at her kirtle.

"I love you more than anything, Stephen."

"More than the throne?" Stephen kissed her.

She returned the kiss. "The throne has nothing to do with this." Matilda held Stephen close to her. "It has been too long since I last held you."

"William, do you think my husband, my dearest Stephen, will be here tonight?" Maithilde sat on the bed, her hands clasped about her knees, and gazed at the stars through the open window. Somewhere under those stars, Stephen was probably making love to Matilda. Maithilde pulled pieces of dry skin off her bottom lip. She did not care if she drew blood. Matilda would pay for her indiscretions. Maithilde would let her think she had what she wanted, but when the time was right, Maithilde would take everything away from her. Maithilde could feel the heat of William as he sat behind her.

William ran his hand up her bare spine, reached around under her arm and pinched her breast.

Maithilde pushed his hand away. "Not now, William. You are insatiable. Tell me, do you think Stephen will return to my bed tonight?"

"Not with Geoffrey gone. Stephen will stay with his mistress tonight, and I will stay with mine." William grabbed Maithilde's shoulders and pulled her back on the bed, holding down her body with his. He held her wrists tightly.

"Do not use that word. It sounds crass to talk of a mistress." Maithilde pushed William away. She sat up, rubbed her wrist, then leaned over and kissed him again. His roughness excited her. He was good for her in many ways. She needed him for soldiering as well as for loving. She giggled as he leaned over and nuzzled her. "You are crude, William."

"You have to expect that from a mercenary." William put his muscular arms around her and pulled her atop of him. "You are a woman as tough in politics as you are in love."

"I use whatever weapons I have to get what I want. I want to be Queen of England, and you can help me get it if you do not fail me as you did the last time. I gave you a simple job and you could not do it."

"I sent my best man to do the deed. He failed. I have not seen him since. I suppose he has run away rather than face me. There will be other ways to kill Matilda and other times. You will be queen."

Maithilde shivered at the thought of having the power of a queen. She would make her own future in spite of the failure of the assassination. "I can be queen if you will be my lover. I get my strength from you."

"Are you using your charms to bewitch me?" William kissed Maithilde, then released her. "I will raise a larger army for your cause when the time comes. You have bewitched me, after all."

"Love can do that, William of Ypes. I am not capable of love, my sweet, but I have a need that only you can fulfill." Maithilde had learned a long time ago that there was no room in her life for love. She did not remember her mother or father ever loving her. Love was for the peasants. She did not need it. Maithilde bit William's shoulder, leaving marks in his war-toughened hide.

"Ow! Which need are we discussing? The need for an army or the need for passion?"

"Both, my dear William. Both."

"Does not your dear husband take care of you?"

"Stephen has his own amusement, as you well know. If you think that reminding me of his liaison upsets me, do not be stupid.

That very same coupling will be used to my advantage when we help Stephen take the crown from Matilda. I only hope he does not tire of her as he has with his other mistresses." Maithilde held back a sigh, lest her bravado be revealed as a cover for the twinge of jealousy that caught her in unguarded moments.

"You amaze me, as usual," William said.

Maithilde straightened her shoulders. "One can not let sentiment get in the way of progress." She grabbed William by his hair and they rolled over together. "Take me again, William. I want a warrior to make love to me. I want to ride to the throne on you." She laughed.

The wind whistled through the great hall, and Matilda pulled the woolen cloak tighter around her shoulders. Even the fires in the fireplaces were not enough to ward off the chill that accompanied the worst blizzard that Matilda remembered. She wondered why her father had called her here instead of to his apartment. Mayhap it was because her father hated to be confined, and they had had to stay indoors for the last three days. She spied him next to the fireplace by the kitchen with a red-nosed courier at his side. The poor young lad was stamping his feet and drinking hot mead. King Henry was ordering the cook to take him to the kitchen for a good meal.

"My daughter!" The king often bellowed, or so it seemed, whenever he was contained by walls. "This message concerns you. Your dear husband misses you and wants you to attend him in Normandy. You are to sail as soon as possible. Here, read this for yourself." King Henry held the parchment toward Matilda, but she just stared. "Are you deaf? Read this. He wrote in Latin, and very well, I might add. He is a scholar as well as an historian and a knight."

"Do not try to be a peddler for Geoffrey's attributes. It does not sway me." Matilda snatched the offensive parchment from her father and read it for herself. Her blue eyes clouded with grey, mirroring the storm clouds that rolled across the sky. "I can not cross the Channel in this weather. It is the dead of winter. Does he think me the fool who entertains the court? I will not put my life in jeopardy for this . . . this arrogant count." Matilda flung the parchment into the fireplace where it bounced off a burning log and clattered to the hearth, scattering sparks onto the stone floor.

King Henry jumped up and stomped on the floor's reeds to kill the tiny fires that Matilda had started. He turned toward his daughter. "My dear child, you will not go in a raging blizzard, of course." He smiled, but his mood changed quickly. "You will make haste to Normandy as soon as it is possible. You will not embarrass me by your actions, and you will not treat your husband with open defiance. You do not have any choice in this. Geoffrey has called for you, although, for the life of me, I can not understand why he wants to torture himself. You are to be at his side, and you will behave as you have been reared; as a gentlewoman at all times. You will remember you are of royal blood."

Matilda lowered her eyes and tried to keep her anger from showing, for she knew that her father would match her word for word. "Father, may I speak?"

"Could I possibly stop you?"

Matilda smiled. "I do not think so."

"Then proceed."

"I have no desire to leave England so soon after having come here from Germany. I have found memories hidden in the recesses of my mind that were waiting to be awakened by a familiar yet forgotten aroma, sound, or sight. I do not want to be a stranger to my own land, my own people. If I am to rule England, then I must know England."

"You do not convince me."

"Father, imagine riding through a forest that had been forgotten. Suddenly the odor of moss, fresh after a rain, reaches out and tugs a memory. The memory is peopled with a loving father, a mother who laughs at their child, an older brother, dear Richard, and a twin brother to always have by my side. Both drowned on the White Ship leaving me with only memories. Imagine that memory being found, then lost again, and the return of emptiness. Can you live with the knowledge that sending me to Normandy would do that to me?"

King Henry took Matilda's hands in his. He held them tightly. "This is not about lost memories, my daughter. It is about an illicit love affair."

Matilda gasped. "I . . . I do not understand."

"I know about Stephen." King Henry drew his daughter to him and put his arms around her. She nestled there, her head under his chin. "If I had been more observant when you two were younger, if I had only thought about what might happen if there were no male heirs to carry on, if I had not tried to control the future so much, then mayhap I could have seen . . ."

"What Father?" Matilda held her breath, waiting to hear her father confess to a mistake.

"I could have seen that you and Stephen would have made a perfect union for the preservation of England. I am afraid that I have misjudged badly." King Henry shuddered. "I have a vision of a great and deadly battle on the very land that I want to sustain."

"Why do you fear so? You are King Henry of England. Do what must be done to keep this island safe." Matilda pressed her lips together to keep from crying out. The King could not be rushed into bold thoughts.

"If I had only played the matchmaker for you and Stephen. Now, it is too late."

"You are the King. You may do whatever is necessary to keep the crown." Matilda held her breath.

"I can not go against the teachings of the Church. There can be no breach of a marriage contract."

"There are ways, Father. Declare an unholy union because of Maithilde's adultery, and then Stephen would be free. We can dispose of Geoffrey some way. He could be bribed with gold. You have the gold, Father. Please help me. Please help England."

"It would be a fragile England built upon deceit. Besides, it is unlikely that the Church would be comfortable with such a plan. It is a thin plan at best and would break in time. You only ask this of me because you think you love Stephen."

"I do love him, Father. It seems so unfair that our servants can marry whom they choose when we permit them, and I can not. I love Stephen with all my strength. I can not lie, Father. I am willing to do anything to stay with Stephen."

King Henry looked into Matilda's eyes. "Stephen has little land, no power of his own, and no strength. I will not take that risk, Matti. You will go to Normandy when the weather breaks. You will treat your husband with great affection. Without him, you will have no chance for the throne. If I hear that you have not taken me seriously, I will be disappointed in your knowledge of politics. I have asked that Brian fitzCount accompany you to Normandy in order to help you, let us say, to make life there more tolerable. He and his men will serve as an honor guard. They will also be a deterrent to those who do not wish you to gain the crown."

"I will not go."

"Then you will not rule England, for you will have no power. You have a choice: you may go to Normandy and make it pleasant, or you may stay here and lose the crown because of your stubbornness. Which is it to be?"

Matilda looked at her father with her mouth agape. She closed it so that her father would not see her shock. Her eyes narrowed. "I can not believe you are doing this to me."

"Your passion for Stephen has no place in the quest for the crown. You have been better taught. Act the part of the 'Lady of England.' "

Matilda started to speak, but could not. She did not like to lose an argument and rarely did except to her father. Should she reveal that Maithilde's talk could be construed as treason? As much as she wanted Stephen and England, she could not do anything dishonorable to Maithilde.

"Do not look at me that way. It will do you no good, for I have spoken." King Henry said.

There was nothing for Matilda to do but follow her father's judicious advice. She believed, at that moment, that she knew where her stubbornness had come from. Her only recourse was to be gracious in defeat. "Yes, Father." Matilda left the great hall with tears in her eyes that made the stones in the walls quiver.

It seemed that the days flew and stood still at the same time. Before Matilda could recover from the surprise of being forced to Normandy, she was directing Ella and the servants what to pack. She had her favorite tapestries rolled and wrapped, making certain the one from Stephen was double wrapped in linen for the trip. Her clothes, books, and furniture had been readied for the journey. It seemed that fate had dealt Matilda the same blow twice. She was forced to say farewell to Stephen, again, and this time Matilda was the one who seemed to feel the pain more. Every moment possible had been spent with Stephen, and when she was not with him, she thought about him.

The day came when amidst a cacophony of activity, Matilda had to allow herself to be placed on the ship by her father. She had kissed Adelicia and King Henry all the while looking at Stephen. Matilda believed he was there to make her miserable.

Matilda leaned across the side and watched the grey-blue water swirl past. She watched the water separate her from England, her family, and Stephen. Each mile took her away from Stephen and changed her life. A lone sea gull swooped down looking for a meal. The graceful bird had the freedom that she did not have. She watched as the bird followed the ship for awhile, then turned and flew away. It emphasized her loneliness. Matilda had asked Stephen to stay away from the dock, but he had not. He had stood on the pier his face stone-like, apparently afraid to show any emotion. She had stolen side long glances at Stephen. Her father had stood next to her, his hand on her elbow while her luggage had been loaded aboard ship. Matilda did not know whether he had been trying to support her or control her.

Matilda turned to cross to the other side of the ship and ran into Brian fitzCount. "For the sake of my sanity, quit following me."

Brian fitzCount blushed, his freckles getting darker. "I am sorry, my lady."

"Are you my friend or my guardian?"

"I am both, my lady."

"I need no guardian." Matilda felt like a child who had been naughty and was now under the watchful eye of a nurse. It made her peevish.

"Then I will be your friend."

She shot Brian a quick glance. He was serious. Matilda turned away from him and stared at the sea. When she moved away from the railing to avoid being sprayed by a wave, she stepped on his foot. She felt clumsy and that made her short tempered.

Matilda put her hands on her hips. "You are worse than a puppy, for you dog me constantly. I will not leap into the great grey sea. Although I would prefer that to my present fate." She smiled at Brian fitzCount's astonished face. He was too gentle for the likes of her. She watched Brian bow and move away from her. She was sorry that she had treated him so badly, and she called to him. "Brian, forgive me."

The smile she got from Brian made her chuckle. He seemed so eager to please her. As she turned back to the sea, she vowed to be nicer to Brian. She licked the salt from her lips and smiled for the first time since she had left England. Brian was comical without trying.

Geoffrey's castle in Normandy was similar to what Matilda was used to except the stones were darker, and she wondered whether it was because they were a different type or just older. She looked around the apartment. The tapestries on the walls were her favorites brought with her from Germany to England, and now to Normandy. A new tapestry had been placed across from the sitting area above the fireplace at the instructions of Matilda. It showed an Arabian princess being swept away by a dark prince astride a delicate but powerful horse. The princess smiled, and Matilda knew that she was happy to be with her prince. A Moorish castle, white in the moonlight, was in the background.

The tapestry had a special meaning for her because it had been a parting gift from Stephen. He had said, "I wish that were us," had strode from Adelicia's chambers where they had met secretly, and had closed the door behind him before she had been able to speak. At that point, she had been close to tears, a rare thing for her.

A knock on the door broke her thoughts of the past, and she looked at Ella. "I will answer that and discreetly leave," Ella said.

Geoffrey stood in the doorway more handsome and more manly than Matilda had remembered. The straw-colored piece of hair still slipped out of place and rested on his forehead, causing Matilda to blush at the thoughts that raced through her mind. She pushed the ideas away, for she felt disloyal to Stephen.

"May I come in?" Geoffrey asked.

His gold tunic made his eyes look greener, and Matilda was surprised at the quickening of her pulse. "Of course. Is this not your castle?"

"It is. I hope I have chosen well for you."

"You have. The apartment is much larger than the one I left." Matilda tried to cover her nervousness with a smile and extended her hand. "Do come in. I am happy to see you."

"Really? To what do I owe this change?" Geoffrey closed the door and took both her hands in his. "It is pleasant, I have to admit." He turned her hands upward and kissed both her palms. "Are you an imposter? What have you done with the real Matilda?"

"Do not make sport of my attempt to arrive with sweetness on my tongue and love in my heart." Matilda tried to keep her anger from rushing forth, but she could hear the hardness in her voice.

Geoffrey laughed. "Ah, the old Matilda is with us after all."

"Old? How unchivalrous of you, my dear youthful husband." Matilda no longer smiled.

"I do not really mean anything by that. You are more heavenly than any woman I have ever seen. I was taken by you when we were married, but now you are even more angelic." Geoffrey pulled her into his arms. "Would you stand by my side and help me hold Normandy against our common enemies?"

"I . . . I . . . you confuse me, Geoffrey. Why the amiable disposition? It does not fit our personalities." Matilda was perplexed by her response to the warmth of Geoffrey's body next to hers.

Geoffrey's voice was soft as he spoke. "It is in the interest of our countries for us to be in alignment, and we may as well be congenial. It would serve my nerves better."

Delicate laughter burst from Matilda. "I do not think you have to worry about your nerves. However, I am not against a small truce between us." Matilda flicked a piece of lint off Geoffrey's woolen tunic and placed her hands on his chest. "I believe that you have ordered me here for political purposes. I suppose you have heard rumors of an uprising, and you believe that the presence of King Henry's daughter will stop that?"

"I said as much a moment ago. There appears to be a small problem with one of our nobles. He wants to do battle for a piece of Normandy and Anjou. Mayhap the threat of Henry will change his mind."

"You wound me, Geoffrey, with your reference to my father. Am I not enough of a deterrent in my own right?"

Geoffrey chuckled. "You certainly are, but having King Henry standing with us will help."

"Who is this person trying to cause trouble?"

"It is nothing to worry about now that you are here. His castle is a day's journey west. If he knew you as I do, he would go on a crusade and leave us in peace."

"No, he will not. You speak of the Count de Rouell. He will not be deterred by my presence." Matilda tapped her fingers against Geoffrey's chest as she tried to remember the lay of the land. "Where do you think Count de Rouell will choose to attack?"

"It might be here," Geoffrey said.

Matilda nodded in agreement. "If this castle were to fall, then others who are loyal to you would be vulnerable to further attacks from Count de Rouell. How many followers has he?" Matilda's cheeks were flushed.

Geoffrey pushed the errant strand of hair away from his forehead. It slid back down. "He has mayhap fifty or sixty loyal knights who would like to gain more lands of their own."

"I have brought Brian fitzCount and twenty fierce English knights. We could stop Count de Rouell." Matilda smiled at Geoffrey. "Allow me to protect this castle. You will have no worries."

"You surprise me, my gentle wife."

"Do not be absurd." Matilda stepped away from her husband, her anger controlling her movements. Why did Geoffrey seem to bring out the anger in her quicker than any other person? It was irritating not be able to control her emotions. She swore to work on her temperament — later. "I am not gentle. You ridicule me, once more. English women have learned military warfare by listening to their fathers or their husbands plan battles. English lords have often had their ladies make war upon enemies while they were gone. It is necessary for survival. Besides, since my father has decided that I am to rule after him, he has been teaching the fine points of warfare to me incessantly."

Geoffrey laughed uproariously. "I can imagine the great Henry and the stubborn Matilda discussing warfare. It must have created small wars every time you two conversed. You were reared in Germany. Did you have problems there?"

"Yes, and I was trained there, as well. We had enemies to fight for ourselves as well as for the Pope. As you know, we were charged with the protection of the Pope and the Holy Roman Empire." Matilda wanted Geoffrey to believe that she was capable of fighting a battle, but she could not understand why it was important to her to impress him. "I am good at military strategy. I fought battles for my first husband and I won. I will never lose any battle, for I will never quit until my enemy is dead or I am dead."

"Your father has told me of your victories. With you beside me, we will conquer our enemies."

Geoffrey pulled Matilda to him and kissed the top of her head. He held her close enough so that she could feel his heart beating as quickly as did hers when she went into battle. She wondered if the chance of a small war excited him, or if she did. She pulled away from him, and he let her go.

"It will take time," Geoffrey said.

"I have good knights with me. It will not take much time at all. In fact, mayhap we should charge him."

Geoffrey grasped her hand again. "I did not mean to speak aloud my private thoughts."

"Really? What did you mean?"

"I meant that if you were to allow me to love you, it would take time. I understand you still believe that Stephen loves you." Geoffrey studied Matilda's face.

Matilda pulled her hand from his grasp. "Do you not love someone else?"

"I thought I did, but after marrying you, being with you, I find that no other woman can match you. I can not play the lovesick fool. My pride will not let me, so if you ever decide to . . . to tolerate me, then tell me." Geoffrey turned to leave.

"Geoffrey, do not make me feel so inadequate. It is not fair." Matilda tried not to let her voice crack.

He did not turn, but placed his hand on the door latch. "You will never be inadequate, Matti. I will leave in the morning to return to Anjou."

Matilda winced as the door slammed behind Geoffrey. She had been twice pierced in a single second, by the use of Stephen's pet name for her and by the finality of the closing door. "How can my love for Stephen be true if I am enamored by Geoffrey?" The sound of her voice was loud in the quiet room and underscored her loneliness. She had thought to ask Geoffrey to stay, but for what purpose? She was afraid to ask, for she did not want to deny her love for Stephen.

There were names for women who loved men indiscriminately, and she did not want to be called one. Her mother's face flashed before her, and she felt her cheeks turn hot. Even in death, her mother's teaching guided her. Matilda could not explain her feelings to herself, so she decided not to try.

Brian fitzCount could not force his horse to go faster. The news was old, and he felt that time was against him. It seemed that the spring flowers mocked him as he rode past them. Brian looked back at the flowers as they waved in the current of air caused by his horse. He noticed that spring came sooner to Normandy than it did to England, thus the time for warfare was here. Brian fitzCount had spent the winter watching over Matilda on her daily rides outside the castle walls. He knew he would never speak of his feelings for her because it would be useless. She was no more than a dream for him. He was faithful and would be brave for her sake, but there would be no hint of impropriety from him. He smiled as he thought of the local peasant girls willing and waiting for any of the foreign knights to make love to them. They were young and not worn by time. He was no monk, but Brian knew that he would not marry a second time, and he struggled to gather the face of his dead wife into his thoughts, but he could not.

It was just as well. He had to forget his youthful past, for he wanted to serve Matilda until the end of his life. He would protect her with his own life as King Henry had bid him to do. He had sworn to Mary, Mother of God, to follow Matilda into Hell if necessary.

Brian remembered the conversation he had overheard and dug his heels into his mount's rib cage even though he knew the horse was going as fast as it could. The memory of the words he had heard caused his pulse to race. If anything were to happen to Matilda, he would feel that he had failed his mission. He had left the peasant girl at the inn where her father worked and had ridden out of the stable just as the sun came up. Brian laughed at the memory of the girl's confused look as he pushed her aside before their lovemaking had commenced. He remembered the straw sticking him in the backsides as he sat quietly. She had pulled at him while he listened to the knights talking below him as they got ready to ride. Brian could not remember the girl's name, but if it had not been for her and the promised romp in the hay, he would never had overheard the plot against Matilda.

Brian clattered up to the castle gate and yelled for the gate master to open up. He dropped off his horse next to the nearest entry to Matilda's apartment, ran up the steps and, without proper courtesy, burst through her door.

Brian noted with some pride that Matilda was quick, having the instincts of her father and grandfather. She was out of bed and had a five inch dagger unsheathed and poised in front of her before Brian was to the end of her bed. He froze waiting for her to realize who he was. It took her a moment to recognize her protector. Matilda struggled to calm down, then she lowered the knife to her side.

"I am sorry to startle you, my lady, but you must know that Count de Rouell plans to attack this castle tomorrow at dawn. We have very little time to prepare."

"From whom do you get this information?" Matilda pulled on her robe and tied it, then slipped into low cut, soft shoes that she wore only in the apartment.

"I was . . ." Brian was embarrassed at the memory that flashed into his mind. He cleared his throat, then began again. "I overheard Count de Rouell's knights. They did not know I was in the stable the same time as they were."

"How accurate are their statements?"

"Very accurate, for they spoke with the authority of those who had helped with the plans. We must prepare for the worst," Brian fitzCount said. "First, I want to send one of my most trusted soldiers to warn Count Geoffrey of Anjou."

"It would be a waste of needed man power to send one of your knights. I will send Ella to Anjou. She and a few of our servants will be more likely to get past any spies or murderers who might be between us and Geoffrey." Matilda gestured toward Ella who was watching the two of them from her bed.

Brian shook his head. He had trouble imagining a woman, other than Matilda, doing what should be done by a man. "That would be too dangerous for her."

Ella threw back the covers and stood. "I do not think so. I can ride like the wind, and I will race time to get to Geoffrey. Leave us to get dressed, sir."

"Go, Brian, and make ready as quickly as you can. Let no one leave the castle other than Ella and her faithful Welsh companions, for we do not want their spies to pass the word that we have been warned. Any battle that comes will be at Count de Rouell's expense. Go! You have much work to do, and so do I." Matilda smiled. "I love little wars."

"I am always amazed by you, my lady." As Brian left the apartment, he noticed the sun had topped the castle wall and shone in through the glass windows.

It would have been difficult for Matilda to sleep that night even if she would have had time. She moved through the castle from area to area checking with the men about their weapons and with the women who would take care of the wounded. She found herself repeating instructions about the use of the medicines and knew it was because she was nervous. She looked at the calm faces of the women and hoped that she had chosen well. The butcher's wife was young, but already she had been instrumental at organization, and she knew anatomy. Matilda was pleased with the young woman's instruction to the others about the dangers of infection. She prayed the woman would do as well when the real test came. Matilda had been accustomed to tending the wounded while under the tutelage of her mother and the Arabian physicians.

The next day, in the pre-dawn, Matilda moved from merlon to merlon checking the arrow loops and the knights who waited behind each slit. The sight of the men, covered from head to toe in chain mail, quivers full of arrows, and determination on their faces made her feel secure. She said words of encouragement to them. She did not expect them to answer her, even though some did, because she knew from experience that each warrior had to have a quiet time before the battle in order to make peace with God.

Matilda walked up to Brian fitzCount and stood next to him. When he acknowledged her presence, no doubt interrupting his own prayers to do so, she spoke. "I expect the onslaught to arrive from the east. At least, I would do so in order to have the sun behind me and mayhap to conceal my arrival as long as possible. We do not have as many soldiers as I would like with Geoffrey and his men in Anjou. I do not have to tell you to wait until the enemy is close so that no arrows are wasted. I will be behind the second merlon from here so that we can communicate. I feel this will be a lucky day for all of us. God be with you, Brian."

Matilda looked toward the east where the sky was getting lighter and scanned the area where sky met earth. She could see no movement nor could she see any shapes that had not been there the morning before, but she knew by the quietness of the birds and animals that their habitat had been invaded much as hers soon would be.

She moved toward the slit in the thick, stone wall that had been placed there for the shooting of arrows. The slit on the outside was small to prevent the enemy's arrows from coming through. The slit on the inside was wider that gave the archer the advantage of movement and increased the angle by which an arrow could be fired.

Matilda tried to hide the excitement breaking rhythmically within her like waves cracking against a rocky shore. A tiny bead of perspiration trickled down her back. She could not scratch it through the chain mail, so she had to ignore it. The sun would not come up fast enough, and she tapped her arrow case noisily until she realized that the knights on either side of her were frowning.

She pulled an arrow from the quiver and ran her thumb down the trimmed goose feather on the shaft and smiled at the memory of the young girl who had brought her the feathers. The child had said that they were the nicest feathers she could get from the goose. They were fine feathers and Matilda vowed to tell the girl as soon as the battle was over. She hoped there would be a battle.

Matilda was afraid that Count de Rouell would not come. The waiting could continue until Matilda would have to lead an attack against the Count's castle. It was better to be attacked as long as it were expected. Matilda thought about the two men in her life, listing them in order of proximity. Geoffrey was an excellent warrior, but even if Ella rode her horse hard all the way to his castle, it would take at least a day and a half. Matilda would get no help from Geoffrey for at least three days. She would have to win this battle without him. However, Geoffrey would be helpful if Count de Rouell tried to put them under siege.

Matilda wondered what Stephen would be doing had he been here to fight by her side. She smiled at the thought of fighting, then loving when the battle was over. She felt her cheeks flush at the dream of her lover by her side. She looked around to see if anyone noticed, then remembered that she was wearing her helmet.

Stephen's face flashed before her, and she took it as a good luck omen. Together, she and Stephen could conquer the world.

The sun and Count de Rouell's knights appeared at the same time. Matilda was unsure that it was, at last, a reality. As soon as Brian fitzCount appeared, moving along from merlon to merlon with last instructions to the archers, she knew. He finished, then whispered to Matilda to be careful and was gone to take his former place on the battlement.

The standard bearer came closer until Matilda could make out the azure chevron with sable cinquefoils on a field of gules. It was definitely the standard of Count de Rouell. The knights continued riding closer, and by their casual attitude as they rode, Matilda could see that they did not expect the castle to be ready to receive them. A ragtag band of serfs followed on foot behind the knights, armed with old swords, clubs, and a pitchfork or two. She grinned at the rabble. They looked far more weary and underfed than her own serfs.

Matilda held her breath as she waited for the army to come closer. She raised her arm high above her head and held it there, ignoring the long sleeve of her kirtle as it tumbled back to her shoulder revealing the mail beneath it. When de Rouell's army came within three hundred feet, she would to drop her arm straight down as the signal to her men to shoot. Matilda felt like a spider waiting to trap its dinner.

Count de Rouell lead his men closer to her web. From her vantage point, she could see that he was well armored. His chain mail hauberk was covered by a tunic of azure and sable, and his helmet was rounded after the new fashion, better to ward off blows. A triangular shaped shield, half as tall as he was, effectively covered him while he was on horseback.

Count de Rouell held his sword high. The sun shone off it as he rode up and down the front lines while at the same time coming closer. When he passed the invisible line that Matilda had drawn in her imagination, she would be like the spider and snatch him. Matilda took a deep breath. It would not be long now. "Come closer, de Rouell," she whispered. "That is good. A few feet more." She watched de Rouell glance toward the castle, and she froze like a rabbit hiding in a thicket. He continued to move toward them, seemingly unaware of her trap. It was at this moment Matilda lowered her arm. Two dozen arrows rained down on the startled men. She let fly her first arrow, for she had already chosen the knight she would target. Matilda's arrow found its victim. He fell from his horse and did not move. Five other knights followed her victim's lead, and Matilda smiled as their souls left their bodies. She quickly nocked an arrow and studied the chain mail of one confused knight. Her father had told her of the weak spot in hauberks and she aimed for it. She pierced the knight under the arm on the right side. He would not die from the arrow, but he would probably die from the infection.

By the time she had spent her last arrow, the remainder of the knights had fled, following a trail blazed for them by the serfs. Matilda counted twelve left behind. All appeared dead, but they would be left until it was certain. The sun was barely past the ten o'clock point in the sky and the skirmish was over. The surprise had been turned.

"Come with me," Brian said. "We have several casualties. An arrow caught a lad in the shoulder, and there are some knights who are not doing well from loss of blood. One knight has red streaks going up his leg already. There are minor injuries which, as you know, can get serious. We have blisters from the chain mail, as usual. I think the men will feel better if you see them."

"I am glad my mother taught me nursing skills, so I can be of service. Thank God for the Arabian medical knowledge." Matilda wriggled out of the quiver she still had slung over her shoulder. She smiled as she handed it to one of the squires. "Will not Geoffrey be surprised when he finds I have killed one enemy and wounded another?"

"You did? I had no idea. . . ."

"Dear Brian, you did not think that I could do what I said I would. I have been in training for years and I will be the next ruler of England. If I am to be a leader of men, then I must be able to fight like one and think like one." Matilda moaned inwardly. Would she have to prove herself over and over to both her enemies and her friends?

The iron smell of blood and hot metal assaulted Matilda's nostrils, but she had long ago learned to ignore both. What she could not ignore were the moans and screams from the men whose wounds were being treated. She sang the Christmas Mass to herself to drown out the sounds of the men, and although it did not seem appropriate, could think of nothing else that worked as well. Matilda had taken only enough time to wriggle out of her chain mail and put on an old kirtle. She hurried to the great hall and set immediately to work. She knelt next to a man she knew only as David ap Thomas. From a dark wooden box the butcher's young wife placed next to her, she removed a pair of shears. Delicately, she cut away the bloodiest portion of David's under tunic. It was stiffened and dark brown with dried blood. David lost his hold on reality and slipped into a dark world that knew no pain. She was glad, for it made her task easier.

Matilda listened for David's breathing while she worked, for if the breathing stopped, she would waste no time before going to someone else. The young woman who helped was well trained. Matilda crushed and mixed the powders for a poultice, while the young woman washed the jagged opening in the warrior's side with boiling water. Matilda looked over and could see the white of the rib beneath the flesh and muscle tissue. The woman was doing well and did not seem to be getting sick.

"You are doing a fine job," Matilda said. "What is your name?"

"I am called Mary."

"You have talent that goes beyond any training I have given you." Matilda smiled at the blush she saw creeping upwards from Mary's neck.

Matilda had learned from her mother that bubbling water often kept a wound from festering, and she was pleased that Mary knew to do the same. Matilda took a folded cloth covered with dark powder from Mary and placed it on the wound. She held it while Mary bound strips of material around the man's midsection.

If David survived, it would be a small miracle. Matilda knew a lot of medicine, but so often the men died days or even weeks later of the green disease that made them rot like death before death came. The physicians from the Mediterranean kingdoms were excellent. One, Abdulla sim Baba, had worked with Matilda's mother when her mother had been a young girl. Matilda hoped she would be as good with medicine as her mother had been. She spent a lot of her gold to keep the chest filled with the medicines that her mother had taught her about.

Mary helped her fold the leather packets and replace them in the chest before they moved to the next man. Her mother had taught her to take the time to replace each bag carefully. It would be a disaster to mix the wrong herbs, for they were poisons.

Matilda laid on the feather mattress and tried to sleep, but so much had happened in the last forty hours that sleep would not come. She was tired; tired down to the marrow of her bones and yet sleep avoided her. The servants had drawn a bath for her, but the soak in the tub did nothing to still her mind. She listened to the emptiness that surrounded Ella's vacant cot and hoped that she had been successful in her ride to get Geoffrey. Ella was too young to know the difficulties to come. Today was only a sample of what might be.

Sleep did come, finally, fitful in the dark and full of dead knights begging her to help, always the chest empty of medicines. She rolled in the covers of her bed and awakened in a sweat just as dawn appeared, a greyish white light in the absence of the sun. As soon as it was daylight, Matilda slept a sleep without dreams. The daylight was receding when she awakened. She was confused as to whether she had been asleep or not, but as soon as she saw the torches in the sconces flickering from the walls and the tray of food on the table covered by a cloth, she knew it was evening.

She sat up and screamed. The man in her bed leaped up. He reached for his sword, but knocked it, clattering, to the floor. The door banged open. Two guards rushed in, swords unsheathed and held at ready.

"For God's sake, Matti, do not frighten me so!" Geoffrey's grin was contorted with fright.

Matilda looked from the face of her husband, who tried to calm himself, to the faces of Geoffrey's guards who stood in confusion at the end of the great bed. She tried not to laugh. She stuffed the bed covers into her mouth, but she still uttered a strangled, choking sound in spite of her efforts.

"You may go." Geoffrey waved the guards away.

Matilda watched as they backed from the room. She imagined they were trying to erase the strange scene of their count standing in his night tunic next to his countess who had the bed clothing pulled up to silence her laughter. She could guess that they did not want to know why she screamed. It was none of their business what the count did to the countess.

Matilda glared at Geoffrey. "What are you doing here?"

"You sent for me."

"I sent for you to come to my aid, not sneak into my bed! What ever possessed you?"

"I do not know. Mayhap I thought you might like my company, but certainly I was wrong. I have ridden all night and I, too, am tired. Since it seemed natural to spend the night with my wife, I slipped in here. Actually, there is no other place for me, since all the apartments are full of my soldiers, as well as Brian fitzCount's men. Do not scream at me any more." With that discourse, Geoffrey climbed back into bed and turned his back to Matilda.

Matilda placed both feet in the middle of Geoffrey's back and shoved. She laughed when he hit the stone floor, scattering reeds, and uttering an oath to God. She laughed harder when his head popped up over the edge of the bed and he glared at her.

Geoffrey propped his elbow on the bed and put his chin in his hand. "Did you really kill one of de Rouell's knights?"

Matilda gazed at him. The strand of hair that was always out of place was still out of place. It made her want to brush it back. His expression was that of a youth, and she wanted to hold him. He was handsome, and his eyes looked dark, though she knew they were green. The eyes seemed to touch her soul, and she glanced away before she fell under his spell.

"I killed him." Matilda was startled at the harshness of her voice.

"You killed him?" Geoffrey grinned. "How? Did you kick him to death?"

Matilda laughed, and leaned forward to pull Geoffrey back into bed. She liked him in spite of the circumstances of their marriage. She wished he would not be so charming. "My dear husband, I may invite you to my bed, but do not ever assume that position yourself."

"Do not worry." Geoffrey rubbed his lower back. "I fear the kick of a horse much less than the kick of Matilda."

"And I fear nothing; not man, not beast."

An arm wrapped itself around Matilda, and before she could pull away, Geoffrey kissed her. She turned her head away, and he nuzzled her neck. "What is wrong, Matti? Do I not please you?"

She lay quietly, barely breathing. She could feel her pulse quicken. She hoped that it would not betray her, for Geoffrey did please her.

"I am your husband. I am enchanted by your beauty and your ability to fight. I find you exciting, but I am puzzled by your reluctance. Am I that undesirable?" Geoffrey brushed aside her dark hair and kissed the nape of her neck.

"No." Matilda saw Stephen's face flash before her. She felt miserable at her betrayal of Stephen's love.

"Then why do you not desire me?"

"I think I do."

Geoffrey rolled over onto her, turned her face to him and leaned down to kiss her.

Matilda turned away from him. "But if I let you love me, then I will feel like a whore."

"What?!" Geoffrey placed his hand under Matilda's cheek and turned her to face him, again. "I fail to see how being with your husband can make you a whore."

Matilda was determined to explain her feelings to her husband as best she could. "Please do not be angry with me, Geoffrey. I am trying to explain my feelings. It is difficult, for I feel a stranger to you." Matilda's eyes closed to shut out the intense green eyes of her husband.

"I am listening."

Matilda turned her head. She felt a hot tear slide across her temple. "I have loved Stephen too long to forget him." Matilda cringed as Geoffrey rolled away from her.

Geoffrey sighed. "You are stupid for an intelligent woman."

"I do not understand." Matilda stared out the window at the darkening sky that matched her mood.

"I will not betray you, but Stephen will. He wants the crown of England for himself."

"Now you are stupid." Matilda wiped away the residue left by tears. "Stephen loves me, and he would never do anything to ruin that love. If anyone wants the crown of England, it is his wife. She is the greedy one, not Stephen." Matilda pushed back the thought of deception by Stephen even though in the darkest part of her mind, she agreed with her husband.

"There is no hope for us, then, except that we are bound together to battle for our lands. I feel sorry for you, Matilda, for you know not what wars you create within yourself in the name of love." Geoffrey slid out of bed.

"Where are you going?" Matilda asked.

"Do you care?"

"I do."

"I am going for a long walk. I have things to think about. I may have to ask your father to come to help us. We will have to stop Count de Rouell before others join him. He is powerful, and even though you stopped him, he will be anxious to try us again. We can not afford to lose Normandy."

"Will you come back to me?"

Geoffrey stood at the end of the bed. "I do not know if three of us can share a bed."

"Three of us?"

"It seems that Stephen sleeps between us." Geoffrey pulled a woolen cape about him and left the room.

Matilda buried her face in the pillow so that she would not see him go.

CHAPTER
V

ATILDA AWAKENED ABRUPTLY. A shiver cascaded down her spine — a warning that she was being watched. She turned her head toward the window and saw that Ella was staring at her. Matilda relaxed the hand that was already reaching for her dagger under the pillow. Is this what it meant to be king? To always be on the edge, even in sleep? Did her father sleep on the boundary of wakefulness? She pushed her hair away from her face. It always fanned out across her pillow as if it had a life of its own, often attacking her in the night.

Matilda stretched her arms, the momentary wariness gone. "Good morning, Ella. What kind of day is it?"

"The rain comes in such sheets that it distorts the view." Ella sighed.

"Why the sigh? Did you want to ride with me today?" Matilda threw the covers back and sat up. She cocked her head sideways and studied Ella. There was something about the way Ella was twisting her hands that alerted Matilda. "You look like someone who has a secret. This weather is terrible. I desperately wanted to ride. So, what is your secret?"

"I fear to tell you this, Matilda."

"Is there to be a second attack from Count de Rouell? Good. I want to be the one to send his black soul to Hell."

"Matti! You should not say such things. What if you were to die with that blasphemy upon your lips?"

"I would not care. The count's death would be a gift from God." Matilda tried not to laugh at Ella's consternation. She enjoyed teasing Ella, especially about her beliefs. Matilda was religious up to a point given the training by her mother, but Ella went beyond the Church. Ella still invoked the gods from the old religions just in case they had power.

"Mayhap Hell is too good for Count de Rouell. After all, the devil must have some pride about the company he keeps."

"Matilda! You are horrible." Ella frowned. "Besides, there is something much more important to tell you and much more pleasant."

"Tell me! Is Father coming?" Matilda slipped out of bed. She stretched again and wriggled her toes, wrinkling the linen cloth that covered the reeds next to her bed. She hoped that her father was on his way. Adelicia had hinted in her last letter that he might visit. "Is Father here?"

"Two days away. The courier arrived just minutes ago."

"Ah, then we have no need to go out in this rain except to prevent boredom. Did the courier say how large of an army he had?"

"He said more than fifty."

"Is your dark-haired knight with them?" Matilda asked.

Ella smiled. "I hope so, but I know not."

"We shall have to prepare more food. I did not expect so many men. Father knows that a large army can be a deterrent to war. Make haste. I need to be kept busy so that time will fly like the arrow."

Ella clasped her hands together. "You have not seen Stephen since you left England."

The thought of Stephen caused Matilda pain. He had become a memory tucked away in the dark corner of her mind. Matilda frowned to erase poignant reminiscences. "Father will not bring Stephen. He does not want me to see him."

"But he is a knight and a warrior."

"The better to leave him in England to guard the throne," Matilda said.

"Is that wise?"

"It is only his wife we have to fear, and even she is not stupid enough to attack King Henry. He has too many loyal subjects. It is I who have to fear her for more reasons than one. But come, let us rejoice through our preparations. My father comes."

"Luck is with you to have your father for most of your life," Ella said.

Matilda looked down at Ella, who knelt before her, tying her slippers. It surprised her to hear Ella speak of her father since she did so rarely. Matilda felt her heart twist for the lady-in-waiting who had become her friend. "Do you miss having a father, Ella?"

Ella nodded, her fingers busy with the leather ties on Matilda's slippers. "I have always wondered if Mother would have lived longer had Father lived. She had a hard life without Father. Of course, he was an enemy to our king."

Matilda winced. "How can you be so matter of fact about the circumstances of your life? If I were thrust from the position I have now to being a handmaiden, I would feel like murdering my father's killer. I was angry enough when I was forced to marry a mere count after being an empress."

"My mother taught me that even though we were once titled and owned lands, the circumstances of our lives had changed. If we were to survive, we had to make do." Ella held out her hands. "I was also taught that a lady never had sun-burned hands, ragged fingernails, or callouses. I feel lucky to have none of those problems. Your father was kind to my mother to let us both have positions within the palace. It was, no doubt, the result of my mother's friendship with your mother."

Matilda leaned over and took Ella's face between her hands. "I was too young to realize that my father had killed yours. I saw you as a companion, someone to share my darkest secrets, and someone to care for me."

"Politics meant nothing to two small girls in a huge castle." Ella took Matilda's hands in her own. "Remember how we used to comfort each other whenever the noises of fighting, drinking, and yelling awakened us in the night? In a way, we are still doing that."

"Yes, we are."

Matilda raised her face to the hot sun and closed her eyes. She enjoyed the warm breeze that whispered past her ears and lifted strands of hair away from her face. She was perspiring and wondered whether it was from the sun or because she was anxious to see her father. She pulled at her kirtle, then fanned her face with her hand. The gnats buzzed around her head. She clapped her hands together, killing a few, but not eliminating the problem. Dancer, knowing her hands were off the reins, pranced beneath her. Mayhap he was curious as to why they were not on a hunt. Matilda tightened the reins and pulled him around in a tight circle to show him who was in control. When he settled down, she patted his neck.

Dancer was the first to know when the army was close. Matilda loosened the reins when he snorted, anticipating the tossing of his head as he caught the familiar scent of horse and man. He tried to dance again, but Matilda squeezed his ribs to remind him that the bit would pinch the inside of his mouth if he did not stop. Dancer shook his head trying to dislodge the bit. He snorted again as the men came closer. Matilda watched his nostrils flare to better catch the scent coming on the wind. He stopped suddenly and stood still, waiting for battle or the hunt, as he had been trained.

Matilda stood in the stirrups. Her breath caught in her throat. "Brian, is that not a cloud of dust on the horizon?"

"Yes. In spite of yesterday's rain, the land is dry enough to raise clouds. The grass is so dry that it crackles beneath our feet. I fear we will have a hot summer here. I would prefer summer in England." Brian shielded his eyes with his hand. "I think the courier told us the wrong number of men."

"Mayhap to confuse any spies we might have in our midst." Matilda eased herself into the saddle and watched the cloud. It did not seem to move any closer. She tried to hide her impatience so Brian would not think of her as a child at Christmas. She hoped she sounded casual. "Shall we ride to meet them?"

"Not yet. I think we should wait until we see the standard. If it not King Henry's colors, we will have a different problem," Brian said.

Matilda nodded. She turned to look down at Ella who rode a smaller horse. Ella was twisting her long braid around and around her fingers.

Matilda laughed. "Are you nervous?"

"So much so that I can barely sit here. I thank you for allowing me to come with you, although I might have been calmer at the castle. What if my Edward is not in attendance to the King?" Ella shifted her gaze from the dust cloud to Matilda and whispered, "Worse, what if he does not love me anymore?"

Matilda placed her hand on Ella's arm. "Who could not love you, Ella? He is probably more concerned about your loving someone else. There are many men who watch you walk about the castle. He is as faithful to you, Ella, as you are to him. If he is not, I will have someone take care of him for you."

"No! I would never want him harmed." Ella's face was white.

Matilda was sorry that she had caused Ella discomfort. She had forgotten that she was viewed as powerful by others, mayhap because she was so used to having power. "Please, I am just playing a game with you. A poor one, I think." She smiled at the woman next to her. Matilda flinched as Brian slapped his leg and yelped with pleasure.

"It is King Henry's colors!" Brian picked up the reins, ready to move out. "I see the chevrons of gold, gules and azure held high. That sight alone should make Count de Rouell run and hide."

"Oh, do you feel it? The ground trembles in fear for King Henry!" Matilda felt her heart vibrating off her rib cage, matching the quivering of the ground. Whenever her father appeared, she felt an excitement that welled up inside her until she felt that she would burst. The feeling would not go away until her father spoke to her.

Brian laughed. "I feel it. The ground always trembles for the King. He arrives shortly, escorted by the quake of many horses' hoofs."

It looked to Matilda as if a rainbow had fallen to earth. The knights' tabards were in bright colors, a contrast to the parched earth. The sight of the King and his army filled Matilda with pride. Careful, she said to herself. Pride goeth before the fall.

Her father was magnificent. He rode in front between the standard bearer and the king's first lieutenant. King Henry was taller than either of them. Matilda could tell her father not only from his position and height, but also from his raven black hair that matched hers. She could wait no longer. She kicked Dancer in the ribs and tore down the knoll toward her father. The horse quivered beneath her. Not only did he match her excitement, but his pace matched her heartbeat. The wind in her eyes prevented her from seeing the figure break away from the front lines to match her speed, closing the gap. When he was near, he shouted her name and Matti turned the galloping horse toward him.

King Henry pulled up tight on the reins and almost brought his huge stallion to a sitting position. Clouds of dust swirled around the stallion's legs and mixed with the dust from Dancer. King Henry ignored protocol and the dust and leaned over to grab Dancer's reins before Matilda swept past him. With one powerful arm, he pulled the horse to a complete stop.

"Father, I am so glad you came." Matilda leaned over and put her hand on his, partly from a need to love and partly from a need to regain her balance.

"I have missed my daughter more than I ever thought possible. Look who I have brought with me, and who is my second in command." King Henry turned Matilda toward the advancing calvary.

"Not Stephen?" Matilda looked at her father with wide eyes.

King Henry frowned. "No, I did not bring Stephen. I brought someone more loyal, Robert of Gloucester. He implored me to allow him to fight for you and for Normandy."

"Dear Robert." Matilda looked at the lone horseman who approached. "My dear brother. I wonder if Robert loves me as much as I love him."

"Robert has always cared for you. When you were sent to Germany, he was unhappy for weeks, maybe for months. He will be a great help to you when you rule England. You may trust him with your life."

Matilda nodded. "So I shall."

Robert rode up to Matilda. His tabard was a rich brown, which brought out the brown flecks in his hazel eyes. He sat on his horse like the prince he should have been. He bowed from the waist, restricted by his hauberk. "My lady."

"Robert, do not play the subject with me. I am only your Matti, still a younger sister to my older brother, my only brother, since William and Richard drowned." Matilda grabbed Robert's hand and held it to her cheek. Robert had the black hair of their father as well as his looks. However, he had the hazel eyes of the countess to whom he was born.

"I hear that my sister has done well as a soldier and has surprised Count de Rouell with her prowess."

Matilda shrugged. "It will be a bigger surprise to him now if he attempts it again with most of the English knights here to stop him. Although I would prefer to kill him myself."

King Henry's and Robert of Gloucester's laughter burst forth.

"How dare you two laugh at me!" Matilda crossed her arms. "I promise you that I will kill that man if given a chance. It would be the ultimate hunt."

"I believe you." Robert turned to King Henry. "I do not know why we are here. I do not think Matilda and Geoffrey need our help. I think it is an excuse for a visit."

"Mayhap," King Henry said. "I care not. It is good to see Matti again. Come, Daughter, it has been a long trip. Lead the way to the great hall first, for I am hungry. You always do well at preparing banquets." King Henry turned his horse and rode away before Matilda could answer him.

Matilda hurriedly turned Dancer and followed her father before the King's knights could catch her and enveloped her in another cloud of dust. She slapped her horse on the rump and leaned forward, willing him to catch up with her father. She loved the rhythm of Dancer's pounding hoofs against the hard-packed earth.

The king turned as Matilda closed the distance between them. He laughed and drove his horse forward. Matilda was reminded of the races he had run with her twin, William, in the sunny days before death had changed history. She chuckled to herself when she saw King Henry slowing. It was a familiar trick by a father who expects to win easily. She would show him a trick or two. She was closing the gap rapidly. He glanced back, and Matilda saw his astonishment. He was a proud man, adverse to losing.

"To the edge of the woods!" King Henry shouted over his shoulder to Matilda who was close to passing him. "Let the shadow be the finish line."

"All right. You have met your match!" Matilda leaned forward and shouted to Dancer. He leaped ahead of King Henry's horse with a burst of speed.

"You can not win, Matti." King Henry slapped the reins back and forth against the sides of his horse's neck, and the animal lurched forward.

The horses matched stride for stride and crossed the line between shadow and sun at the same instant. Matilda was pleased that there could be no way to determine the winner. She did not want to lose nor did she want her father to lose. She and her father let their animals slow from a gallop to a trot and finally to a walk before they pulled the reins back to stop.

King Henry shifted in the saddle and looked at Matilda. "You continue to surprise me, Matilda. Your abilities are still growing. You have the heart of a man within the body of a woman."

Matilda watched the leaves dance overhead as a breeze threaded its way through the trees. She wanted to tell her father that he underestimated her. She did not like the idea that he thought of her as a man within a woman's body. She was a woman, and she liked it that way.

Matilda squared her shoulders and looked at her father. "It should not surprise you that I am capable, for I am more than the offshoot of a sturdy tree, the issue of a great king. I am a strong woman. I am intelligent, and I have been well educated. I should be able to match you in whatever you do." Matilda rubbed Dancer's neck. "I wish I had won."

"Maybe next time you will." King Henry took Matilda's hand. "I am not used to you as a grown woman. Mayhap I do not want to admit that time has passed and that I am getting old."

Matilda brushed aside his comment as nothing more than a man making conversation. She did not want to think of her father as being mortal. "You will be here for many years." She looked at the army that closed the distance between them. "Let us ride. I do not want to be covered with dust."

King Henry rode slowly with Matilda riding next to him. "Do you ever wonder about the future? I believe that the young live in the future, and the old live in the past. I try to forget the past."

"Father, sometimes the younger generation lives in the past. I think of the past every day, nay, every hour."

Matilda took a deep breath and let it out slowly. She chose the next words carefully. "I want to return to England."

"Your place is here with Geoffrey. Together you are to protect this land that your grandfather ruled."

"England is my home."

"No." King Henry's lips were set in a tight line. "We may have a problem in England, Matti."

Matilda's head snapped around and she stared at her father. "What kind of a problem?"

King Henry rode in silence, his face a shadow of conflicting feelings. "It is only an undercurrent of distrust that I perceive, mayhap brought on by a furtive glance or a lull in conversation when I enter a room. It is like a whisper in the dark that makes one wonder if it has been dreamed."

"Are the barons sorry they swore to put me on the throne? I have no illusions. I fear that I will have to fight my way to the throne, and I will be happy to do so, for I shall win. If the barons will not support me, then I must hope that they will not work against me. They are not to be trusted?"

"I do not want to accuse them of that, but when the time comes, it may be difficult to maintain their allegiance to you under pressure from other quarters. We must think of a way to prevent Stephen from taking the throne."

"Stephen! He will not take the throne. I am surprised that you say that, Father."

"I agree that he is weak."

"He is not weak."

"Do not let your heart cloud your mind, Matilda, for you could lose everything. Stephen is weak, but he would be a popular choice for king if there were a movement away from your ascension to the throne. We must think of something."

"Do you not think it would be good for me to go back to England so that I can be a visible reminder of the future?" Matilda waited, holding her breath.

"Mayhap later, but not yet. I think you need to prove yourself here in Normandy. Of course you have defended the castle, but there must be more victories to convince the doubters that this was not a one time occurrence."

"Perchance fortune may smile upon me, and others here will want my death." Matilda felt bitter because her father had casually dismissed the idea of her return to England.

"You are teasing your poor, old father."

"You are neither poor nor old, so do not try to get my sympathy." Matilda looked toward the eastern horizon from where Count de Rouell had appeared. There were no knights on horseback, no charges toward them, and no screams from pain, at least not today. "There will be others who will come. The future will involve bloodshed."

"You will be ready, Daughter. I will help you." King Henry reached for Matilda's hand and held it in his. "There is something you must do. You must seem the loving wife, even if you are not."

Matilda's heart jumped at her father's words. "What do you mean?"

King Henry stared at Matilda. "I mean that you must forget your infatuation for Stephen."

Matilda removed her hand from her father's. His attitude was infuriating, but she pushed her anger back. She needed to change his mind. "Do not be so condescending. It is not infatuation. I love Stephen, and had I not had such a foolish father trying to make marriages that could not work, then I would not have to find love elsewhere." Matilda closed her eyes. This meeting with her father was difficult. She had looked forward to it for so long. "I do not want to talk about this now. It will spoil our reunion."

"We have to talk about Stephen. You must not continue with this affair. I order it to stop." King Henry's voice was harsh.

"Stop! How could I have anything started? I am separated from Stephen by many miles." Matilda grappled with her emotions. She could not obey these orders that her father threw at her. "You might as well order the blood to stop rushing through my veins or my heart to stop beating. I can no longer control my love for Stephen any more than I can control my beating heart."

"You can not expect to gain the confidence of the barons unless you stop this affair," her father said.

"Oh, magnificent King Henry, how can I do what you do not do? You have had liaisons that have produced sons and daughters who carried your looks, but not your name. My dear brother, Robert, is such an offspring."

"Matilda! It is not the place of a well-bred woman to talk of such things."

Matilda smiled at his discomfort. She was glad he found her words shocking. She had parried words with him, and now it was time for another thrust. "I am no different than you, Father."

"It is not seemly for a woman to have affairs." King Henry's heavy, dark eyebrows were almost pulled together as one, his frown was so intense.

"I am not an ordinary woman. It is because of you that I am not, and I do not intend to behave as other women do."

"Listen to me. I am telling you, as your king, you will give up this destructive affair with Stephen. You are destroying your chances for the throne." King Henry threw up his hands. "You can not flaunt yourself. You can not have a lover and be a ruler."

"Am I not already breaking tradition? Why not behave as a man? Marriages are merely for alliances. Love comes where we find it and the two are never the same. Am I not entitled to some happiness? There will be so little of it in my life, for I will be fighting to gain and keep England," Matilda said.

"I can not let you do this. I know this illicit love will cost you the kingdom."

"You can not stop my love any more than you can stop the wind. But, at the cost of my happiness, I will see Stephen no more. He will no longer come to my bed, for you are my father and my king, and I must obey you."

A breeze rose and rippled Dancer's mane, then Matilda's kirtle. She hoped that King Henry would not see the sparkle of tears in her eyes. She shook her head to deny the validity of her father's request because she dared not speak.

"You will see that I am right." His voice was subdued, almost tender. "I do wonder at your ability to keep your promise to me. For this reason and others, I will require you to remain in Normandy for a while longer."

Matilda stared at her father, eyes narrowing. "Do not think me weak. If you are strong, so am I, and if I am weak, so are you. Let us ride on to the castle now. I have no wish to discuss Stephen with you. I desire that you never talk to me of the matter again."

The king winced. He cleared his throat. "That is fair enough, Daughter. Your point is well taken. Let us ride."

Ella moaned. "You are not eating enough to keep alive. It has been almost a week since your father arrived, and you have not even gone hunting with him. He has asked you faithfully each evening and again each morning. What ails you?" She motioned for the servant to remove the untouched tray. "If you persist in this behavior, you will wither and look a century old."

"Please, just leave me. I do not want to talk about it." Matilda waved Ella away, then sat in the window seat and stared at the grey sky. She felt that she had worn out her brain, as well as her heart, worrying about Stephen.

Ella crossed her arms. "Why did you promise such a thing if it is to be the death of you?"

Matilda recoiled at the feeling that she had deserted Stephen. If she had really loved him, she could not have given him up. If she did not really love him, then she was no better than a common woman who took men to her bed. Matilda swung around to face Ella. "I had to. My father is right. The truth is that I want the crown more than I want Stephen. I only hope I can convince my over-wrought heart."

"I think love is worth much more than the crown with its problems. You know not that you will be able to keep your promise to your father. The way you act now, if Stephen stepped through that door, you would not be able to resist him," Ella said.

"I know. I was in too much haste to please my father. I know not what to do. Mayhap it would be to my advantage to stay here and make certain I never see Stephen again." Matilda shivered at the memory of Stephen's touch and his voice.

"If I thought I could never see my Edward again, I would want to die. I can not tell you the happiness I have had since he has arrived. But, I am being selfish to talk of my joy when you are so devastated." Ella kissed Matilda on the top of her head, and folded her arms around Matilda's shoulders. "Could I trade my happiness for your pain, I would. Maybe Stephen's wife could have a most convenient accident."

"I have thought that, too, but though I have murder in my heart, I can not have murder on these hands." She held her hands in front of her and studied them. "I am happy that one of us is content." Matilda patted the arm wrapped about her. "I am strong. I will get over Stephen if I will it so."

"I do not believe you."

"I will prove it. Get my hunting outfit, and see if my king will wait for me. Today, I take out my frustrations on the deer in the woods to erase the thoughts of the dear in my heart. I will not see England for a long time. I may as well make the best use of my time. I will hunt the trails that my grandfather used to tell me of. Mayhap his ghost will send me a large stag today." Matilda willed the vision of Stephen from her mind.

"I will go fetch a messenger to ask King Henry to wait for you. I am relieved that you have chosen bliss instead of brooding." Ella moved quickly toward the door, then paused. "It is a very good day for a hunt. Do not change your mind, Matilda."

"Go, then, before I do." Matilda laughed as Ella swung open the door and scurried from the chamber scattering reeds as she went.

Matilda sat astride her horse as she had become used to doing and held Dancer steady with one hand. If her fellow hunters noticed anything amiss, Matilda guessed they were either too polite to make reference to it or they were not wont to invoke King Henry's wrath. She looked at the gathering of King Henry's hired huntsmen who mixed with Geoffrey's. John Fitz Gilbert le Marechal was in charge of King Henry's horses. He growled orders while at the same time he fretted over the welfare of his animals. If ever a servant was seen mistreating a horse, he was castigated and spent the rest of his life as a field hand. Matilda's eyes sparkled at the sight of John Fitz Gilbert le Marechal and his horses. He was one of the most loyal knights that King Henry had. She had often heard her father say that he wished all his knights were as strong and as honest as Sir John, even though at times it was difficult for the king to listen to his honesty.

Together both rulers had no fewer than six huntsmen along with their assistants as well as five horn blowers, twenty sergeants whose only job was to beat the cattails, and too many dog handlers to count. Dogs were everywhere nipping at each other, their hackles up with excitement. Several archers were on hand in case the king or the count tired of hawking and wanted to shoot game instead. Matilda shook her head. It was a small army that had begun the morning by having an outdoor breakfast with their king.

King Henry rode toward Matilda, his normal pace slowed by frequent stops to talk with his knights. Matilda was not certain of how he would react to her emergence from her self-imposed exile. She knew that he was aware of her presence because he kept glancing her way. She would let him make the first overture and set the tone for the day. She watched as her father rode closer. Why did she always feel like a child around him? She was a woman, capable and strong. The child-like feelings should have vanished long ago, but alas, they had not. Matilda wondered if all women felt this way.

Her father rode toward the falconer, who with his assistants, stood waiting patiently for the duck hunt to begin. Matilda was more excited than usual, for one of her talents happened to be in falconry. She had been expertly trained by her father's falconer, then she had learned the finer points from Geoffrey's falconer. She caught herself wanting to surprise her father with her newly honed skills. Matilda silently chastised the child in herself for trying to win approval from her father.

In order to forget her momentary lapse, she looked around for Geoffrey. He turned, caught her eye and smiled. She returned the smile in spite of herself, for she was rapidly becoming enchanted by him. The sun shone off his hair, giving him a halo affect. Matilda laughed. He was no saint. He saluted, then was distracted by a question from Brian fitzCount. She wondered whether or not Geoffrey would be proud of her newly honed hunting skills.

Matilda was brought out of her revelry by Dancer's welcoming nicker to King Henry's horse. Matilda watched her father ride to her. She bit her tongue to keep from speaking first. He would have to make some concession to her pride.

"Daughter, it is a fine morning to hunt. Tell me, are you ready for your hawk?" King Henry pulled at the top of his heavy leather glove to make certain it was on tightly.

Matilda held up her left arm where a similar glove protected her small hand. The glove went to the elbow and was stitched with heavy thread. The talons of the peregrine falcon were sharp. "I have a favorite hawk, Father. See, she sits quietly on the arm of Geoffrey's falconer."

King Henry looked back toward the falconer he had just left. "He told me that was the best trained hawk of them all. He will allow just a few people to hunt with her. I, of course, am one."

Matilda smiled at the naturalness of her father's arrogance developed from the habit of his every wish being granted. She decided to use his conceit against him. "Are you going to choose your hawk first, or do I?"

As expected, King Henry waved his hand in a gesture of magnanimous assent of king to subject. "Of course. There is a nice little hawk being held by that young boy."

Matilda smiled. "I think not. It is too tame. I did learn falconry while in England with you."

"Yes, that is so. A hawk too large will be difficult to handle."

Matilda motioned to the head falconer. She tried hard not to smile as he came toward her, but the corners of her mouth lifted involuntarily. She leaned down in the saddle and held out her arm. The falconer nudged the hawk gently from his arm onto hers. The peregrine falcon did a little sidestep hop, shifted from foot to foot, then settled. "She is a pretty bird." Matilda carefully straightened. From the corner of her eye, she saw her father's surprise.

King Henry stared down at the falconer. "Is it wise to let her lady have the strongest bird? I thought you told me that only a select few were allowed to hunt with this hawk."

The falconer glanced at Matilda, then bowed to the king. "I did, your majesty. The empress is one of the few."

"Really?" King Henry stared at Matilda. "Have you been keeping a secret from me?"

Matilda used her ungloved hand to smooth the slate grey feathers on the peregrine's back. "I kept no secret. You assumed that you were the best falconer. Mayhap I have usurped your hawking prowess." Matilda pretended to be looking at the speckled chest of her hawk. She rubbed her finger over the patterned breast of the bird.

King Henry chuckled. "A challenge? We shall see which hawk brings home the most ducks." King Henry turned to the falconer. "Bring me the best bird that you have left. I will still win." He pointed toward the sky. "When the sun reaches its zenith, then we shall have a count."

"What do I get when I win?" Matilda grinned at her father.

"You want to wager? Then we will make it worth while. If you win, I will take you back to England with me."

"England?"

"Well, it would not be a bad idea to take you back." King Henry leaned down and took the second best falcon onto his gloved hand. He quietly whistled a tune and the bird sat still.

Matilda's grin was gone, replaced by a serious countenance. "If I lose, then will you leave me here?"

"Naturally. A wager is only good if the bargain is kept."

Matilda ran her finger down the bill of the hawk, checking the sharpness of her black-tipped beak. She looked around for Geoffrey. He was by the hounds, and she could barely see him for the dust they had raised. "All right. It is a wager worth everything to me."

Matilda looked at her father and smiled. "I will win. Prepare to lose to your daughter, King Henry."

"Then let the hunt begin!" King Henry shouted.

Matilda watched as everyone leaped into action. The swirl of color heightened her excitement. The falcon fluttered her wings. Matilda leaned toward her falcon and sang a few bars of the song with which the bird had been trained. The peregrine settled down immediately. Matilda rode forward, following her father. The dogs had been turned loose to flush the ducks from the marshes. Matilda rode off to the right to give herself and her bird more area. She removed the falcon's hood, sitting still while the hawk's golden eyes adjusted to the light. Matilda thought that her eyes looked like precious jewels.

The sound of flapping wings brought her attention to the task at hand. Matilda whispered to her hawk, "Do your best, for you are my passage to England." Matilda held up her arm and signaled the falcon with a whistle. She turned her face away from the whirlwind created by the flapping of the hawk's wing as she took to the sky, rowing her way upwards. Matilda slid down from Dancer and watched the graceful, pointed wings as the hawk cut through the air, making dainty orbits above her.

Matilda spied a duck and whistled a command. Her falcon circled above the hapless duck, dove, and latched onto her back, then brought the fowl back to earth. She dropped the duck gently at the feet of her mistress as she swooped by and landed on Matilda's upraised and gloved wrist. Matilda reached over with her ungloved hand and wiped a drop of blood from the talons. Matilda looked over to where her father's falcon was coming in with her first kill. "I wish they would hurry up with the dogs and flush some more ducks. We need a lot of kills, do we not?" Matilda ran a finger across the silky head of her peregrine. "Will you win for me today?"

The sun was directly overhead when Matilda heard the prearranged signal for the hunt to stop. She looked at the mound of ducks in front of her and was struck by the thought that it may not be enough. She chastised herself for doubting not only her hunting skills but that of the falcon. With head held high, she bid goodbye to her falcon as the falconer retrieved the tired and bloody hawk. Matilda watched his face for a sign of approval, but she could read nothing in his stone-like features. She watched him disappear into the crowd of his helpers with the hawk.

Matilda turned toward the sound of hoof beats. Her father, followed by John Fitz Gilbert le Marechal, Geoffrey, and Brian fitzCount rode toward her. She wanted to count the ducks that the huntsman assigned to her had strung up, but she did not want her father to know that she was anxious. She greeted the men with a smile and a small curtsy for her king.

"Matilda, I do not wish to embarrass you, but it is quite probable that my falcon's kill today was a record. The falconer said so himself."

Matilda would not allow her father the satisfaction of her curiosity. She waited, but saw her dream of returning to England eluding her.

"Do you not want to know the record?" King Henry's grin was wide.

"Certainly." Matilda waited for the number that surely bested hers.

"My falcon has killed five ducks in the short time of the contest." King Henry turned to Geoffrey and pointed to his left. "I see by the ducks over there that Matilda has done well. I see at least three hanging."

"Father, my kills are over there." Matilda pointed to the king's right, then watched as he counted once, then twice.

King Henry's mouth gaped. "Matti! There are seven ducks. Are they all yours?"

"Yes, Father." Matilda allowed herself to laugh at his astonishment. She started to say something when she noticed Geoffrey's flushed face. She was instantly contrite that her happiness had brought him dismay. Of course, her father had probably told him of their bargain. "Geoffrey, would you ride with me back to the castle?"

He nodded, dismounting quickly to hold Dancer for Matilda as she swung up. "I know the bet that your father had with you."

Matilda adjusted the reins so Geoffrey would not see her nervousness. "I am sorry," she whispered. She noticed her father studying her and she blushed.

Geoffrey ignored protocol and rode out before the king with Matilda riding by his side. When they were out of earshot of the entire hunting party, which seemed to have been held back by King

Henry, Geoffrey spoke. "It seems that we are at cross purposes, again. Your father told me he did not expect you to win. He does not know that your . . . your infatuation for Stephen drives you beyond what is expected. I am surprised that you did not deplete the entire duck population for miles to make certain that you would win."

"I . . . I wish I had not made that silly bet with Father. Geoffrey, if you do not want me to go to England then I will not go." Matilda felt her heart twist. Why must she love one man and be married to another? The fates had been so very cruel.

"I will not stop you. In fact, it will be good for you to face Stephen. Maybe you will find out that he does not love you." Geoffrey started at Matilda's quick intake of breath. He frowned at her. "I do not mean to hurt you, but you know not what love is. Stephen does not love you."

The anger that surged through Matilda caused her to reach out and slap Geoffrey across his arm with her hawking glove. "How dare you say such a thing to me."

Geoffrey grabbed the glove and jerked it from Matilda's hand. "I know about Stephen. He will be your ruin someday."

"You know nothing," Matilda snapped.

"You make it difficult to love you. Enjoy your sojourn to England. May things work out for you." Geoffrey used the glove to slap his horse on the flank. He left Matilda glaring after him as he galloped off swinging around the hunters that obscured him from her view.

CHAPTER
VI

HE SHIP BOUNCED AND CREAKED to the point that Matilda feared for her life. She clung to her father's strong arm and buried her head in his shoulder. It was colder than normal for an August channel-crossing. She would not have been standing at the railing except that it was worse to sit on the backless, wooden benches. She could not help wondering if God intended her to die as her twin brother, William, had died. She shivered. She always shivered when she imagined William's final breaths taken on the sinking White Ship near this same spot.

King Henry wrapped his arm around Matilda. "Would you like me to take you elsewhere?"

"No. I want to see England as soon as possible. I want to see the land for which I yearn."

"Is it just the land for which you yearn, or something else?" King Henry looked down at his daughter.

"I am so tired of bouncing around that I could almost give up the kingdom for a strip of non-bobbing land. I yearn for dirt, nothing more." Matilda held onto the railing as a wave tossed the small, wooden ship upward, held it suspended for a long moment, then sent it sliding at enormous speed down the other side. Matilda gasped for breath.

"You are more of a soldier than a sailor, I see."

"If my legs were meant to be on the sea, then I would have a fish's tail like the mermaids we hear about from travelers. The sea has already claimed several of your children. I hope I will not be claimed as well."

King Henry looked out to his left, his eyes unfocused. "Yes, the sea took the crown prince among them. In one mad moment a piece of my immortality died, and the future had to be re-done." King Henry held Matilda tighter. "I will not think on the past. I have you here, and the future is within my arms."

"You are certain that the barons will meet with us next month?" Matilda asked.

"I will order them to appear before us again." King Henry stood steady with his feet planted apart, still holding Matilda with one arm and gripping the railing with the other while the ship shuddered beneath them. "I do not want to think of anything other than surviving this trip. I thought the Channel was placid in August. Is the devil driving the boat today?"

"Land would look sweeter than all the gold and jewels in your treasury." Matilda bent over the rail, hoping to lose what was left of last night's dinner, but the spray of salt water caused her to gasp instead. The moment was gone when she could get rid of the stone that lay in her stomach. She brushed hair from her face and looked toward the prow to make certain it had not splintered after the last crash against a wave. She thought she saw a dark shape ahead of the ship. Given her mood, she believed it to be one of the ugly sea monsters that frequented the Channel. Suddenly, the darkened blob had meaning. "Oh, look, Father! There is land!"

"Sweeter words I have never heard. Praise be! It appears none too soon, for I think that I would lose my kingly breakfast before too much longer, and Robert would never let me forget it. He rides this storm-tossed boat as if it were a smooth-gaited horse. He never sickens."

Matilda laughed. "And I thought King Henry was invincible."

"No one is invincible but God," King Henry said.

"Again, look, Father. The land gets closer and looks better to me at the same time. I can see people waiting at the docks. It will not be too soon for me."

"Do you see Stephen?" King Henry asked.

"Father, you promised he would be sent north to help keep peace there." In a moment of guilt, she had asked her father to send

Stephen away so that she would not see him. Her father had promised, in an off-handed manner, and she had felt less guilty.

Matilda looked away from the docks and down at the deck. How could her father be so cavalier about his promise? She did not trust herself to appear calm if Stephen were there to meet the King's party.

"He is keeping peace in several places. If he felt the need to be in the south of England, he would be here. If he needs to talk with me, then he will have to meet the boat. He is your cousin, Matti, and one of my aides. You will have to meet with him, nay, even be in the same room with him at times, so you must get used to seeing him. He will have to be a memory."

"A living and breathing one. A most difficult kind to forget."

It seemed much too long before the ship docked and Matilda was helped to dry land. She felt like her legs were made of willow limbs, and she could hardly wait to be placed in a wagon. The ride to the closest inn would take only an hour, but Matilda wondered if she would make it. She sat quietly on a crate and waited for the trunks to be placed in the wagon that would take them inland to their castle. Ella sat next to her, not speaking. Her mouth was ringed by a greenish-white color, and Matilda felt sorry for her. These trips were always worse for Ella. She would not eat for an entire day before sailing.

The number of people who were here to meet the ship surprised her. Among the throng that had to be held back by her father's guards, were the local fishermen, their wives, and their children. Matilda wrinkled her nose at the strong fish smell that permeated the air. She imagined the clothing of these villagers to be beyond laundering. They were dressed in various shades of grey and silver and looked much like the fish they caught. Matilda wondered if they were attracted to fishing because their faces were fishlike, or if they were fish-like because they spent most of their lives with fish.

The men talked loudly, pointed to various activities, and jostled each other for a better view. The braver children slipped out of the grasp of their mothers and wove their way to the front of the crowd wriggling in between the legs of the men. Some children were even braver and waved at Matilda. She smiled and waved in return, delighted by the gentle smiles. The women stood silently, watching her intently. Matilda wondered why they did not talk, wave, or smile. Was their life difficult? She had no concept of how they lived or how they loved.

Gulls screamed above them, diving toward piles of discarded fish guts. They fought with wings, beaks, and feet for the choicest pieces of meat. Matilda did not know which was the worst, the deafening screech of the gulls or the fish smell that saturated everything. She was sure that if a rock were taken from the shore, it would smell of fish no matter where it was taken.

A loud crash caused Matilda to turn toward the sound, and she groaned when she saw that it was her box of books that she took everywhere. Fortunately, the top had not burst open. She watched the man who dropped the crate get boxed about the ears by the captain of the ship, and she was not sorry. He should not be so clumsy with valuables.

Matilda heard her father's booming voice above the noise. He was talking with several servants about the luggage, gesturing and giving orders in rapid, staccato sentences. A rush of admiration for her father surged through Matilda, and it surprised her. She loved the power that he had, and she knew at that moment she wanted the same power. Everything she had learned throughout her life seemed to come together for her. She knew that she was ordained for greatness, and she said a silent prayer to God asking for his guidance.

Stephen had not met the ship and to Matilda it was worse than she had expected not to have him near. She wondered when the inevitable meeting would come. She turned toward the sound of horse's hoofs beating the ground as it neared. Matilda's intake of breath at the sight of the man caused Ella to turn to look at the rider also. Matilda's throat constricted, nearly cutting off her breath, and her palms were sweaty before she realized it was not Stephen.

Matilda did not know whether she was relieved or sorrowed. "It is not him."

"No," Ella said.

"I fear that I am not over my love." Matilda wondered if she could live with just a throne for comfort. She forced herself to remember that only a few moments ago she was basking in her father's power. She was determined to replace her longing of love for longing of power.

Ella put her hands on her hips. "Mayhap if your husband would act like one and live in the same castle with you for longer than a week or two at a time you would have no reason to love Stephen."

"It is not Geoffrey's fault. I told him to leave me alone. I do not want to be a wife to Geoffrey, and he will not force me. He left the day after the hunt because of me." Matilda shrugged. "I do not know what I am to do. I may not be as strong as I would like. My only hope is that Stephen will stay north. Will you help me, Ella? You may be my only salvation."

"I will help you, of course. Right now, I will be glad to find us a bed that is not floating on water. I feel as if the land were haunted. It bobs. Will it never stop rolling and bouncing?"

"I hope it will, and soon. I will be happy to get back to London. I have missed my step-mother. If she were not so frail, she could have come to Normandy with Father. There will be no babies this year for her. Her letter said that she lost another early in her term. Poor Father. He did not know about this baby until it was already gone."

"How many does this make?" Ella asked.

"At least three. I do not understand, but some women can not carry children. I have wondered why I have not had any. Although in some ways it has been a blessing." Matilda sighed. "I just hope that William the Conqueror's line does not end with me."

Ella shook her head, auburn braids swinging. "I do not think God will let that happen. You know it is ordained that you rule England. I know your heirs are meant to rule as well."

"I find comfort in your beliefs, and I hope you are right. It is a great risk and depends on support from the nobility. It should be interesting to see how the barons act at our meeting in September." Matilda pointed at a jerking wagon pulled by two horses that looked as if they had been pulling plows only a few minutes before. "Look, our wagon has arrived. It is ghastly, Ella. It rocks like the boat did." Matilda clasped her hand over her mouth. She spoke through her fingers. "When I am king, I will outlaw boats."

The day of the meeting with the barons was beautiful and warm. The sun streamed in through the two-story stained-glass windows in the chapel. Matilda was there early anxious to have time alone before she met the men who were to swear fealty to her again in her quest for the throne. This time she had a stronger commitment to her father's strategy than she had had before. She had started her quest with a desire to please her father more than to please herself. Now she wanted the throne for the power of it. She wanted to lead England. She wanted to make her father's dreams her own.

Matilda walked across the chapel to the alabaster statue of the Virgin Mary. The chards of color from the windows played across Matilda's saffron-colored kirtle as she sliced through the man-made rainbow. She stopped before the statue of the Virgin studying her delicate face and slender hands. She had known the pain of losing a son and ultimately a kingdom of heaven on earth. Would she understand the need for Matilda to have a kingdom, too? A different kind of kingdom, to be sure. Matilda wanted to pray for guidance, for her instincts told her there were many who would rather Stephen rule. The rumblings and the reports from her father's spies confirmed her worst fears.

She frowned. Whispering to the statue of the Virgin, she confided, "I am as capable as Stephen. I am as capable as any man, and yet there is prejudice against me because I am a woman. Who will believe that I am my father's child in hunting, in fighting, and in politics? Who will lay aside their doubts and support me because of what I can do, and not because of my sex? Mother, Mary of God, I pray to you. Help your daughter in need."

The sound of footsteps caused her to turn toward the small doorway that led to the hall and her father's apartments. Adelicia appeared and looked around the chapel until she spied Matilda standing in front of the statue. She smiled and crossed the short distance. "Your father sent me to make certain you were ready. He will be down in a moment, and the barons are to appear soon after. The King has made sure that all barons are present. I must warn you that Stephen is amongst your supporters."

Matilda's hand flew to her mouth. "Stephen is here?"

"Yes."

Matilda took a deep breath. "It was to be expected, sooner or later. I am ready. I have willed for myself a heart of iron."

Adelicia adjusted the silver girdle that encircled Matilda's waist. She stepped back to view her adjustments. "You are sure? I do not think love can be stopped so completely."

"Controlled, my dear step-mother, but not stopped. Love has to be killed, and I can not commit murder."

"You must be careful, lest love become a complication. You can not compromise the crown for the mere love of a mere man."

"What words do you speak? This is my own Adelicia speaking politics and intrigues? You hate this kind of talk, and never discuss the woes of the crown." Matilda's eyes sparkled with mischief as well as sudden tears; tears for Stephen.

"Matti, do you tease me? I am concerned about you, for your father has told me of possible plots against you. I fear even for your life. More so since that horrible arrow struck you down. Some would like to see you disposed of soon." Adelicia blinked rapidly, her eyelashes wet.

"I am not worried about my life, yet. Too many men fear King Henry. After his breath leaves his body and his soul flies to Heaven, then I will have to watch behind me," Matilda said. "It may be a woman I need fear more than any man."

"You mean Stephen's wife?"

"Yes, I do mean Maithilde, for she is ambitious. Ambitious people are dangerous, especially when they drive another person." Matilda grabbed her step-mother's arm. "I hear footsteps. Is it the King?" She looked toward the door from which Adelicia had appeared.

"There he is." Adelicia curtsied.

Matilda curtsied as well, and held the pose until her father spoke.

"Arise, my lady, and daughter. You do unnecessary homage. No one is present but us three." King Henry motioned toward two large chairs placed to the side of the altar, slightly in front of it. "Matilda, you are to sit between the altar and me."

"But, Father, these chairs are the same size and height. Is there not one for Adelicia?"

"I am not to be here, Matti. It is for you and your father to work out the barons' loyalties. I will take my leave of you now. Please come to tell me what happens. Have supper with us in our rooms." Adelicia kissed Matilda on the cheek and moved swiftly away, disappearing down the hallway.

"Now, Father, tell me what subtleties you have planned for this meeting. I know you think of every tiny detail." Matilda eyes twinkled.

"Such as?"

"The chairs and their placement."

"The chairs are placed to the side of the altar to signify God's plan for you to be the first female king of England. The chapel was chosen for the same reason. The size of the chairs indicates you are equal to me. A smaller chair, which is normal for a queen, would only emphasize that you are just a woman, not a ruler."

"You are very thorough."

"The future of this country depends upon a peaceful ascension. Please, sit."

" I should have a false beard like the female Egyptian pharaoh." Matilda sat and arranged her kirtle so that one dainty slipper showed. She pulled her foot back as if it had been burned. She had forgotten that she was to repress her femininity.

"I do not think a beard would be attractive on you, Matti, although it might keep you warmer in the winter."

"You are playing politics to make certain that I inherit the throne."

"A king is nothing more than a man; mortal in life, but immortal if he has heirs, for his lineage is carried through the centuries. A part of him lives in each generation, and the historians invoke his name in their works."

"A vain desire."

"Yes, but not uncommon. Everyone wants immortality. Even our peasants have children for that reason. I could not do this, though, if I thought you incapable of being king, Matilda. Hush, I hear the barons approaching. Watch the double doors at the entrance to the chapel. They come through there."

Matilda glanced sideways at the king, and felt peculiar to be at the same level with him. She tried to calm her heart that hammered away, vibrating her rib cage. She wondered if the noise from her heart would betray her to Stephen, for she had already refused once to see him since her return. "What does it take to kill a love?" Matilda asked.

"You spoke?"

"Not really." Matilda watched the door as it was pushed open by two castle-guards. She held her breath, for Stephen was first through the door. He was so handsome that she feared her face would reveal the truth, and he would have to discount the lies that her note had told him. His black hair glistened in the sunlight that shone through the windows. Matilda clenched her hands together in her lap to keep from reaching for Stephen. She forced herself to pull her eyes away from Stephen's and look at the others who had entered behind him. As expected, Brian fitzCount was next to her brother, Robert. She caught Robert's eye and gave him a nod. He winked at Matilda, causing her to bite her lower lip to keep from giggling at his impudence. Robert had always been flippant when it came to ceremonies. Mayhap it was because of his illegitimacy. He was the living reminder of his mother's broken commandment. Maybe after that broken rule, mere rules of man seemed unimportant. Of all her father's bastard children, Robert was the only one she really liked. He was unpretentious, and thus, seemed more royal than any of the others.

Near the front was Sir John Fitz Gilbert le Marechal, his sandy hair belying the darkness of his person. He was made of strong mettle, and could be cold and hard if necessary. He was a trusted knight to her father. Matilda wondered if they would ride off to heaven together.

The other lords and barons fanned out behind Stephen. Matilda was aware of a multi-colored crowd that mirrored the stained glass windows behind her, and they seemed as formidable as the grey stone walls of the chapel. She felt closed in, and she quickly realized that the freedom she had would be swept away in a few moments when the barons swore fealty to her. With the crown would come responsibility.

Matilda glanced at Stephen. He would have much to lose. Would he lose gracefully or let his wife shove him into civil war? Matilda pushed Stephen from her mind. She had a responsibility to her father. The King deserved his immortality.

"You know why you have been summoned here." King Henry leaned forward in his chair. "Today, I wish to have confirmation of your intent to support my daughter, Matilda, as the next king of England. If she were not capable, I would not propose such an historical event." King Henry paused and looked at the crowd before him. His frown was fierce as Stephen was the first to step forward and kneel before the royal pair.

"I wish to pledge my everlasting support to Matilda, the next King of England. It is my belief that God wills it so and that I, as his vassal, must help his destiny. I will swear to uphold King Henry's wishes because of divine intervention." Stephen stayed on his knees, his dark hair sliding forward and nearly covering his face.

Matilda clutched the arms of the chair and willed her body to stay seated against all her desires. She stared at Stephen's arms and remembered, painfully, the last time they had held her. She almost cried out, but was mercifully distracted by Robert of Gloucester as he knelt before his father and half-sister.

"It is my duty to do as my father and King desires. It is my duty as a brother to protect my sister in her quest. I will do so with a happy heart and with love for both King Henry and Empress Matilda."

Matilda smiled at Robert as their eyes met — his hazel like his mother's eyes — Matilda's the blue of their father's. He was her protector, and Matilda trusted him above all others.

Brian fitzCount knelt so quickly and quietly that Matilda was startled when his youthful voice clattered against the stone walls of the chapel. "I can neither call upon God's divine will nor can I call upon familial relationships, but I can attest to Matilda's ability to lead men in battle. I can attest to her strength and intelligence. For these reasons, I know she can lead this great country as well as any man. I must support Matilda as the rightful heir to King Henry's throne." Brian fitzCount's freckles darkened against his pale skin as his nervousness increased. His auburn hair was also a startling contrast to the dark haired gentlemen around him, hinting at an ancestor or two from the northern countries across the Channel. He stared at Matilda briefly, then looked away.

The rest of the afternoon was a blur of words and faces for Matilda as the many barons of England pledged support to her. She watched their faces, stared into their eyes, and wondered which ones she would have to face in battle. Such hypocrisy from some of those who were kneeling before her did not surprise Matilda. She would not hesitate to do what was necessary to take her place in history. It was at this moment that she knew she could kill any of these men if they prevented her from ruling. She knew not who her enemies were, but she knew she could kill them. Except for Stephen. She caught herself and refused to let the thought surface. She was glad that she would not have to worry about Stephen.

Her eyes moved from face to face, but no traitors could be acknowledged. She glanced away from Stephen who stared at her.

Heat pushed up from her neck to her cheeks, and she knew she was flushed, so she forced herself to concentrate on what was being said by the baron who bowed before her. The speech was not as elegant as Brian fitzCount's or her brother's, but the man sounded sincere. She slipped back into a daze for the rest of the testimony and did not hear any more words except those of Sir John le Marechal. He was intriguing to her with his harsh voice and short, to the point, speech. He used none of the lilting phrases and long winded words of some of the knights. She was glad that he was so practical. She might need someone who acts instead of talks.

Her father dismissed the barons after a short speech. Matilda was pleased to escape on her father's arm. In the small hallway leading to their separate apartments, she asked, "What do you really think, Father? Did we forestall a civil war?" Matilda stepped in front of her father and stopped.

"How can I predict the future?" King Henry asked.

"I am not asking for a prediction. I am asking for your opinion based on your experience. I want to compare your ideas to mine."

"I think that if Stephen is pushed by his wife and because of her liaison with William of Ypes, some of her relatives, and those she tries to purchase, you could have trouble. I think that if we plan things correctly and you have children by your husband, then you will have Geoffrey's support and there will be no problem. But let us not talk of politics. I am tired. I want to eat dinner with you and my dear Adelicia. I have ordered your favorite dishes and your favorite fermented mulberry juice. Tonight we celebrate quietly, for we have won a victory."

"I wish that I did not have to have a child by my child husband," Matilda said.

"You would deny me my heirs?"

"Oh, Father, of course not, but I wish there were another way." Matilda sighed and pushed her hair away from her face.

It was late when Matilda returned to her own apartment. Ella was absent, and she smiled at the thought of Ella walking in the moonlight with her lover. Matilda slipped out of her kirtle and let it fall to the floor. She unhooked her stockings from the garters that were pinching the skin at her knees. She kicked them under a stool. They were ghastly things and she hated them. Her night chemise was laid across the bed and she grabbed it, grateful to be rid of the daytime clothing. She held the chemise above her head, put her arms into the sleeves, and let it slide down her body until it touched the reeds on the floor. It was warm in the room so Matilda pulled open the windows until they were flat against the inside stone wall. She leaned out, inhaled the clear air, and looked at the moon for a long time before leaving the window to climb into bed.

The full moon shone in through the window making the room as bright as day. Between first sleep and deep dreaming, sounds invaded her mind and forced dreams to explain them. There was a light knock at Matilda's door. She dreamed that a sword was striking her chain mail. She tried to push the swordsman away, to no avail. She came out of the dream frustrated and perspiring, her body tangled in the linen sheets.

A breeze came through the windows, and Matilda realized from the position of the moon that she could not have been asleep for long. The soft knock that was the cause of her dream came again to startle her. She stared at the door. Would it be one of the barons ready to murder her in her own bed? She laughed at her imaginary fears and got up to open the door.

The shock at seeing Stephen was immediately replaced by absolute bliss. She had no time to think of the consequences when he pulled her to him and kissed her with the pent up passion of months of denial. He shut the door and kissed Matilda again.

Matilda pushed Stephen away and stepped back. "I can not do this, Stephen. You have to leave."

"I do not understand why we can not have what has been ours in the past and is ours now. We belong together," Stephen said.

"We do not belong together. I have promised my father that I would not see you again. I must keep my promise."

"How can the words you said to your father overcome the feelings that surge between us? It is unnatural for him to ask that of you. Does he not understand the depth of our feelings?" Stephen put his hands on the door on both sides of Matilda, trapping her neatly. Matilda shivered as he looked down at her, the odor of his freshly washed hair bringing back memories of stolen evenings. When he placed his cheek against the top of her head, she wanted nothing more than for Stephen to make love to her. Matilda was barely aware of his hands until they slid down the rough planks of the door and held her by her arms.

"Can you deny what was meant to be?" Stephen kissed her temple. "Your father tried to play God when he arranged my marriage and yours. We were meant to be together and you know that."

"Stephen, what is done is done. You are married and so am I. Even though it is to the wrong people, my father is correct. I can not afford to give any of my enemies an excuse to keep me from the throne." Matilda wanted to pull away, to send Stephen out of her apartment and pretend that this night had never happened, but she stood still, savoring the familiar warmth of his hands on her.

"You still love me."

"It does not matter. What matters is England and my promise to my father, my king. I must be trustworthy."

Stephen whispered into her ear. "Am I not worth breaking a promise to a stubborn, old man?"

"You are being unfair. First you are too close to me for my senses to work properly. Second, you are asking me to choose between my love for you and my love for my father. I have tried to choose the love of my father, but you will not let me." Matilda pushed Stephen's hands from her arms, but only succeeded in having him lower them to her waist. She trembled and leaned against his chest. The feel of his muscles beneath his tunic brought back a deluge of passions that surged forward and broke through the dam of resistance. Matilda clutched Stephen's tunic, hanging on like a drowning woman. Please, she thought. Someone come and help me be strong.

"Matti."

The sound of her nickname dissolved the last of her resolve. She pressed against Stephen. "I love you too much to refuse you any longer. I want what was once ours." Matilda felt the heat of her body against him, and she knew that the victory was his. She smiled as he picked her up, carried her to the bed, and laid her down. The moonlight shone off his black hair, and she pushed his hair away from his face so that she could see more of him. She felt his kiss on the frown that she knew marred her face, but even that did not help her relax. Matilda knew that time was on his side. This battle was lost to Stephen.

Ella sighed and rolled over, putting her arm out to find Edward. He was beside her, snoring lightly, his bare arms flung above his head. She forced her eyes to open and sat up, dragging the cover with her. "Edward! It is nearly dawn! Wake up, you must get me back to my lady unseen!" Ella pounded on Edward's chest. "How can you sleep so? Wake up, Edward."

"I can not. I had a very exhausting night."

"Edward, do not be so crude. Help me to dress. Where did I put my kirtle? Have you seen it?" Ella looked around the tiny room that Edward shared with another knight. "Get up and light a lamp so I may see." She reached for a mound of something that looked like her kirtle, but it was a sleeping cat. The cat scratched at her, and she jerked back her hand. "How can you just lie there? Help me."

"I find you fascinating when you are upset. What difference will a few moments make? Your mistress will know that you have been gone the night. Have you not been with her for most of your life? You said she was like a sister to you." Edward handed Ella her kirtle, then squirmed around on the pallet.

Ella grabbed the kirtle from him, slipped it over her naked body, and felt around for her undergarments and her hose. Ella slipped on her soft, leather shoes, a gift from Matilda, and started to rise. Edward grabbed her around her middle, pulled her to him, reached up the back of her kirtle and patted her bare bottom.

"Once more, Ella, before you go."

"Do not act the goose. I have to get my lady's bath drawn, and your cousin is sure to want to return to his bed before dawn. I am also to help her resist the charms of a certain gentleman." Ella looked toward the curtain in front of the door. "Do I hear your cousin returning?"

"He will not return until tonight. Maybe not then. He has found solace in another bed. It has worked out very well for us." Edward held tightly to Ella. "Why will you not marry me? Then we will not have to put out our poor cousin."

"I will not marry you until you have a position with Matilda's army. I can not choose between you and my lady. She would allow me to stay with you and serve her step-mother, but Matilda is everything to me. Besides, she needs me, for reasons I will not reveal."

"I have need of you, too."

"Need of me? After last night? Well, never fear, I will arrange something soon, I promise." Ella pushed his arms away and pulled down her kirtle. She stood, holding a bundle of undergarments.

"I will walk with you if you will give me time to dress," Edward said.

"I have no time for that. I will have to get back, unseen, by myself. If I am lucky, no one will guess where I have been. It would be unseemly for my lady to have been unattended for the night, although she does prefer it from time to time." Ella pushed aside the cloth door covering and slipped from the room.

It took only a few minutes to walk across the courtyard and climb the steps to the corner tower. One of the guards discreetly turned his back to her and did not acknowledge her as she passed near him. She was at the top of the stairs just outside Matilda's door when it opened. Ella slipped behind a stone pillar, holding her breath until the person passed by her. Certain it was safe, she peeped out and recognized the tall and handsome Stephen. She had not been missed at all.

Ella opened the door slowly. Matilda was still in bed, but from her movements, Ella knew she was not asleep. "My lady, have you slept well?"

"Hardly at all, Ella. I have been so worried about you. Where have you been?" Matilda stretched her arms out and yawned. "I am glad you are safe. I thought you had been kidnaped."

"If I have been kidnaped, then I hope I am never rescued," Ella said.

"How was your Edward?"

"How was your Stephen?"

"How did you know?" Matilda sat up in the bed and patted the place next to her. "Come and tell me all about your adventure, and I will tell you mine."

"He is wonderful. He wants to marry me, but of course that depends upon you, my lady." Ella crawled onto the bed and like sisters, they traded confidences.

"I can not give you up, Ella, so that means I must acquire Edward as my knight. Is he good with horses, or is he better at marching? What place should I make for him?"

"He is good at love," Ella said.

Matilda giggled. "I have no job like that, or I would take Stephen with me wherever I go."

"He is excellent with horses, Matilda. He did not get to go with the calvary to Normandy, and I believe he missed the horses more than he missed me."

"Then I should leave Dancer behind for his love." Matilda grinned at Ella's feigned shock.

"Oh, do not tease me so. He is good with Dancer, too. Remember when Dancer had the injured foot? It was my Edward who tended him, so I know you could use Edward in the calvary." Ella stared at her mistress so intently that Matilda could no longer hold back her laughter.

"All right, I promise to take Edward with us wherever we go. One of us should have happiness in a mate. I am sure that when I explain it to Adelicia, she will be more than happy to let Edward be a guardian for the both of us."

Ella took Matilda's hand in hers. "I am distressed that you are not happy. If I could change your life for you I would."

"I thank you for the thought. I envy you, for your happiness is easily obtained. You should marry as soon as possible, so I will talk with Father tomorrow. I am certain he will let me take Edward to help build my army."

"Can you not have happiness with the man who just left your bed?" Ella asked.

"I have broken an oath to my father, and so my love for Stephen is tainted. How can I be happy with that? I am miserable without Stephen and unhappy with my choice. I let my strength ebb as Stephen held me, but I do not care. I will continue to see him."

"I will keep your secret." Ella leaned over and patted Matilda's hand. "Love deserves to be saved. I am so happy that I want you to be happy."

"Bless you, Ella. It cheers me to know that you side with me when no one else does."

"We will have a grand time together, sharing conspiracies of love." Ella swung her legs over the side of the bed. "May I draw your bath now? You must see Adelicia today. She has asked that you break the fast with her. In my haste to get to Edward, I forgot to tell you."

"I forgive you, considering the circumstances."

Matilda hurried down the long hallway toward Adelicia's apartment, although she did not know why she wanted to hurry. Mayhap she was afraid that she might see her father, and she was not certain she could face him. When the door was opened for her, Matilda looked around the room. She was relieved to see that her step-mother was alone.

As if in answer to Matilda's unasked question, Adelicia said, "I thought we should be alone, so I sent the servants away. Come and sit." Adelicia leaned across the wooden table and indicated a chair that was opposite her. She waited for Matilda to sit, then poured a cup of hot broth for her. "You look like you have not eaten for a week." Adelicia pushed a plate of small cakes toward her. "These are fresh from the pantry."

Matilda shook her head. "I am not hungry."

Adelicia's eyes narrowed as she studied Matilda. "These are made with clover honey."

"Later."

"You have refused your favorite cakes? I know not what is wrong with your appetite. I have never seen you so reticent, except when ill. You are not ill, are you?" Adelicia leaned toward her step-daughter and took her hand.

"I am all right." Matilda picked up the cup and blew on the hot broth. She did not want to eat, but if she did not pretend to do so, Adelicia would be even more concerned than she was now.

Adelicia pushed the cakes closer to Matilda. "I know you too well, and I can see you are unhappy about something. Please confide in me so I can help you."

A tear slid down Matilda's cheek. She brushed it away quickly, but Adelicia had seen it. "I am sorry, Adelicia. I am not myself. It is because I have betrayed my father's wishes. I have let Stephen make love to me against the orders of the king himself."

"Is that all?" Adelicia said.

Matilda felt her mouth gape. "Is that all! I hardly expected such a cavalier attitude from one so pious."

"It is a realistic attitude. What can your father do to you? He certainly will not accuse you of treason, for then he would have no heir. My feelings are simple. I believe in love, and I think that one should marry for love. I have seen so much unhappiness because of arranged marriages. Naturally, I do not think you should have a married man as a lover, but that is also the result of an arrangement. I was lucky enough to love your father, but what if I had been married to someone whom I would not have loved? I can not imagine the misery."

Matilda's mind was in a whirl. She had never expected Adelicia to agree with her. Adelicia always agreed with the king in all matters, until now. Matilda could only believe that it was because of Adelicia's kind heart. Adelicia was a simple person who followed the laws of King Henry and the Church. It was unlike her to break either, even in conversation. She hoped that Adelicia would not feel guilty about their talk. If only she had not let Stephen into her chamber. Her weakness was at fault, and she was angry with herself for not having control. How would she rule a kingdom when she was so wanting personally?

Matilda put the cup down with a bang against the plank table. "I wish I had never met Stephen. He has caused me as much heartache as love."

"I believe that is the way with all young lovers. Even I had bouts of misery whenever your father was away from me. I still do, but I know he will return to me. Marriage does provide that assurance." Adelicia smiled at Matilda's frowning face, then leaned over and brushed an unruly strand of hair away from Matilda's eye. "All the wishing in the world, all the anger you generate will not change what has already been."

"I am breaking God's laws," Matilda said.

"That did not bother you before, so I think you should be resigned to your fate by now. You can not use that as a deterrent. It is too late. Besides, it did not work for you in the past, and it will not stop you now." Adelicia waved her hand to dismiss Matilda's doubts. "God's laws are broken by our own priests, so I hardly think God will be watching you when he is so busy with them. Matti, you have had so little chance for happiness that I want you to have it now. Once you sit upon the throne, you will no longer have any peace and very little chance for real love." Adelicia closed her eyes and shook her head. "There will be no peace and very little happiness."

"Think you I should go on seeing Stephen?"

"I will not tell you what you should and should not do because only you know the circumstances. I would not, however, let your father know if you can prevent it. It would be better for him." Adelicia leaned back against the brocaded fabric of her chair. "Let us talk of more pleasant things and forget this problem of yours."

"That is fine with me. You have become a most trusted ally for me, Adelicia. I love you as much as any daughter could love a mother."

"You know how to bring a tear to my eye. I have always wanted to become a mother, but it will not happen."

"Someday," Matilda said.

Adelicia turned away. "No, Matti," she whispered. "I have chosen to take the herbal drink that prevents a baby from growing within me."

Matilda was not certain that she had heard correctly. It took her a moment to realize that she had heard Adelicia's words. Matilda felt the shock of learning someone's long kept secret. Her eyebrows were raised, and she was aware that mouth was open. Adelicia loved babies. She was always the first to visit a newborn. The women who worked in the castle, even the women of the village always received a gift for the baby whenever they gave birth. Matilda shook her head to rid herself of the shock of hearing Adelicia's secret. "But how could you do that? How could you deny yourself the joy of a child?"

Adelicia stared out the window, refusing to meet Matilda's eyes. "I felt it was better to have no baby than to have one, learn to love it, then have it die. I could not endure that kind of pain."

"It is a fact that some babies die, but some live. We are proof that some of us live," Matilda said. "To not have a child because you are afraid of chances of survival is to deny life."

"You do not understand, Matti. I would take a chance if I were not married to King Henry. Do you not know that if I were to have a child, there would be many who would plot to have it killed? It would upset the plans of Stephen's wife, Maithilde, for one." Adelicia turned to Matilda, eyes bright with tears. "I could not stand that."

Silence dropped like a castle gate between them. Matilda leaned forward and took Adelicia's hands in hers. "I understand. These are dangerous times. I have to fear for my own life. I want you to know that if ever you have a son, I would gladly step aside for him and let King Henry's line continue. I would fight for your son and protect him."

"I know you would. It is not you I fear."

"Does it work well?" Matilda asked.

"What?"

"The herbal mixture."

"Most of the time, but I would not advise you to take it. It causes a lot of bleeding, and I do not think you should take that chance. I will not let you have it, for it can make a woman barren."

"It sounds too dangerous for you, too. I think my mother taught me about it. She told me it was a poison. Can you not stop taking it?" Matilda asked.

"I am careful, and I have never felt ill, just weak at times. Promise me that you will not do what I have done, Matti. I do not want you to take a chance. You must have children."

"Do not worry about my taking any medicine, for I have never conceived. I probably never will, which is unfortunate for King Henry's line when I get the throne." Matilda shrugged. "If I thought I could have children, I would have to submit to Geoffrey more often." She laughed at the blush she brought to Adelicia's cheeks. "Do not play the delicate lady with me. I know that you enjoy love making as much as I do. I was surprised to find that Geoffrey can be exciting." She grinned at her step-mother. "Come, let us talk of more pleasant things, such as hunting."

"I do not find hunting a pleasant topic, Matti, so let us talk of the next Christmas court. It will be here in a few months."

"And think how fast time has flown since I learned to love Stephen. It was at last Christmas court that I knew I loved him. Yes, let us talk of Christmas court." Matilda smiled in anticipation and for a memory.

In another part of the castle, Maithilde sat in the window alcove, staring through the glass, but seeing nothing. She tapped her fingers against the seat, tapped her foot, then jumped up and crossed the room to sit at her dressing table. She looked into the polished metal mirror and saw a pretty woman with a frown that seemed quite natural. Brown hair cascaded down her back and brown eyes looked back at her.

"Am I so ugly that Stephen can not tolerate me? Why must he continuously seek out the enemy to love?" Maithilde watched her reflection speak as she spoke. "Unfortunately, you have only questions and no answers," she said to the mirror.

Maithilde was still seated in this position when a knock interrupted her contemplation. She looked toward the door. "There are never enough servants. Where is one when needed?" Maithilde slammed the mirror down, then sorry that she had mistreated such a rare and expensive item, picked it up and checked to see if she had bent the shiny metal. Satisfied that she had not, she laid it on the table more gently this time, then stomped across the room and answered the door herself.

"Yes," Maithilde said, more annoyed that she had opened the door to an underling. She glared at the young boy who shifted uncomfortably in front of her.

"I have a message for you." The young servant bowed, his hair sliding forward. A soiled, brown tunic hung upon his thin body and his hose were torn. His feet were covered by worn leather shoes. A dirty hand held out a piece of sealed parchment.

"Wait here until I tell you to leave." Maithilde took the parchment carefully so that she would not touch the hand that held it. She noted that the servant watched her with curiosity. She was irritated with his staring, so she walked quickly to her dressing table. She scooted a powder jar aside, picked up a silver-handled knife, and broke the seal. She read the message and smiled, then picked up a quill, wrote two lines, and signed her name. She re-folded the parchment and laid it aside. She took a candle and held it over the flap so that the tallow would drip onto it. Maithilde turned her hand over and pressed her signet ring into the soft accumulation of yellowed fat. She snatched up the parchment and returned it to the servant.

"Take this back to your master as quickly as possible, and do not stop to tarry about the kitchen or I will have you hanged for a spy." Maithilde stared at the young man until he turned, ran from the doorway, and bolted down the length of the corridor to the steps leading down and to the outside.

Maithilde pushed the door shut, crossed the room, kicking the reeds as she went, and watched out the window as the servant appeared in the courtyard. He slid across the yard and out the gate before anyone could speak to him. He was known as a servant to William of Ypes, and it was assumed that William was a follower of King Henry. There was no reason to suspect treachery.

When the sun had been down for more than a half an hour, two cloaked figures rode from the back gate and around a hill. Maithilde looked over her shoulder at the hulking castle that lay behind them. Someday it will be mine, she thought. She and William's escort did not ride far before entering the forest. It was noticeably warmer in the woods out of the cold fall winds, and Maithilde no longer hunched over. When they emerged from the woods on the edge of grazing land, the wind attacked them again. She pulled her fur cape tighter around her. When I am queen, she thought, I will not spend my winters in this forsaken place. She and the knight stopped at a wattle and daub hut with a simple thatched roof. The knight, who had not spoken the entire way, did not speak now, but got down from his horse and helped Maithilde dismount. She handed him the reins. She took no notice of him, instead letting her attention focus on the mean hut. She would have to secure better quarters for her trysts. Men did not seem to take into consideration the finer points of comfort.

Maithilde did not have to knock on the door. William was standing in the doorway with the firelight from a small fireplace at his back. He stepped forward and wrapped his arms around her, but she pulled away.

"Not out here, you fool. I do not need spies taking tales back to King Henry, or that adulteress daughter of his."

"You are not one who can discuss adultery in that tone of voice." William laughed, pulled Maithilde inside, and shut the door.

"Do not pull at me like that. I am not a wench, but a lady." Maithilde jerked her arm out of William's hand.

"Did I make my mistress angry? Let me apologize. You must remember that I am nothing more than the bastard grandson of Robert de Frisian. You are looking at the man who twice failed to be appointed as the Count of Flanders because of my dear mother's indiscretion."

"Spare me your history. I am only interested in one thing." Maithilde moved toward the table. "Is it safe to sit upon this humble stool?" She sat down without waiting for an answer, her back to William.

"You are interested in two things, or am I being used by you?" William moved behind Maithilde. He placed his hands on her shoulders, then moved them down her arms.

Maithilde pushed his hands away. "Let us discuss business first. Your communique said that you had several barons who were against Matilda. Who are they, and can they be trusted?"

"Your naivety amuses me. I will not give you their names, but you can be assured that they do not want a weak female leading their country."

Maithilde glowered. "You would be wrong to miscalculate Matilda's abilities. I wish I could find a way to get her out of England. The longer she remains in England, the more followers she collects. Many of the barons swore a second allegiance to her."

"Including your husband," William said.

Maithilde waved her hand as if to brush the words away. "He thinks he loves her, but when the time comes I will convince him that he should be king."

"You do not understand politics as well as your adversary. Some of the very same barons who have sworn to help us were on their knees before Matilda in the chapel a mere two days ago. I have done what I promised I would do, and now I want to collect what you promised me."

Maithilde looked around the dirty cottage. She wrinkled her nose at the odors. "I do not feel like making love tonight."

"I did not ask whether or not you felt like it. If you want my continued support, you had better find it in your heart to love me. Unless you treat me as you did when we first met — when you wanted me to perform acts of treason for you — then you may find yourself in the interesting position of defending yourself in King Henry's court."

William kissed the back of Maithilde's neck, placed his hands on her shoulders, and slid them underneath the neckline of her kirtle.

Maithilde winced at the word 'court'. "What makes you think that King Henry would believe that we are anything more than lovers. I was not entirely stupid. Take your hands out of there." Maithilde twisted around and faced William. "I am not a peasant girl that you can maul."

William smiled, his teeth white against tanned skin. "The parchment has your handwriting and signature plus your seal."

"Do not be a fool. I said nothing about a conspiracy. I merely said that I would meet you. I can be most innocent when I have to be. How could a poor, ignorant woman like me even think of usurping the throne, let alone have plans and followers for such a thing."

"You would not be the first woman to crave such power or to attempt such a thing. It would be best that in order to preserve your intrigue, you should bed me tonight. I can do more for you than Stephen." William leaned over and kissed Maithilde's hair, then her mouth. He pulled her up from the stool and held her. "We make good lovers."

Maithilde stood on tiptoe and draped her arms around William's neck. She had better take no chances with his loyalty. Besides, he excited her, and an empty bed held no comfort. "I can stay the night, for Stephen will be detained by his mistress. You are so right. We do make a good pair."

"Of traitors," William said.

"Better lovers."

"If Stephen ever dies . . ."

"Do not even speak of such things for fear your thoughts will become real. Without Stephen, I can not become queen."

"Then you do not love me," William said.

Maithilde shrugged. "What has love to do with anything? Love will not get me the crown. Even if I could love you, I could never marry you."

"Because you are married?"

"Because you are a bastard with no future other than skull splitting — a small war here, a small war there. I have to have better than that."

William pushed Maithilde away and looked into her eyes. There was no hint of merriment there. "You do wound me with your cutting words, Maithilde."

"I believe in telling the truth."

"You believe in nothing but Maithilde, but I accept that flaw in you. Now, enough talk, for I need you." William pushed against her.

Maithilde's voice was hoarse. "Then make me need you."

CHAPTER
VII

ATILDA HAD BEEN ASTONISHED when she had realized that she and Stephen had had almost an entire year of happiness, but now it was marred by the decision she had had to make. Time was once more her enemy. Time was a man-made contrivance, but it was God who skewed it to suit his own design. Matilda had decided that no matter how she and Stephen had schemed to stay together, God had sent her a double-edged gift.

She waited for Stephen in the cool woods at their favorite meeting place. The dank odor of half-decayed leaves drifted about Matilda. She sat on a mound of moss and listened to the sounds the creek made as it fought its way across the stones. Sunbeams bounced off drops of silver water that danced in the air before diving back to the creek, merging and losing identity. Sun streaked through the leaves and made its way to the floor of the woods. Above Matilda, a chorus of birds sang. It was here that she felt closer to God than she ever had in a cathedral.

He had twisted her life once more, and she was almost afraid to be angry, but not quite. She had talked with God in irate tones, but had given up when he did not answer her prayers. It was like talking to her father when his mind was made up. God was stubborn, too.

Matilda leaned against a tree and listened to the insects buzz about her. She felt like the castle was in another country when, in fact, it was just beyond the forest. Matilda looked at her stomach. It was not obvious to anyone but her that a future heir to England's throne was implanted there. She placed her hand on her abdomen, but there was no change that she could discern other than a tightening of flesh. She smiled at the irony of having a baby after all her barren years. Mayhap God meant for King Henry to be assured of an heir to carry on the line of William the Conqueror. She could not look upon Stephen's child as a punishment. This was a lovechild and could be thought of as a gift.

Dancer snorted. His ears were forward, and he watched the path down which they had come. A few minutes later, Matilda heard the soft clop-clop of hoofs on the leaf-strewn path. Stephen appeared astride his favorite stallion. He smiled as he dismounted.

"I received your message. Why did you say it was urgent that I meet you? Are you all right?" Stephen dropped to the grass next to Matilda and grasped both her hands in his.

"I needed to talk with you privately. I am all right, but you must know that both our lives will be changed, and I can not predict the outcome." Matilda wished she had better news for him. She did not like to see Stephen frown.

"I do not like the words that you speak."

"This is difficult for me. I must return to Geoffrey immediately in order to preserve my honor and your integrity." Matilda turned her head so she could not see Stephen's eyes.

"I do not understand. I thought you would be allowed to stay for as long as you wanted, and as long as your father was ignorant of our love. Has he found out? Is Geoffrey insisting on your return? We can think of reasons for you to stay here. I can not lose you. You mean more than life to me." Stephen reached for Matilda's chin, turning her face toward him.

"I am going to have your baby in March," Matilda said.

Stephen stared at her. He gently pulled Matilda to him and held her. "Are you certain?"

"I am very certain."

"What should I do?"

Matilda pulled away from Stephen and looked into his eyes. "I want you to agree with my plan, for I have spent sleepless nights deciding the future of my child. I must go to Geoffrey and convince him to accept this child as his own. He will know, of course, whose child it is. I will ask both of you not to reveal that you are this baby's father." She hoped that he would see the wisdom of her decision and would support her.

"A difficult price to pay for an indiscretion. My love has given me a child I can not claim, while my dear wife is pregnant again and giving me a child I have to claim, but I know is not my own. Mayhap, she will miscarry this one as she did the last one. Matilda, I have been faithful to you."

"Oh, Stephen!" Matilda kissed him. "Does not your son, Eustace, give you pleasure?"

Stephen buried his face in her shoulder. He nearly cried and his voice was pained. "He is kept from me. Justice seems not to have been served in my case. I feel that I have lost and lost and lost."

Matilda grimaced at the sound of Stephen so close to tears, yet she was upset that he was not behaving more manly. She pushed that idea away with the excuse that Stephen had not been prepared for what she had known for the last month. Of course he was close to tears. She had just taken away his unborn child and told him that she must return to Geoffrey. She had killed their dream.

Matilda held Stephen tightly. "What have you lost, Stephen? I will always love you no matter where I am."

"I have lost you because time and distance will dull the memories of what we have. I have lost it all. Can you not stay with me? We can go to Scotland and live with your uncle, King David." His voice was muffled.

"No, Stephen. There is no use arguing or pleading with me, for I have already started the arrangements for the trip back to Anjou. I will beg Geoffrey to pretend to be the father. If I am persuasive enough and give him all that he wants, then I will be . . ."

Stephen's head snapped up and he pushed Matilda from him. "Give him all he wants?"

"Just so. I am in no position to bargain." Matilda sighed. "I have loved you far too much, Stephen, and now I must pay for my happiness. I will leave for the shore in two days, and sail in five. Please, do not try to stop me. Do not try to see me, again. It will be difficult enough, leaving you."

"What can I do to convince you to stay?"

Matilda shook her head. "Nothing."

"Can I not convince you to run to Scotland?"

"You do not have the strength. You are too conventional. We part here, my love, with great sorrow, but I will love our child as I have loved you. I will have a living memory of you."

"What will I have of you? I am left with nothing."

Stephen put his head into his hands and stared at the ground. "You are trading our love for the throne of England."

"That is no surprise to you, Stephen."

"I know, but I managed to forget it these last few years." Stephen leaned over and placed his hand on Matilda's abdomen. "I will have nothing, and you will have our child as well as the throne."

"I have lost, too, but it is more difficult to see." Matilda turned Stephen's hand over, drew it to her lips, and kissed his palm. "Please help me by leaving now. I want to have a painting in my mind of you leaving my favorite place. Go on before I cry and give you an ugly memory."

"You are certain?"

Matilda nodded.

Stephen rose without another word, mounted his horse, and rode back down the trail from which he had come. He never looked back.

Geoffrey stepped closer to the bed and pulled back the curtain to get better lighting in order to see the slender figure resting there. He looked down at Matilda whose hair was braided neatly in two black plaits that contrasted with her white skin. Long lashes lay on her cheeks that were paler than usual and her lips looked drained of life. "Ella, does she always look this pale?"

"No, sir. The trip was very detrimental in her condition. The trip across the Channel was much worse than the one we took away from here just a year ago August."

"Do see that she is well cared for. I have sent for a mid-wife to see her tomorrow." Geoffrey wanted to be angry with his wayward wife, but he found he could not. She had either the audacity or the desperation to arrive at his castle bearing Stephen's child. Geoffrey thought of the two possibilities. With Matilda, it had to be audacity. He wished he could leave her, but she had crept into his heart like a disease. She was difficult to love, and he wished he were not so captivated by her. He could no more control his love than he could capture the mist.

"When Matilda awakens, make certain that nothing places stress upon her. I want no one to visit her unless she feels well. If she worsens, send for me. My apartment is down the corridor. I will return when she has recovered. One other thing; do not tell her I was concerned."

"Sir?"

"I have my pride, Ella." Geoffrey took one last look at Matilda and left.

Each day since Matilda's arrival, Geoffrey had checked on her. He wondered if she guessed the power she held over him. Geoffrey closed the chamber door quietly and looked toward the window alcove. The weather was unusually warm for August, and the air blew hot across the room as it had for the entire week since Matilda's arrival. She sat on the bench in an alcove next to the large window of her bed chamber trying to get the last of the morning air before the sun hit its meridian. He smiled at the picture presented to him.

She leaned against the stone wall, her feet propped on the bench opposite with her kirtle pulled up above her knees. It emphasized the small mound below her waist. Geoffrey could not fathom why he desired her more than ever he had. His heart thumped harder. She was beautiful. He watched as she brushed back a wisp of hair that was plastered to her forehead. Geoffrey moved closer. She did not hear him. He looked out the window to see what Matilda saw. The woods looked as hot as the castle grounds. There was no feeling of relief there, either, since a muggy fog-like mist arose from the trees, getting thicker as the sun drew the moisture out of the leaves.

"You look like a peasant girl with your kirtle pulled up like that," Geoffrey said. His voice sounded too harsh and loud to his ears.

Matilda turned quickly. "I did not know you were near-by." She put her feet down and the kirtle slid to her ankles. "You should not sneak up on people like that. You might hear something you do not want to."

"This is my castle. I go where I want. I hardly think you are in a position to criticize your husband and the father of your child." Geoffrey stood in the archway of the alcove, blocking any exit that Matilda might have wanted to take.

"You are not the father of my child! I told you in the letter who the father was."

"You begged me to take you in so that your virtue and the quest for the throne could both be preserved. You did not even give me the time to give you an answer. Were you afraid I would turn you away?" Geoffrey asked.

"I did not expect you to be chivalrous, especially in these circumstances."

"You underestimate my love for you."

"Oh, do not take me for an idiot." Matilda turned away from Geoffrey.

"It is because you are not an idiot that makes me want to love you. You make it difficult for me, however." Geoffrey moved closer to Matilda, much as he did when trying to snare a quarry.

"Do not talk of loving me, Geoffrey. I hardly find your attempt at humor amusing. Just allow me to stay here. I can not let King Henry's grandchild be brought into this world illegitimately."

Geoffrey turned the quick stab of pain into anger. "I will not talk again of loving you. You are not worth the effort. You use me, my dear, and so I will use you." Geoffrey's voice was cold.

"I was honest with you. I told you this child belonged to Stephen. I am not using you."

"No? Which other convenient husband did you have in mind to be your bastard's father?"

Matilda reacted so quickly that Geoffrey was stunned. She was off the bench and slapped him hard before he had time to grab her upraised arm. She stood glaring at Geoffrey, and he felt the heat on his cheek that was fast becoming welts. He did not know who was more surprised; Matilda or himself. She still held the offending hand in an upward position. He hesitated. He had never fought a woman before, and he did not know how.

Geoffrey neither moved, nor spoke, transfixed by the burning blue eyes of the woman before him. Slowly, he let out his breath, almost a sigh. He noted that Matilda looked from side to side; a small, trapped animal that had not given up hope of escape.

The small alcove was getting smaller. Matilda moved quickly and pushed Geoffrey using the upraised hand as a gateway to freedom.

"You are not going anywhere." Geoffrey pulled down her hand, and pinned her arms to her side. "I have told you before that I have pride. I should have you publicly beaten for what you have just done, King Henry's daughter or not."

Geoffrey felt his catch squirm, and he tightened his arms around her. He could smell the rosewater she used to wash her hair. He wanted to kiss her, to make her love him, but he knew that he could not. He could only hope for tolerance from Matilda, but that was better than no emotion at all. He was angry with her for not being thankful to him, and he felt the urge to show Matilda he could control her.

"I could have you right now, for you are my wife, and you must do my bidding." As soon as the words were uttered, Geoffrey realized his mistake. He watched her eyes narrow, and he winced as she dug her fingernails into his thighs.

"Do not try or I will kill you the first time you are unguarded. Let me go," she hissed.

Geoffrey was shocked by the abhorrence in her voice. He was confused, for when they last parted she had not hated him, but had almost agreed to love him. Mayhap it was her pride. He had left her, and now she had to take whatever he would give her. Geoffrey was at a loss as to how to handle this captured wildcat.

"I will let you go when you agree to act like a lady, and to share my bed."

"May the Virgin Mary preserve me!"

Geoffrey burst out laughing. "Do you realize the incongruity of that small prayer? I should think calling on Venus is more appropriate."

"As you wish. May Venus damn you, Geoffrey! Why do you want me to share your bed? Can you not find a wench who will be happier with you than I ever could be? You speak of pride. What man forces himself upon a woman who can not abide him?" Matilda laughed. "You are still a boy after all."

"You no longer make me angry with that taunt. I do not care what you think." If Matilda knew he loved her, she would use it as a weapon to control him. "You will share my bed tonight, so prepare yourself by bathing."

"By bathing! You are despicable. You are not talking to one of your peasants. You know that I bathe daily. I have no fleas and no lice, my dear husband, unless I get them from you . . . you . . . you old boar. Now let go of me." Matilda tried to jerk free.

Geoffrey smiled. "If I am a old boar, then you are my Countess Boar. Yes, I think that fits you rather well. Do rest this afternoon and eat hearty so that we may have a good night." Geoffrey let his arms drop. He bowed to Matilda, sauntered across her bedroom, and left.

Geoffrey pulled the door shut behind him and leaned against it, letting out a sigh. He smiled when he saw Ella coming up the stone steps with a tray of food and drink. "Has she been eating well these last two days?"

Ella looked startled and tried to curtsy, but was waved up by Geoffrey. "She did not eat much the first day, but yesterday and today she has done better in spite of the heat. We are not used to this type of weather, your lordship."

"I know that you serve your mistress well. See that Matilda gets the best of whatever the kitchen has. If she wants for something, send word to me and she shall have it. She is feeling better and is angry with me. This Matilda is not one who can be dealt with easily."

"I will tell her of your kindness."

"No, do not do that. The mere mention of my name will make her strike out like a wild cat." Geoffrey rubbed his thigh where Matilda's nails had dug into his skin through his tunic.

"Sir, if I may be so bold as to speak?" Ella gazed at Geoffrey, holding her gaze steady.

"Go on."

"She does care for you more than she wants to admit. If you will give her time. I know she can be difficult. . . ."

"That she can be."

Ella licked her lips. "If you will give her time, she will learn which man is true to her." Ella curtsied to end the conversation.

Geoffrey understood her reluctance to speak further. He moved down the hallway, then turned, and called back, "See to it that she is in my bed chamber tonight."

Ella giggled. "Yes, sir." She opened the door to the apartment, crossed the room, and put the tray on a table by the window alcove. Mayhap she could help ease Matilda into Geoffrey's arms without a fight. Ella said a prayer, then plunged ahead. "The fresh air will help your appetite, my lady. I think that Count Geoffrey has become so much more handsome than when we last saw him. He is no longer the boy. You are a lucky woman." Ella looked at the figure that stood beyond the table. The scowl on her face was enough to scare the devil himself. Ella wondered if she had said the right thing, but it was too late now.

"How can you be so blind? Do you not know what kind of man he is? He is a barbarian."

"But Matti, he has inquired about your health each day since we arrived. Why, the very day we came, when you were in such an exhausted slumber, he came to make certain you were all right. He sent for the midwife to see to you."

Ella took the linen cover off the tray and held out the finger bowl for Matilda. "Come, this is the best food in the castle. The apple slices are in cream. Count Geoffrey rode out and picked the apples himself. He knows where the best fruit trees are." Ella asked God to forgive her for the lie she had just told. She told another. "He ordered the cook to give you cream from the best cow." Ella did not dare look at Matilda directly for fear the words would stick in her throat. "It is time you ate. You must have a healthy baby. I hope it is a boy. If you are not healthy, you will have a girl child."

"I am healthy enough to have twin boys, Ella, but I do not want to eat now. I am too angry." She turned to Ella. "Did he really inquire about my health? Daily?"

"Yes, he did."

"Do you think he is sincere?"

"Very much so. He loves you."

"Ridiculous. He needs my army, not my arms. I am still angry with him. He is so pompous. Take away that food."

"You must eat, Matti. I made certain that the blankmanger was prepared just as you like it." Ella felt perplexed. She had an inkling of what Geoffrey might have to contend with when it came to Matilda's stubborn anger.

"Do not look so dispirited, Ella." Matilda smiled for the first time that day and sat down in front of the tray. "It does look tasty." She took a bite of the chicken custard. "It is flavorful, but I do not think their kitchen help is as good as ours." She took her eating knife and stabbed a slice of apple and nibbled it. She grinned. "This is a good apple. I should thank Geoffrey. No, that would make me too subservient. Did Edward take care of Dancer for me? I do not think he enjoyed the voyage."

"My Edward has never been on a ship that did not make him green from illness. He was at the back of the ship with Dancer the whole time." Ella shook her head and poured mead into a tankard.

Matilda giggled. "I am sorry, Ella, but I meant my horse, not your husband."

"Oh, my. Are we not a pair? I worry about my husband, and you worry about your horse. Of course, you could worry about your husband, also." Ella knew she was being bold, and she worried about a reprimand.

"Ella, you have been fooled by Geoffrey. He is nothing more than a lustful youth. The last thing that Geoffrey of Anjou feels for me is love. He would rather see me dead. At best, killed in a victorious battle for Normandy and Anjou."

Ella shrugged. "He did allow you to come to Anjou, and in your condition, too."

"He reminded me that I did not give him time to reply, which is true. He also reminded me that I have to do everything he asks. It could be interesting if I were in the mood to train him, but I do not think the boy knows the difference between love and lust," Matilda said.

"Do you, Matti?"

Ella stood still and waited for the wrath that was sure to come. When the silence stretched out, she bit her lower lip and ventured a look at the blue eyes of her mistress. Matilda was staring out the window. "You should not have said that, for now I have to answer and I have no answer. When I am with Stephen, I want to be with no one else, and I can think of nothing else, and yet . . ."

"I am sorry that I spoke out of turn. It is not my place to question you."

Matilda turned and grasped Ella's hand in hers. "You are more than a lady-in-waiting to me. I feel that we are friends, and with friends, one must take the occasional jarring question."

"I am still sorry that I made you sad. Friends should be more considerate."

"Think you that Geoffrey cares for me?"

"I believe he is enchanted by your beauty," Ella said.

"It certainly is not my personality. We seem to get along as well as two old tom cats. He has been most generous. I should be more tolerant. You know, Ella, I can not understand why he can make me forget about Stephen."

"I can."

"Do not play games." Matilda pushed a piece of almond around the plate with her knife.

"Would it not be nice to be in love with your husband, as I am?"

"That is a pleasure reserved for other than royals, I fear."

"He loves you."

"Mayhap he is just lonely, and I happen to be here."

"That is a beginning," Ella said.

"The only beginning I want is the assurance that the throne will not be difficult to keep. For that I need Geoffrey, or so my father insists. I wonder if I do need him."

Ella shook her head to clear the tangle of thoughts. "I do not know anything about politics, but I know about people. If you do not start being nicer to Geoffrey, then you may alienate him more than just politically. You might make it difficult for him to be a father to your child."

Matilda dropped her knife with a clatter against the table. "Please explain your meaning."

"You may need help in the rearing and protection of your child, especially a son. It would be tragic if Count Geoffrey refused to take that responsibility because of your actions toward him. To love the mother is to love the child."

"You are more astute than I have credited. You are right, of course. I do have to think of King Henry's grandchild, and so I must put aside my personal feelings."

"If that is possible for one as stubborn as you, Matti."

Matilda smiled. "So true. It will be difficult, but my stubbornness can be put to good use. I will be so charming that my dear husband can not turn out either of us."

"That will be interesting to see. I can not believe you will survive long."

"But, Ella, I will have to survive for the sake of the child. As soon as I finish supper, I will go to him. I shall enjoy my last hour of freedom before the sun sets, for as darkness falls, I will give myself to Geoffrey."

Ella snorted and put her hands on her hips. "Do not play the victim of rape with me, Matti. You know as well as I do that you do not mind Geoffrey's hands on your body."

Matilda wadded up her napkin and threw it at Ella, who caught it easily. "Ella, you are incorrigible. All right, I choose to see it as an adventure with an interesting prize at the end. Why should I not make the best of things? Although, I feel guilty for not suffering

longer without Stephen." She picked up her knife and stabbed another piece of apple. "It will be an amusing game."

Ella shook her finger at Matilda. "If you play games with a
man's heart, you might be sorry later."

"Sorry? Never!"

Matilda leaned against the wall outside Geoffrey's apartment.
The stones felt cool through her kirtle. She whispered to the column that stood before her like a sentry. "I can not be too sweet. He
knows my nature and it would not do. I will have to resist enough
so that the trap will work. It will be easy. He is just a boy, after all."

Matilda tapped gently on Geoffrey's door. She was startled when
it was opened quickly by Geoffrey himself. "My dear Countess,
how nice of you to call upon me. I am honored."

"Do not be absurd. I was ordered to be here, and threatened, no
less, so spare me the false courtesy." Matilda swept past Geoffrey and
stopped halfway across the room, unsure of where to go. She hesitated then went directly toward the alcove and the open window.

The sun had set. A warm breeze pushed past Matilda and rippled
the tapestry on the adjacent wall. She sat on the bench at the open
window and looked out toward the twilight. It struck her that she
was homesick for England and the certainty of her father's and
Adelicia's love.

"Would you like some claret? It is a very good vintage." Geoffrey
was held out a gold cup.

"I want nothing from you."

"Except that I pretend to be your child's father, and that I help
you in a possible civil war at your father's death. No, do not pretend
that you want nothing from me. You may as well accept a little
wine. It is the least you can expect from me."

"Then, I must thank you for it." Matilda heard a bird cawing from
far away. The sound underscored her loneliness in a lonely world.
"What do you want from me? I know that besides my fortune and the
power inherited from King Henry, there must be something else."

Laughter from Geoffrey startled Matilda, and she looked at
him from the corner of her eye, not daring to look at him directly,
for fear he was mad.

"My dear wife, I want what most husbands want, a loving and
dutiful woman to do my bidding, a woman who will manage my

castle while I am fighting, and, if necessary, a woman who can lead an army into battle. And yes, a mother to the many heirs we will need to insure our line."

"You are disgusting," Matilda said.

"Are you not capable of all the above? Which part can you not do?" Geoffrey extended the claret yet again.

"I am capable of all that you ask, but I find it abhorrent to think of myself as the wife of a boy, and mother to your children." Matilda took the claret and concentrated on sipping the drink, staring out the window at her past.

A powerful hand shot out and grabbed Matilda's arm, bringing her to her feet. She spilled the claret on her aqua kirtle, making a red stain over her heart. Geoffrey's other hand grabbed the nape of her neck, and he pulled her toward him. He kissed her before she had a chance to react. She pushed the nearly forgotten cup against his chest and tried to pull her head away, but his grip was forceful. When at last he loosened his grip, she stepped back and threw the remainder of the claret into his face.

The red liquid ran down his face and dripped off his chin. "Why did you do that?"

Matilda's feelings tumbled together. She wanted to laugh at Geoffrey's astonished face, but was afraid of his reaction. She wanted to push him away, but his kiss stopped her. Her voice rose above its natural register. "Do you think I am impressed by force? I am not some moronic tavern wench, you stupid . . . stupid . . ."

"I treat you as you treat me. I am Count of Anjou, not a page who is used to groveling at your feet. Mayhap I expect too much. I believe you should act the lady." Geoffrey went to the wash basin on a table next to the bed. Matilda watched as he poured fresh water into a pewter bowl and splashed his face. He groped for the linen cloth folded next to the bowl and dried his face. He dipped the corner of the towel into the water and walked back to Matilda.

She stood in the alcove, rooted to the spot by shock that increased as Geoffrey tried to wipe the red stain off her kirtle. Matilda looked down and watched the stain enlarge and turn to light red, but it would not disappear.

"I seem to be making things worse," Geoffrey said.

"Do you mean your cleaning ability or your attempt at lovemaking?" Matilda's tried to suppress a smile. She watched Geoffrey try to wipe the stain without touching her breast, which was impossible. "Here, hand that to me. You are just making it worse. I do not believe a stain such as this can be removed. This kirtle is destined to be given to a servant." Matilda made a swipe across the kirtle. "It was one of my favorite colors, too, but never mind. It was not new."

"Do you want me to send for another kirtle? Forgive me. I am awkward around you."

"No, I am to spend the night with you, so I will remove this." Matilda deftly slipped the kirtle over her head, wriggled out of it, and laid it on the bench behind her. She was aware of Geoffrey watching, and she felt an unaccustomed shyness that caused her to blush. She sat down.

"The stain has soaked through to your chemise." Geoffrey sounded hopeful.

"No, that I will not remove." Matilda glanced at her husband.

Geoffrey dropped to his knees before Matilda and grasped both her hands. He took on the sorrowful look that Matilda had seen on the court jesters. "'O queen, it is for you to be fully aware what you ask: my duty is to obey. Through you I hold this kingdom, for what it is worth. . . .'"

"Oh please stop!" Matilda laughed. "You butcher the intent of Virgil's famous work. I can not let my favorite poem be so used. Stop your tongue before I stop it for you."

"'Well, you have made the storm, I must lay it. Next time I shall not let you so lightly redeem your sins.'" Geoffrey buried his head in Matilda's lap.

"What game is this, my young fool? I can carve the Aeneid into pieces as well. Listen: 'I, too, have gone through much; like you, have been roughly handled by fortune; but now at last it has willed me to settle here. Being acquainted with grief, I am learning to help the unlucky.'" Matilda grabbed Geoffrey by his flaxen hair and pulled his head up from her lap. "Do not tease me so! Have you a book of Virgil? If so, I would dearly love to hold it, for I have never been able to have a whole copy. Only the first book has been mine."

"Do not tell me that I have found a way to your hardened heart? This is difficult to fathom. If you will come with me, we can sit in bed and read the text by candlelight. I have had four of the books copied by the monks at Bec. Come."

Geoffrey rose and, still holding Matilda's hands, pulled her to a standing position. He led her to the armarium and opened the broad door carved to resemble the columns and sainted statues of a cathedral. On the shelves within rested more than two dozen books, each bound in leather of varying colors and stamped in gold with their Latin titles and author's names. He took out a small text bound in dark green suede and opened it to show Matilda the vellum sheets.

"You have books and not scrolls!" Matilda touched the pages gently with a graceful hand. The lambskin felt smooth. "It is the most beautiful book I have ever seen."

Geoffrey closed the book and pressed it between Matilda's hand. "It is yours."

"I can not accept a gift from someone whom I have . . . have . . ."

"You must accept it as a token of my friendship for you, and of my support in your quest for the throne. Please, I know of no other way to make you happy."

Matilda rubbed the nap and watched it change color with the change of direction. "I do not know how to thank you after I have been less than gracious."

"Do not thank me with the tears welling up in your eyes. I have been told that Matilda does not cry. I meant to make you happy."

"You have made me happy. The tears escape from a heart that is overflowing with gratitude and shame for having been the child that I accused you of being. Can you forgive me?"

"If you forgive my stupid attempts at trying to tame a wild thing with force instead of gentleness."

"You are poetic, for a barbarian." Matilda stood on tiptoe and kissed Geoffrey's cheek that felt cool beneath her lips. "Let us sit and read together. It is a moment we can share and preserve for fond memories in the dark days that lie ahead." Matilda moved toward the bed, climbed the small stool, and sat on the linen sheets. She patted the bed beside her. "I wish to share this gift with you."

Geoffrey took a book of red suede from the armarium, and closed its door before joining Matilda. He did not need the stool since he was more than six feet tall. He was beside her on the bed with an easy vault. "I should tell you that the books are only two quires in length and hold just two books of Virgil's *Aeneid*. I want you to have all that I have."

"You have given more to me than I have to you." Matilda leaned against the pillows and squirmed until she was comfortable.

"I will accept only the first book. You should keep the other. I am being overly sentimental, but that way the set is only complete when we are together."

"Do I detect a hint of love from my countess?"

Matilda turned a page of the book, the crackling sound piercing the silent room. "I do not know. Mayhap a deep friendship is forming. I missed you after you left me in England, and again when I left you in Normandy."

"Is that why you fell into Stephen's arms?"

Matilda looked down at the pages opened before her. She traced the first illumination, the letter 'T', inked in red and green and outlined in swirls of gold. "I can not explain my love for Stephen. I can not explain my feelings for you. When I am with you, I tend to forget him. I hope that I do not go to Hell because of my torn heart."

"You will not go to Hell because of that. It is not the worst sin. I think you are a virtuous person, and that God has plans for you and your heirs. I do not think God would make you a king, then let you spend eternity in Hell." Geoffrey kissed Matilda on her forehead and lay back against her pillow.

Matilda rested her head against Geoffrey's shoulder. "I began this evening as a deception."

"I do not think so. I think your ire was real."

"Oh, yes, that was real, but I had intended to trick you into thinking that I was fond of you."

"It has worked."

"But it is not a deception any longer. You have melted my hardened heart, though, I do not know how."

"My 'Ice Queen' has been replaced by a woman? Mayhap motherhood has softened you in preparation for the gentle task at hand." Geoffrey kissed her cheek. "I do not care for the cause, just the result, as long as I am the recipient."

Matilda turned a page of the book she held. "I shall strive to spend the winter with you in peace. Unless, of course, Count de Rouell decides to attack. Then I shall vent my anger on him."

"I pity the Count."

The passage of time for Matilda that year was not by the counting of days or weeks, but by books shared with Geoffrey and the size of her abdomen. Matilda was surprised, almost daily, by the extent of Geoffrey's understanding of the classical authors. The ritual of reading at bedtime was comforting to Matilda, but it had taken her nearly all fall and winter to admit that she looked forward to this time spent with Geoffrey.

Matilda was also surprised at Geoffrey's gentle concern for her health. It took most of the winter for her to believe he was sincere. She did not acknowledge that she liked his concern until one night when she was stood by the fireplace, her hands against her arched and aching back. Geoffrey had just come into the apartment, stamping snow off his boots.

"Matti," he said. "What ails you? Is your time to deliver here?"

She had laughed at the look of terror on his face, told him he could relax for a few weeks more, and then gratefully let him rub her back. She conceded that Geoffrey pleased her. After that, she began to seek his company.

The winds were still howling and snow attacked the stone walls of Castle LeMans in the early morning hours of March fifth, in the year of our Lord, one thousand, one hundred and thirty-three. Matilda was oblivious to the wailing of the outside storm for her own storm was raging inside her.

"Push, my lady! Push again. I can feel the head. Again!"

The stern voice of the mid-wife cut through the pain, and Matilda pushed with the strength of ten, not because she was ordered to do so, but because she had to. Nature would not allow any other course.

The curved, open seat of the birthing stool cut into her thighs. Matilda held a rope tied to the end of the bed, and pulled as if she were reining in a wild horse. She blinked to rid her eyes of sweat. Her hair stuck to her forehead, neck, and breasts. She wished it had been braided.

"Once more! Once more!"

Matilda could not wait for the last order, but pushed as if another person were ruling her body. The strain was beyond anything she had ever felt before. She let a small moan escape. There was a swoosh and amid the cries of joy around her, she heard a strong cry of anger. A child had been thrust into a cold world from a warm one.

Matilda sank against the tall back of the birthing chair and relaxed, unable to move. Ella wiped her face with a cold cloth before helping her into bed.

"It is a boy! King Henry has a grandson," the midwife said.

Matilda smiled in spite of feeling that credit for her son's birth seemed to go to King Henry. "His name is to be Henry, in honor of my father. He will be a great king, too, for he is descended doubly from William the Conqueror."

"We will prepare for his christening, my lady." Ella rung the cloth again and wiped Matilda's face and neck. "This is truly a great day for England and Normandy."

"Your husband is awaiting entrance, Empress. May I let him in?" the midwife asked.

Matilda nodded, the tired smile an indication of how difficult the last twenty hours had been. She closed her eyes to wait for her husband. The sound of the door opening was followed by Geoffrey's soft footsteps as he crossed the room.

Geoffrey took her hand and squeezed. "He has the copper hair of your ancestors. He is handsome, too, and will make a fine king."

"I think so. Please send a message to my father. He should know as soon as possible about his first grandchild."

"I have already made the arrangements. My sealed letter is being sent at this moment. I had only to insert the name of the child, for the rest was written as you labored." Geoffrey took Matilda's hand. "You look tired. Are you feeling all right?"

"I am exhausted, but I have never been happier."

"I shall leave you to sleep. I want my wife to be rested for our son's christening in three days."

"Our son?" Matilda asked.

"Of course. I have loved his mother. Now, no more talk. You sleep." Geoffrey kissed the listless hand of Matilda and quietly slipped from the apartment.

Matilda's eyes closed, a smile graced her face. She was doubly happy. A son for England had been born.

When she awoke, it was to the cry of a demanding and hungry baby. She propped herself up on one elbow and looked across the room where the nurse was walking the child back and forth.

"I am sorry my lady. I have sent for the wet nurse, but she is slow in getting here."

"I did not order a wet nurse. Give him to me. I plan to nurse my own child." Matilda sat up and arranged the pillows behind her. "Give him to me."

"As you wish, but it is most unusual. Are you sure that you want to? It makes the breasts sag."

Matilda pulled the sheet down to her waist. "See this scar? With a scar like this, no man would notice sagging breasts. Give him here. I want this baby to have royal milk. I want to feel the nourishment flowing from me to him." Matilda held out her arms. The nurse placed young Henry in them, clucking all the time like an angry hen. Matilda felt the warmth of the baby in her arms, and she leaned down to rub her cheek against his fuzzy head. The action caused her breast to rub against the baby's cheek and his head swung around. He gripped the nipple and instantly sucking sounds replaced the crying. "See? He knows what he wants already. I shall see that he gets anything he wants."

"What shall I tell the wet nurse?"

"Tell her to wet nurse another child, but go ahead and pay her. I am sure she needs the money for her own child." Matilda kissed the top of her baby's head. His hair tickled her lips like down feathers.

"Her baby died at birth, my lady."

Matilda looked up, startled. "Oh, I knew not." For the first time, she knew what it meant to lose a child even though she had been a mother less than one day. "I am so sorry. Give her my regards and wish her well."

The nurse smiled. "I will, my lady. She is my own daughter."

"Will there be other children?"

"I hope so. For a woman to be barren is to be incomplete."

"I understand that now, but I never did before." Matilda looked down at the tiny pink mouth working rhythmically between shorts naps. Suddenly, he wrinkled his face up like an old man and began to cry. He turned away from the nipple and screamed. Matilda gasped. What had she done wrong? "Nurse! Is he sick!"

The nurse folded her hands across her stomach. "No, my lady. Give him your other teat. That one has run out."

Matilda awkwardly shifted the baby from one breast to the other. She was relieved when he searched for the nipple and found it. He stopped crying in mid scream, shuddered, sighed and sucked. Matilda laughed. "I am stupid about babies. I have never been around one before! Nurse, would you send for my husband? I miss him." She looked out the window. She was shocked to find that the sun had not yet risen.

The door burst open and Geoffrey rushed in, his night tunic flapping. He was pursued by the nurse who was shushing him. "My lady is well. I keep telling you that!" The nurse looked at Matilda. "Tell him, my lady, that you are not dying. He would not listen to me."

"He is hard headed, that is true. Leave us, and I will see what I can do with him."

Geoffrey's face turned red. He stammered. "Women die after having children. I thought. . . ." He pointed to the window. "The sun has not risen. I thought there was an emergency."

"I am too strong to let a baby kill me. I want to die either a very old lady or on the battlefield."

"On the battlefield? You are not normal, Matti."

"I am to be the first female king of England. Why should anything I do be normal? Except having children." Matilda patted the bed. "Come and watch little Henry eat. He has an appetite fit for a king."

Geoffrey sat on the edge of the bed as if he were sitting on a nest of eggs. He leaned over and looked at Henry. "Why is he so red?"

"He is embarrassed at his father's entrance." Matilda started at the realization that she had inadvertently spoken the lie of the baby's parentage. It seemed so natural that she would think of Henry as belonging to Geoffrey. Throughout the winter months, she and Geoffrey had planned for the child and talked about him as if he were Geoffrey's son. Thus, the use of the term 'father' in regards to Geoffrey rolled off her tongue easily.

"Matti, you wound me."

"Think of poor Henry. Less than one day old and his father acts the fool. The child will have a difficult life."

"Maybe his beautiful mother can make up for his awful father's shortcomings." Geoffrey reached out and tentatively touched the baby's cheek. "Your father will be here as soon as the weather allows him to cross the Channel."

"It will be a happy day when grandfather and grandson meet."

CHAPTER
VIII

MAITHILDE RAN HER FINGER across the dent in the mirror's metal surface. She had thrown it once too often. She had wanted a new one, but Stephen had refused to spend the money. Well, no matter. She would be queen, if her plan worked, and then she would have many mirrors. "Stephen, you fret too much. You need to act, not think. King Henry is in Normandy playing grandfather. He is old and travels slowly." The summer breeze blew across the table where Maithilde sat before her mirror, making circular motions with her fingers as she rubbed softened lard into her cheeks and throat.

"You could force your hand at this moment. King Henry is too far away for you to worry. He is past the age of death and will soon be gone. His regent, whom he left in charge, is a supporter of yours, albeit secretly. The time to strike is now." Maithilde continued working the lard into her skin while watching Stephen pace in and out of range of her mirror. "You are not afraid of your Uncle Henry, are you?"

Stephen stopped pacing. He was a reflection in Maithilde's mirror. "It is not a question of fear, Maithilde. It is a question of timing. It is better to fight a weak opponent than a strong one."

"You believe King Henry to be too strong? He is satisfied to play grandfather to a baby and would not be so willing to fight. Besides, a well-placed spy could agitate Geoffrey enough to fight King Henry for Normandy. It would not take much." Maithilde wiped her fingers on a linen cloth, then opened one of her many jars. She studied the contents, dipped her little finger into the cream, and smoothed the silvery ointment under each eye.

"It is an interesting idea. It might work to have Geoffrey cause the King problems. The King's forces would be split between England and Normandy. His regent could be convinced to be less than helpful." Stephen paced back and forth once again. "No! I can not go against my uncle. He reared me after my father died, and he made certain I was given the same consideration that his own children were given. I can not let you force me to make a mistake."

Maithilde put the pot of cream aside and picked up her hair brush. "You are a stupid, stupid weakling. I will have to arrange the uprising myself. That dear cousin of yours will not take away my right to the throne. It is bad enough that she has stolen my husband."

"Do not be absurd, Maithilde. You have not been my wife since before Eustace was born. Or was it William? Or Mary? Do you think I care?"

Maithilde whirled around and hurled her brush across the room. It hit Stephen in the shoulder, and he stopped pacing. She did not care that he stared at her with a look of contempt.

"You do not know for whom William was named, do you? He could have been named for your grandfather or his real father!"

"Young William is not mine, so I have to assume the little bastard belongs to your lover. You have no taste, Maithilde, to settle for a common soldier."

Maithilde's anger pushed her to a murderous rage, and she wanted to kill Stephen. She was furious because without him, she could not be queen. In her frustration, she turned her back to him so that she would not have to look at the man she hated, but needed. She saw her face in the mirror and was shocked to see it contorted into a gargoyle-like visage.

Stephen bowed. "Do forgive me for taking leave of you. I have a more comfortable bed in which to lie tonight, one that is not so dangerous." Stephen moved toward the door, and hesitating, pulled it open without using the latch. "Do you always leave your door open?"

Maithilde turned the mirror so that she could not see herself. She glanced over her shoulder. "Of course not. You were last through the door. This time, see if you can close it properly." She smiled to herself as the door slammed behind Stephen, causing dust to fly.

The girl heard the door slam from her position behind the stone column. With trembling hands, she held her skirt wrapped tightly about her so that it would not reveal her hiding place. She waited until she was certain Stephen had gone, then slipped through the shadows and down the back staircase, the opposite direction from Stephen. At the bottom of the stairs, Sarah hesitated, waiting for a small group of knights to pass. One knight winked at her and she curtsied. He would not remember her, she hoped, for he had never been near Queen Adelicia while Sarah was in attendance to her. Nevertheless, Sarah held her head down, letting the cowl hide her face while praying that he did not feel like testing her virtue.

The knights were laughing at a comment one of them had made, and Sarah continued to stare at the floor. She wished that she were anywhere but here. It seemed like a long time before they forgot about her and moved on. As soon as they were gone, Sarah ran along the edge of the great hall toward the kitchen, skirting the hounds that were not supposed to be inside. She was afraid of dogs, and she eyed them with trepidation. Fortunately, they slept, twitching now and then as if on a hunt. Sarah would feel more comfortable when she could give up this duty. If her lady Adelicia had asked her to meet with the ghosts in the forests, she would have. She would do anything her lady asked. Without the queen, Sarah would have been left to starve after her mother died. The children of prostitutes were not treated kindly.

Sarah hesitated at the kitchen door, took a deep breath, and tried to walk casually past the servants who were rushing to and fro. She bit her lip. She wished Queen Adelicia had sent her to talk with the ghosts in the woods. They would be easier to deal with than spying on Maithilde and Stephen. The thoughts of Maithilde's temper made Sarah hurry through the kitchen past the cooks and their boy helpers. The odor of meat cooking in the big pots at the edge of the fireplace did not make Sarah hungry. Her stomach seemed to have turned upside down.

She was almost across the hot and smelly room when someone grabbed her arm. Sarah turned to find herself looking into the red and sweaty face of the meat cook.

"Be a good girl and go fetch the butcher." The cook shook his head, his jowls jiggling.

Sarah was so relieved at the request that she hurried through the propped-open door. She walked past the chickens scratching in the garden to the small building close to the kitchen. She looked in the door and saw more than a dozen hares hanging against the back wall along with a pair of geese and a half-dozen ducks. Sarah wrinkled her nose at the smell of blood. The butcher was skinning a hare with sure strokes that showed he had skinned countless animals in his career. Sarah twisted a piece of her kirtle around her finger as she waited for him to acknowledge her. Would he never speak? She had to hurry, but she also had to do what the meat cook had asked her. To have disobeyed him would have drawn attention to her.

At last the butcher laid the skinless hare aside and, as he reached for another, he bellowed. "What do you want? Can you not see I am busy?"

"Sorry to trouble you, sir, but the meat cook asked that you go see him. He sent me."

The butcher grumbled and slammed his knife down. "I got better things to do than to run to the kitchen every half minute."

"Yes." Sarah turned and ran to the stable. She sneezed as she rushed through the door. Hay dust always made her sneeze. She rubbed her nose with the back of her hand. The dust danced in the light that came through the cracks of the wooden sides. As soon as Sarah's eyes had adjusted from the summer sun, she saw a man straddling a bench against the stone wall at the back of the stable. He was stitching two pieces of leather together with a large needle. He looked up briefly, glanced around, and nodded. Sarah was almost to him when she saw that he was missing two of his fingers. It did not seem to interfere with the repairing of a bridle. She breathed easier. Queen Adelicia had said to talk to no one but the man with the missing fingers.

Sarah glanced around the stable, then whispered. "I have a message for our queen."

He looked up at her, his eyes narrowing as he studied her closely as if to catch her in a lie. "You are a young one. Why did the queen send a child?"

Sarah stared back at him, letting him know that she really worked for the queen. She prayed that her nervousness would not make him think she was untrue to her queen. She took a deep breath. "I am not known to Maithilde or Stephen. I was put in service for the first time here. I have never worked in the queen's chambers."

"Our queen is wise and clever." He returned to his stitching. "Speak slowly so that I can remember each word," Terence said. "Come closer. You will have to speak softly."

Sarah moved nearer to the man whose face was as leathery as the materials with which he worked. She leaned down and whispered what she had overheard into his ear. The man never dropped a stitch. When she was finished, he laid his work aside. Within ten minutes he was leading a saddled horse from the stable. Sarah waited until he had ridden from the stable, then she slid the bar into place on the back door. She watched through a crack as Terence rode slowly through the side gate, obviously a trusted servant whose ride would arouse no suspicion. He was cautious, however, for Sarah noticed that he kept to the side of the castle opposite Stephen's apartment until he was behind a knoll. Sarah breathed a sigh of relief when he disappeared. She looked around and slipped out of the doorway. The laundress would be screaming for her if she did not hurry. Sarah liked the job of washing sheets. The work was not dirty and it gave her access to all the apartments in the castle. No one could identify the young girl who carried so many sheets that her face was hidden. She would feel much safer, though, when Queen Adelicia called her back to her services.

Adelicia felt the heat of anger on her cheeks, and she wished she could be calmer. She rarely showed a temper. She knew the servants were unaccustomed to this behavior from her. She watched them scurry about their nightly duties with perplexed looks. They tried to please her, but could not. Adelicia wished she could contain her anger.

It was past midnight, and she had not been able to sleep. Action suited her purpose better, and she had her lady-in-waiting arouse the staff. She had splashed cold water on her face to lessen the red spots, but it did no good. She had dressed and paced the room to wait for the servants to prepare her materials.

"No! Not the vellum, it is too good for the likes of them. Give me common deer hide. Send for three messengers and have them make ready. One is to go to Normandy and meet with the King."

Adelicia watched as the servants pulled forth her writing instruments from velvet lined boxes and laid them on the table. Her favorite bronze pen had been cleaned and sharpened after the latest letter to her beloved king and the ink pot had been refilled.

"Do you wish a clerk to do the writing?" Joseph asked.

"Not at all. I wish this venom to come straight from my heart through my hand and to those traitors." Adelicia sat and waited for Joseph to place the deer hide before her. It had been scraped to a smooth finish by pumice stone brought from Italy. The sides were trimmed to a straight edge so that a t-square could be used to form light guidelines.

The queen pulled back the flowing sleeves of her outer kirtle and reached for the pen. Having been taught penmanship by the abbess of the convent where she had been reared, she wrote quickly, but neatly. She chose to write in Latin rather than her native language because of the terseness, strength, and economy of word. She always thought angry words were more forceful in Latin.

Two hours later she was ready with three messages. She read them once more to make certain that there were no words unsaid, especially the one to Maithilde, for that was whom Adelicia had thought of as she had penned the document. There were no mistakes. She was pleased, for the abbess had never allowed her to cross out mistakes, but made her rub them away with a smaller version of the same stone that had been used to prepare the parchments. She folded each parchment into thirds and waited while Joseph prepared the softened tallow, then she turned her hand and imprinted the tallow with the top of her ring. The indentation was especially deep in the seal on the letter to Maithilde.

Dawn was barely pushing the night sky away from the earth. Adelicia watched from her upstairs window as the riders departed for their three different destinations. A cool breeze ruffled the sleeves of her kirtle as the queen waited for them to disappear.

Servants clustered around each other at the edge of the great hall and watched their master, Roger, Bishop of Salisbury. Yetta had her hand covering her mouth, and she grimaced as the Bishop of Salisbury's face got red, then darker as he bellowed for his own messenger to send for Maithilde and Stephen immediately. He stomped and stormed and raged. Some servants scattered to other sections of the castle far away from the Bishop's apartment, but Yetta and the older servants stayed close. They knew it would be worse if the Bishop wanted something, and they were not there to provide it. Then the quiet came. Yetta looked at her husband, Francis. His eyes were wide. Yetta, Francis, and the older servants disappeared as the younger ones returned.

The day was grey. A fine mist coated every item of clothing as well as the hindquarters of the horse upon which Maithilde was riding. She frowned, then forced the frown away. She had noticed the lines across her forehead just a few days ago.

Stephen rode beside her with an entourage following a discreet distance behind them. "I wonder what the Bishop wants."

"It had better be very good news, like the King's death." Maithilde was irritated that Stephen watched her with peripheral vision. Why could he not look at her directly? Maithilde pulled her hood forward trying to preserve at least one spot of dryness. "Somehow, I do not think we can be so lucky. This rain is dismal."

"I do not think that you should be so concerned with the death of King Henry. I find it unbecoming a lady of your rank."

"Dear Stephen, just because you are a weak-willed and weak-minded person does not mean that I should suffer for it. The only thing for which you will strive is a wench to help you pretend you are a man."

Stephen rode in silence, then he said, "I feel sorry for you, Maithilde, for you have never been content with what you have. You look for what ever it is that you want, but find the wrong thing. The problem is that you are not intelligent enough to know it is wrong for you. You do not even know that you are not intelligent. Someday you will pay for your ignorance."

"I hope you die," Maithilde said.

Stephen reached over and grabbed the reins of Maithilde's horse and brought him to a quick stop. Mud splattered up and speckled both their cloaks. "You are so ignorant, my dear, that you forget. You can not be queen without a king. You are the wrong Matilda." Stephen's teeth were clenched as he spit out, "Do not forget it."

Silence was heavy for the rest of the ride. The only sounds were the steps of the horses and the occasional splash as clumps of mud fell from the horses' legs onto the road. The Bishop's castle loomed before them, camouflaged by mist. For the first time, Maithilde noticed an ominous air about the palace. There was no color in either the stones that formed the walls or in the gardens that were planted with vegetables, but not flowers. She shivered, not from the dampness, but from a foreboding. She did not believe in premonitions, nor did she use a soothsayer to divulge the future. However, there was something wrong. She shook the thought from her mind. It was merely a feeling brought on by a grey day.

The gates were open in anticipation of their arrival. Maithilde licked her lips. The Bishop always set a fine table. Mayhap he had arranged entertainment for them. Maithilde hoped so.

The party rode through the court yard and up to the doors to the great hall. Maithilde waited until Stephen dismounted, then called sweetly, "Dear husband, would you do me the honor?" She held out her arms so that he could take her by the waist and lift her from her horse. As Stephen lowered her from her mount, he released her sooner than he should have so that she dropped, not too gracefully, to the ground. He whispered in her ear, "Do not play me for your fool. I have ways to make you look the more foolish for doing it."

Maithilde could not retort without sounding like a shrew, a fact that she wished to keep hidden from the Bishop. She forced herself to smile as she walked with Stephen through the door into the hall.

Stephen and Maithilde were in front of the main fireplace drying their clothing when the Bishop entered. His usual bland expression, made more so by his pudgy, baby face, had been replaced by a scowl.

"Roger, how nice to see you." Maithilde extended her hand for him to kiss. She was startled when he ignored her, and she flushed at the insult.

"It is not nice to see you," the Bishop said. "You have caused us great distress. As regent for King Henry while he is in Normandy, you have placed me in an awkward position. You will soon receive a message from our queen. You will not like the contents any more than I cared for the contents of mine."

"I do not understand," Maithilde said.

"Do you understand treason? Do you understand execution?" the Bishop asked.

The flush was replaced by a bloodless color as Maithilde knew in a flash that the ever present spies had overheard her conversation with Stephen a few short days ago. Maithilde gasped. "I . . . I . . . What am I to do? How can I convince her ladyship that . . . "

The Bishop's eyebrows were drawn together. "You will deny everything. I have already dispatched my own messenger to try and clear this mess of your making. If you are born under a lucky sign, then mayhap Queen Adelicia will follow my advice."

Stephen rubbed his temple. "Are you saying that Queen Adelicia found out about a discussion that occurred in our private apartment? Explain this further."

Maithilde shot him a scathing glance. "Do not be so naive, Stephen. There are people everywhere who would sell information for a price. We have our enemies, too."

"You two are about to lose your heads over this indiscretion. I will have to work long and hard to undo the damage you have done by your inability to wait until the king is dead before you take the throne," the Bishop said. "I have already arranged to visit the queen on your behalf."

"I am sure that it will cost us a small fortune for your favor." Maithilde spit the words out with such vehemence that both men were silenced.

The Bishop was first to break the quiet. "You have no choice. If you would rather worry about money than having your head sliced off, so be it."

Maithilde shuddered. Her hand went to her throat. "No, please. Do not mind me." Maithilde smiled. "I find it difficult to think straight, especially when the queen has been told untruths about Stephen and me."

Stephen hissed at his wife. "Leave me out of this."

"I am afraid you are in this as much as your wife is," the Bishop said. "Without you, Maithilde would have no cause."

"When are you leaving? We should go with you," Stephen said.

"If you do, you may be imprisoned until King Henry returns or until Queen Adelicia orders me to have you beheaded."

A short, sharp cry escaped from Maithilde. The Bishop continued, "I have sent for you to tell you to stop trying to rush the future. If you persist in lusting for the throne, you might end up in the Tower instead. I am ordering you to play the part of the faithful subjects. If you forget what I have told you, the next time I will not be helpful. I believe that stupid people should be eliminated."

The Bishop looked at Maithilde. "Are you stupid?"

"No, sir." Maithilde felt like a naughty student being reprimanded by her tutor.

Stephen cleared his throat. His face was ashen. "How much influence do you have with Queen Adelicia?"

"I think that she will soon calm. She seldom becomes angry and is uneasy maintaining anger. I may be able to appeal to her religious sense, although, when it comes to protecting King Henry, she is no longer the sweet honey, but the stinging bee. I will do what I can." The Bishop shook his finger at Maithilde. "Might I remind you that I do this not for you, but as insurance for my future."

Maithilde stepped back from the accusing finger. "What are we to do until you return?"

"You will go back to your apartment and stay there until you hear from me."

"But . . . but I can not," Maithilde said.

"We will do as you say." Stephen pinched Maithilde.

The parchment from Queen Adelicia was waiting for Stephen and Maithilde when they returned from the palace of the Bishop of Salisbury. A servant stood in the doorway and held it toward Maithilde as had been his custom in the past. Maithilde saw the confusion on his face when she would not lift a hand to take it. The servant stood, shifting from foot to foot. His face showed relief when Stephen came forward and jerked the parchment from his hand and slammed the door.

Stephen flung the parchment onto the floor at the feet of Maithilde. "Here, this is your doing. You may have the pleasure of unsealing that which may seal our fate."

Maithilde kicked the parchment. "How dare you behave that way toward me."

"And how dare you to place my life in jeopardy with your untimely ambitions. Pick it up, or I will put you down on your knees to read it. Do it now."

With eyebrows raised, Maithilde glared at Stephen. "I will do so only because I am curious, not because of your threats." Maithilde retrieved the parchment and walked to her dressing table.

She pushed aside the various pots and jars and laid the tri-folded deerskin before her. She stared at the seal, then took her fingernail and popped it open. With trembling hand, Maithilde shoved the invidious skin away from her. It pushed against some of the containers on the table, and they crashed to the floor.

Stephen turned away from the window toward her. "Do you suppose the three days and three nights of rain is a bad omen for us? Do you think the angels cry for us?"

Maithilde gasped. "I hope not."

"What does the queen write?" Stephen asked. "What does she say about me?"

"She says nothing about you."

"Then what does the message contain that distresses you so?" Stephen grinned. "Have you been chastised for trying to become queen before your time? Are you not happy that I am safe?"

"You are less than a man. I can see the relief upon your face. Let me tell you that, if I lose my head, I will make certain you lose your head first. I want to enjoy the sight." Maithilde kicked the parchment toward Stephen. "Here, read it for yourself so that your joy may be multiplied." She absently chewed on a fingernail while watching Stephen's face.

Stephen picked up the parchment and unfolded it. "It is written in Latin. You know I have difficulty reading Latin."

Maithilde quickly pulled her little finger from her mouth, but she saw that it was not fast enough to prevent Stephen from noticing she had chewed her nail down to the quick. "You can read Latin as well as any of us. You just want to hear my fate with my own words. I am not afraid. The queen merely states that if we are plotting treason against the king, we shall be executed." Maithilde choked on the last word.

"My dear, it says nothing of the kind. It says that you have been subversive in your actions ever since the unhappy day you wed me. It says that you alone are responsible for all the unrest that has occurred in England, and that you alone will bear the brunt of the executioner's ax. I think it is worded plainly. Our queen wants you dead. I do not have much hope for the Bishop of Salisbury to save you. Mayhap you should flee for your life."

Maithilde's heart pounded. She refused to let Stephen see her trepidation. "I will not flee. That would indicate guilt."

"Well?" Stephen asked.

"I am not guilty. Or at least I will make certain that such thoughts of obtaining the throne are withheld from even you, dear Stephen, until the time is right. If I survive beyond King Henry, then I will actively support you for king against my nemesis, your other Matilda. Now leave me. I have much to do."

"Do you not want the pleasure of my company, dear Maithilde? Do you not want someone to hold your hand and comfort you in your time of dire need? Someone who is refined and not an ill-kempt soldier?"

"Get out!" Maithilde reached for a convenient jar, but fumbled about without getting one into her grasp. Most were on the floor. "Get out!"

"My pleasure. I do not wish to stay with the doomed and the damned." Stephen bowed and exited, his laughter echoing behind him as he closed the door.

Maithilde finally found a jar and threw it against the door. She watched the blue glass splinter. She turned away from the newly released white blob that slid down the plank.

The Bishop of Salisbury waited in the great hall for the queen to send for him. The last week had been torturous. Even his appetite had fled for a day or two. He tried to appear calm, but it was difficult. He felt like a man being crushed between two great forces. If ordered, he would have to obey the wishes of the queen and execute Maithilde. It would be his duty as regent for King Henry, but an execution would ruin his plans for the future of England. The Bishop did not like Maithilde, but she was necessary. He knew that Stephen would not have the strength of character to lead a civil war against Matilda without his wife beside him.

"Women." The Bishop of Salisbury spoke to a hound that lay in front of the fireplace. "It is always women who mess up the plans of men. Now I have to convince one woman that another is not traitorous so that I can help keep yet a third woman from the throne. Damn, damn, damn to all women." The Bishop paced, the reeds beneath his feet crushed under his ponderous weight. He spoke to the dog, again. "King Henry has given me a weighty job, and Maithilde has made the job even stonier."

The Bishop turned, startled to find Queen Adelicia quietly coming toward him. He noted that her quiet demeanor fit her usual placid disposition. He could tell from the look on her face that she knew why he had come. He could feel the beads of perspiration break out on his temples and across his bald pate. He wished his face were not flushed. He reached up and tried to tame the fringe of grey hair that ringed his head.

"My dear Roger. How nice to see you." Adelicia held out her hand as he bowed and kissed it with his thin lips, the only thing about him that was thin.

"My lady, you look lovely as always."

"Let us sit here by the fire. It is so damp with all the rain. I hope you find the chair comfortable. I had it brought down from my apartment. I felt that our conversation would be more private here," Adelicia said.

"A shrewd move, my lady. We can see anyone before they even get close enough to hear us."

"I know that you are here to discuss Maithilde and Stephen. Proceed." Adelicia sat down and waited for the Bishop to make himself comfortable.

"You waste no time," the Bishop said.

"I am curious as to your position."

The Bishop hesitated. "My position, as it always has been, is to preserve England in the manner that King Henry wishes."

"Of course," Adelicia said. "I do not question your loyalty, just your motives."

The Bishop started to lick his lips, but caught himself in time. He did not want to appear nervous, or worse, insincere. "I have come to discuss the possibility that someone wanted to place Stephen and Maithilde in danger."

"What do you mean?"

"I have talked with them, and I believe them to be totally innocent of any treachery. I believe that someone wanted to split King Henry from one of his allies in order to weaken the kingdom."

"Do not be absurd, Roger. Maithilde is hardly a friendly supporter of the King." Adelicia looked away from the rosy face of the Bishop.

"I am speaking of Stephen. He has been like a son to King Henry, and you know his temperament. He would do nothing to harm the man who reared him." The Bishop waited, not breathing. He could see the first splinter of doubt in Adelicia's face. "I admit that Maithilde is ambitious, but she is not stupid. She knows the price of treason."

"Really? I do not agree with you. If you had read my message clearly then you would have realized that my fight is not with Stephen, but with that awful Maithilde. She is the traitor to the king."

"I think you misjudge her. I repeat myself, but I think she is the innocent victim. Maithilde would never presume to have the power to overthrow the king," the Bishop said.

"She is right about that." Adelicia leaned forward. "Might I remind you that a certain conversation was over-heard?"

The Bishop shrugged his shoulders. "Who can trust spies, my lady? They work for money, so what can their motives be?"

Adelicia's eyes fluttered. "My source, I feel is trustworthy."

"Mayhap, then, a misunderstanding or a conversation in which only part was heard. I believe that the question of her treachery is enough in doubt that you, as a Christian, can not take her soul before its time without grave consequences to your own soul."

The intake of breath from the queen was audible across the short space between the two chairs and the Bishop was pleased. The sudden, sharp thrust of religion into the conversation had the desired effect and the Bishop pressed on.

"It would be difficult to explain an execution based upon a conversation supposedly held in the privacy of their own apartments, without any semblance of an army raised, and without any hope of winning. It would be even more horrible to imagine a wrong done to an innocent person if one had to confess to such an act."

"I can see that. If I am wrong, could I spend eternity in Hell?" Adelicia whispered.

"I think that you are so innocent, my lady, that God would forgive you." The Bishop waited for the look of relief upon Adelicia's face and then continued. "But, of course, how could you ever forgive yourself? It would be a dreadful burden to bear for the rest of your life."

"I see. Naturally, I understand that you are well-versed in these ecclesiastical matters, but I am still concerned about my king." Adelicia leaned forward and looked intently into the Bishop's eyes.

The Bishop had difficulty keeping his lips from curling upwards into a wolfish smile. He felt certain about the outcome of the meeting. A little flattery would assure his success. "Your king is strong. He has won many battles, including one for the throne. You have no need to be concerned for King Henry, although I find that admirable."

Adelicia tapped her fingers against the wooden arm of the chair. "You are right about the King's strength. Mayhap I have been hasty for no reason."

"I do not think that protecting your husband is a sin." The Bishop spread back his lips, the closest thing to a smile that he was able to muster.

"Do you believe it would be sinful for me to ask that you behead Maithilde?"

The Bishop shifted in his chair and waited a moment before answering to make certain his voice did not reveal his shock at her persistence. He would have to tread carefully. He cleared his throat. "It would be inappropriate. It may lead people to believe that King Henry is old and weak, which he is not."

"I see. I have sent for the king. I hope I was not too hasty," Adelicia said.

"I think not. He has been gone long enough. I will also send him a message and tell him that there are charters that need his attention."

"Then we have nothing more to discuss. Maithilde is safe from the executioner, for the moment." Adelicia motioned toward a servant who was posted next to the kitchen door. "I have taken the liberty of having a meal prepared for us. I have a fine piece of venison that needs an appreciative palate. Will you be my guest?"

"It would pleasure me more than you can imagine," the Bishop said.

CHAPTER
IX

ATILDA HAD SMILED at her father's urgency in asking her to Normandy so that he could see his first grandchild. She and the baby had made the trip to Normandy before the child was four months old during an early heat wave in June. She had worried about the heat, but to her surprise, little Henry cared only that he be fed whenever he wanted to eat. She had only relinquished the baby to the nurse to rest her tired arms. He was healthy as well as heavy. Matilda had wondered at her inability in following tradition. She was supposed to let the nurse care for him more. She had decided that he must be protected, and she could do that better than anyone. She understood Adelicia's fear of losing a child better for having had her own child.

Matilda had looked down at the baby in her arms and knew that if anything happened to him, the pain of his loss would supersede any pain she had had at the end of her affair with Stephen. The trip to Normandy had been slow because of the heat and the wagons. They could have ridden faster on horseback, but it would have been more difficult with little Henry. They had arrived just a few days after her father had made the trip from England instead of the same day, which had been the original plan. Matilda had been surprised at how many goods had to be hauled about just for the baby. He seemed to have more things traveling with him than she had.

Matilda stood in her father's private quarters with Henry in her arms. She marveled at three generations in one place; a fact she had found difficult to believe. Matilda's father looked so tired and much older, seemingly all at once. The most telling sign had been the silver mixed amongst his black hair. Matilda hesitated before placing the squirming baby into her father's still powerful arms.

King Henry looked down into the eyes of his tiny namesake. He held out a large finger near the baby's hand and smiled when the tiny fingers closed over his big one. He pushed the linen wrappings aside and watched as little Henry's legs thrashed about.

"He will be tall and strong, Matilda. I never thought I would see a grandchild during my lifetime. It has made all the battles I fought and all the pain worthwhile, for now England has you and your son to follow in my footsteps."

"I will do everything that I can to assure you it will continue, Father. I will give my life, if necessary, to do your bidding." Matilda touched her son's arm with her finger. His skin felt as soft as a flower petal. "You hold the mighty future in that diminutive bundle."

King Henry nodded. "I will start training him immediately for his future. First, be rid of all these clothes that restrict movement. Your mother taught me that babies should be allowed to kick and squirm about like the baby animals of the wild. Look at the horse whose young stand in minutes, and remember the doe whose fawn is ready to run soon after birth. Let the little Henry exercise as nature intended. He should be fed whenever he wants." King Henry smiled again at the solemn face staring at him. "He stares intently. It makes him seem as old as time itself."

Laughter burst from Matilda. Her laughter increased at her father's curious look in her direction. "I am sorry, but it is odd to hear the King of England discuss the care and feeding of a baby."

King Henry said, "He is destined for greatness."

"You act like a jester rather than a king. I find it wonderful. Give little Henry to his nurse, and we will have something to eat. I am tired and hungry after our journey. I seem to want to eat all the time." Matilda pointed to the infant. "He takes everything from me."

"As all children do."

"You are to rest while you are here, Father." Matilda waited for the transfer of the gurgling baby to the woman who was hovering nearby to make certain that the child would not be damaged.

Matilda took her father by the arm and led him to the next room. She almost pushed him down onto the stool, but even she would not have attempted that. "You are to eat regularly and sleep. Adelicia sent me a message to that effect and has asked that I make certain you do those things."

"She worries too much," King Henry said.

"I wish she could have come with you. I miss her."

"She is terrified of ships and refuses to cross over. Where is Geoffrey? Did he not want to come to Normandy?"

"He thought there might be an uprising instigated by the dear King of France." Matilda sat across the table from her father. She picked up a napkin and placed it on her lap and took her eating knife from its sheath on her girdle. "You are not eating." Matilda motioned to the servants to be quick about serving her father the rest of the dishes. "I would have let them serve the eels you ordered, but Adelicia told me the physician said you were not to have any more. They make you ill."

King Henry grumbled, "I am king. I should be allowed to do whatever I want."

"Just where policy and wars are concerned. You know Adelicia watches you carefully. I have been instructed to stand in her stead."

King Henry took his eating knife from its sheath and had laid it on the table. "Will Geoffrey be able to prevent the French from invading?"

Matilda nodded. "Of course. Geoffrey is an excellent warrior."

"He will be a great help to you if you have to fight for the throne." King Henry took his knife and pushed food around on the plate. "Turnips. Must we always have every meal overrun by turnips?"

"You like turnips."

"I never liked turnips. I just said I did for Adelicia's sake."

"Oh, Father. You are behaving badly. If you do not want turnips, then eat something else."

King Henry took a bite of chicken and chewed slowly. "Geoffrey will help you fight for the throne if you have to do so, will he not?"

"I do know not. He is strange and moody and seems self-centered. I am not certain he sees that my controlling England will help him."

"I need to teach him some basic facts of survival."

"It is too bad you did not secure the throne for your heirs with an alliance between Stephen and me. I think that would have been the prudent step to take," Matilda said.

"You say that because of your lust." King Henry looked at Matilda, eyebrows arched and waited for her reaction.

"My lust!" The old guilt at loving Stephen and Geoffrey at the same time exploded from Matilda as anger. "How much you do not know. You are not the wonderful politician you think you are." Matilda threw down her napkin and stood.

"Sit down."

Slowly enough to irritate her father, Matilda sat down as commanded. "If I fight a civil war, it is because you could not control the future even with your manipulations of marriages and lives."

"You forget that when I had Stephen marry Maithilde your birthmate was still living and would have been king." King Henry turned away from Matilda.

Matilda saw the familiar sadness in her father's face, and it wrenched her heart. She understood his loss better now that she had her own son to protect. She placed a hand on his arm. "I am sorry about William. Destiny has been unkind to leave a king without an heir. There should be no reason for me to have lived and my twin to have died."

"Daughter, I would not trade your life for William's. I have once again found my future in yours, and now, with the infant Henry, I am assured of it."

"I fear it will be a battle to live up to your expectations. I will fight to the death for my son. He alone has strengthened my resolve," Matilda said.

"Enough talk of death, daughter. Let us go for a hunt this afternoon. It is a fine June day and the heat of noon will make my bones feel young again."

"Your wish will be granted. Mayhap if we hunt ducks, I might even let you win."

"I know you better than you think I do. You would never let me win. The desire to be the best is too strong in you, Matilda."

"Then I shall not embarrass you twice. We shall have a picnic instead."

"As you wish, Matilda." King Henry laughed.

A month passed before Matilda thought a day was pleasant enough for her father and son to be outside. The woods felt cool as Matilda rode along with King Henry, some of her servants, and several of her knights. The sun barely cleared the horizon, but the day would be hot since it had not cooled down during the night.

"The stream is not far and it is comfortable there, Father." Matilda fanned her face with her hand to keep the gnats away.

"I think your idea of leaving that stifling castle and eating outdoors is admirable. I have always had difficulty with this weather. It is not like England." King Henry shifted in his saddle and grunted.

"It is better for your health to get you out of that oppressive apartment. Even the breezes seem to have forgotten us." Matilda let Dancer's reins lay slack against his neck. He did not have his usual spark and plodded along like a draft horse.

The leaves on the trees drooped and seemed without life, not stirring as the riders passed beneath them. The buzz of insects took the place of the usual song of the forest birds, and their sound was irritating.

The stream was not as noisy as usual, but there was enough water to splash across rocks and create small whirlpools. Matilda thought it felt refreshing by the stream, but not much. The riders climbed down from their horses and waited for servants to spread flaxen coverlets on the grass next to the stream. The horses were unsaddled and fettered by the squires and everyone settled down to enjoy the coolest place available. The servants were close enough to be called upon when needed, but at a distance discreet enough to afford both societal levels some privacy.

"I have always loved Normandy, Father, but I fear that I miss England. I never thought I would say that about our barbaric kingdom," Matilda said.

"An unsettled land and an unsettled people, our England, but I love its ruggedness." King Henry leaned closer to Matilda. "I have waited until now to tell you this, but I have to return to our homeland."

"Why, Father? It seems you have only arrived." Matilda looked into her father's face. "Is anything wrong with Adelicia?"

"No, my dear." King Henry speared a chunk of meat. "I have to attend to some things that only I can do. My regent, Bishop Roger of Salisbury, is of no use to me in this matter." He bit into the meat.

Matilda laid her hand on King Henry's arm. She felt a shadow had just been cast across the happiness of the last few weeks. "I do not believe you. I do not think you would leave your grandson so soon if things were not amiss at home. You may as well confess to me, for I will hound you until you do." Matilda dropped her voice to a whisper, so the devil would not hear the trembling. "Calm my distress and tell me straight out what is wrong."

"I have received two messages in the last three days. It seems I am needed at home by both my queen and my regent. There is nothing wrong, but my presence would keep the kingdom intact." King Henry patted Matilda's hand. "I am getting old and have not much longer to live."

"Father, do not say such things!"

"It is true, and while I love you and my grandson more than ever I thought possible, I desire to die in the land where I was born. I need to see England again."

"Do not speak of your death. You are strong and powerful. Our family is long-lived and so will you be. If you must return to England, do it because of reasons of state, not because it is a place to die."

"Adelicia has written that Maithilde and Stephen have talked of my overthrow, but then an interesting message from the Bishop of Salisbury says that Adelicia was mistaken, and she has recanted her first story. He thinks that she is becoming nervous without my presence. He is requesting I return for that reason, if no other." King Henry looked across the stream.

"Is he suggesting that Adelicia is mentally weak?"

"I believe he hints that. I do have a responsibility to my country and to my wife. For that reason, I will leave within a fortnight." King Henry leaned over and kissed Matilda on the cheek. "It is more difficult for an old man to leave his children than a young man."

Matilda studied her father's face. It was more lined than she remembered. She was shocked to see how much more silver had threaded through his hair in the last few weeks. Even though the muscles were still powerful, they were sinewy and the skin was not as elastic as it had once been. Her father was still a handsome man, but in his last years, as he had said. How could her father be young when she had grown past her own youth? This could be one of the last moments she would spend with him, but if that were so, then she would make it a happy event for him.

"So, Father, let us not talk of parting, but of the fun we have had in the past. Do tell me of things I should know. Tell me stories of William, my grandfather, who claimed England."

"I have told you those stories before."

"I never tire of hearing them." Matilda smiled at her father. She loved to hear stories in his resonant voice. He began with the story of her grandfather's invasion. She leaned forward and listened to the part of the story where her grandfather had crossed the Channel faster than anyone else. She loved the tale of the slings that had been designed by William the Conqueror to hold the war horses as they traveled by ship. Soon she had traveled back in time and place. She looked at her father who had stopped speaking.

"Are you lost in another world, Matti?" King Henry held her hand.

"I was just re-living the past, Father. I shall be sorry to see you leave. Let us stay here until dark, so that our time of peace may stretch out." Matilda squeezed her father's hand. "Tell me about my mother. She was much more royal than either you or I, what with her being sister to four kings!"

"Do not forget that she was wife to a king and mother to an empress." King Henry's eyes were full of mirth.

"You tease me. I am a mere countess now, although I have to admit that I still use the title of empress."

Matilda glanced at the baby who slept on a linen sheet near his nurse. "My greatest title, though, is that of mother."

"That is how I shall remember you. I will think of you as mother and protector to my grandson."

"Father, you talk as if we will never meet again." As soon as she said the words, Matilda was sorry. Her worst fear, which she tried to keep hidden even from herself, had slipped out. She was devastated by the look on her father's face. They both knew that when they parted, it would be forever.

Her mind wondered back over the last few happy hours. Little Henry slept peacefully the entire time, and Matilda was able to concentrate on her father. She leaned back against the tree. It was a bitter-sweet time for her. She thought back to this morning when they had ridden out. Now she knew why King Henry had wanted the picnic. He had wanted to soften the news he had for her. Or maybe he had wanted to soften the news for himself.

Adelicia opened the stained glass window of Cotton Hall. She did not want to see the cheerful colors. She ignored the blast of cold air that whipped past her. For nearly three years since he had returned from Normandy, Adelicia had worked to keep her husband healthy, guarding him from anything she thought would hurt him. She had failed and the tears flowed.

Mist arose from the snow, making its own colorless cloud. It was like being enveloped in a death shroud of whitest linen. Adelicia turned and looked toward the woods. Only the trees closest to the edge of the forest could be seen. They appeared lacy and black as if in mourning, for in fact they were. King Henry, the First, was dead on this day, December First, in the year of our Lord, one thousand one hundred and thirty-five. Adelicia could not stop the flow of tears and she did not try. She stared out the window and re-lived Henry's last moments one more time.

"Henry," she had said, "whatever is wrong?" Adelicia had felt helpless as she looked at her husband's ashen face. "You have such a fever. I have already sent for the court chirurgeon."

"I think I ate something I was told not to," King Henry had said.

"Do not tell me that. You would never be so foolish. Have you been where there was sickness? I have tried to keep you away from the ill. What did I do wrong, Henry?" She had held his hand, trying to take away the pain, but nothing would take away the guilt she had had.

"You have done nothing wrong. I was the foolish one and ate some eels when I knew that they would probably make me ill."

"You have recovered before and you will do so again," Adelicia had told him. She had prayed at this moment, and then was horrified that she had had so much fear.

"No, this is much worse. I have sent for the Barons and for Robert of Gloucester. The time has come. I want you to stay with me until the end. Do not cry," the king had said. "I am not afraid of dying. I look forward to seeing my father, my brothers, and my sons. Tell Matilda she is to come immediately, but only if Geoffrey is in a strong position to protect her."

"I will tell her, but it is an unnecessary request," Adelicia had said.

The Barons had stood next to King Henry's deathbed and pledged to support Matilda once again, at the king's insistence. They had stood by his side, casting giant shadows against the tapestries while life left the king in the middle of the night. Robert of Gloucester, alone amongst the men, had let tears fall against his chest, soaking his tunic.

Adelicia knew that Robert's love for Henry had been quiet and heartfelt. She had felt sorry that he had been robbed of his sire.

The wind howled like the ever-present wolves. Adelicia was brought back to the empty present. She closed the window, happy to shut out the unhappy world. It was an unhappy world without her king.

Adelicia moved toward the table where her writing box was waiting and picked up the vellum parchment. The black border had already been inked around the edges by one of the clerks. Adelicia would write to Matilda and a few others, but the clerks would send out other messages to people of lesser importance. Within a month the world would know that England had lost its king, and the strife would begin.

Though the room was cold, as it usually was in the winter mornings, Matilda stretched and pushed the covers down below her stomach. She placed her hands on the little bulge beneath her night chemise and laughed quietly. Even the snow storm that rattled the windows and frosted the inside glass could not change her mood. Geoffrey moved, but did not awaken. Matilda looked at him, then pulled at the end of a feather that was sticking out of a pillow casing. It fanned out as she released it, and she leaned over to tickle Geoffrey's nose. She giggled as he swatted at the feather.

Geoffrey opened his eyes and rolled toward her. "What a pretty sight so early in the morning." Geoffrey nuzzled her neck.

"What a charming man you have become." Matilda kissed the top of his head.

"I have to be, or my lovely wife will cut off my ears."

"I would do no such thing. I would cut off your head, for I would not waste my time on mere ears."

"You look pleased with yourself today. What is it that you might be trying to hide from me?" Geoffrey patted her abdomen.

"Only that I think I will make you a father again."

"Is that an invitation, or are you telling me something?"

"I am telling you that I will probably have your child next summer when it is very hot. I think some time in July. I do not know why I seem to like to suffer in the hottest months of the summer. Ah, but yes, this is the result of that raucous night last October when we both celebrated too much, argued too much, and made up too passionately." Matilda laughed aloud. "I think I will always treasure the memory of you that night."

"You dare make fun of the father of your two sons, and now mayhap a third? For shame, Matti. Have you no respect for the father of your children?"

"Three children? Do you still care for little Henry now that I have given you your own namesake?" Matilda asked.

"I will always think of Henry as mine. He will carry the title of Count of Anjou and Duke of Normandy when I die, for he is my eldest son. Geoffrey will carry other titles, as it should be with the second born."

"Your kindness is considerable. I thank you for that. Someday I hope to repay you." Matilda twisted Geoffrey's unruly curl around her index finger.

"You already have, and now you tell me you will repay me again with yet a third son."

"Do you think you can order sons from me? What if God decides it should be a girl?"

"If she is beautiful like her mother, then I will not care."

"And if she is ugly like her father, will you still love her?"

"You are a wicked one this morning. If you were not carrying such a fragile package, then I would . . ."

Geoffrey stopped at the sound of knocking on the door. "What could be so urgent that we are interrupted this time of morning?" He threw back the covers and crossed to the door. When he opened it, a servant stood there with a snow-covered messenger with ruddy cheeks. The messenger held out a familiar tri-folded parchment. Geoffrey took it, and without saying a word, closed the door. He leaned against it for a moment, then moved back to the bed and slid under the covers.

"What is it?" Matilda asked.

Geoffrey handed her the parchment without saying a word.

"The border is black. Oh, my God. It is Adelicia's writing and her seal. There has been a death. Please, please let it not be my father." Matilda hesitated before breaking the seal and opening the vellum. Tears obscured the words as she read them a second time, hoping they would change.

"Tell me," Geoffrey said.

"The king is dead. He died the first day of December. He was buried as is custom three days after." Matilda clasped the parchment to her. "He never knew that I was about to give him a third grandchild. I wish he had. When I last saw him, I knew that it was the end. I knew it. It has not been three full years since last we talked." Matilda slid under the woolen covers and turned her back to her husband. The corner of the vellum pricked her skin, and she was glad for the pain.

Geoffrey placed his hand on her arm. "I am sorry, for now the conflict will begin. It is only a question of where Stephen will strike first, Normandy or England. Which of us will he think the weaker and try to overthrow?"

"Stephen will not do that." Matilda's voice was muffled from both the pillow and her tears.

"You have not been his mistress for more than three years. You no longer know him."

Matilda winced at the truth. Why had God handed her such a complicated and difficult life? She owed it to Geoffrey to be truthful, no matter how bitter it was for her.

"I have reason to believe that his wife will try to talk Stephen into taking the throne, but he may still hold some feelings for me. He did promise to support me on two different occasions. He is a gentleman. He will keep his promises." Matilda turned and looked at Geoffrey. "Surely he loved King Henry as much as did I. He will follow his wishes. I know this to be true, for my heart says it will be."

"Do not believe your heart, Matti. Believe your head."

"Please keep everyone away for today. I can not bear to listen to their words of consolation that will bring forth a fresh torrent of tears. Except Ella, of course. We seem to find comfort in each other, and our sons play together so well."

"I will command it for you," Geoffrey said.

Stephen shivered. He wondered why the weather had to be against him. Things were going to be bad enough, and he wished that King Henry were still living. He did not want the conflict that was sure to come. Sleet, freezing rain, and snow mixed together beat itself down on the riders who rode with heads bent and fur lined capes drawn tightly about them.

Stephen was in the lead, his brother Henry, the Bishop of Winchester, close behind. The trip from London had been accomplished in record time, for Stephen had had no communique on the where abouts of his cousin, Matilda. The winds made speech impossible.

"There!" Roger, the Bishop of Salisbury said. "The door opens. Dismount and enter. I am quite frozen. It would have suited us better had the king died in summer. I have trouble riding in all this horrible weather."

The Bishop of Winchester laughed. "You have trouble riding because your gluttony has made you fat."

"How unkind you are." The Bishop of Salisbury frowned like a petulant child.

"Roger, I am but truthful." The Bishop of Winchester laughed again at the rotund figure straining as he descended from his horse. "You are the personification of one of the seven deadly sins."

The Bishop of Winchester dismounted and turned to his brother. "Stephen, you have to be firm with William de Pont de l'Arche. He takes his job as treasurer seriously. He is old and was loyal to King Henry. Above all, do not threaten him with violence, for he is stubborn and will choose to die rather than reveal the secrets of the locks."

As Stephen handed the reins to a groom, he nodded at his brother's words, trying to concentrate on all that Henry was telling him. If his performance did not ring true, l'Arche would see through it. It was imperative that the treasury be in his control.

Stephen and the bishops were met at the huge wooden entrance by two servants of William de Pont de l'Arche. The men threw open the doors and bade them enter. Stephen crossed to the fireplace quickly in spite of his cold and stiff body and stood in front of it along with his companions. He wondered if he would ever be warm again.

It was not long before William de Pont de l'Arche joined them in the small library. "It is my pleasure to have you as guests in my castle," William de Pont de l'Arche said, "However, it is unexpected on such a wicked night as this. To what do I owe the honor of this occasion?"

Stephen could not think of the delicate speech he had prepared for the guardian of the treasury. He shook his head, but the pretty words would not come, so he stated simply, "I have come to ask you to hand over the treasury of England, for I am king."

The old man squinted, and his lips pressed together. He looked from one man to another. Finally, he spoke. "You do not look like King Matilda."

The old man's impertinence as well as his reference to Matilda caused Stephen's guilt to be registered as anger. "Listen here, you old fool. I will have you . . ."

"Stephen, do calm yourself before you cause problems greater than what you can handle." The Bishop of Winchester placed a restraining hand on Stephen's shoulder. Stephen shrugged it off; the weight of his brother's hand offensive to him.

The Bishop of Winchester smiled. "Dear old William. Do you not know that our King Henry had recanted his wish that Matilda reign after him? Why, I have brought you a witness to that very speech King Henry made. I have brought none less than the Bishop of Salisbury to reveal the truth of King Henry's last words. Tell him, Bishop Salisbury."

The old man looked from one bishop to the other. "This had better be convincing, or the soldiers will slit you from one end to the other, men of God or not. I have lived long enough to know that the religious dress can sometimes hide a man of sin."

Stephen saw the Bishop of Salisbury's face turn from pink to white, and Stephen almost snorted at the bishop's cowardness. He watched the Bishop of Winchester poke an elbow in the fearful Bishop of Salisbury's belly.

The Bishop of Salisbury stepped forward. He rocked back and forth on tiny feet that did not look as if they could hold the weight above them. The Bishop of Salisbury cleared his throat. "It is true, sir. I was King Henry's regent and trusted by him. I was at his side at the end." The Bishop took a deep breath. "You do recall we were told that King Henry was disturbed with Matilda and her husband because they did battle in Normandy without his consent?"

"Yes, I do recall that," William de Pont de l'Arche said. "However, I also know that he sent part of his treasure to them."

Stephen stepped forward. "That was for his daughter's children. I know that he sent it for their security since Empress Matilda and Count Geoffrey were using their own funds for fighting."

William de Pont de l'Arche's eyes narrowed. He looked directly at Stephen. "It still seems that he was on friendly terms with his heirs."

Stephen winced at the choice of words the old man had used, for he did not want to emphasize the relationship of Matilda to King Henry, and he glanced away.

"He was a kind man, mayhap to a fault," the Bishop of Winchester said. "Listen to what our good friend here has to tell us. He was witness to the king's last words, after all."

The Bishop of Salisbury cleared his throat a second time, his fat chin quivering as he did. His voice registered higher than normal as he spoke. "Yes, King Henry was kind, and he was an excellent ruler. He always put England first. In doing so, he decided that the country would be better served by putting Stephen in charge."

The Bishop of Winchester spoke. "You know, of course, that our own brother, older than Stephen by five years, has willed that we follow the orders of the king? He would naturally be next in line, but Theobald wants what his king wanted."

Stephen wondered if that information would sink into the consciousness of the old man. He put his hand on William de Pont l'Arche's shoulder. "I do understand that King Henry wanted you to continue to be treasurer. He knew you could be trusted. He told me this several weeks before his death. I did not expect to have this conversation with you so soon. I was reared by King Henry, and his death can be likened to the death of a father." Stephen was glad to see the old man's eyes flicker. He had broken through the man's resistance.

"Stephen has also had the Londoners elect him king," the Bishop of Winchester said. "It was overwhelming to see the masses of people beg Stephen to lead them as their king had wanted."

"I have always done whatever King Henry wished." William de Pont de l'Arche stood straight. "I can not doubt the word of two bishops, one a regent, and King Henry's own nephew, so I must hand over the treasury and crown to you, since you have been named king by the populace of London as well as your own brothers."

Stephen caught something in the old man's voice that sounded like resignation. Good, he thought. The old fox knows he is outnumbered and outsmarted. Stephen smiled at William de Pont de l'Arche. He felt immense relief that he would not have to kill the old man. "Thank you. You are as wise as King Henry told me you were."

The Bishop of Salisbury rubbed his protruding belly. "Now, could we trouble you for a little supper? We have ridden long and far in a short time, and we are famished."

"It would be my honor," William de Pont de l'Arche said.

Stephen was shocked that in the three short weeks since King Henry's death, he had come this far in getting the throne. It was three days before the birthday of the King of Heaven. Stephen hoped, somehow, that this was a good omen. He had no desire to see Matilda come toward him with an army.

Stephen hesitated at the door to the Abbey, then began his walk toward destiny. He walked down the stone paved aisle, his footsteps echoing against the thick walls of Westminster Abbey. It seemed as if the stones were talking to him, but he could not tell what they were saying.

Stephen thought about the strength of the building. He wondered if his name would live beyond the Abbey or if the Abbey would exist beyond his name. He was going to take his place in history along with his grandfather, William the Conqueror, and King Henry the First, his uncle. The coronation might make him king, but could he hold onto the kingdom against Matilda's onslaughts? Would she invade this "graceless island," as she called it? Probably not, for she would not have much of an army. By the time she could raise one, it would be too late. He would already have made policy, shored up his power with friends, and the people would be used to King Stephen. Matilda was finished. Stephen sighed for his personal loss. She was a far better companion than his wife, but then there would be other women.

Stephen stopped at the altar and watched flickering candles make dancing shadows across the altar cloth. His brother, Bishop Henry, stood on the dias. Since he was not yet king, Stephen walked to the bishop rather than make the bishop walk to him. Stephen wondered how long it would take him to get used to people bowing to him and granting his every wish. His wife was already acting more royal than Matilda ever had.

Bishop Henry clapped Stephen on the shoulder in a rare show of camaraderie. Stephen was offended by the rare gesture since he was sure it was not because of love from one brother to another, but merely as part of a staged setting. He knew he should feel grateful that his brother helped him, but he knew Henry's motives. Stephen felt like a highly tuned war horse and could hardly stand still as he and his brother waited for the Archbishop of Canterbury to arrive.

"The Archbishop is really here, Henry, is he not?"

"He is here, although it was somewhat difficult to convince him that he should change sides since he had sworn an oath to King Henry." The Bishop of Winchester flicked a piece of fuzz off his tunic. "So dear brother, we told him the same story we told others."

Stephen looked across the space that separated him from the observers. "I see so few people."

The Bishop of Winchester followed Stephen's gaze. "There was not time to gather a great number since it was more important to get you crowned as soon as possible."

Stephen shook his head. "I should have more people here to support me. Counting you, Henry, there are only three bishops in attendance. There are no abbots, no priests or nuns, and only enough barons to count upon one hand."

Stephen knew that the small number of people in the huge cathedral emphasized how little support he actually had. Contrary to what Bishop Henry said, it seemed that support for his ascension to the throne was weak. If Stephen had to fight against Matilda, he might lose his throne. "There are not enough allies here," Stephen hissed. He felt very alone.

"It does not matter the number in attendance only that you get crowned," the Bishop of Winchester said. "Now go and think like a king, for you are about to become one."

CHAPTER

X

 SHOULD BE KING! How could Stephen do this to me?" Matilda whirled around with the parchment in her hand and used it as a weapon to sweep the supper dishes off the table. A pewter goblet bounced across the floor and clattered against the fireplace amidst the crashing of silver and gold platters and utensils. Matilda glared at Geoffrey. "He can not do this to me, to my father, or to my son. I will see him dead." Matilda kicked a pitcher across the room so hard that it hit the stone wall, bounced back and spun around until it finally lost momentum.

The noise was loud enough that Matilda did not hear Geoffrey cross the room. He could tell she was surprised when he wrapped his arms around her from behind and pinned her arms to her side. "Matti, stop this!"

"He can not take the crown from me! I will have his head for treason. I will fight him until England is mine as it should be."

"Calm yourself. Remember that you are carrying another child of mine. You knew Stephen would take the crown. You knew that." Geoffrey held her tighter, but it felt like holding a writhing river of fire.

"Let go of me." She spoke through clenched teeth.

"Only when you quiet down, Matti." Geoffrey waited for her to stop fighting. His arms, although strong, were getting tired. "Matti, there is nothing left on the table to throw. I would rather that you not destroy the furniture for it is the best I own."

He felt Matti slump against him. "Are you all right?" Geoffrey turned her toward him, and she buried her face in his broad chest.

"You were right about Stephen. He never loved me. I was a diversion, someone to entertain him during the boring hours of court. He made a mockery of me, Geoffrey. I gave him a son, and he gave his son nothing, not even a kingdom."

"I will help get England back for you."

Matilda raised her head from Geoffrey's chest. "You amaze me. You give my son your name, and now you will help get England back?" She looked at Geoffrey with accusing eyes. "Why?"

Geoffrey looked down at her tearless eyes. He loved her strength, her pragmatic nature, and he loved her. He could not tell her this, for when he did she became distant. He supposed it was because of the old problem that haunted her. He would never understand why she felt that she betrayed Stephen by enjoying her husband. As much as he wanted to ignore the fact, Matilda had loved Stephen and trusted him. She would not love or trust any other man for a long time, if ever. He had to answer her question.

"It is a matter of protecting my lands. Without the strength of England, then Normandy and Anjou are in danger. Stephen will try to take Normandy. The question is not whether, but when."

"It will be soon." Matilda's eyebrow raised, an outward indication of an inward anger.

Geoffrey saw the need to turn her anger into a productive behavior. "You will have to fight Stephen in England as well as Normandy."

"I know." Matilda pulled away from Geoffrey and paced back and forth in front of him. It was her habit whenever she had to think. "He will claim to be Duke of Normandy as well as King of England." Matilda raised a fist and shook it at the ceiling. "How I wish I were in England or Normandy instead of Anjou." She began pacing again. "We must plan our attack carefully. I have to think about the best way to gain back my crown." Matilda went to the window alcove and stared out the glass. "I do not think I have much of a chance to beat Stephen in England without help from Robert of Gloucester."

"Will Robert help you?" Geoffrey asked.

"He is my brother." Matilda hesitated. When she spoke her voice was strong. "He swore to uphold my right to be the ruler of England."

"At the same time as Stephen swore to do so?" Geoffrey asked.

A sharp intake of breath was Matilda's answer.

Geoffrey, lost in thought, tugged at his lower lip. "Robert is still in Normandy at Caen, is he not?"

"Yes."

"If Robert said he supports you, then he will." Geoffrey moved to the window and stood beside Matilda. He smelled the rose petals and spices that she always placed in her bath water. It brought memories of passionate nights surging forth into his consciousness. He only wanted to hold her, to make love to her, and forget the ensuing battles. Geoffrey put his arm around Matilda and kissed her fevered temple. "Matti, Robert will help you. He has nothing to gain by helping Stephen."

"He could gain more land." Matilda leaned into him.

"I have known Robert by his reputation, and it is impeccable. He will support you, but the question is when. He has to make certain he will not lose his head to an executioner." Geoffrey felt Matilda shudder.

"Stephen had better not lay a hand on Robert, or I will slice that usurper up in tiny pieces myself. I would die for Robert, and gladly, if I could kill Stephen."

Geoffrey had no doubts that Matilda would be capable of following through with her threat. "How can we best use Robert and his knights?"

Matilda pursed her lips. "That is easy. Since Robert is in Normandy, I could take a chance and count on Stephen not to move against me. I should invade in order to stop the troops that Stephen will already have in place in London, Lincoln, and Winchester. Stephen is bound to have people loyal to him in strategic palaces."

"Winchester, for certain," Geoffrey said.

"Of course. His brother, Henry, is bishop there." Matilda waved a hand. "I know that he will hold others to his cause, but I have my followers as well."

Geoffrey dropped his arm from Matilda's shoulder and pulled at his lower lip once again. "It should be done in two waves. First, you should lead with troops, then I should follow to finish."

"I will set about to raise the troops, but I can not ride with them until after the baby is born. If I get enough men gathered before the birth, then you will need to lead the first assault. It will take us long

enough to react to something for which I should have been ready."
Matilda turned from the window. "When the snows have been long
gone and summer is at its zenith, then the difficult job of regaining
the throne will commence. I should not have let love blind me. I
will never make that mistake again."

He would fulfill his part and help Matilda. "I will send a trusted
knight to take a message to Robert. He will surely have information
that can help us in our fight."

"There were many loyal to my father who will be loyal to me. I
am only sorry that it will take so long to get my hands around
Stephen's treacherous throat."

Summer came hot and humid in Anjou in the year one thousand one hundred and thirty-six. Throughout the month of August,
the weather had been the worst of the summer with no breeze to
bring relief either in the day or at night. The leaves on the trees had
turned brown on the edges, and they hung curled with no life. Crops
had died from the drought and the heat. Animals had to be slaughtered so that they would not starve to death. The coming winter
would be difficult for the peasants with less grain and meat than
usual.

Matilda lay on the bed with little William next to her. He was
sleeping after having just finished nursing. She ran her hand across
the top of the baby's head just to feel the reddish-blond fuzz. "Ella,
he has hair the color of his father's and little Henry's. He is only a
month away from birth and look how strong he is." Matilda shook
him until he opened his eyes, then she held her finger next to
William's hand. He grasped it, and Matilda tried to pull away. "I
can feel the strength of generations of knights in this one tiny hand."

"I am sure you can, Matti. He is a beautiful boy. All three of
your sons are handsome, but then so are their parents." Ella laid
aside her sewing to watch the infant.

"You have a beautiful son, too, Ella. He has a sweet disposition
like his mother. I love him as much as my own." She sat up and
looked directly into Ella's eyes. "I will protect him as my own."

Ella's face reddened. "Edward and I have sworn to each other
to protect your sons as our own, too."

Matilda nodded and felt comforted. She leaned against the pillows and kissed the top of William's head. She was fascinated by his

hair and loved the feel of the down on her lips. She had kissed him so much on the top of his head that she thought maybe he would go bald. If anyone ever harmed this child or any of the others, including Ella's son, she would be like a wild cat and scratch them to pieces.

"I wonder about the future for our little sons. Mayhap it is silly, but I gave my children names of their ancestors for strength and wisdom." Matilda rubbed her finger up and down William's arm. It seemed to stimulate him and he kicked his legs. Matilda remembered her father's advice about not wrapping babies in swaddling cloth. She never had.

Matilda thought about the future and the tremendous task ahead of her. She would risk everything for her sons. She looked out the window as if to see the future, but saw nothing. "If I can not beat Stephen, then the fates of my sons are bleak."

"I believe that God intends for the throne to be yours. You will have it." Ella picked up little William, who was sound asleep, and placed him in his cradle.

"I seem to have doubts at times, but then I tell myself that God wants to test my mettle." Matilda crossed herself. "He has certainly devised a unique way to test me."

Ella waved her hand nonchalantly. "Geoffrey has had a victory at Lisieux. Your brother is in Caen. In another month you will be strong enough to lead an army into Normandy to help reclaim what is yours. Then you will take England."

"I hope so."

Ella rocked the cradle with her foot. "Hope has nothing to do with it. You told me that yourself. You said an army was the only thing that would get you what is rightfully yours."

Matilda laughed. "It is not fair to throw my own words back at me." A knock on the plank door startled Matilda. She sat up and motioned for Ella to answer it. Placing her hand close to her dagger, she watched as Ella hurried to answer the door. Ella took a message from a young boy covered with road grime. His hair, plastered with sweat, stuck to his head. He looked exhausted and Matilda felt sorry for him. She called out. "Go to the kitchen and tell the cook that Empress Matilda sent you. You stay and rest before returning to . . . to . . ."

"Count Geoffrey of Anjou," the boy said.

"Let me see the message." Matilda sat up and pulled her kirtle into place. She held out her hand in spite of the impropriety of calling a messenger to her bed. She smiled when Ella intervened.

Ella took the scroll, nearly jerking it from the boy's hand. "Go to the kitchen at once." She shut the door and hurried to her lady. "Here, Matti. It does have Count Geoffrey's seal. I hope it is good news."

Matilda reached for the parchment, opened it and read, frowning as she continued. She looked up at Ella. "You will have to find a wet-nurse for little William. I have to get my army together and ride to help Geoffrey. He needs me immediately."

"How badly does he need your army?" Ella asked.

"It is an even battle thus far, so in order to win he needs more men. I must get there quickly, and yet I know it will take weeks to gather men. Geoffrey took mine. I was too stupid. I should have begun immediately to replace my army." Matilda threw the covers back and swung her legs down. "Who can I get to gather an army for me?" Matilda swung her feet back and forth as she thought. "I will do it myself."

Ella put her hands on her hip. "You are in no condition to ride about the country."

"God in Heaven, Ella. I am fine. If I ride to the nearest castles, I will be all right. I know that the peasants have babies and go right out to work the fields again. I am hardly delicate. Send for your husband. I will ask him to gather the knights that are here. I will meet with them at noon. He can also go to the farthest castles and carry the message for me. Please hurry for time wasted can not be regained, and time will get my crown returned." Matilda slid off the bed, her shoeless feet making no sound as she crossed the room and looked down at her sleeping son.

Ella shook her head. "You are not ready to ride so soon after William's birth, Matti. It is not good that you do this."

"I will have to do this. I can not afford to let Geoffrey down. He is a part of my strength." Matilda was struck by the irony of the situation. "Is it not peculiar that I go to save the man I did not want to marry, and I fight the man I loved? How close love is to hate. I hate Stephen and if I ever see him . . ." Matilda shook her head. "I was very foolish."

Ella twisted a braid around her fingers. "We are all foolish when in love. It is a miracle when love works."

"I resolve to never believe in the miracle of love again. From this point onward, I will believe only in myself. No longer will I be controlled by love."

The late September sun glinted off the shining chain mail of the knights as Matilda looked behind her. They moved as one northwest toward Normandy. Clouds of brown dust rose behind each horse and each foot soldier until there was a haze that floated skyward. Standards fluttered in the breeze at the head of each knight's collection of rag-tag vassals and mercenaries; the colors made miniature rainbows. Matilda looked to her right where the bearer rode with Geoffrey's standard flying. The flapping of the standard made the four rampart lions of gold appear alive. The field of maroon reminded Matilda of dark red blood. She wondered how many battles she would have to go through and how much blood would be shed before she had her kingdom. Death would, of necessity, claim some of the knights. Pushing these thoughts from her mind, Matilda concentrated on the villagers that lined the road into town.

Whenever the army passed near a village, the children and dogs trailed behind them raising more dust and adding to the noise. The muted thunder of the war horses' hoofs vibrated Matilda's breast bone, and she was sure it vibrated the breast bones of the peasants who came out of their huts to watch the spectacle. Some of the women held up their babies to see. Matilda's nerves were sharpened from excitement, and her senses were heightened. She was certain that the sight and sound of a marching army must intoxicate people with fright.

When Matilda saw Geoffrey's camp in the distance, it was at the end of a hard four days' march. She was filled with trepidation at the inactive camp. As she reached the edge of the camp, the guards, they alone in armor, recognized the standard of their leader, the Count of Anjou. They saluted as Matilda and her entourage rode through camp. She glanced from one tent to another, recognizing some of the shields and lances that were stabbed into the ground in front of the tents identifying the knight inside. Matilda was shocked and angered that the knights and their squires were sitting around playing knuckles and bones instead of being in armor. The shouts she heard from them were of gambling, not of war. Why on earth did she leave her son, climb on a horse, and don chain mail for Geoffrey if he did nothing more than lay around? Geoffrey had better have a good explanation for this.

She looked past the rows of tents with banners flying from the tops and scowled. This was not an army at war. Anger surged through her, giving energy to her weary body, and she urged Dancer forward at a faster clip. She moved out in front of the knights who had come with her, loosened the reins, and dug her heels into Dancer's ribs. The standard above the largest pavilion matched the one she carried. It was Geoffrey's. Matilda did not pull back on the reins until she neared the huge tent. The guards recognized the colors she carried, although they looked perplexed. They stood aside as the rider brought the horse forward. The knight that appeared at the tent opening waited for the horse to stop before helping the armored figure to dismount. He did not have time to hide his surprise when he discovered it was the Empress.

"We believed you would come, but not so soon and not in chain mail," Griffith fitz Thomas said.

Matilda handed her helmet to him and rubbed the bridge of her nose. It was sore where the nose piece had rubbed against the tender skin. "We expected to encounter enemies and we did, but it was a small battle not worth discussing. We killed a few. Where is your lord? I need to plan with him."

"I have terrible news for you. The Count has been badly injured. He is in a great deal of pain," Griffith said.

Matilda seized his arm. Her first concern was of the campaign. What would happen to the knights if their leader died? They would not follow her, she was certain of that. Her second concern was a tentative feeling that she would miss the father of her children. Matilda was pragmatic. It was too soon to despair. "What type of injury?"

"His foot has a deep wound from a pole-ax, my lady."

She breathed easier. That type of wound was dangerous, but could be dealt with easier than a wound to the trunk. "Get my chest of medicines from the squire." Matilda pushed past Griffith and stepped into the tent that seemed dark to her after having been outside. The odor of rotting and infected flesh was unmistakable. Matilda could not help but clamp her hand across her nose and mouth, but she dropped it quickly to her side. It would do her no good for any of the men to see her in a squeamish state. She had to be stronger than any other woman, or any man, for that matter.

The tent was oppressive to Matilda. It was all she could do to keep from running away. As her eyes adjusted to the darkness, she could see Geoffrey on a pile of furs and linen sheets. She looked at the two knights who were in attendance along with a squire. "This will never do. Get some air in here. Open the tent flaps and raise one of the sides. Get me some clean linens. These are disgusting. Boil some water and get me a gallon of wine. Why do you stand there looking like fools? Do as I say and do it now."

"Boiling water? Do you want soup?" Sir Corydon fitz Pyke asked.

Matilda looked at the knight and frowned. "Do you not know anything? I thought you had been to the Holy Land. Do you not know that boiling water helps healing? Now move quickly, for your stupidity may cost your Lord Geoffrey his life. Where is the chirurgeon? Did he not come with the army to tend to wounds?"

Sir Corydon fitz Pyke called over his shoulder as he left the tent. "Count Geoffrey dismissed him. He said that the chirurgeon knew nothing about medicine. Do you want me to get him?"

"Certainly not. If the Count does not want him, then neither do I." Matilda muttered to herself, "He has not kept up with the new medicine of the Arabs."

Matilda moved toward Geoffrey, but the sound of metal against metal as she moved made him stir and groan, so she stopped. "Get this chain mail off me."

A squire, trying to tie up one side of the tent hesitated, his hands on a leather strap, and not knowing quite what to do, continued with the job at hand.

"Get this chain mail off me!" Matilda's voice cracked across the small space between them.

As if struck by lightning, the squire let go of the strap. The side of the tent slipped down and hit the ground with a thud that shook the entire tent. Geoffrey thrashed his arms at the sound.

"Fool! Get over here. Can you not do anything right?" She stood still as the squire rushed over and cowered with uncertainty before her. Matilda's anger changed to amusement as she realized the squire was unsure of where to place his hands in order to grasp the hauberk.

"Pull the coif off first, please. It will make it easier to do the mail." Matilda bent her head forward. She wished she could see his face, but the light touch of his fingers on her shoulders as he grasped the coif was enough to cause her to struggle to keep from giggling. She felt the coif roll off her shoulders and head. She reached up, pulled the linen covering off her hair. Her hair rippled down her back and she was immediately sorry that she had loosened it, for strands caught in the metal rings of her chain mail.

Blushing, the squire helped her pull the hauberk over her head. She almost laughed at his obvious relief to see that she had a tunic underneath just like the men did. She held her lower lip in her teeth while the squire hesitated but a moment, then knelt behind her to unlace the chausses that protected her legs. Again, she noticed that he was relieved to see that the tunic came down to her knees. He waited to see what she expected him to do next. He stood holding the hauberk and chausses, then turned away. He glanced back at Matilda.

Matilda was smiling at his discomfort. "Have you not helped a woman in battle dress before?"

"No, my lady."

"It is not uncommon for a woman to lead an army. Many have led armies throughout history. I could name several for you."

"I know that women have had to defend their lord's castles and lands, my lady, but I am new. I do not know what is proper," the squire said.

Matilda looked at the squire for the first time. He could not have been much more than eleven years in age. "In time of war you are to treat a woman warrior as you would a man. We are no different. Just put the chain mail on that rack over there next to the Count's. Now go back and tie up the side of the tent. I see that my husband is in bad condition and needs my attention."

Matilda knelt by the pallet that was covered by a pile of fur and linen covers, glad that the autumn air was filtering through the putrid-smelling tent. She failed to notice who placed her chest of medicines next to her. She was relieved that Geoffrey still slept. It would be easier for her if he continued to be in the land of dreams. She leaned down and pulled aside the sweat-soaked and stained linen coverlet. Matilda had to turn away as the source of the rotting smell was uncovered. She swore at the ineptitude of the foolish chirurgeon.

"Get me some incense, perfume, anything," Matilda said. She spoke to no one in particular, but knew that her orders would be followed. "I need someone to help hold my husband down while I work with him."

Two knights stepped up. Matilda nodded as Sir Griffith knelt next to Geoffrey's head and placed his hands gently on Geoffrey's shoulder and arm. Sir Corydon knelt on the other side and did the same.

"I will use the hot water to mix a poultice that I will place directly on the wound. First I will have to clean the entire area with the wine. Do not ask me why, but it has often worked to keep cancrene away. It has been used by my mother many times." Matilda held out her hand and the young squire gave her the wine. She let the wine trickle over the wound. Geoffrey groaned and tried to sit up, but Sir Griffith and Sir Corydon pushed him back down.

Matilda clenched her teeth when Geoffrey groaned, but she held his leg down with her knee and continued to pour until blood flowed with the wine, making it darker. She stopped and leaned back. Sweat dripped down her forehead and into her eyes. She wiped her face with the sleeve of her tunic.

"Get a new pallet prepared and fresh linen. Burn this disgusting mess." Matilda opened her medicine chest and took out a small packet and bowl. Within minutes she had prepared a cloth with a hot, dark green cataplasm that she laid across the oozing wound. It was not until the fresh pallet had been prepared and Geoffrey had been moved that Matilda stood and walked outside. She flexed her shoulders and rubbed her neck. She was too tired to rest. She hoped that would come later. Matilda placed her hands at the small of her back and bent against them. She ached all over, but it was nothing compared to what Geoffrey was going through.

Daylight was starting to fade as Matilda paced back and forth. A light breeze blew across her sweaty face and body, chilling her. She shivered and glanced toward the west. The sun had almost disappeared, and the sky was darkening. Matilda turned and looked across the encampment where the men were preparing to bed down for the night. Small fires, randomly placed, flickered like candles at a Christmas Mass. Matilda wondered how many men would die tomorrow without one of their leaders. She turned, went back into the tent, and knelt next to Geoffrey. She watched his face and felt his forehead with her wrist.

Matilda knew what must be done, and she stood. She walked outside and motioned for Sir Corydon and Sir Griffith to come to her. She watched the greybeard, Sir Corydon, move as quickly as he could, and she wondered why he was fighting along with younger men. His experience, however, would be of help to her. She wished that Brian fitzCount were here instead of in Anjou guarding the castle. Brian was quiet, but his observations were true. He would always answer straight when asked what he thought.

Her attention was drawn to Sir Griffith and she wondered how competent he was. He was tall and gaunt with cheekbones that threatened to push through his skin. He looked like he could eat entire herds of cattle and never gain weight. As he came toward her, Matilda noticed that he seemed to be in constant motion. He even fidgeted as he walked.

Matilda acknowledged their bows with a half-hearted gesture. She was getting more exhausted by the minute. Because of this, she got right to the point. "As commanders of these men, do you think this army would follow me into battle tomorrow without the Count?"

If the men were startled, they hid it well. Sir Corydon did not hesitate. "You brought more than fifty men. If you talked to them, mayhap they would follow you north, but I am not . . ."

Sir Griffith spoke quickly, "The knights who follow the Count are discouraged after losing the battles at Lisieux and Sap, especially Sap where the Count was wounded. We should have waited for your troops, but we underestimated the enemy's resistance. If we ordered them to regroup and attack those same two cities once more, they would . . ."

"It would be difficult. I understand," Matilda said. "I am not a warrior honed by the fires of battle. You and the other knights follow Count Geoffrey. Give me until morning to think about your words. Thank you for your counsel."

Matilda re-entered the tent. At the door, she hesitated. "Come and see me before the sun rises. I will have a decision then."

As Matilda passed the candles in the tripod on either side of Geoffrey's pallet, they flickered. She had ordered the light so that she could watch her husband throughout the night. She dropped down next to Geoffrey's pallet and stretched out on a pile of furs covered with linen sheets. She was asleep before she could form the first thought in her mind about tomorrow.

It was nearly dawn. Matilda had curled up, her head on her arms. When Geoffrey groaned, she awakened and watched him. His eyes opened, then closed. He opened his eyes again and stared at Matilda.

"Good morning, Geoffrey."

"You are here."

"I arrived several hours ago. Together we could have routed Stephen's supporters, but now . . ."

"I took a pole-ax in the foot. Is it still there?" Geoffrey coughed.

"The chain mail helped keep your foot, but the infection is very serious."

"You are a well-trained nurse, almost magical. I have faith in you, Matti."

"Geoffrey, I want to take you back to Anjou. I can not lead the battle without you, and we have no one who is good enough to be second in command. Robert is still in Caen and I left Brian fitzCount in charge of our castle." Matilda took his hand. It felt like hot, dry parchment. She was sorry that she had been angry with him earlier for dragging her away from her new born son.

"I wish I felt well enough to argue with you but to be truthful, I fear I will have to battle death instead of Stephen." Geoffrey closed his eyes, his pale lashes looked dark compared to the pallor of his skin.

"We shall return to Anjou in the morning." Matilda pulled the linen covering around Geoffrey's shoulders. He seemed so thin and frail.

Geoffrey shook his head. "Turn tail and run? That does not sound like you."

Matilda sighed. "It has to be. I can not take the chance. Too many men would be killed, and too much would be lost. I do not want to lose my first real battle against Stephen's forces, so I shall talk with the men right away. They should know as soon as possible that we return to Anjou."

"I am sorry, Matti, but I can not think about anything right now. I am too ill."

"I know. It will be a long time before you are well, but you will live. I have the medicines." Matilda leaned down and lifted the poultice.

Geoffrey winced. "Promise me that you will not remove my foot. I would rather die than be a cripple."

"I would rather have a cripple than be a widow a second time," Matilda said.

Geoffrey opened his eyes. "Does this mean you love me?"

Matilda smoothed the linen sheet that covered Geoffrey. She was reluctant to admit love. "I might be saying that." She saw Geoffrey smile, then look past her toward the sound of footsteps.

Sir Corydon and Sir Griffith appeared out of the early morning light and stood before Matilda.

"My lady, you arranged for this meeting," Sir Griffith said.

"Yes, I want the Count carried on a litter. He is too ill to ride, and it is too rough to place him in a wagon. Sir Griffith, you are to take care of this."

"Yes, my lady. I will get the best men," Sir Griffith said.

"You, Sir Corydon, are to assemble the knights before me. I have an announcement." Matilda watched the knights leave, then looked down at Geoffrey. He watched her. "You should be sleeping."

"So should you, Matti. Have you rested?"

"I can not. It is difficult to turn an army away from a battle, especially one that is the beginning of a fight to get back my crown."

"I wish I could encourage you to go on without me, but it would be foolhardy." Geoffrey reached for her hand and held it to his cheek.

"I know. I will announce a retreat as soon as the knights have assembled. Our time has not yet come." Matilda felt an emptiness within her. Her dream for the throne was postponed. "We will move out at dawn. I will give you a drink to help you sleep so you will not be in pain."

Matilda rose and walked outside the tent. She was startled to see the commanders had already gathered in silent groups. They stood before her, faces solemn, eyes watching her closely. Their shoulders sagged and tunics hung listlessly from their shoulders, and she saw that they suspected the truth. Even the banners seemed to know they would not see battle and hung heavily off the poles.

"I can not lead you into battle without Count Geoffrey and win, so we are going to return to Anjou." Matilda looked from one silent knight to another. "Do you have something to say?" She waited. "Then we will move out as soon as possible."

A knight wearing colors Matilda did not recognize, stepped before her. "My lady, may I speak?"

"Yes, of course," Matilda said.

"We feel we could win with you leading us and with one of us in Count Geoffrey's stead."

The knight knelt before her. He was young, so young and with his youth was hope, but no experience.

"I appreciate your faith in not only me, but in yourselves, however I feel our first duty is to Count Geoffrey. I can not go into battle and care for Count Geoffrey, too. Without him, my cause is lost. I have nothing more to say. You are dismissed." Matilda watched the knights leave in twos and threes. They said nothing, and she said nothing, for fear her disappointment would show. It was going to be a most difficult winter.

Geoffrey's castle at Anjou was cold, but Matilda did not notice as she walked back and forth in front of the fireplace. She felt like a wild cat housed with a bear. Geoffrey had been grouchy since he had been well enough to hobble around the castle, often following her while she tried to manage the servants.

Geoffrey had the nerve to ask Matilda to entertain at a time like this. She turned toward Geoffrey. "I do not feel like having an Easter Court. I did not feel like celebrating Christmas and yet we had guests. I will only celebrate the day of my sons' births. Henry is in his third year and were it not for my sons, it would be a bleak period in my life." Matilda crossed the room and stared out the window.

"I even hate the snow this year for it keeps me from my duty."

"Come and sit down. We will play another game of chess."

Matilda waved away the suggestion. "Chess is but a game of war. I am tired of games."

"I did not ask you to turn back the army. I did not ask you to stay and bathe my foot with your herbs and potions, and I did not ask you to stay in my castle all winter."

"And I did not ask that you put your foot under someone's pole-ax so that they could slice it up."

"Yes, I did that on purpose so that I could limp around all winter. Do you think I like being a cripple? Remember, I said I would rather die." Geoffrey moved a pawn and took Matilda's knight.

Matilda walked back to the chessboard and stood looking at the pieces. She reached down, moved her bishop and took Geoffrey's rook. "You said that you would rather not have your foot removed. I did not remove your foot."

"I had Christmas Court because I needed some diversion and now I need diversion still since I am not healed well enough to wear a boot. Without a boot I can not ride, so I would like to have Easter Court." Geoffrey stared at the chess board.

"You want me to have to put up with your loud and unruly barons and their entourages? Do I not have enough to think about without having to arrange for your friends for a month or more?" Matilda had become increasingly tired of hearing Geoffrey's daily complaints. She had tried to contain her thoughts and dark looks whenever Geoffrey moaned. She knew his foot hurt, for the wound had been deep, but surely he had more strength of character than what he showed. It was a good thing he never had to give birth or he would have had no more than one issue.

"I do not need a bunch of knights drinking mead and falling drunk all over the great hall."

Geoffrey picked up a captured pawn and twirled it between his finger and thumb. "Mayhap it is beyond your capabilities. Mayhap you can not plan such a banquet or play the proper hostess."

Matilda put her hands on her hips and tapped her foot. "Mayhap it is beyond reason to ask such a thing."

"If it is my will, then it must be done." Geoffrey leaned back against the brocaded cloth of the chair.

Matilda's eyes narrowed and her mouth clamped shut in a tight, straight line. She watched Geoffrey as he shifted his leg, which was straight out in front of him and rested on a cushioned stool, and waited for him to realize that he could order her to have Easter Court, but he would be embarrassed by the results. She was so angry with him that the usual barrage of words would not slip off her tongue.

Geoffrey became increasingly uneasy. Matilda would not let a smile escape as she realized he found her silence more dreadful than her angry words. She had discovered another way to control Geoffrey. She waited and watched Geoffrey as he twirled a bishop around and around.

"Let us continue our game of chess," Geoffrey said.

"Continue our game of chess? Why should I play at war on this stupid wooden board with wooden men when I should be taking England? The only game worth playing is with real soldiers for real countries."

"You can do nothing at this time."

"I can do nothing? My dear uncle, King David, at least did something."

"He came up against the largest army within the memory of man." Geoffrey shifted in his chair and rubbed the muscle in his thigh. "It was said that Stephen had as many as ten thousand men against King David."

"He could afford to hire ten thousand men. He did it with my treasury. He steals from me. He will pay for it." Matilda picked up the king from Geoffrey's side of the board and looked at it. Her voice was acid. "He will pay, for I am not yet beaten." She snapped off the head of the chess piece and threw both pieces into the fire. She sat silent and watched as the flames absorbed the decapitated king.

"King David did not desert me. He is one of the few men who had the decency and the fortitude to support me because of his oath to do so. Dear Uncle David, I hope that you may survive Stephen's assaults."

"Stephen's assaults? King David did very well actually, and I think Stephen did rather badly politically," Geoffrey said.

"What do you mean?" Matilda asked.

"Even with his ten thousand men, Stephen had to placate your uncle after the invasion and capture of Newcastle upon Tyne. Stephen had to give King David the tax rights to Newcastle just so he would not destroy it. He also had to give King David the huge lands of Cumberland and Westmorland." Geoffrey moved his leg again. He frowned, his irritation with his leg becoming more evident.

"It really was not Stephen's to give." Matilda could no longer watch the discomfort on her husband's face. She knelt and began to knead the cramped muscle. "I can not believe that Ranulf, Earl of Chester, would be very happy about Stephen giving his lands away."

"Exactly. An asinine move by Stephen. It was not much better for him to give King David's son the earldom of Huntingdon, for he has not given Stephen any sign of homage."

"So our spies have told us." Matilda smiled. "Stephen took an army of ten thousand men and came back with a lot less land, no oath of fidelity from my uncle, and has made an enemy of Ranulf. It cost Stephen dearly for that little episode."

"Your time will be soon, Matti. You will get back the crown of England with my help."

"Thank you, Geoffrey. I am counting on you. The two of us together should take Normandy and England from our nemesis." Matilda smiled as she moved another chess piece and took Geoffrey's knight.

CHAPTER
XI

THE DELICATE SPRINKLE OF RAIN did nothing to hide the happiness of Stephen's wife, and she sang as she dressed for the midday meal in the great hall. Preparations had gone smoothly even though she had to order one of the young men beaten for drinking too much mead. The days just before Easter had gone well and Maithilde was pleased. No one could say that she did not do as well, nay, even better at the arrangements than the witch in Anjou.

Maithilde motioned for her servant, Jane, to come and comb her hair. Maithilde sat quite still and watched in the mirror as Jane expertly untangled Maithilde's light brown hair.

"Does my mistress wish to have her hair plaited for this joyous occasion?"

"Call me by the proper greeting. I am queen." Maithilde made no attempt to hide her wrath.

"Yes, my lady."

"Good."

"Does my lady wish to have her hair plaited?"

"No, I think not. I wish to wear the new style. Let it hang loose and down the front. I have been blessed with a lot of natural tresses. I shall be the envy of many." She chuckled. "I imagine I shall be the envy of one particular Countess in Anjou. That makes this day doubly good." Maithilde adjusted her kirtle. "This morning's crowning will make history. My name will live forever in the mouths and writings of the chroniclers. Not so, Matilda's. She will be forgotten."

"It is appropriate that it should take place at Westminster Abbey, my lady," Jane said.

"All of London is mine and soon all of England and Normandy will be mine." Maithilde leaned forward and stared into the mirror. "I will repay the adulteress for all that she took from me." She licked the end of her little finger and smoothed an eyebrow.

"Yes, my lady." Jane continued to comb Maithilde's hair. She was still combing it when Stephen entered the apartment and waved her away.

Maithilde watched the girl leave and anger swelled inside her. She always resented Stephen's intrusions into her rooms, but most of all she resented the way he ordered her servants about. She started to protest when Stephen blurted out a string of words.

"That traitor, Robert of Gloucester, is not here at my Easter Court." Stephen slammed his fist down upon the dressing table in front of Maithilde and the pots and jars bounced.

"Robert is not here?" Maithilde forgot her anger. Stephen's face was crimson with rage. She was more concerned than angry. There had to be some reason for his absence. "I had hoped that Robert of Gloucester would see the futility of his sister's wishes. It would be better to have him here. We need him, for next to you he is the wealthiest and most powerful man in all of England and Normandy. Are you certain he is not on his way?"

"Normandy is not so far away that he could not be here. Look at this." Stephen held out a small parchment. "He sent word that he is unable to attend."

"Mayhap there is trouble from Count Geoffrey, and he has to stay to protect Normandy for you," Maithilde said.

"He would have told me if that were true. He is loyal to Matilda. He is so faithful that he will obey the stupid oath that he gave to King Henry. I will have to fight him unless I can get him to see that I am, by the will of God and the people, king."

"That is something to think about later. I am to be queen with or without Robert's presence." Maithilde placed a large sapphire and gold ring on her finger. "I am ready. You must escort me even though it does gall you to do so."

"I will be happy to play the part of the king to his queen, and I expect you will do likewise. I have more problems than even you could give me. I have to worry about Robert." Stephen held out his arm for her to take.

"I should think that you would have been more concerned at Christmas Court when you were crowned. There was hardly anyone of importance here at that time. We have more nobles, barons, and knights here now that I should think you would be content. Obviously you have a stronger following than you had then. I would not worry about one man." Maithilde rose from the dressing table and placed her hand on Stephen's arm. "We are assuredly doing what God intended."

"My triumph will not be complete without adding Matti's own brother to my growing list of supporters."

"Matti, is it? Do not use that pet name in front of me ever again." Maithilde's lower lip protruded.

Stephen dropped his arm, letting Maithilde's hand fall. "You are unsure of yourself, are you not? Matilda is of no consequence to me except as an enemy. She was merely a diversion because I have a shrew for a wife. Now, as king, I can have any woman I want."

Maithilde would not let him see that he irritated her, although there was no longer enough feeling left for Stephen for her to be angered by his taunts. "You are of no consequence to me either. I have my own entertainment. The only reason you are important to me is so that I can be Queen of England. Within the next hour, I will be the queen and my son . . ."

"My son in name," Stephen said.

"Our son, Eustace, will be the crown prince and through him my life shall continue," Maithilde said. "Mayhap there will be another heir for me in six or seven months."

"Breeding again? You drop children like a sow."

Maithilde slapped Stephen hard. The red welts that her fingers made on his cheek gave her pleasure. "You are the swine."

"Do you know the difference between you and Matti? Do not be so bold as to frown at the use of my pet name for her. I am king and can do what I wish. The difference between you two is that you wanted to be queen, but you did nothing on your own to get there. Matilda wants to be king and she is willing to fight for it. She is a more fearful enemy than any I could have." Stephen stared at

Maithilde. "Make certain that you look the part of a queen and are fit for a king. I do not want to have to have you replaced."

"Do not be absurd. If you are trying to frighten me, do not bother, for I could poison you in a minute. However as long as you are necessary to me, you will be safe." Maithilde smiled at Stephen's consternation. She was always quicker with a retort. She pushed the tight sleeves of her chemise up and arranged the resultant wrinkles. The sleeves were stylishly over-long.

"It seems we are at our usual impasse, so I suggest we go to the coronation and be done with our conversation. I am supposed to escort you. It is time to go." Stephen held out his arm and Maithilde placed her heavily jeweled hand on the woolen cloth of his tunic. Even though Stephen's tunic was brown, it was richly embroidered with red and blue thread on a gold border. She had insisted that he wear the dark color so that her own saffron gown would look bright. The sleeves of Maithilde's gown were designed so that they opened wide at the wrists, trailing nearly to the floor in fluid ripples whenever she moved. Her chemise was a rich blue, the tight sleeves showing beneath the wide saffron-colored kirtle. The longer chemise fell to the floor, showing at least eight inches of blue.

Maithilde and Stephen moved out of their apartment and walked down the many corridors to Westminster Abbey where Maithilde would become queen before Easter Mass. She hoped the Archbishop would not drag the Mass out as he was wont to do.

The banquet to celebrate both Easter and Maithilde's coronation was so crowded with the dignitaries of England, Normandy, and Scotland that even in the great hall people invariably bumped into each other. Maithilde was smiling and acknowledging curtsies from the ladies who were present. The barons bowed to her at her every turn. Her neck hurt from holding her head high. She felt a place between her shoulders tingle from holding her back straight. She would not lean back in the chair since she wanted to look the part of a queen.

Everything she touched was fit for a queen. The cloths on the table were new and as white as goose down. Dishes made of pewter and gold had kept the smiths busy full time for a month to be ready for this one banquet. The finest meat and sauces were available, and courses were continuously served to the guests so that none would be in want.

Maithilde sat at the table to Stephen's left and constantly glanced at the trays being brought from the kitchen. She frowned. She waited for one of the servants to pass near her and she asked, "Where is the mutton that I ordered?"

The servant hesitated. "My lady, the mutton has all been eaten. It was most tender and most popular."

"Then get some more," Maithilde said.

The servant's eyes shifted away from Maithilde to the floor. "There is no more, my lady, since we have scoured the lands about here and have taken nearly every last sheep."

"I do not want excuses. My guests must not think we are unable to feed them properly. Get some mutton and place it on the table," Maithilde hissed.

"Yes, my lady." The boy placed his platter of beef in front of Brian fitzCount who sat next to Maithilde.

"I do not think my lady has anything to fear from her guests. The banquet is excellent," Brian fitzCount said.

Maithilde leaned toward Brian. "Is it as good as what King Henry used to have?"

Brian hesitated a fleeting moment before answering. "My lady, this is a banquet fit for a queen."

Maithilde laughed. "So it is. Do you find it surprising that I am sitting here instead of Stephen's dear cousin?"

"Not at all," Brian said.

"Do you find me more attractive than the other Matilda?" She leaned over and placed her face close to his, her light brown hair contrasting with his auburn hair.

Brian's freckles grew darker and he blinked. He swallowed once. "You make a beautiful queen. I am certain that your beauty will make history just as the beauty of Helen of Troy is still celebrated in our time."

Maithilde leaned over and whispered into Brian's ear. "I hope so."

"Tell me something," Brian said.

Maithilde tilted her chin upwards so that she would appear younger and looked into Brian's eyes. "Yes?"

"Why does the Archbishop of Canterbury look so angry?" Brian nodded toward the man who sat several people away from Stephen.

"My husband is trying to placate King David of Scotland. In order to do so, he has let the Scottish Prince Henry sit in the place the Archbishop customarily occupies. The Archbishop has always fancied himself on the right hand of the king and God. King Stephen fears that the Scottish king will turn against him and side with his niece," Maithilde said.

"Why does he think that?" Brian asked.

"Because of the oath that was given to Matilda, but of course, that means nothing. You gave such an oath, did you not?" Maithilde leaned against Brian fitzCount. The muscles in his arm was firm. She liked the feeling of strength.

"I did."

"And yet you are here, eating Stephen's food and paying homage to your new king and queen." Maithilde watched Brian's neck redden as the blood pushed up past the collar of his tunic. She watched Brian like a cat does when playing with a mouse.

"That is so."

Maithilde leaned close to Brian. "Tell me what you have been doing since I saw you last."

"My lady, I have been helping my father tend his lands and overseeing his servants. I did travel a bit," Brian said.

"Where did you go?" Maithilde asked.

"Actually, my father sent me to Normandy to check on some of our holdings there."

"I did learn of your trip. Someday I hope to visit Normandy after we take it back."

"Most of Normandy is still in control by the English." Brian reached for a cup of wine, but was stopped by a well-placed hand.

"Yes, but Geoffrey has already made one aborted foray into Normandy. I heard that he was badly injured. When Geoffrey heals, he and Matilda will undoubtedly try again." Maithilde looked at Brian through half closed eyes. "Do you not think so?"

"I do not know. I am not much interested in politics or games of war." Brian let his hand drop to the linen table cloth.

"King Stephen worries that Robert of Gloucester still supports his sister, Matilda."

"Mayhap he is just keeping watch over his lands because he fears an invasion from Count Geoffrey and Empress Matilda," Brian said.

"Empress?" Maithilde could not keep the bitterness from her voice. She hated it when people still referred to Matilda as Empress. She would tolerate no one placing that woman above her. "Matilda is a mere countess now, and I am a queen. I have surpassed the high born Matilda. I find it fascinating that you have always been interested in Matilda." Maithilde traced a scar on Brian's hand with her forefinger.

Brian glanced down at his plate and stared at the streaks of sauce that were left. "The lady about whom you speak has been twice married and thus unavailable to me."

"She was unavailable to you because she was the mistress of my husband, not because she was married." Maithilde watched Brian turn red again. She was glad she had provoked him. He was another of Matilda's stupid admirers. Harmless, but irritating.

"She was unavailable to me because it is against my beliefs to interfere in the marriage vows of others."

"You are too, too good. How can you win favors from a lady if you are too good?" Maithilde laughed. "You blush like a young girl. Do I embarrass you?" She watched Brian sit as still as a stone, waiting, no doubt, for someone to rescue him.

Maithilde whispered in his ear. "I must have embarrassed you, for you can not answer. What a dear sweet man you are, and one that I find highly interesting."

"Did you notice how many people have come to pay their respects to you?" Brian asked.

Maithilde looked away from Brian and across the great hall where row upon row of tables had been piled high with food and drink. "It is quite a spectacle is it not? I have outdone even King Henry."

"It is a great celebration of our Lord's Resurrection," Brian said.

"Oh, that. Yes, and a great celebration of my crowning as well. We will have a long and peaceful reign. My son, Eustace, will become king, and my lineage will continue unbroken for centuries to come. I have started the greatest of all lineages for England."

Brian cleared his throat. "King Stephen arises."

"What could he possibly say that we would want to hear?"

Stephen held up his jeweled chalice and waited for the great hall to quiet. "My friends and countrymen, I am honored that you have chosen to be with me today on this joyous Easter. Queen Maithilde has also asked that I extend her appreciation at your attendance of her coronation. I wish to humble myself before you and propose a toast." Stephen held the chalice above his head. "Here is to my friends and supporters. The crown is truly on my head where it belongs. I foresee a long and prosperous peace, and I thank you for both."

Maithilde smiled as the great hall came alive with shouting and the banging of pewter plates and mugs against the tables.

Maithilde sighed. She spoke to no one in particular. "My happiness is full and I am content."

His sleeping alcove was peaceful except for the soft snoring of his cousin who shared the space. Brian was glad to be away from the celebration at last. He had had to stay until the host and hostess had retired, and he had not been long behind them. Brian had much writing to do and daylight would soon be here to reveal any riders leaving the castle.

Brian fitzCount sat at the small table next to the curtain that blocked the hallway from the sleeping room. He left one candle lit, but sat in front of it to shield the light from anyone who might be passing by. The scratching of the pen sounded loud enough to Brian for it to waken even the drunken knights who had celebrated long and with enthusiasm.

He had almost finished when he heard a shuffling in the hallway. If he blew out the candle, someone might notice the absence of light, so Brian shoved the parchment under the pallet on the reed covered floor and lay down. He pulled his cape to his head and appeared to be sleeping. He watched with squinted eyes through the crack under the curtain as the person walked past the alcove and into the garderobe down the hall. The odor from the cesspit below the garderobe wafted down the hallway and into Brian's nostrils. He found it offensive, but then what was a person to do? The garderobes were a necessity of life.

Just as Brian was concerned that his mystery person would not give up his seat in the garderobe, that very soul stumbled back down the hallway, and as Brian listened, the footsteps faded away on the stairway to the lower level of the castle. Brian tried not to awaken Paul James who slept like the dead, as the young often do. With a few more scratches, the document was done and Brian quickly sealed it with the candle wax and his signet ring. He knelt down and shook the sleeping Paul James until he awakened. Without a word, young Paul took the parchment, stood, and stretched, his eyes betraying the need for more sleep.

Brian put his hands on Paul's shoulders. He remembered when the lad had been born, and he remembered when his uncle, from his death bed, implored Brian to watch over him. He was not watching over his youthful cousin very well. "You will have to be careful, and you will have to get to Normandy as quickly as possible. The passage has been arranged. The ship leaves in two days. If there is any doubt about your safety, then do not go through with this."

"I will get to Robert as quickly as possible. You can depend on me. Robert will be here before you miss me." Paul James took the parchment and slipped it under his tunic. He pushed aside the curtain and left the alcove, slipping down the corridor in the shadows.

Exeter Castle stood on a hill overlooking the Exe River and the town that had sprung up around both river and castle. The wattle and daub huts housed businesses as well as the owners. There was no space save for the streets; each hut built next to its neighbor and sharing a common wall. The thatched roofs looked like a giant, flattened hay stacks.

The Countess de Redvers pushed back a strand of grey hair and squinted. She would not mind growing old if all her body parts worked. She could see just fine whenever she did embroidery, but to see beyond the Exe River was difficult. Lately, she had noticed that the river itself was becoming less and less like a river and more like a smooth, silver band cutting through the low hills. The trees in the distance no longer had individual leaves, but had puffs of spring green on the ends of brown trunks.

As long as she could still see the details in her husband's face and her sons', she would be content. She would take whatever God had given her as a burden. She hoped that she would be able to manage the burden the count had placed on her.

The window was narrow and the countess had to lean against the thick stone, which made up the support for the lintel, in order to see to the left. From the second floor of the gate house and the most fortified section of the castle, the countess had a clear view to the bottom of the hill. The grass was beginning to show the green of spring. Soon, the first flowers would be in abundance. The countess longed to have the lilacs in bloom, for they were her favorite.

The countess frowned. The knights under Stephen had surrounded the castle for a week. They were trampling the new grass and her lilac bushes. The Exe River ran straight north after making a turn from the northeast close to the site of the castle. The countess nodded approval at the clever placement of the castle on the highest land by her husband's grandfather.

She rolled the name of the castle around in her mind. The sound of Rougemont was like a soft piece of music to her. The countess looked down the green grassy hill that contrasted with the name that meant red hill. Of course, the earth had a reddish cast to it. Mayhap that is why the name had been derived. Mayhap it was from blood that had been spilled here.

Stephen was coming, she was certain of it. He had to come and try to take what he thought was his. The knights that had charged in ahead of Stephen pointed out how little control he had over his own men. The countess clamped her teeth together. She was determined to do all that she could to protect Rougemont from Stephen for her Lady Matilda. Her husband had left her in charge when he went out for one last time to get grain. It was unfortunate that the siege had begun while he was outside the castle walls.

Had it only been a month since Easter? Had it only been two months since her husband took this castle back from Stephen, brought in the knights, and fortified it? They had been conspicuous in their absence from Stephen's Easter court.

Her thoughts were broken by sounds of running and the heavy door banged against the stones. She turned in time to see a young man burst through the door followed by her two sons. She smiled at the sight of the strong sons of a strong father. Edgar and Arwyn were not twins, but were often mistaken for each other. Both had the blond hair, light blue eyes, and ruddy complexion of their Saxon ancestors from their mother's family. The countess had noted on many an occasion that her sons were like her in coloring. In them, she could see her father and her brothers. Edgar, the oldest by thirteen months, was taller, and Arwyn had a heavier body mass.

The countess was proud of them both, and she had spoiled them, but it did not seem to matter. Their dispositions were cheerful and both were such natural leaders that they were never at a loss for followers.

"Countess! Countess de Redvers!" A young knight pushed his way into the room and bowed down before the countess, but did not stop his narration as was customary. "The King and his army are coming! I see them across the long field. King Stephen's standard bearer carries a cross pattee of gules on a field of white with gules and white streamers. I know that to be the king's colors. The two hundred men who hold us in siege are about to be joined by thousands more. I can not believe it, but I saw the standard of Robert of Gloucester."

"Arise, my good knight, and tell me something I did not expect. It is well known that when my husband seized the Castle of Exeter that King Stephen would not stand by in idleness. We have been well fortified, for my husband prepared for such an invasion." Countess de Redvers waved her hand as if to shoo away a fly. "It is a fact of life."

"You see, my mother is ready for war and though my father is sequestered in his castle on the Isle of Wight, he left this castle in capable hands. " Edgar fitz Baldwin said.

"We have no need to fear the siege. The springs run full even in the summer. The castle garrison will fight long and hard for my mother. She has been kind to them. You are too new to know this, but ask the others," Arwyn fitz Baldwin said.

"So let King Stephen come with his soldiers. We are safe on our hill behind the hand hewn stones. Let the firebrands fall on us, for the youngsters in this castle have instructions on how to put out the fires." Countess de Redvers signaled the young man that he was free to leave. He backed toward the door and stopped. "If I may ask, why were you not surprised about Robert of Gloucester's alliance with the king?"

"I can not answer that without betraying a confidence. You may go." The Countess de Redvers watched as the young man left, closing the door behind him.

"Do you think we can hold off the king's men?" Arwyn watched his mother's eyes.

Unflinching, the countess answered her son. "It is possible, but unlikely, for eventually we will run out of supplies. We can only hope that Robert of Gloucester keeps his word to us as we have to his sister. We must be prepared to fight if Stephen loses patience with a siege." The countess looked from one son to another. It was obvious from their faces that they were ready.

Autumn leaves fell throughout the woods and rustled under Dancer's feet as Matilda led the way down a path. Geoffrey was behind her, riding his bay mare. A discreet distance in front and behind them, rode an entourage of Geoffrey's knights. Matilda did not like their presence, but she tolerated them. It would be disastrous if she were kidnaped by Stephen's forces. All would be lost, for she would have no hope of escaping Maithilde's clutches. Matilda grimaced at the thought of Stephen's wife. The day was too beautiful to ruin by thoughts of her.

"How does it feel to be riding in spite of your injury, Geoffrey?"

"It feels good to be free of that dreary castle. It is a wonderful day for a ride, and soon I shall be in fine fighting shape again. It surprises me how one injured foot can take so long to heal and be such an impairment to one's fighting skills."

"I, too, am very happy to rid of the castle walls. I never thought you would heal. My best medicines were not very good." Matilda turned in the saddle to look over her shoulder. She rode astride like a warrior and could not see Geoffrey well. She watched the horse's gait and smiled at the improvement in Geoffrey's abilities.

Geoffrey pointed abruptly. "Look! Someone comes."

Both pulled back on the reins of their horses and waited for the rider.

"There are others with him. I hope we have not been ambushed." Matilda laid a hand on the dagger hidden in her sleeve and looked about for the knights who accompanied them.

"He sees us and waves. Mayhap it is a friend," Geoffrey said.

"We need a friend." Matilda stood in the stirrups and watched the rider as he came closer. He rode slowly and slumped in the saddle. As he got closer, Matilda could see his grey hair. He could not be too dangerous. "Greetings to you, Stranger."

"I, a stranger? Surely you have not forgotten so quickly one of your father's best friends and a supporter to Empress Matilda, rightful heir to the throne?" The grey-haired man stopped before her.

Matilda stared at him. She removed her hand from the hidden dagger. "Sir Baldwin de Redvers! And what brings you to my husband's lands? How did you get to Anjou without one of our knights telling us of your coming? Who is with you?"

"My faithful friends, who will be faithful to Empress Matilda and Count Geoffrey, are with me. My warring knights, who wish to strike at Stephen who tries to claim Normandy, have followed me here. No call of king to him from me, but usurper who takes what is not his to take. We have come, my lady, to help you reclaim what is yours." Sir Baldwin bowed his head.

"My most humble thank you is hardly enough. Please, you and your men must join us in Geoffrey's castle. Tell us of news from England while we ride." Matilda pulled on Dancer's reins, and he turned, tossing his head and nickering softly. Dancer flared his nostrils and inhaled the scent of strange animals.

"It is good of you to join us in our efforts. My humble castle is open to you for as long as you wish. Now tell of why you are here and how it came to be," Geoffrey said.

Sir Baldwin looked back over his shoulder at the three knights behind him and motioned for them to follow. Matilda was glad to see that Geoffrey's knights were alert and studied Sir Baldwin's movements carefully. The old count settled in his saddle riding between Geoffrey and Matilda. The three struck up a leisurely walking pace for ease of conversation and for Sir Baldwin, always a good story teller, who paused until he was certain that he had his hosts' attention.

"It was my desire to take back some of the castles that Stephen had taken from the rightful heir to the throne, so I decided on Castle Exeter mainly because of the springs inside that normally would have been impervious to a siege, but alas . . ."

"Why do you say it normally would have been impervious to a siege?" Matilda leaned forward to better hear the tale.

"The drought of last summer dried up our springs until there was but a trickle of water. I have never seen such dry, sun scorched lands. Dust covered everything, but I am getting ahead of my tale of woe."

"Go on," Geoffrey said.

"I had many men who helped lay in supplies to offset the siege that would certainly come. My dear wife and two sons are instructed in warfare. I thought that one last trip into the countryside for grain was necessary, but I did not expect a traitor to go to Stephen and tell of my plans. I was outside the castle when a force of two hundred imprisoned the countess in Exeter Castle. I could do nothing without being captured, so I left to find my good friend, Judhael de Totnes."

"Judhael de Totnes?" Matilda could see Judhael de Totnes and her father, heads together, discussing affairs of state. It was sad to think that those scenes could never again be played. "A good friend to my father as well."

Geoffrey smiled at Matilda. "Yes, and a supporter of yours. I am told he swore an oath to you before your father, not once, but twice."

Sir Baldwin nodded. "That is true. He supports Matilda. I called on him for help. In the meantime, the two hundred men were able to secure the town of Exeter, but not the castle, for my wife was doing well and it held. However, Stephen came himself with hundreds of men, including your brother, Robert of Gloucester."

"My brother? Are you certain of that? How odd." Matilda pursed her lips.

"Not so, when you hear the rest of the tale." Sir Baldwin continued. "For weeks my wife held the castle from the enemy. Acting on information supplied by Robert, Judhael de Totnes and his men managed to blend themselves into Stephen's army and undetected, got a message into the castle to the countess. At a pre-arranged time, the countess ordered a sortie of arrows and firebrands to rain down on Stephen's army. All the men who followed Judhael in support of our Empress were able to slip into the castle."

"Stephen has many problems. He does not have the support he thinks he has. Good news for us." Geoffrey laughed.

"Judhael had enough men to help in the holding of the castle. They were a welcome relief to the weary knights and the fighting was renewed with vigor." Sir Baldwin spurred his tired horse.

Matilda slowed Dancer to keep abreast of Sir Baldwin. "There are more spies than just my brother. Else there would not have been such an easy time in entering the castle."

"True, my lady. Many men fight for you and hate Stephen. They feel that you have more of a head for the doings of the country and a better eye for battle than has he. Besides, our King Henry wished it so." Sir Baldwin bowed his head again.

"On with your story. We are impatient for news," Geoffrey said.

"The lack of water forced the countess to give in, but not until three months had passed. It was not until after the huge wine cellars were completely dry that she had to surrender in order to prevent the many deaths of our loyal friends."

Matilda grinned. "Wine? How very clever."

Sir Baldwin chuckled. "That she is. She ordered all the cooking to be done with wine, bread was made with it, men washed in it, and it was even used to put out the small fires from the firebrands that the enemy lobbed over the walls."

"She is a strong woman, and I admire her as I do my own strong woman." Geoffrey winked at Matilda.

"Even more so, you will think, after I tell you the next part." Sir Baldwin shifted in his saddle, then swatted at a horse fly. "The Bishop of Winchester, Henry, acted like no man of God for he was cruel beyond belief." Sir Baldwin shook a fist at the sky. "The angels wept that day."

"Stephen's brother can be cruel when he sees profit for himself." Geoffrey slowed his pace, for Sir Baldwin's horse could barely place one foot before another.

"He changes sides quickly as it suits him. Do continue for I am most anxious to hear this tale," Matilda said.

"When at last the wine had run its course and was no more, my countess had to send not one, but two envoys to plead their case to Stephen. Both times, in spite of their emaciated frames, sagging skin, and dull eyes, the Bishop of Winchester counseled Stephen to send them away without so much as one word." Sir Baldwin sighed.

"Nor a drop of water to drink," Matilda said.

"You are right. Not a drop of water, not a morsel of bread."

"A most vile bishop." Geoffrey shook his head.

"Next my dear wife did the only thing that she could in order to save those inside Exeter Castle. She came to Stephen with bare feet, ashes smeared about her head and face, and she cried in genuine pity for those she left dying of thirst. She, too, was sent away by Stephen on the advice of Henry, Bishop of Winchester."

Matilda's mouth dropped open. "Henry is an unspeakable devil in God's dress. There are no words that can describe him."

"Were the lives all lost?" Geoffrey asked.

"It was the men of Stephen's own army who begged Stephen to be merciful, for many of the men inside the castle were related closely to the men outside," Sir Baldwin said.

"What could they say that would turn the viper?" Geoffrey slapped a fly on his horse's neck. The fly dropped to the ground.

"They had to appeal to his vanity," Matilda said.

"You are right, my lady. The knights who fought with Stephen said that it should be enough for the castle to be surrendered to him. He should remember his humanity and that he was all-powerful. He did not have to show it through the death of the half-dead. Stephen was also reminded that these were men who had never sworn homage to him personally and were only following my commands," Sir Baldwin said.

"I do not understand this." Geoffrey leaned over to examine the speck of blood on his mount's neck. "How could Stephen's own barons and knights argue that he had no right to expect loyalty?"

"It is curious," Matilda said. "Is his claim to the throne so tenuous that not all subjects are expected to be loyal? I find this heartening."

"It is peculiar. What did Stephen do about the situation?" Geoffrey asked.

"Stephen allowed the men to leave the castle unharmed complete with their arms. His brother, Bishop Henry, was livid and swore that Stephen was making an unpardonable mistake."

Matilda laughed. "I have to agree with Bishop Henry this time."

Sir Baldwin nudged his horse. "I have taken this as a sign of weakness. I did enjoy taunting Stephen and his brother by using my castle on the Isle of Wight as a place to attack Stephen's ships because they have to pass close by. Some were fooled by my lights and were ripped apart by the chalk needles that are close to shore. I have sunk many a ship, but alas, I had to flee, for I received word from Robert of Gloucester. . . ."

"My brother? What did he do?" Matilda asked.

"Your brother warned me that Stephen was launching an attack from Southampton to invade my island. I sent my dear countess north to her people, for she can not tolerate the Channel crossing, and here I am with a few faithful men." Sir Baldwin waved his arm back to take in his friends.

Matilda's eyes glistened with excitement. "This is a most interesting story and helpful in explaining the workings of Stephen's inept mind."

"He is weaker than we thought. Mayhap wrenching Normandy from his grasp will not be difficult. He will invade Normandy, which is good, for this means that his forces will be strung across two continents. We should begin our plans for an attack in the spring," Geoffrey said.

"What of my brother? What is he doing at Stephen's court?" Matilda asked.

"Do you not know?" Sir Baldwin's eyes widened in surprise.

"She knows. She is testing you," Geoffrey said.

"Ah." Sir Baldwin nodded. "I have helped him send messages back and forth to our compatriots."

"Is my brother well? I would think he should be careful if he is playing the game of spy." Matilda chewed on her lower lip. If anything happened . . . She refused to finish the thought for fear the fates would hear.

"He will soon be safe, for he has plans to return to his castle at Caen in Normandy. We spoke about it before I came over on the ship," Sir Baldwin said.

"Good. We will meet with Robert soon." Geoffrey's horse jumped from the bite of a fly on his rump, and Geoffrey had to place weight on his sore foot. He groaned.

Matilda sucked in her breath at Geoffrey's obvious pain. "Geoffrey?" He shook his head and she said nothing. Sir Baldwin waited for Geoffrey to right himself. "You will have a chance to meet Stephen as well. I hear that he plans to come to Normandy in the spring to lead the out-landish mercenary army."

"You mean that despicable William of Ypes is still in his employ? I understand the Flemish army he brought to England has done Stephen more harm than good. The English hate the mercenary army from Flanders. So you think they will be here next?" Matilda smiled at the irony of Stephen having to use William of Ypes. It must irritate Stephen to have to rely on his wife's lover. She hoped it pained Stephen. She should have been more aware of how Stephen used people. She did not want to dwell on the past, so she turned her attention back to the conversation between Geoffrey and Sir Baldwin.

"Without a doubt, Stephen will appear on our shores. He has to fight us for Normandy," Geoffrey said.

"With a mercenary army. Mayhap he can not get enough nobles to go against us." Matilda let the reins slacken and Dancer took his head. She pulled him back, causing him to do staccato steps in protest.

"Mayhap not," Sir Baldwin said. "The English hate the Flemish mercenaries and with good cause. They have created a lot of destruction and havoc. Stephen has had many of his own friends turn against him because he brought them over."

"Good. His stupidity helps us." Matilda held the reins tighter.

"Come, you and your men must be tired after your journey," Geoffrey said. "It is but a short distance to our humble castle where we can make certain you have good wine and food and a place to rest."

CHAPTER
XII

STEPHEN PACED BACK AND FORTH in front of the freshly turned garden inside the castle walls at Lisieux. He stopped under a tree and stared through the branches that crisscrossed the grey March sky like a black spider web. No hint of spring yet showed in the skies of Normandy. Stephen pulled his fur-lined, woolen cloak tighter about his shoulders. A cold breeze from the north ruffled his hair and he shivered. His feet were cold even though he had put on boots lined with fur that matched his cape.

At times he wondered why he wanted to take Normandy from Geoffrey and Matilda. It had been a damp and miserable spring, and he wished he were anywhere but here. The political advantage did not seem to make up for the physical discomfort. He wished he could count on Robert of Gloucester to take and hold Normandy for him, but he had not seen any overt sign of real support from Robert. He tried to think about Robert's personality and what he might be thinking, but the thoughts became jumbled. He did not understand people.

He shook his head to clear thoughts that felt like cobwebs, twisting and threading their way around his mind and blocking out any sense he had made of things. He wished he were back in England where the people treated him like their king instead of being forced to be in Normandy where the barons were cold-hearted. They were too quiet whenever he talked with them, and it made him nervous. He was a simple man used to straight talk and straight answers. The barons in Normandy did not talk. How could he know what they were thinking? A group of them had left less than an hour ago. They had met with him for two days, including Robert of Gloucester, and Stephen knew them no better than before. He had summoned William of Ypes to meet him hoping that he better understood their taciturn manner.

Stephen kicked a wayward clod of dirt back toward the garden and watched as it crumbled. He was irritated that he had to depend on William for advice, but there seemed to be no other person who would tell him the truth. Stephen was aware that William enjoyed telling him the truth if it were unpleasant. Well, he had some truths for William that were unpleasant and for once, the tables would be turned.

Stephen looked up as a shadow fell across his path. He waved his hand to dismiss the bow that he knew would be cursory at best. "Good day, William." Stephen's eyes narrowed. He would enjoy complaining to William. "We have need to discuss your army. I have been advised by the Norman nobles that your men's behavior is despicable. I hold you responsible for the army that you command, and I expect immediate changes. Stop your men from their pillage and mayhem. It was abhorrent in England and is so here in Normandy. I can not placate my Norman supporters much longer. We must make ready to fight Geoffrey of Anjou and Matilda."

William stood in front of Stephen, his arms folded across his broad chest. "My men are anxious to fight, and we should be doing so instead of sitting around this place eating, drinking, and getting soft. They spend half the night gambling with knuckles and bones, then sleep half the day. Whenever we try to take them out and about the countryside to practice war, the Normans complain. If the Normans had any sense, they would join us in full force with armies instead of supporting us with words that can not kill."

William of Ypes spit on the ground. "We should attack the Count and Countess of Anjou instead of waiting for them to come here to push us out. My men are trained warriors and need activity. Your Norman supporters expect us alone to attack Geoffrey to re-gain their castles."

"That is not the issue. Control your men. They act like barbarians."

"You need to control your own men who act as spies while pretending to support you."

Stephen felt his face getting red. William's manner was insolent and it rankled him to the point where Stephen could no longer be civil. "What do you mean?"

"I am talking about the brother of your enemy."

"Brother of my enemy? Robert of Gloucester? Why do you accuse him of spying?" Stephen asked.

"Because he is. Why do you think he brought his army to Exeter to 'help' you with the Countess de Redvers and sent not one man in to fight?"

"We were strong enough without his men. He merely gave me the honor."

William spat at Stephen's feet. "An honor hollow of meaning. How did Judhael of Totnes manage to mingle with your men and get inside the castle? He had the help of Robert of Gloucester."

"Absurd."

"Think you that because you broke an oath to Matilda twice over that all men do the same? Robert is an honorable man and unlike you, he has kept his promise to Countess Matilda." William's look was contumelious. "Do you believe he would choose you above his own sister whom he has protected all his life?"

Stephen felt his face get hotter. "I find these accusations difficult to believe. I demand more respect from you. Remember that I have the ultimate power of life and death over you, so do watch your insults. They have not gone unnoticed."

William bowed. "So sorry your majesty. I have listened too much to your wife."

Stephen raised his fist and held it in front of William's face. Stephen no longer tried to control his hatred, and his eyes flamed with loathing.

"You may fight against me or with me," William said. "I would suggest that at the rate you are losing supporters, I am more valuable to you than Robert. He is the spy, not I."

Stephen lowered his fist, turned from William, and stared at the barren branches of the trees. He clasped his hands behind his back and paced before speaking. "I shall set a trap for Robert. I will send word for him to join me within the month to help with the battle plans against his sister. As soon as Robert arrives from Caen, he will be executed as a traitor to the crown."

Stephen smiled grimly. "You will be happy to do the deed, I assume."

"I will do the deed as long as I am not included on the list of traitors, your majesty."

"Then come and drink to our joint success. Geoffrey of Anjou's attacks on my Norman supporters have been vicious and has left many wounded and dead."

"Do you have many supporters left on this continent?" William asked.

"I have a habitual enemy of England turned friend. The King of France has recognized that I am Duke of Normandy rather than Geoffrey."

"Has he sent any troops to fight for you? Has he agreed to shed blood for your cause? His kind of support is worthless."

"He has no need to send troops, for we can manage without him."

"Then his words of support have no strength. It is easy for the King of France to say you are the Duke of Normandy rather than Geoffrey, for it costs him nothing. That kind of support will not last."

Stephen did not want to believe William, but in the back of his mind he had to agree. Stephen pushed the thought away and promptly forgot that he had ever had it. "William, I do not like your implications."

"I am being realistic. Dreams do not win battles."

Thoughts of possible intrigues were giving Stephen a headache. "Enough."

"It is true, Sir Robert. I have heard the both of them with mine own ears, and I have the best of hearing." The young man stood before Sir Robert, at attention, hands held rigidly at his side. He was dressed in a rough tunic of non-descript color, the original color having been obliterated by the stains of daily life. His feet were bare, toughened by the weather and the earth. Next to his feet was a small bundle, similar in color and texture to his tunic.

Robert stared into the boy's light blue eyes. He seemed too young to be counterfeiting, but one never knew in these days of strife. "Why should I believe that one as young as you would walk all the way from Lisieux to Caen to tell me this astonishing news?"

"I got rides from some people, sir, and it is only one day's distance, sir." The blonde haired young man waited for the next question as he had been trained to do.

"Why would you, obviously a son of England, be in Normandy and in the service of Stephen?" Robert asked.

"I was allowed to better myself by accompanying the king on his travels to Normandy. I am now the first assistant to the cook."

"You want to betray the very man who gave you this opportunity? This does not sound like a reliable source." Robert stared at the young face before him.

The boy shuffled his feet. "It was, as I found, a dubious honor. The queen is demanding and difficult. She has been known to send back most of her meals to be prepared again."

Robert laughed, a booming laugh much like his father's. "I admire you for your honest interpretation of personalities. I am not so astute."

The young man shrugged his shoulders. "Thank you."

"What is your name?"

There was a look of pride in his face. "My father is Master Dafid, the head cook to King Henry the First and now head cook to King Stephen, although he has stayed in England. I am Patrick."

"Well, Patrick, why am I to believe you?"

"I feel that since my king, King Henry, wanted his daughter to be the next king that my alliance should be with her, however, I am but an insignificant servant and could do nothing to help her until now." Patrick's gaze never wavered.

"Why do you feel a desire to help the Empress Matilda?"

"I like her. When I was a young boy, she was kind to me and made certain that she tasted the beef I had basted for Christmas Court. She told me she would. Unlike many people, she kept that promise. I would like to repay her."

"All right. I believe you." Robert tugged at his ear as if to make certain it was working properly. "It is to pass that I am to be tricked into joining Stephen at Lisieux, and he will have me executed as a traitor? How ironic that I am to be considered the traitor when he is the usurper. Patrick, it would be safer if you stayed in my care and worked with my cook. Would that be satisfactory?"

Patrick nudged the bag at his feet with his toe. "I brought all my worldly goods, for I am not a supporter of anyone but Empress Matilda. My contributions can not be much."

"Without your keen ears, I would be soon on the far side of the grave. I think your contribution is great. You will be rewarded with a piece of silver and my gratitude."

"Thank you, Sir Robert. You are true royalty in spite of your birth."

Sir Robert was startled at the boy's candor. "You are refreshingly honest."

The June rain was warm and promised that summer was here, but it kept Matilda in the castle instead of outdoors where she had been teaching young Henry to ride. She stood at the door that led outside and looked toward the Western sky, but could see no assurances of a clear afternoon. The clouds still churned in the sky like boiling water. The color was the same as pots with shades of pewter darkening into charcoal. She walked back inside. It had been a boring morning, and there had been no news of Geoffrey's latest foray into Normandy. If it had gone as the rest had, the news, when it came, would be good.

Matilda had barely started across the great hall toward the kitchen when she heard the cry for the gates to be opened. She crossed the room to the windows on the courtyard side and watched as Geoffrey and his knights clattered across the stone paved yard and into the stables. She smiled, for she could tell by their jubilant manner that they had won yet another victory. She continued to the kitchen, ordered a meal to be prepared for the men, and went upstairs to her quarters to await Geoffrey. It would be more than an hour, for it was her husband's habit to bathe and eat before joining her.

She made certain that there was wine. Geoffrey would talk more if he had a good red wine to drink. She added a small log to the fire in the fireplace. In spite of the early summer's warmth, today was damp. She stood and inspected one of the tapestries for signs of the disgusting mildew that she hated. Finding none, she sat next to the table that held her books and picked up the maroon leather one that she had been reading. It was the best way for her to pass the time and soon the story had transported her across the centuries and back to ancient Greece where men fought wars for kingdoms.

Matilda was jerked to the present by the banging of the door as it met the stone wall.

"I am sorry to be so noisy, but I can not contain my exuberance." Geoffrey crossed the room and pulled Matilda from her chair and into his arms. "I have such good news for you, Matti. It will warm your heart."

"Your victory against Stephen is complete?" Matilda's eyes sparkled. "Has he fled Normandy?"

Geoffrey sat and pulled Matilda onto his lap. "Dear lady, do you remember how Stephen's Norman knights resented his use of William of Ypes and his Flemish madmen?"

She slapped the hand that had pinched her bottom through her kirtle. "That is old news, Geoffrey. They took their men and went back to their own castles leaving him without help."

Geoffrey rubbed his hand where Matilda's slap had turned it red. "They had good reason, what with those Flemish mercenaries killing off the good Norman and English men who were supposedly on Stephen's side."

Matilda squirmed until she found a more comfortable position on her husband's lap. "More indication of Stephen's lack of leadership. He could not keep his own army from killing each other. He was stupid to hire William of Ypes' mercenary army." Matilda impulsively kissed her husband on the cheek. "They only have loyalty to silver."

Geoffrey grinned. "Speaking of silver, I have been given two thousand marks by your dear cousin, Stephen, to seal a truce."

Matilda sat up and stared into Geoffrey's eyes. "A truce! But Geoffrey, I do not want a truce, I want Normandy and England. Not a truce! Never would I have agreed to such a thing. Never!"

"We need silver to finance our own assaults into England. I made Stephen give me the year's truce money in advance." Geoffrey pulled Matilda to him.

"It is silver from my father's treasury and thus mine in reality. I hardly find that something to celebrate." Matilda slid off Geoffrey's lap.

Geoffrey held out his hand, palm up. "It is silver in hand, not in a vault in England. Do I not get a thank you for getting this much?"

"Yes, of course. I was just disappointed. It seems that we have made so little progress."

"Does the control of Caen by Robert and Bayeux by me sound better?" Geoffrey asked.

"Is this true?"

"It certainly is. As of now we have recovered a portion of our stolen lands and better yet, Stephen has already boarded his ship and has set sail for England."

"Then Normandy can be ours again." Matilda grabbed Geoffrey by his face and kissed him.

Geoffrey returned her kiss. "He left William de Roumare and Roger of the Cotentin in charge of keeping order. Mayhap we should concentrate on England. We do not have to worry about Normandy. It is as good as ours."

Matilda clapped her hands together and whirled around. "It would be my pleasure to invade England. I think the time is right for a meeting with Robert and a message should be sent to my Uncle David. It would help if he could irritate Stephen from the north."

"An excellent idea to have King David of Scotland attack Stephen on the northern front while we work from the south. I will send for Robert." Geoffrey pulled Matilda back onto his lap. "But first, can you help quench the fires of passion in this lonely soldier?"

Matilda responded by pulling Geoffrey to the floor.

The sounds of battle surrounded King David like the cloud of dust that rose over the plain. Grass had been trampled by men and horses until it no longer existed, making a scar on the earth that would last almost as long as the scars the men would bear from this battle. King David, holding his pole-ax high, the attached banner tattered and listless, rode his war horse back and forth along the thin line of battle.

"You must not fear Stephen's men, for they are no better than you! Arise and fight, my gallant warriors! Let not the sounds of arrows force you to flee. This land was given to Empress Matilda by King Henry. Let us take it from the usurper. Fight!"

"Listen to me, King David! The battle is lost!" Sir Hugh fitz Smith galloped beside King David. "Look at the men. They lie dead, bodies full of arrows from Stephen's men. They can not arise. Save yourself, my King, for we can not go on without you."

"No! I will not. I have to fight to the death. It would be cowardly of me to leave these brave boys!" King David shouted over his shoulder as he urged his tired horse into a trot. "I should die with them, and I will fight to the death."

"You can not die. Scotland needs you. Come with me and we will ride to Carlisle where we will be safe." Sir Hugh shouted over the sounds of metal hitting metal and the screams of the dying soldiers.

"Safe? How can I be safe from God's eyes? I can never be safe." King David reined his horse to the left and galloped down the thin line of battle, oblivious to the arrows that swished past him, but miraculously fell away. He barely noticed Sir Hugh racing after him through the ever present cloud of dust raised by the battling soldiers. King David ignored Sir Hugh's shouts for him to stop. King David knew that even with chain mail, a well placed arrow could kill him, and he wished for the arrow that would bring his end and peace. He had failed his sister's daughter. He had failed in his duties to Empress Matilda.

King David spurred his horse, but Sir Hugh gained pace with him, leaned over, and grabbed the bridle of the King's horse. The horse reared and Sir Hugh's hand was jerked upwards. King David knew that Sir Hugh had to let go before he was thrown from his horse. Taking the opportunity of the moment, King David continued racing down the line of battle, a halo of spent arrows falling around him. He looked over his shoulder in time to see Sir Hugh move his heels into his horse's ribs with a quick jab. The horse leaped sideways, then forward before settling into a run.

King David kicked his own mount in the ribs, but Sir Hugh caught up with him and grabbed the bridle a second time, pulling the horse to a complete stop. Sir Hugh watched him as one might a mad man.

The king's booming voice could be heard over the sounds of battle. "You can not stop me. I am the King of Scotland."

"I stop you because you are the King of Scotland. Without you there is no Scotland. If you think there is death now, wait until Stephen fights your son for your own lands. There will be death that you could have prevented. Come with me. Sound the retreat," Sir Hugh shouted.

King David nodded. "Sound the retreat."

Sir Hugh rode along the front line to the bugler. As the notes for retreat drifted across the battlefield, he returned to King David and galloped away with the reins of King David's horse in his possession. The king was forced to grasp the saddle, squeeze his knees against the ribs of his horse, and hang on as best he could. When they were far enough away so that a stray arrow would not hit them, and the noise was muted, Sir Hugh stopped.

"I will not abide your audacious manner any longer." King David's voice was harsh. "I have failed my men, my son, and my lady, Matilda. I am not fit to live."

"It would be the coward's way out to die. Your pain would be eased, but hundreds, nay thousands of men would suffer after you. Women would weep and wail for lost husbands and lost sons. The war would continue without you to lead us to peace."

As King David looked back at the rows of knights and Scottish tribesmen trooping back toward Scotland with heads down, he felt guilt rise until it nearly choked him. "I have failed my oath to King Henry and to Empress Matilda. I can not be king."

"You have to be king. Scotland can not be Scotland without its king. Come, let us ride to Carlisle and we will rest, then we will talk. Your son will join us as soon as he is able."

King David allowed Sir Hugh to lead his horse. It was easier to let others make the decisions.

The reins were returned to King David when Sir Hugh seemed satisfied that he acquiesced to the trip. The king was glad that Sir Hugh respected his feelings, and both men rode, heads down without speaking for the rest of the day and into the night, leading what remained of their army northward to safety. The unnatural silence made the army appear ghost-like to the peasants who observed the dark shadows slide past them. To the king, even the August night seemed to exude a depressed and phantom-like air. The moon was partially hidden behind dark clouds, and there were no stars to guide the riders to the castle gates.

King David gave the signal for the commander of the guard to open the gates, and the army rode in without the usual joyous cries of victory. Quietly, the men were given food and a place to rest, the horses groomed, watered, and fed without any questions about the battle. Bad news could wait.

The sun forced its way through the night, breaking it apart as King David stood at the window and watched nothing. The rays of light sprayed across the rolling hills and illuminated the king. He blinked and turned from the window. Sir Hugh watched him.

"It was a terrible battle, and I could do nothing to save those bare-chested men from the arrows of Stephen's army."

"The Scottish barbarians were doomed by their primitive beliefs and the promises of their equally barbaric magician. You could do nothing to convince them they were not invincible," Sir Hugh said.

King David's sigh became a shudder. "I should have refused to let them go into battle with me. They are not trained in warfare of this type. They refuse to wear armor, and I should have refused to let them fight."

"That would have been an insult to them. They are your people, also. To deny them the right to fight for Scotland, for your son, and for Empress Matilda would have said to them that they were not true citizens."

"A pity. There were many youthful men who will not have wives or children to carry their names into the future. How can I tell the people that their future has died on the battlefield in defeat; that my shame will live into history?" King David's voice faltered.

"The shame of Stephen will live on far longer, for he betrayed a king's trust and usurped the crown of England. He took what he promised to help the Empress keep. You may have lost a battle, but you are still an honorable man. That you are an honorable man will carry more weight in the pages of history."

"Honor will not save a country, unfortunately, and neither will honor save me. I am too old to lose battles. To see men die hurts me more the older I get."

Sir Hugh nodded. "It is because with age we must confront our own mortality."

The air coming in through the open window was chilly and reminded Matilda that another winter was on its way. She leaned over and pulled shut the window. Yet another winter was on her without a chance to invade England to reclaim the crown; another winter with Stephen spending her treasury to kill her friends; another winter to remember broken promises.

"Mother, you look like you are going to cry. Are you going to cry?" young Henry asked.

"I will not cry, but I am sad. Some bad things have happened to our friends."

"Give me a sword and I will kill the bad people." The prince swung an imaginary, two-handed sword above his head and brought it down with real force against his mother's enemy.

The noises he uttered convinced Matilda that the enemy was indeed dead. She held out her arms and Henry ran to her. "Some day you will have a chance to kill all the enemies you want, but until you are older, I must do it." She held him so tightly in her arms that Henry started to squirm. She let him go.

"Why?"

"Because a very bad man broke his promise to your grandfather, King Henry, and he will pay for that broken promise." Matilda kissed the top of Henry's head. At times like these, her heart was filled with so much love that it felt as if it would burst.

"Who is the bad man? I want to kill him." The prince's eyes were wide as he stared at his mother.

She looked into eyes that were a reflection of her own. "You have lived too short a time to think of killing enemies just yet."

"I have lived a long time," young Henry said.

Matilda smiled at her auburn-haired offspring. "Five summers may seem a long time to you, but you will have to wait a few more before you are allowed astride a war horse."

"How many?"

"I know not. It depends on how well I fight," Matilda said.

"Will you kill our enemies?"

"I hope so." Matilda smiled.

"Who will you kill first?" Henry asked.

"I will kill Stephen, for he is our worst enemy."

"Do you hate him?"

Matilda looked at her son. He studied her with the intensity of a priest in confession. "I hate him. He is the usurper and has taken the throne away from me and subsequently from you."

"Who is he? Why did he do that?"

Matilda hesitated. Such questions from one so young. "He is our cousin, and he took the throne because he is weak, and his wife is strong."

"Did you always hate him?"

Matilda blinked rapidly from the surprise of the question and tried to think of a way to answer her son. She did not believe in lying to him. "No, Henry, I did not always hate him, but I do now. He has caused our country and our loyal friends much pain."

"How?"

Matilda sighed. This child was always full of questions, and he would not stop until all questions had been answered to his satisfaction. "It is very complex, but I will explain as best I can. Let us sit by the fire. I think autumn will come early this year."

Without a word, the young prince waited until his mother was seated, as he had been taught, and then flopped himself on a fur rug at her feet.

It amazed Matilda how he could sit like that for hours while she told him the stories from the priests or stories of the family that had been told to her. He was going to be a wonderful king, mayhap one of the finest. She sat in a brocaded chair and arranged her kirtle to cover her ankles and keep out the ever-present draft.

"The usurper, Stephen, was once a . . . a very good friend. He made promises to your grandfather and to me that he did not keep. Many friends have died or have been defeated in battle. I sometimes wonder at God's plan."

"Who has died in battle, Mother?"

"A Count named Ernulf was hanged along with ninety-three of our loyal friends. He was very old, nearly eighty years he had been on this earth. I was told that my friend, William fitz Alan, the castellan of the Castle Shrewsbury had declared his support again for me, and so Stephen attacked the castle. William fitz Alan's Uncle Ernulf convinced him to flee to Scotland with his wife and children," Matilda said.

"Was he a coward?" Henry asked.

"No. One of the most difficult things to learn is when to retreat so that the war may be won in spite of the battle being lost. Count Ernulf knew that in order to help me, he had to let William fitz Alan and his family flee. Count Ernulf defended the castle well, but to no avail for it fell to Stephen." Matilda stared into the fire. The flames showed her a story of an old, but proud man who gave his life so that her father's dream might live.

"Mother! Mother!"

Matilda looked down at her feet where Henry was seated, tugging at her kirtle.

"Is Stephen a coward for hanging an old man?" Henry asked.

"Stephen is finally acting like a man, although 'tis a pity he chose Count Ernulf's death as a way to prove his manhood."

"I will pray for Count Ernulf's soul," Henry said.

"That would be kind of you."

"Are you also sad about King David?" Henry asked.

Matilda looked at her son in surprise. "What do you know of King David?"

"I heard the knights talking about it."

"Were you in the great hall again bothering everyone?"

"Not everyone, Mother. I only listened to the best knights who tell the best stories." Henry's eyes were wide.

Matilda laughed. "I see. And who are the best knights?"

"The ones who win, of course." Henry looked at her as if she had no common sense. "They said that Uncle David was a broken man. Is he broken like my good bow?"

"He is not broken exactly like your bow. King David is very unhappy because his men were not well-trained and they were killed. Stephen won a battle that was very important to us."

"Did we lose the war?"

"No, but we are farther from winning than we were before. It will be a long and difficult winter, for I have to wait for a better time to invade England."

"I want to go with you when you 'vade England."

Matilda leaned down and brushed a strand of hair from Henry's forehead. "Let us hope that you are still too young."

England in December was bitterly cold in the year 1138, and Stephen pulled his woolen cloak tighter about his shoulders as he stood before the fireplace in his apartment.

"I do not wish to see my brother. Send him away." The servant opened the door just enough to slip out without letting warm air escape to the cold corridor. Before the servant could shut the door, it was pushed open by Henry, Bishop of Winchester. The door banged back against the solid rock wall and Stephen winced as the bishop stepped inside.

The bishop glanced around the room before he slammed the heavy door shut. Stephen waited, not knowing whether to summon the guards or not. Stephen reached for his knife, but hesitated. The likelihood that Henry would have the audacity to assassinate him was remote. He waited for the color to fade from his brother's purple face. When it did not, Stephen thought that mayhap Henry would die. The thought was not unpleasant for it would spare Stephen the confrontation he was trying to avoid.

"You . . . you . . . ungrateful bastard, you are unfit to rule!" The Bishop's face was still dark and his hands were at his side, clutching his robes. "The Empress Matilda has more honor than you!"

"You are not to speak to the king unless spoken to."

"You are no king, merely an usurper, an oath breaker. I should have known that once you broke an oath to Matilda, you would soon break your oath to me."

Stephen stepped back. "I swore no oath to you."

"You agreed to make me Archbishop of Canterbury. Do not lie to me, for God knows who tells the truth here."

Stephen felt trapped. He had not wanted to face Henry, but here he was asking questions and making accusations that Stephen could not defend. "I agreed to nothing. You kept talking and talking about it incessantly. For more than two years since our last Archbishop died, you have hinted and nearly begged. . . ."

Bishop Henry stepped closer to Stephen and in a soft, but savage whisper he said, "I did not need to beg from my own brother, did I?"

This time Stephen refused to step back. He could feel his brother's hot breath on his face. "It is better that I placed Theobald of Bec in that position, for he is feared by no one."

"Of course not. He is too stupid." Bishop Henry spat out the words.

"Unlearned, but not stupid. He will not try to run the kingdom." Stephen held his breath, waiting for Henry's reaction.

"He is hardly educated well enough to have such an important position. He can barely read Latin, knows no French, and has never learned to read English." Bishop Henry's face darkened. "He is totally unsuitable."

"He will be an asset to me." Stephen could no longer tolerate being this close to Henry, and he stepped away from his brother.

"This ridiculous decision shows that you are incapable of making proper ones. If it had not been for my advice, you would not be as far as you are now and you do know that." Bishop Henry closed the narrow gap between them.

"You did nothing but yap at me like a barking dog. 'Do this, do that.' Always you were at my elbow telling me to whom I should lay siege, and whom I should hang. You would not allow me a moment to think on my own." It was Stephen's turn to have the color rush to his face.

"I had to tell you these things, for you were in danger of losing whatever you had gained. Your chivalry was taken as a sign of weakness by enemy and friend alike."

"I do not believe you."

"After my advice to hang Ernulf your men were quicker to obey. Do not deny it, for you yourself remarked about it. And where is Ernulf today? He is in another world where he will not bother you by attacking your backside when it is uncovered." The Bishop moved away from Stephen and the heat of the fire.

"Ernulf was a good man. It was difficult to make that decision."

"You did not make that decision. I did. Had you been left to make it, he would have lived as you let Count Baldwin de Redvers survive."

"What harm did Count Baldwin do? I have his castle."

Bishop Henry rolled his eyes toward the ceiling. "What good did that do you? He went on to plunder your ships from his castle on the Isle of Wight, and he has crossed over to side with Matilda. He will be a continuous threat to you and the throne."

"The only reason you want to be Archbishop of Canterbury is so that you could be second in command." Stephen loosened his cloak. The room seemed suddenly too hot.

"I do not deny that," Bishop Henry said. "It is the rightful place for the king's brother."

"It is dangerous for the king."

Bishop Henry stared at his brother until Stephen glanced away. "You know not what danger is. If I choose, I could be much more dangerous to you if I sided with Matilda than if I were Archbishop of Canterbury."

"Treason does not become you." Stephen removed his cloak and tossed it on a bench. He wished he had made Henry Bishop of Canterbury. It would be preferable to this meeting. He felt the sweat trickle down his back.

"It is not treason to follow King Henry's wish and side with his chosen ruler of England." Bishop Henry sat down on the chair beside him and looked up at his brother. "You see, I sit, for I do not think you are the real king of England."

"You can not sit in the presence of the king unless invited to do so." Stephen's rage obliterated rational thought. He clamped his lips together in colorless anger.

"I have no king as of this moment. Do not try to murder me, for I have more friends than you do. Oh, I did forget. You are too weak to murder your enemies." Bishop Henry peered at Stephen.

"I could kill you right now."

"No, for that would take a decision to kill. You do not have the courage to be king. You waited until I was out of town to choose the Archbishop of Canterbury." Bishop Henry rose and moved toward the door. "I have no need of your kind of king. Empress Matilda has more courage." Before he could be dismissed, Bishop Henry was out the door. It closed heavily behind him.

Stephen stomped across the room and pounded his fist against the closed door. He should have his brother murdered, but he knew he would not.

CHAPTER
XIII

VEN IN THE DARK Matilda could see the shores of England. She gripped the wooden railing tighter and leaned forward. The water slapped rhythmically against the timbered bow as the ship glided silently toward shore. The spray drenched Matilda's kirtle below her heavy cape, but she did not feel anything. She looked to her left and could barely see the two dozen boats that were in tandem with hers.

She did not notice Robert standing next to her until she saw his hands on the railing. "How long have you been here?" Matilda asked.

"A long time. You had such a look of joy on your face that I could not disturb you. You appear child-like as if the greatest gift in all the world had been given you." Robert put his arm around Matilda's shoulder.

"I am about to receive the world itself. I can hardly believe that we invade England at long last. I am happy, even though I expect the task to be difficult and fraught with heartache. It is a sobering thought to have England divided. I blame Stephen for that."

"It has been four years since our father died. That is a short time in the scheme of things, but such a long time in our lives," Robert said.

Matilda leaned against her brother. She shivered even though his warmth permeated her cloak. "You are certain that Adelicia expects us."

"Yes, I sent many messages to Arundel Castle. How convenient it is that she is on the coast. Her new husband, Count William de Albini, made certain Stephen's spies are told we plan to follow William the Conqueror's lead and land at Hastings. We said that you were a sentimental woman and wanted to follow in your grandfather's footsteps."

Matilda's laughter floated out to sea and was lost in the wind. "It is true that I wish to follow my grandfather's lead and invade England."

"So you shall. We have bribed Stephen's sentries in case Stephen thinks of Adelicia's castle. Of course, Sir Baldwin de Redvers is nearby with his knights on his well-fortified Isle of Wight." Robert squeezed his sister. "I know we can be successful, for Stephen has made many enemies, including his own brother, Bishop Henry."

"Stephen has been stupid enough to turn other bishops against him by devious means. Even that stupid traitor, Roger of Salisbury, will never get over his near death from Stephen's treachery. Imagine thinking that the fat old boy was against him. I had heard from Adelicia that Roger was involved in a plot to assassinate King Henry," Matilda said.

"I have always wondered about that plot. He does not seem intelligent enough to have been involved directly." Robert looked into the darkness. "I was told that Maithilde could not wait to be queen, and that she instigated the plot."

"Adelicia should have insisted that Stephen and Maithilde be beheaded. It would have saved us a lot of trouble." Matilda rubbed the salt spray from her cheek. It felt gritty. She licked the salt from her lips.

"She probably did not want to execute Stephen for fear you would never speak to her again," Robert said.

Matilda jerked her head around to stare at Robert. "Is my love affair with Stephen going to haunt me throughout my campaign for the throne? How was I to know that it would cost me a kingdom?"

"No one could have foreseen the future, Matti."

"Mayhap, but I should not have been so weak. It will never happen again." Matilda leaned forward and looked toward land. A dark outline seemed larger than before. She felt her heart beat faster. "Is that a light I see?"

Robert leaned over the railing. "Where? I see nothing."

"I see nothing now. Mayhap I wished too much for land," Matilda said.

"No! Look, there is a light. It is higher than we are. I do not understand," Robert said.

"Is it a signal?"

"I hope not, for that would mean trouble. We did not plan to have any signals in order to avoid suspicion."

Robert leaned forward as if to see better. Matilda smiled to herself. "Then it has to be the castle. I would guess that Adelicia has prepared for our coming and has a bonfire on top of the walls. Dear Adelicia. I have not seen her for so long that now the time is near, I am close to tears."

Robert brushed a strand of wet hair away from Matilda's sea dampened face. "You must be very tired."

"I am too excited to be tired. I may never see the other side of consciousness again." Matilda gripped the railing and leaned out farther.

"You are a strong woman." Robert kissed her cheek.

"Secretly, I am afraid, but not for my own life." Matilda placed a hand on the kissed cheek.

"You fear for your sons," Robert said.

"How did you know?"

"I fear for my daughter and her husband." Robert's whisper was almost lost to the wind.

"I am sorry that I involved you and your family."

"I would not have been a happy subject to Stephen, for he is not the true ruler of England. I have to follow my conscience, and furthermore, I love you too much to ever desert you. I should have known you would be a leader, for you used to lead me around when you were a little girl."

"Robert, I am certain I did not." Matilda smiled at the thought.

Robert placed his hand over Matilda's lips. "You must be quiet now for we come close to the shore and our voices carry on the wind."

Matilda nodded. The flapping of the sails gave way to the sounds of creaking as the sails were lowered. Matilda placed a hand over her heart to deaden the noise of its loud and rapid beating. She did not know she was not breathing until she became dizzy. She took in great gulps of salty air and noticed the smell of damp earth near the sea. She imagined that England smelled even fresher and more wonderful than either Normandy or Anjou. She let a tear slide unnoticed down her cheek.

The sound of grating brought her from her reverie. Several men jumped from the boat to pull it ashore. England! She was home.

Matilda stepped through the archway and watched the light move toward her across the great room. She forgot the chill of the trip across the channel, the fear of the deaths to come, and the battles ahead. She felt safe. She wanted to forget the present and the future and slip into the past.

The candle light was too bright for her eyes and she blinked, but it was welcomed nevertheless after the boat ride through the dark. Matilda did not have time to get used to the brightness before she was enveloped in the arms of her step-mother.

"Matti, how I have waited and prayed for this day."

"And I, too," Matilda said.

"Please, I have made your bed with mine so that we may talk the night through like two young girls, for I knew that you would not be able to sleep." Adelicia hugged Matilda.

"You know me too well." Matilda held Adelicia's frail body gently. "I wish we were never apart." Matilda leaned back and looked at Adelicia. "Do I detect a glow? You seem to shine from within. Is it your husband, William, who makes you this way? Where is he? I must meet him."

"He and Miles of Gloucester are out telling lies about where you are to land. They also patrol the shore to keep Stephen's sentries away." Adelicia slipped her hand into Matilda's.

"You love him very much, do you not?" Matilda asked.

"I have been twice blessed. Some women never know one love. I have loved and been loved two times." Adelicia led her step-daughter across the great room and up the stone staircase that hugged the inside wall of the room. At the top they moved past two other doors before stopping at the third. Adelicia tapped lightly. At Matilda's questioning look, she smiled. "You will see."

The door was opened by a nurse and at that sight, Matilda's mouth dropped open. "I do not believe it!"

"Believe it, for you will in the middle of the night when she cries for my breast. I am like you and did not want a wet nurse. She is hungry all the time. I could not send you a message to tell you of her birth. I did not want to take a chance that someone might see the messenger and know that we were still on good terms."

The two women moved across the room toward the cradle. Matilda leaned down and pulled back the comforter. The flickering light from the fireplace made shadows across a tiny face. Matilda tilted the cradle until she could see the infant in better light. "She is beautiful."

"I named her Hope because that is what we need right now."

Matilda smiled. "You are happy."

"Yes, and I plan to have several more babies. I no longer have to fear for their lives."

Matilda sighed. "It must have been difficult for you while married to my father."

"No, Matti. I loved him more than life itself. I lost a part of myself when King Henry died. I suppose I am trying to get a piece of myself back by having babies."

Matilda knelt down and placed her slender finger next to the baby's chubby hand. "Look, Adelicia. Little Hope has taken hold of me. May I hold her?"

"Of course." Adelicia picked up the baby, and put her in Matilda's arms. "I will tell her of Empress Matilda, ruler of England, who held her this most important night."

"How odd that you should talk of this night as making history. I suppose that it will become part of the story tellers' repertoire." Matilda gazed at the baby in her arms. She felt a pang of loneliness that she knew could only be eased by her own children.

"You have successfully invaded England. It will be just a short while before you are on the throne." Adelicia's eyes were bright with tears. "There are many barons and earls who have been angered by Stephen's outlandish actions. They have come over to your side. It is an impressive list."

A draft from the opening of the door caused Matilda to turn away in order to protect the baby. She looked over her shoulder and watched Robert and Miles enter with a stranger following them. Matilda stared at the tall, thin man who towered above her brother and Miles. The stranger's curly, brown hair wrapped itself around his head like a sheep skin. His long nose seemed to fit in with the thinness of his face. At first, he did not look handsome, but as Matilda continued studying him, he appeared better looking. She decided it was his eyes. They were intelligent and observant and made up for any flaws.

"Robert and Miles with a stranger in tow. Who might this be?" Matilda whispered to Adelicia.

"Why, Matilda, that is my very dear husband." Adelicia crossed to William, took his hand, and led him to her step-daughter. "Matti, I would like you to meet my dear William. He has sworn to help you in any manner possible."

William bowed. "My lady, it is an honor to have you in our castle. I am your humble servant."

"You have already done a great service to me and I thank you for it." Matilda extended her hand, holding Hope in one arm.

"My pleasure." William kissed her hand.

The baby grabbed Matilda's dark braid and the adults laughed. Matilda laid her in the cradle and covered her with a linen sheet that had been embellished by Adelicia's embroidery. Matilda ran her hand across the colorful threads and smiled at the memory of Adelicia trying to teach her the fine art without much luck. Mayhap she would have a better student in little Hope.

Robert took Matilda's hands in his. "We have good news for you. There are many barons who have sent word to William that they are ready to support you."

"Wonderful. Who might these honorable men be?" Matilda found comfort in Robert's hands. She liked the feeling of warmth and strength.

"I do believe that Roger, Bishop of Salisbury, is one of your supporters."

"Really? How interesting. Can Bishop Roger be trusted or does he continue to be a spy? I would not want to give Stephen any advantage."

Miles of Gloucester spoke. "William and I have made some inquiries and the story has been the same from several good sources."

Matilda was surprised to hear Miles speak since it was a rarity for the quiet man who was a discerning observer and an invaluable advisor to her. "What stories?"

"It seems that Stephen's advisor convinced him that Bishop Roger was plotting against him and supporting you. Bishop Roger has been busy the last four years building castles in strategic places without leave of Stephen. Waleran of Meulan and his friends used this as proof that he was ready to help you in a war against Stephen."

Matilda chewed on her lower lip while she digested what her father's former constable had told her. "What of Bishop Roger's son, Roger le Poer? Does he follow in his father's footsteps to my side of the invasion?"

"He does." Miles rubbed his bearded chin. "It was he who stocked the castles with provisions and armed men. It has made Stephen nervous, especially since Stephen has run out of King Henry's treasure."

"Treasure!" Matilda exploded. "Stephen stole my treasure and spent it all in his attempt at the throne!"

Robert put his arms around Matilda and held her still. He whispered in her ear. "This is not the place to throw things as I know you do when this angry."

Matilda ended her tirade as quickly as it began, not because Robert stopped her, but the noise had awakened the baby. She immediately felt chagrin. "I am sorry, Adelicia."

Adelicia moved toward her whimpering baby and rocked the cradle. "It is all right, Matti. She will go right back to sleep. When you think of Stephen, instead of being angry that he took the treasure, think of how sad it is that he had to use it to buy people's loyalty. He did have to buy loyalty, you know." Adelicia continued rocking the cradle even though the baby was quiet. "You have others who will come to your aid once it is known that you have invaded."

"Who else can we expect to help us?" Matilda asked.

William cleared his throat. "Many, for Stephen is taking, but he has nothing to give. He has devalued silver and gold. The Barons long for the genius of King Henry through his daughter."

"As the treasure wanes, so does Stephen's power."

Matilda laughed. "Some good must come of his taking from me."

Robert put his hand on his forehead. "William has told us that Stephen ordered the many bishops and barons that are under the protection of his court to attend a council. Stephen argued with the very same bishops and the barons he had vowed to protect. The fight that followed erupted into a small war and Stephen imprisoned them."

"It was the most unchivalrous thing to do. His actions astonished us," William said.

"How I ever loved him. . . ." Matilda said.

"Let us not dwell on the past, Matti, for we have to look to the future. I will take my best knights and leave for Bristol Castle to make contact with our supporters." Robert pulled his cape tighter about him. "We have many men who will fight with us. I need to tell them we have landed."

"I fear for you." Matilda grabbed Robert and leaned against the broad chest of her brother. Robert held her, wrapping his brawny arms around her. The memory of her father's sturdy frame and strong arms flashed before her and left quickly before she could grasp it. "Please be careful. There are spies everywhere."

"I have twelve good men. Brian fitzCount has control of Wallingford to the Northeast. He stands between us and Stephen. Miles has been invaluable in his knowledge of King Henry's true friends. He also knows the terrain so well he could find a black cave at midnight on a moonless night," Robert said.

Matilda giggled at her brother's description. She looked at the dark haired Miles whose cheeks were pink from embarrassment. "I place my faith in you as did my father."

Miles' cheeks got redder. "That is an honor I do not deserve, my lady."

"To the contrary. I do not deserve you." Matilda turned to her brother. "Did you say that Brian fitzCount is a supporter? This information confuses me. He has been to Stephen's court. I was told that Maithilde was quite fond of him."

Robert nodded, his shiny hair glistening in the light from the fire. "It is true that he is in Maithilde's favor, much to his chagrin, but that is to our advantage. We tease him about his charms that enchant Maithilde. Have no fear. You can count on him to be a true supporter of yours and not a fair-weather friend as some will undoubtedly become."

Matilda's memory coasted back to the time that the auburn haired man had pledged his support. "I am glad that dear Brian is still with us."

Robert pulled a map from his pocket and spread it on the table. Miles moved over and held down the western edge while William held down the other side. Robert pointed to the placement of castles. "We also have most of western England, but we will have to fight our way to Windsor Castle."

Matilda looked at the marks on the map that represented towns, castle fortifications, and rivers. "I miss London town. Windsor was always my favorite castle in spite of my being born in Winchester Castle." Matilda felt frustration billow inside until it almost choked her. She stabbed at a mark on the map with her fingernail. "Windsor is mine and I will be in it soon."

"I must congratulate you on your determination and success," Adelicia said.

"Not yet. Wait until I sit upon the throne and wear the crown of my grandfather, William the Conqueror, my uncle, William the Red, and my father, King Henry, the First."

Stephen pulled his horse up short and waited in the forest less than a quarter of a mile from Arundel Castle. A yellow leaf floated down in a zig-zag pattern and brushed against Stephen's arm before it found a place on the ground. Stephen's gaze switched from the leaf to the castle. A few guards could be seen walking along the top of the outer curtain wall, appearing and disappearing as they walked behind the merlons.

The sun was hot, but a cool breeze from the Channel made it a most pleasant day for Stephen. He was close enough to the castle to see the individual stones in varying shades of grey. Some were dark and reminded him of the shadows in the forest and some were nearly white like patches of light. It was a well-built castle. Henry the First had seen to that. He was dead, but in a sense he still protected Matilda through Adelicia. Stephen could appreciate the strength of the castle except that his nemesis was in that castle with over one hundred knights of her own and those who belonged to Adelicia's husband and Robert of Gloucester.

Stephen turned at the sound of hoofs thumping down the path behind him. He looked through the group of his own knights and saw his brother, Bishop Henry, with his own entourage. Stephen rode through his men toward his brother. He hated to have to depend on that arrogant bag of wind. Stephen grimaced because he had to ask Henry for help. He did not have to listen to his advice, however. All Stephen could manage to ask was, "What news?"

Bishop Henry stopped next to Stephen. The ensuing snorting and pawing by the horses kept the Bishop from answering.

The wait did nothing for Stephen's composure. "Did you intercept Robert of Gloucester?" He hated the sound of his voice, for it betrayed his nervousness. He did not want Henry to know he had not felt safe since Matilda had landed in England.

Bishop Henry shrugged. "He has eluded us as the wild wolves often do. He has taken the back trails and has slipped from castle to castle. I am afraid that Empress Matilda has more friends in the western part of England than you do, Brother."

"I hardly think so," Stephen said.

"Do not be so certain about your invincibility. Your army grows tired of receiving devalued silver or sometimes no silver. Your minor wars with the unhappy counts and barons have done nothing to help your cause."

Stephen grabbed Bishop Henry's arm. "You speak as a traitor. I am king. I need have no cause."

"I speak as one who sees the truth. I see another problem since Empress Matilda has managed to invade England." Bishop Henry jerked his arm away from his brother's grasp.

"I hardly call her presence an invasion."

"How absurd you are. Empress Matilda comes here intent upon wrenching the crown from your grasp, and you do not think she has invaded? She came with over one hundred knights. Her brother and his knights, and who knows how many others, plan to join her. You delude yourself if you do not think this is an invasion." The Bishop shifted his weight and rubbed his thigh with the heel of his hand. "I have ridden for more than twelve hours to try and find Sir Robert. He could only have made it to Bristol with help. You are in more trouble than the Empress."

"Do not talk to me of this. I will not hear it." Stephen turned his face away from the irritating influence. "You had better not make me angry, for I will have even you hanged for a traitor."

The woods echoed with the distant thunder of Bishop Henry's laughter. "I sit here and cringe in terror." He leaned toward Stephen and whispered, "Do not threaten me with your ineffectual words, for if I ever feel my life in danger, than yours will be ended. I have more power with my loyal followers than you will ever know. Do not play the king with me, for we both know what you really are."

Stephen's emotions tumbled from anger to fear to denial. He chose to ignore his brother's words as if they had not been said. He looked through the trees at the castle. "I shall lay siege to Arundel Castle until Matilda is forced into my hands."

"That will do absolutely no good."

"And why not?"

"Dear Stephen. Your forces will be split between Arundel and Bristol. You must know that Robert and his army will have to be in siege as well and at the same time."

"How do you know what is to be done? You were trained for the priesthood, and I for the knighthood. What do you know of military strategy?" Stephen continued to stare at Arundel Castle so that he could avoid Henry's eyes.

"I am intelligent enough to know that when my army has dwindled to a third of its size, it would be foolish to further cause its size to diminish." Bishop Henry nudged his horse forward.

"What do you think I should do? Let Matilda run about England gathering her forces wherever she chooses?"

Bishop Henry looked back over his shoulder. "No. I think you should let me escort her and her army to Bristol to join with Robert."

Stephen stared at his brother in spite of his secret resolve not to look at him again. "Absolutely not. You are a traitor, or crazy. Which is it?"

"You are too quick to say no, Stephen. Listen to reason. You can not afford to have your army split. With Robert and Matilda both in Bristol you can lay siege to that castle and mayhap get two birds with one shot." Bishop Henry turned his horse around to face Stephen.

"Allow Matilda to go further into the interior?"

"Yes. If that is what it takes, it must be done." Bishop Henry said. "If you leave her at Arundel on the eastern coast, she can easily get supplies from Geoffrey."

"I know not if she will leave. She can get help from Sir Baldwin, for he has been attacking my ships again from his castle on the Isle of Wight."

"She will go if I escort her." Bishop Henry shifted in the saddle and the leather squeaked in protest. "I could take Count Waleran of Meulan with me. She is fond of him. She will trust me, a man of God."

Stephen laughed bitterly. He hated to admit his brother was right. He still argued, refusing to give an inch to Henry's idea. "She knows you too well, and she will never trust you."

"I am her cousin, and she has always gotten on well with me. After all, I am not the one who made love to her in order to get her kingdom."

Stephen's eyebrows raised. "I find your references to my love life unnecessary. You know nothing about it."

"You are right. It is not worth discussing. Shall I take the initiative and escort our cousin northward to Bristol?" Bishop Henry leaned forward in the saddle and picked up the reins. He waited.

"Do it. I shall take my men and return to Windsor Castle," Stephen said.

Bishop Henry spurred his horse and moved toward Arundel. "I will do as you bid."

Stephen hated the smirk he saw on his brother's face and wondered if he could trust him. It was in Henry's best interest to maintain ties to the king, was it not? Stephen rubbed his forehead. It gave him a headache to think about the intrigues of ruling a country and defeating an enemy.

The October air was cool in the morning, but warmed quickly as the sun rose higher and higher in the sky. Matilda found that her cape, needed in the early part of the ride, was too hot. She untied the cord, pulled off the cape, and laid it across the back of the saddle. She inhaled the fresh air. It was a beautiful day that she took to be a good omen.

"You are very beautiful," Bishop Henry said.

Matilda turned toward her cousin riding to the right and glared at him. He reminded her of insincere men who said whatever they thought would get them favors. If he thought she were naive, he would be mistaken.

"I remember you as a young child, and you were beautiful then."

"Dear cousin, do not try your brother's sweet utterances on me. I have learned the most bitter lesson because of his honeyed words."

Matilda spurred her horse forward. She rode smoothly in spite of the rough terrain, and she was easily out ahead of her large army. She glanced back and saw that her men had moved up to be with her, effectively cutting off the Bishop's escort and Count Waleran's small force.

A dust cloud rose. The road to Bristol had been traveled frequently by different armies the last week and any trace of grass was gone. The urge to be totally free was overwhelming, and Matilda kicked Dancer while loosening the reins. Dancer surged forward and soon the wind blew Matilda's hair out behind her. She felt it pull at her scalp as if it had a life separate from hers. The wind seemed to push the present problems from her mind while the sun washed depression from her.

She looked back when she heard pounding of hoofs on the ground behind her. Bishop Henry had passed all the knights and was closing the gap between them. Matilda kicked Dancer again, and she felt his back muscles bunch up as he got ready to push himself to the limit for her as he always did. Matilda leaned down and grasped Dancer's mane to steady herself. She had ridden him at full gallop before and loved being on the edge of potential disaster.

Dancer, true to his name, flowed across the ground. Matilda could barely see color as a blur of sky and green mixed with reds, yellows, and oranges rushed towards her. She felt as if she had been pushed into another plane. The only sound she heard was the wind whistling past her. Dancer's mane whipped into her face as she bent lower. She loved the sting of it. She looked back and saw that Bishop Henry had dropped farther behind. She laughed and pulled back on the reins slowly until she had Dancer completely stopped. She turned him around and waited for Bishop Henry. Neither she nor Dancer was out of breath.

Bishop Henry rode up next to Matilda. "What were you doing? Are you insane? To be out here alone like this could get you killed by one of Stephen's knights. Nothing would please him more than to have you dead."

Matilda pushed her hair away from her face. "I was riding much too fast for any arrow to catch me. Would my death please you as well?"

"Not at all, for I believe you should be ruler of England as your father meant you to be."

Matilda pursed her lips as she studied Bishop Henry. He had a motive, but she was not certain what it was. She would discover his motive in due time. Of that she had no doubt.

"First a compliment and now a confession? I find this quite entertaining. What trap have I allowed myself to be drawn into?"

"I assure you that I would not be a party to any wrongdoing. I want to help you regain the throne." Bishop Henry's face got red and tiny beads of perspiration dotted his upper lip. He cleared his throat. "I believe you to be the rightful heir."

Matilda almost laughed aloud at Bishop Henry's audacity. His countenance gave away his inner thoughts. "If you think I am going to accept that, then you are certainly mistaken. What reason would you have for betraying your own brother?"

Bishop Henry tugged at the sleeve on his tunic. With downcast eyes, he asked, "Do you know who was appointed the Archbishop of Canterbury?"

"Why, yes. Adelicia told me. I found it peculiar that you were not appointed. I assumed you had decided you did not want the position," Matilda said.

Bishop Henry's face darkened a shade until it was almost purple. "I wanted that appointment badly, but Stephen was against it."

Matilda cocked her head and observed the Bishop's reaction. He was obviously highly agitated. "I do not understand why he designated such an uneducated man to that post when you, his own brother, would have been perfect. Unless, of course, he was concerned about your loyalty. You are more intellectual than Theobald of Bec. Mayhap Stephen feared your influence."

"Do you fear me?"

"Do not be absurd."

"Do you believe that I want to help you? I am not the only one who wants to side with you." Bishop Henry pointed toward the rider who waited behind them. "Count Waleran is here because he wants to align himself with your cause."

"You are telling me that Stephen made enemies of friends and relatives. Why?" Was simple revenge enough of a reason to turn against Stephen? Matilda smoothed a wrinkle from her skirt. "Why do you turn against your own brother?"

"He is ruining the country. I can not stand by and watch that happen. He is no leader, Matti, and you are. You can pull this country back from the abyss. You have the talents of your father and our grandfather."

"Come now, Cousin. I do not believe in your altruistic motives. What do you really want from me?"

"Ah, Matti, you are perceptive. I do want something from you, and I will not deny it. I want to be Archbishop of Canterbury, and since your brother is not a priest, it only seems fitting that I, your faithful cousin, should be appointed."

"That seems fair. What else do you want?"

Bishop Henry smiled. "I have difficulty fooling you, do I not?" Bishop Henry folded his hands together. "I want the power to choose whomever I please to fill the posts in the Church. I want to select the bishops for all of England, Normandy, and Anjou."

"I think that would suit me just fine. I will have enough to do without having to worry about the Church. I believe I can trust you to keep the Church in good condition. You have always done well by her before."

Matilda looked back at the army of knights that had stopped a respectful distance away. "My mother always liked you, Henry. Do you remember how religious she was? When I was a little girl, I used to think she was an angel sent from heaven for me. She was happy when you studied for the priesthood. Did you know she prayed for you every day, and she talked about you frequently?"

"I remember."

"Because of her belief in you, I will believe in you." Matilda believed only half of her own words, but she had no choice.

"Thank you, Matti."

"Thank my dead mother." Matilda heard the bitterness creep into her voice. She resented sharing the past with her cousin, and she especially hated sharing the memory of her mother with him.

"I will say a prayer for her."

Matilda nodded. That much she would accept from this man of God. She slapped the reins against Dancer's neck and urged him forward. She noticed that Bishop Henry followed her lead, mayhap to prevent her from riding away from him again.

Robert burst through the door to Matilda's room while she sat in the window alcove. The noise startled her, and she leaped to her feet pulling a dagger from her kirtle. Her mind would not accept that the person in front of her was her brother.

"Matti, what is the matter with you?" Robert asked.

Matilda lowered the dagger and shook her head. She wished she were not so nervous. She swallowed, trying to get rid of the dryness in her mouth. "I am sorry." She meant it as much for herself as for Robert.

"Forget that. I have wonderful news. The time has come for the deciding battle with Stephen. He has made a terrible mistake, and we are about to take advantage of it."

"What has the stupid man done this time?"

"He has attacked my son-in-law, Ranulf, the Earl of Chester. I have received word that my daughter is in grave trouble. She is still inside the castle at Lincoln, and Stephen has it under siege. Ranulf has gathered his men and asked that we join him in an attack against Stephen."

"Can we do it?" Matilda's eyes sparkled.

"We can do it."

"I will get my chain mail conditioned. I have waited for over a year for this. I thought when we invaded England that was my happiest moment, but this surpasses it by far. How long until we ride forth?"

"You are not going," Robert said.

"Not going!? But why? I am to be a leader, therefore I must lead. Am I not capable? Have I not proven myself in Normandy?"

"All those things are true, Matti, but there is another consideration."

"What could possibly be more important than my leading my knights to victory?" Matilda asked.

Robert took the dagger from Matilda, laid it on the window seat, and took her hands. "Young Prince Henry."

"My son?"

"Your son. All your sons. Listen carefully to what I must tell you. Stay, for if you are lost, then your son is lost."

"I must fight, Robert. Do not ask me to let you and the others do battle for me. I must fight." Matilda's teeth clamped together to keep the anguish from turning to tears. "I have to fight, Robert."

"For whom do you fight, Matilda?"

Matilda bit her lower lip to keep the tears from flowing. They were dangerously close to the surface. "You know the answer. I fight for my son and heir in all things. I fight for Prince Henry."

"Need I say more?"

The meeting place that had been chosen on the outskirts of Lincoln was little more than a wattle and daub hut. It would not be warm enough since nothing in February was ever warm. Even the castles were drafty and miserable in January and February. Sometimes the castles did not warm up until July and then they were cold again by September. Stephen hated being cold. It hurt his fingers.

Stephen looked around at the collection of huts that were crowded together, seemingly leaning against each other to hold themselves up. He was amazed that a growing town like Lincoln did not have anything better in which to house its king for a meeting. It was understandable, he guessed, since most of Lincoln was under enemy control. He would be glad to wrench the castle away from Robert of Gloucester's daughter. It was too bad that her husband had escaped. He would have enjoyed using him as leverage against Robert to push Matilda back to Anjou. Stephen kicked a stone as he walked toward the hut where the meeting was to take place. This business with battles and small wars was getting weary. He wished that it were all over so he could go back to the comfortable life that he had had when Henry was king.

Stephen swore when he stepped in manure, spotting his maroon suede boots. The king should not have to walk the streets like a common peasant. He cursed Matilda for getting him in this situation.

Stepping carefully around the dung that blended with the mud of the streets, Stephen led his entourage through the tiny door of the hut. He bent over as he entered. His eyes took a few moments to adjust to the room, partly because of the lack of light and partly because of the smoke from the firepit. The peasants who lived here were poor and burned animal chips for fuel. Stephen decided the smell was not as bad as the smoke, but neither was pleasant. He fanned his face with his hand to keep the curls of smoke from stinging his eyes any further and found his way to a chair that had been placed at a plank table next to the firepit in the middle of the only room.

Stephen sat down and leaned against the carved wooden chair back and frowned at the half dozen men who joined him around the table. They looked solemn. Several of the men had been arguing with him all day until their yapping had made him as grouchy as an old dog. They refused to maintain eye contact with him as he glowered. Now he would make them speak out in a forum of their peers. He was tired of them, of their doubts, and their constant excuses of why they should not go to battle. He scowled at the one knight who had been the most verbal.

"Tell us why we should not try to take the castle away from our enemies."

The knight, small in stature, but muscular like an ox, and just as slow, shifted in his chair. He studied his stubby fingers, stared at his feet, and coughed. Screwing up his face and almost wincing, he said, "The feast of the Purification of . . ."

"I am aware that The Feast of the Purification of the Virgin Mary is tomorrow. Do not tell me that I have to send my army away because of a Holy Day." Stephen felt angry with this knight who wanted to turn his backsides to the castle and run. Stephen could not tolerate cowardice in men, especially when it was couched in religious terms. "God has an understanding of earthly matters, and we shall fight as planned."

"But King Stephen, it is not good to fight on a holy day. King Henry would always refuse to do so."

Stephen half rose from his chair, leaning on his knuckles. He glared at the coward before him, Count DuWayne of Sleaford. "I am king now, not Henry."

William of Ypes leaned forward, his elbows on the rough hewn, wooden table, and stared at the man who was arguing with Stephen. "My men are here to fight. How stupid you are to suggest to King Stephen that he should turn them back because your cowards want to use a Holy Day as an excuse."

Count Sleaford's face turned red as he watched William of Ypes. His words were spoken in a pinched tone. "My men are not cowards. They are concerned about the wrath of God, not the wrath of man. An army that does not observe the feast days is an army that loses in battle." Count Sleaford turned toward Stephen. "King Stephen, it may bring bad luck to fight on a Holy Day. God expects our observances of special days."

Stephen looked at the knight who sat next to Count Sleaford. He looked like a fish with a protruding set of lips and glassy eyes behind half-closed lids. His mouth opened and closed like a fish when out of water. Stephen half expected to see gills behind his ears. Who was this knight? Yes, a friend to Count Sleaford. This knight was known as Desmond, Earl of Bythm. Another coward, no doubt. He would give him a chance to speak and make a fool of himself. "Do you have a suggestion, Desmond of Bythm?"

The earl nodded. "It would be best if you would send a messenger to Robert to ask for a truce." He glanced at his friend, Count Sleaford.

Stephen followed his gaze and almost snorted with disgust. Count Sleaford sat with hands folded in apparent prayer, his forehead resting on the tips of his fingers, and his eyes closed. He lifted his head and looked at Stephen. Stephen flicked a hand to show that the man could speak.

Count Sleaford tugged at his ear, a habit that over the years had made one earlobe longer than the other. "It would be best to observe the Holy Day, for in doing so you would have time to assemble a larger army for a later attack. We should leave before Robert arrives."

Stephen pounded his fist on the table and stood so quickly that the chair fell over. It hit the floor with a dull thump. "No! I will not leave." His words reverberated off the wattle and daub walls of the cottage. Stephen paced back and forth across the packed earthen floor. He turned and faced the men whose faces still showed the surprise at his sudden anger. "I have laid siege to Lincoln Castle, and I will not retreat in the face of danger." Stephen felt his face get hot; he turned his back to the men and watched the flames in the firepit. He spoke quietly. "When I was young, my father was in the same position as I am today. He chose to flee the avenging Turks at Antioch during the First Crusade. He was branded a coward until he died in battle. I have had to live his shame, and I refuse to make the same mistake."

"We do not hold you accountable for your father's mistake. History has forgotten something that happened so long ago," the Earl of Bythm said.

"I have not forgotten." Stephen faced the men. "We shall continue the siege, and we will fight Robert. We go to hear mass and then we fight. I suggest you prepare yourselves." Stephen left the cottage and forgetting to watch where he walked, stomped through the muck. He stopped outside the small church used by the towns-people. He glanced toward the castle and spying the stained glass window that signified its chapel, vowed the next time he prayed it would be there.

Stephen pushed open the door to the tiny church where the peasants worshiped. His men followed him, William of Ypes in the lead. Bishop Alexander stood next to the local priest and watched while the altar was readied for the ceremony to follow.

"Prepare us for battle." Stephen knelt in front of the cloth cov-ered altar.

"Yes, my king." Bishop Alexander raised his right hand and made the sign of the cross with a graceful hand movement from his forehead to his heart and from shoulder to shoulder. The Bishop nodded to the priest who handed Stephen a consecrated wax candle.

Stephen held the candle during the blessing of the small band of knights who were with him. He tried hard to listen to the Bishop's prayers, but instead he was thinking of the battle before him. He wondered how many more battles there would have to be before Matilda would give up and let him rule England in peace. Stephen realized that the Bishop was waiting for the candle to be handed back to him as the ceremony dictated. Stephen held up the candle, but before the Bishop could take it, the top half of the candle snapped off and fell to the floor, its flame sputtering and dying. It rolled toward the altar and disappeared under the white cloth. The collec-tive gasp from the knights sounded like a gale force wind to Stephen, and he caught the Bishop's look of horror.

The Bishop recovered quickly and continued as though noth-ing had happened. He took what was left of the broken candle, placed it on the altar, and relit it. The flame wavered and then was steady. All was calm once again, and the ritual continued.

Stephen wiped the perspiration off his upper lip and vowed he would listen to the prayers instead of speculating about Matilda. Even when in his own thoughts, she managed to disrupt things. He bowed his head and concentrated on the Bishop's words.

A crash caused all heads to snap up. The noise contrasted with the early morning peacefulness. At first Stephen thought that Rob-ert had attacked before daylight, but what he saw was much worse than an army for whom they were not ready. The container for the Blessed Sacrament had hung by a chain above the altar. The chain had broken and the pyx had fallen onto the altar. The Sacrament, bread to symbolize the body of Christ, scattered across the altar. Some had fallen to the floor. Stephen did not know whether to pick up the Sacrament, so he did nothing. The silence from the knights made Stephen feel totally alone, and he shivered at the black omen from God. He could not hesitate, however, and the battle would begin as planned. No one could say that King Stephen was a coward like his father had been.

The breath of the horses pushed forth from their nostrils like white plumes, and frosted muzzles made the horses appear ghostly as they trotted across the frozen ground toward destiny. The riders sat stiffly in their saddles, heavy, woolen capes drawn tightly about them, their beards matching the frost-covered muzzles of the horses they rode. For as far as they could see, the land was white, and in the distance, the horizon blended sky and earth into one continuous, colorless sheet.

Cold penetrated to the bone, and Robert could not decide which was worse — the lack of color or the cold. Both made him miserable, but he could not let the men know that. He flexed his fingers trying to get some feeling of warmth, but could not.

"How much further, Robert? I am so cold that death would be a relief," Ranulf said.

Robert glanced at his son-in-law. "Riding in full armor protects one from the arrows of the enemy, but protects no one from the cold. I, too, will be glad to begin the battle, for there blood runs hot even on the coldest days of winter."

"Look to the horizon. Do I see the smoke of Lincoln ahead?" Ranulf asked.

Robert stood in his stirrups, the cold forgotten for the moment. "You are right. We will cross at the ford for the bridge will be heavily guarded by Stephen's men."

Ranulf groaned. "I hope that the fight on the far side of the ford will be soon begun, so that I will forget the cold and mayhap not freeze into a statue."

"We will have no time to worry about cold, for we have to worry about conquering England." Robert settled down in the saddle. "There is the bridge over Witham River."

Ranulf sighed. "It does no good to tell me of a bridge when it is useless to us."

"We are going to use the ford," Robert said.

"The water will be full of ice."

"So it is. What do you expect in February?" Robert was beginning to be annoyed by Ranulf's whining. Robert rode to the edge of the river and stopped. He was shocked by the level of the water. The ford had disappeared under the swollen river. The water rushed past him, tumbling and splashing without end. Robert turned his horse away from the river and stopped to wait for other knights to catch up. When the men were settled in around him, Robert stood in the stirrups. Their whispers ceased immediately. He looked out over the more than six hundred knights who had followed him. The sight made his heart race, and he felt a kinship to these men who had all been cheated one way or another by Stephen. They were angry with the man who called himself their king and protector while he helped himself to their lands and treasures.

The men were so quiet, Robert could hear the wind in the bare branches of the trees. It sounded like music from the angels. He shouted. "Inside Lincoln Castle, surrounded by Stephen's army, is my daughter, wife to Ranulf, who rides with me. We are not here to save my daughter, but to save England. We are here because of Stephen's broken promises. We are here because Stephen can not keep the laws of the land that King Henry labored to put into place. No man, common or titled, is safe in Stephen's lawless land. Too many have died because of Stephen. We are here today to take England back for all of us. Matilda will give us back King Henry's laws, and with those laws we will have peace."

Robert was startled by the explosion of cheers from the men. He looked at the row upon row of faces, young and old, handsome and not so handsome, and wondered which ones would not return. He held his arms above his head and immediately the men became quiet. "We are here because you are brave men. You know that there can be no retreat. We can only go forward into the town of Lincoln, forward into victory. We can rely only on our own courage. We must cross the coldest of rivers and fight the hottest of battles. This is just as I would have chosen it! Once across, there will be no going back. We shall have to conquer or die. Are you with me?"

Robert turned his horse and without waiting for a response from the men, rode into the swift-flowing current of the Witham River. The cold water rushed up to Robert's knees, then thighs, then waist. He did not feel it as he urged his mount forward. He did not hear the hundreds of splashes behind him as his knights and soldiers on foot followed him into the fast flowing, ice strewn river. As a unit, Robert and his men rode up the other side of the river, the first men sliding on the snow and the later soldiers sliding in the resultant mud. Ranulf and his knights separated from the main group and rode off to the right. Robert of Gloucester and his men broke to the left and like a silver wave, surrounded Stephen's army, which, in turn had Lincoln Castle under siege.

CHAPTER
XIV

ATILDA PACED BACK AND FORTH. Crackling reeds under foot only irritated her more. At every turn past the frosted window, she looked toward the eastern horizon. "Where is Robert? I have waited many weeks for him. Whatever is keeping that brother of mine?"

Ella sat quietly near the fireplace, mending linen sheeting. "He will return victorious for it is God's will."

"I believe in the will of God, but I also believe in the will of man. Robert should have been back by now — if he has won the Battle for Lincoln. He should have sent a messenger."

"He may not have had any men to spare." Ella continued stitching, made a knot, and cut the thread with her teeth.

"Or else he has been captured!" Matilda's hand flew to her throat. "What if Robert has been captured?"

Ella glanced up at her mistress. "You can be certain that if Robert had been captured, Stephen would have sent you word. He has not, so be assured that Robert is safe." Ella held up her needle, licked the end of the thread, and deftly slipped it through the eye.

Matilda stopped in front of her. "How can you sit there calmly when my future is in the balance?"

"I appear to be calm, but inside are a thousand fingers of fear. I have been lady-in-waiting to my lady since we were both children, and I have never been as afraid as I am right now." Ella laid the material aside. "I have always believed that you were meant to rule after your father. You will be a wonderful ruler, my lady, and one who is fair."

"You have been such a comfort to me, Ella. Do you realize that you and I have spent more years together than any of my family or my husbands?" Matilda reached out and grasped one of Ella's hands. "You have always been by my side when no one else was there. I owe you a great deal, and I never can repay you."

"You owe me nothing, my lady, for you have given me much more than I could have ever given you." Ella squeezed the hand that held hers.

"Are we not a pair of despondent women?" Matilda dropped Ella's hand and moved to the bench in the window alcove and gazed out the window, peering between the patchwork of colors that were interspersed with clear glass. Usually she liked to brighten the grey winters by looking through the colored part of the stained glass, but today she wanted a clear view of the real world, whatever it might be.

Matilda sat at the window for a few minutes, but her nerves could not take the inactivity. She bounced up and paced back and forth once more, paying no attention to the cold drafts that haunted the English castles like ghosts; unseen, but felt.

"I will have to have the reeds changed before long. You are wearing them down with your marching. One would think you were part of the army," Ella said.

"Ah, were it that I were. Fighting to the death would be easier."

"For you, yes." Ella tucked a loose strand of dark auburn hair back into her braid and continued her mending. "I am glad that my Edward is too ill to fight and that he is here with me. I abhor fighting, but it is the way of our world at the present."

"Your Edward is a good knight whenever we are able to use him. I am sorry he is ill," Matilda said. "He has killed a few enemies in his day."

"I long for the days of old when King Henry had peace. The land prospered and we had plenty. I remember laughing a lot more then. You will give us the old days back." Ella looked across the room at the restless Matilda. "Mayhap it was because we were young."

"I do not remember ever being young." Matilda returned to the window alcove and sat down with her back against a wooden shutter and watched her breath escape like ghostly-white feathers. The sky was turning from grey to darker grey in the absence of the sun. Instead of twilight, the sky got darker until Matilda noticed that Ella was lighting the candles on the table and in the sconces.

Matilda held her palm against the frosted pane. She lifted her hand to peer through the "C" shape that was left. The horizon had changed and Matilda frantically blew on the "C" spot to make it larger. She scratched the edges and made the hole bigger.

"Oh, by God and the Virgin Mary in Heaven. I think Robert has returned! I hope it is Robert! An army comes, but it is too dark to see the standard." Matilda blew on the window again, but gave up when the frost reclaimed the spot as quickly as she made it. "Please God, let it be my brother returned to me safe and victorious."

Ella stood, oblivious to the spilling of her mending box and linen sliding to the floor. "I pray that it is so."

"I must go. I can see better from the top of the wall." Matilda ran across the room and jerked open the door.

"My lady, your cape."

Matilda did not slow her pace. She ran down the corridor to the stairs and bounded up them two at a time as she had always done in her childhood when no one watched.

She reached the top of the stairs and paused to check the position of the guards. She saw them placed every thirty feet behind the battlements along the wall and noticed immediately that they were all looking toward the northeast, their bows up and ready for battle.

Matilda gathered her kirtle up to her knees and ran down the wall toward the inner gate house. As she came to the corner of the adjacent wall, she nearly ran over an archer and from the look on his face she surmised he was not expecting a gale force in the form of a woman to be racing along the top of the inner curtain wall. Not hesitating, she continued until she was at the tower with a staircase that went to the top of the inner gate. Pausing only to get a better hold on her skirt, Matilda raced up the wooden steps, noticing the harsh boards through her thin, leather slippers and wishing she had worn her boots.

At the top, she walked slowly, watching the cloud of dark figures drawing closer. They rode along the town wall to the town gate. She could hear a cheer begin as a low, rumbling sound and raise itself to a pitch of yelling townspeople as the gates were swung open. The standard was held high, a sign of victory! The standards were all held high, and wave after wave of knights rode through the town toward the outer castle gates. The drawbridge was lowered, but Matilda barely heard the grating of the chains against chains as the winch was put into use. The knights came closer to the inner castle gate, followed by a rag-tag crowd of peasants, their children, and a collection of mongrel dogs snapping at the heels of the horses. The horses, being well-trained, ignored the paltry attempts by the dogs to start a battle.

Matilda was deafened by the pounding of horses' hoofs on packed dirt and the clanking chain mail. Robert's standard was in front, flanked by the standards of Ranulf of Chester and Brian fitzCount. The iron-tipped wooden gratings were lifted one by one as the castle's inner gate parted for the returning army. Matilda ran to the other side of the wall and peered into the courtyard where men from inside the castle mixed with the men come from the world outside. The shouting and confusion was joyous; the men's voices echoed by barking dogs. Matilda stood at the edge of the wall, oblivious to the shear drop to the inner courtyard. She wanted to speak with Robert, but she knew that it would be more than an hour before he was out of his mail. Matilda watched the celebrants for a few minutes, then walked downstairs. She had something important to do before she talked with Robert and Brian, and she needed to be alone.

The chapel was lit by altar candles and two wall sconces. The shadows always looked to her like ancestors from the past, but tonight Matilda was too elated to wonder if they were friendly. She knelt at the altar and with only the silence for a witness, thanked God, the Virgin Mary, and all the saints for preserving her quest.

Matilda rose after her prayers and left the chapel. She slipped into her rooms, closed the heavy door behind, and walked trance-like to her dressing table and sat. She accepted a chalice of claret from Ella and smiled her thanks. She swirled the blood-red liquid around in the cup and wondered how many knights would not be returning to the castle with their victorious colleagues. She grieved for them, which tempered her happiness. Stephen's face flashed before her, and she wished him dead, then recanted that wish with a prayer of forgiveness to God. She was not certain she wanted him dead. She just wanted him to go away.

Geoffrey's face surfaced in her memory. She wished he could be here to share this moment. She would write to him of the victory at Lincoln as soon as possible. Matilda realized she missed her husband. Time and circumstances had changed her love for Stephen to hate and her hate for Geoffrey to . . . She did not want to use the word love. She would never again be betrayed by that emotion.

"Ella, have you ordered a meal brought here for Robert?"

Ella looked puzzled and glanced at the dining table bowed from the weight of food. A servant placed yet another dish on the table. Ella swept her arms toward the table, hoping Matilda would see the obvious. "Yes, my lady. I knew you would want to speak to Robert privately."

Ella sat on the vanity bench next to Matilda. "You should have seen the kitchen. Everyone was running every which way, and there was tremendous excitement. I never saw so much food prepared so quickly in all my life. The cook's face was flame red, and I thought his heart would blow out the top of his head. And did he yell at the servants! Nothing moved fast enough for him. Even God himself would not have pleased the master chef tonight."

"Why, Ella, what blasphemy! And from such a good girl, too. One would think the devil had twisted your tongue."

"Please do not scold me on such an historic night as this. I am too happy to be scolded, for this victory means that my son will grow to manhood under the guidance of Empress Matilda, and peace will reign. Listen to me babble as do the court jesters."

"I think God is forgiving. Never you mind your jesting. I feel wonderful. I can hardly wait for my dear brother to come to tell me of the battle." Matilda walked to the table. Sipping her claret, she leaned over and systematically lifted the lids on each dish. She wrinkled her nose at the eels, for she had hated them ever since she had learned that spoiled eels had caused her father's death. Thinking of that, she motioned to the servant who stood near. "Take this dish away. We have plenty here for the entire army."

"I forgot to tell them not to send the eels. I am sorry," Ella said.

"It does not matter. It is a silly worry of mine, but I can not tolerate them. Is it not ironic that King Henry lived through battle after battle only to be downed by an eel?"

Ella nodded. "Fate is unkind, even to kings."

The women both jumped at the pounding knock on the door just before it was flung open. Robert burst through, followed by Brian fitzCount and Ranulf, Earl of Chester.

"Dear sister we have made history on the day of the Feast of the Purification of the Virgin Mary. She was with us, Matti. We have been blessed with victory." Robert put his huge hands around Matilda's waist and lifted her above his head.

"Robert, it is more important to me that you are safe than all the victories in the world. Without you, I could not be king. Now put me down!"

Robert swung her around and scooped her up like a child into his arms.

"Robert, put me down. This is not befitting the ruler of England. What are Ranulf and Brian to think?" Matilda wrapped her arms around Robert's powerful neck and buried her face in his shoulder.

"As my king wishes," Robert said. "Although I have to admit that I have never held a king in such a manner as this before tonight."

"I need to speak to Brian and Ranulf, and I do not wish to do it from this position. Put me down, you fool."

"Fool, am I? I, who has conquered Stephen for you? This is the thanks of a grateful sister? Maybe I will not tell you of the surprise that awaits in a guarded apartment down the corridor."

"A surprise? Did you bring me jewels from Lincoln?" Matilda held out her hand and wiggled her fingers. "You know how I love the sparkle of gems."

"Is that all you can think of? My surprise is better than all the jewels in the kingdom." Robert put Matilda down, but kept an arm around her waist.

"Ranulf, can you tell me what surprise awaits me?"

"No, my lady, for my father-in-law would have my head separated from my shoulders," Ranulf said.

"I have almost forgotten what is really important, Ranulf. Tell me how goes it with your dear wife and my niece? Is she gone from Lincoln Castle and safe?" Matilda asked.

"Catherine is safe, I am happy to say, and none the worse for the experience. Her only complaint was that she had missed her sister's party," Ranulf said.

"She should have asked Stephen for safe passage. He is such a gentleman that I am certain he would have escorted her escape himself," Matilda said. "Please, sit down and eat, and tell Ella and me about the Battle of Lincoln. I can wait until later for any surprise you have down the hall." Matilda smiled as Robert pulled out a chair at the head of the table. It was a symbolic move, befitting her new position. She sat and marveled at Robert's understanding of her. She would savor this moment.

The scraping of chairs broke her revery as the hungry men sat at the table. Ella sat to her left and Robert to her right, Brian fitzCount and Ranulf across from her. The only sound was the clanking of the utensils against each other and the silver-rimmed wooden bowls as the hungry men concentrated on eating.

"I can wait no longer. Tell me of the battle."

"I am anxious to hear, also." Ella passed a mazer bowl of broth to Brian and held it while he spooned the juice over a slab of beef.

Robert stabbed a piece of beef with his knife. "The first charge was from us. I decided that we would have to move quickly toward Stephen's lines. The first wave of our fierce Welshmen were turned back by William of Ypes."

"However, Ranulf moved in to the attack immediately," Brian said. "He forced William and his men back and back until that famous soldier, brave beyond words, turned and fled with his army."

"William of Ypes actually retreated?" Ella asked.

"Not only William. Alan of Richmond and his men were the next to fall under the attack by Brian fitzCount and his men," Ranulf said.

"By then the battle was nearly over. Others retreated in haste." Robert chewed slowly. "I was shocked to see that as I brought my men forward, Count Waleran of Meulan fled. I was astounded, for though we had more than a hundred knights, we were outnumbered. I expected much more of a fight."

Brian fitzCount laughed. "Do not forget that Gilbert of Clare almost forgot to take his army with him as he fled."

"William of Warenne turned tail and ran, then Stephen was left with no one," Ranulf said.

"Our cousin fought bravely, Matti." Robert laid down his knife. "He would not retreat and held us off with only a few foot soldiers and a few men from Lincoln town."

"Again and again we flung ourselves at Stephen and again and again he held us off with only a few men until he drove us back," Brian said.

Robert leaned his elbows on the table and looked across the room at the flames in the fireplace. Dream-like he said, "Amidst the noise of battle, the clash of metal swords on metal helmets and the dust raised by hundred of hoofs pounding on the ground amongst fallen and wounded men, Stephen stood and held the line."

"We charged at Stephen, determined to die rather than retreat," Ranulf said.

"He stood like a castle, and we stormed him like a castle," Brian said.

Robert shook his head. "I have never seen the like. He stood like a lion, the bravest of the brave, fearing the attack of no one."

Matilda's mouth opened in surprise, and her hand was at her throat. She tried to deny that her heart beat faster, and she tried to deny she was pleased that Stephen was so brave. She looked from Ranulf to Robert. "Go on with the tale."

"Ranulf shattered Stephen's sword with his own, but a man from Lincoln gave Stephen a Danish battle-axe to replace it." Robert's eyes were focused on the battle. "It is a fierce weapon, much worse than a sword."

"I had been too close to Stephen and had been knocked off my horse." Ranulf waved his knife through the air. "I managed to dodge the axe, but Stephen, grinding his teeth and foaming at the mouth like a wild boar, brought that axe down full force on my helmet." Ranulf stabbed the table with the knife. He left it quivering in an upright position cutting a neat hole in the white linen table cloth.

Ella leaned away from the knife. "How terrible."

"You are indeed lucky to be here," Matilda said.

"The sound was so horrible that I knew I was dying. I was knocked to the ground and my sword flew from my hand. I felt around on the ground for my weapon, but it was useless. I knew I was going to die," Ranulf said.

"And then?" Ella asked.

"Then someone threw a large stone and hit Stephen square in the forehead. It knocked him down. William of Cahagnes seized his battle-axe, and it was over for Stephen. He surrendered to Robert of Gloucester." Ranulf leaned back and pointed toward the door.

Matilda gasped. "The surprise down the corridor — is it Stephen?"

"Yes," Robert said.

Matilda's world stopped as time stopped for her. Time raced back to the last time she had seen Stephen. Had it really been so long ago? Every part of her body tingled as blood rushed through her veins. From far away she heard her brother's voice.

"Do you want to see Stephen now?" Robert asked.

The sound in Matilda's ears quieted. She sat still and tried to gather in her feelings and sort them. She felt her cheeks flush and she hoped no one noticed.

Robert placed his hand on Matilda's arm. "Do you want to see Stephen, now?"

"I do not know."

Robert frowned. "That answer is not befitting the person who now rules England and Normandy."

"There are things you do not know." Matilda blushed. She hoped Robert would never know.

"I was neither blind nor deaf," Robert said. "Whatever you felt for Stephen happened at another time, in another place."

Matilda put a hand to her cheek. It felt hot and her hand felt like ice. Maybe Robert was right. "Yes, we were different people then, were we not?"

"Do you want to see Stephen?"

"I am ready." Matilda waited for Robert to help her from the chair. With her hand on his arm, she walked from her apartment with her heart beating in double time. It was as if she were at the center of a dream and everyone else had faded.

The two guards in front of the door stepped back after Robert nodded to them. A third guard answered the knock by opening the door a crack, then farther when he saw Robert. Robert stepped aside and allowed Matilda to enter first. She held her head up higher than normal, straightened her shoulders, and swept through the door.

Stephen sat at a table, his head held in his hands, his food untouched. His back was to the fireplace and the flickering flames made his shadow dance against the tapestries on the far wall. He did not look up. Matilda had resolved to hate him, but her anger at his deception had not solidified yet. He looked vulnerable and unhappier than she had ever seen him. She felt sorry for him. She forced herself to remember all he had taken from her, including her trust, and then she was ready to face Stephen.

Robert stopped just inside the door and waited, but Matilda waved him away. She listened for the door to close before she walked over to Stephen. Matilda could parry any words of love that he would thrust towards her.

Armed with anger, she spoke. "So, after all these years, we meet once more. There was a time when I hoped to never see you alive."

Stephen dropped his hands at the sound of Matilda's voice, his mouth agape. He stood quickly and bowed. "It is good to see you after too long a time."

Matilda was taken aback by his action. She had expected anything but this. She laughed at the absurdity of Stephen's chivalry. "Ever the gentleman except where it counts."

"What do you mean?"

"You took what you had sworn to uphold. You broke a vow to King Henry twice over. I can never forgive you for that."

Matilda's eyes narrowed, and she did not feel like laughing anymore. Her hands were clenched at her side, nails biting into her own flesh.

"Would you care to be seated?" Stephen moved behind her and pulled out a chair. He was so close to her that she felt his body heat.

Matilda hesitated. "No, I will not be here long."

Stephen whispered in her ear. "I am sorry to hear that. I had hoped we could talk."

Matilda whirled around, put her hands on her hips, and glared at Stephen. "Talk? You usurped the crown, and you hoped we could talk?" she hissed. She was glad when Stephen seemed confused by her and took a step backward. Matilda stepped forward and pushed Stephen another step backwards.

"The days for talking are over. In case you have not yet discovered it, I have you imprisoned. That precludes any former alliances that we had. I can do with you what I want and believe me, my thoughts do not include love. Talk? I think not. I should have you beheaded, and then we would see how much you would be able to talk." Matilda stepped away from Stephen in disgust.

Stephen reached for Matilda's hand. "I can not undo the wrong that I have done to you, Matti. If you will let me, I will try to explain."

Matilda glowered at Stephen until he pulled his hand away. "I need no explanation. I know why you did this. You let your wife do your thinking for you. You let Maithilde manage your life and in so doing, you lost control of it. I do not care about what happens to you anymore."

"I did not want to hurt you or to take the country, but I now like being king. . . ."

"Ha! You are no more than a counterfeit king."

"I wanted to be like King Henry. I remembered how wonderful he was, and every battle I fought was fought so that I could be a great warrior like your father."

The use of her father's name by Stephen made Matilda want to rip his lips off his face. She felt the muscles in her jaws tighten as she fought the impulse. Her hands were clasped together as if each were preventing the other from doing damage. Matilda breathed deeply.

When she no longer felt the urge to destroy Stephen's face, she spoke through gritted teeth. "Do not use the good King Henry's name to sooth my ire and make me forget my anger with you. It has the opposite effect on me. Do you think I am still a fool? I have aged and am no longer a young and impressionable girl who falls in love. The quick way in which you went through King Henry's treasure proves that your motives were not altruistic after all." Matilda felt as if she were suffocating, and she needed to get away from Stephen. She walked to the door as quickly as she could without seeming to have to escape.

"Wait." Stephen caught up with her and put his hand on Matilda's shoulder. "I need you."

"You needed my kingdom, not me."

"Please talk with me. Am I not the father of your son?"

All of Matilda's breath left her as she gasped. Through her anger at the mention of her son, she said, "Take your hand off me. Geoffrey is his father. Geoffrey alone, not you, has given Prince Henry food, clothing, shelter, an education. Geoffrey alone has given Prince Henry leave to his titles and his lands. You are no father to that child. You have given nothing. All you have done is take what was his through me."

Stephen lifted his hand away from her shoulder and stepped back. "I can change that. I can give our son his due, in time."

"Do not mention my son to me again. I do not want his name corrupted by you."

"I still love you."

"Do not play the wounded lover to me, Cousin." Matilda turned and faced Stephen. "I have no feelings for you, anymore. Whatever I felt for you is gone . . . gone with your broken promises and my broken dreams."

"You do not understand." Stephen took Matilda's face lightly in his hands and kissed her gently on the lips.

Matilda let him kiss her, but she did not return the kiss. She tried to let her mind wander back to a happier time, for she wanted to see if she were still in love. It was worth the risk. If she were still in love, then she would deal with it. When his lips felt like cold stone against hers, she knew the hatred she felt for him was genuine.

Matilda felt the wooden door against her back. She reached up and pushed against Stephen's chest while twisting her head to the side. "Get away from me."

"You still love me."

"You egotistical bastard." Matilda shoved harder and forced Stephen to step back. "I loathe you." She turned and pulled open the door.

"Matilda, please do not leave me. I love you. I spend my nights crying out for you," Stephen whispered.

Matilda turned and looked into Stephen's dark eyes. She felt the old desires trying to return, and shuddering, she escaped through the doorway. Ignoring the presence of Robert and the guards, she turned once again. "For which Matilda do you cry? Which of us causes your pain?" She grasped the latch and started to slam the door, but controlled herself. Stephen would never know that he had stirred emotion in her.

Matilda trembled as she walked down the corridor to her own apartment. She was glad that Robert remained silent. At the door she looked at her brother and smiled.

"How was our cousin?" Robert asked.

"Unchanged. It is I who have changed. I see him for the manipulator that he is. I wonder how I could have ever loved him."

"Love is not something we can control. I, too, have loved unwisely. Mayhap it is our fate to be ruled by heart and not by head," Robert said.

Matilda grabbed Robert's arm, stopping him in mid-stride. She tugged on his sleeve. "You have loved unwisely? Do not make me resort to court gossip for my information. Do tell, Robert."

"Never, for I would not want to reveal my stupidity to my little sister. Now, let us rejoin our friends before you learn the secrets of my past."

"You are no fun at all."

Matilda's eyes popped opened, and she sat up in bed, pulling the bed curtain aside. Through the frosty window, she could see that the dawn was no more than a lightened sky in the east. The sun would probably refuse to break through the clouds yet another day. She threw back the linen sheets and heavy woolen and fur covers and stretched her arms above her head. She glanced away from the window toward the opposite wall. The table against the wall was covered with her writing instruments and sheets of vellum, some folded and sealed. The stub of a candle was on the table, so short that its shadow, formed by the low flickering flames from the fireplace, was almost nonexistent. Matilda remembered reluctantly blowing it out and climbing into bed even though she had not been tired.

Matilda slid to the floor and stepped gingerly across it, wrapping her arms around herself on the way to the fireplace, her frosty breath leading the way. She felt driven to continue her writing, but the thought of the warm bed was tempting. Matilda picked up a poker, stirred the fire, and placed a log on top. It was too early to expect Ella to rise and summon the servant to do the fire. Matilda waited until the warmth from the log pushed the dampness away from the table before she sat down to finish the writing she had begun several weeks ago. She folded back the sleeves of her night chemise and lifted the lid of the inlaid box. If she had not been so careless last night, she would have taken time to put her writing tools in the box where they would be protected.

After lighting a candle, Matilda placed a clean sheet of vellum exactly as the nuns had shown her. She remembered Sister Ethel

Rose telling her that in order to write legibly, she must have the vellum perpendicular to the bottom edge of the writing surface. She remembered, with chagrin, that Sister Ethel Rose had also taught her to take care of her pens. She was supposed to clean the split nib so the ink would not dry and ruin it.

She picked up the bronze pen and tapped it against the table. Dried powder dropped from the nib. Matilda apologized to Sister Ethel Rose and reached back into the box for another pen, vowing to clean it this time.

Matilda shook the ink pot and was pleased that it sounded half full. She took the ceramic plug off the top and peered in. The ink was still smooth. The servant who mixed the soot and water had done a good job. There was still much to do, and Matilda felt her energy was endless.

The only sound Matilda heard was the scratching of her pen as she let the Latin phrases flow. Her plans, as well as her writing, had to be flawless and well thought out in advance. Matilda sat still, head bent over her work. Every now and then she pushed a strand of hair away from her face, but it immediately fell across her cheek again.

"My lady, why are you up so early? Do you never rest?" Ella asked.

Matilda jumped at the sound of Ella's voice, and she almost spotted the vellum.

"I am sorry! I did not mean to startle you."

"That is all right. I need to stop. My shoulders are sore." Matilda laid down the pen and leaned back her head until the muscles in her throat were tightly stretched.

Ella picked up an ivory comb. She pulled it through Matilda's hair with long strokes. "Today you ride out to meet with Bishop Henry."

"Yes. I wish it were not such a dreary day. I heard the rain beating against the windows most of the night." Matilda opened her eyes and stared at the ceiling, keeping her head tilted back. She loved it when Ella combed her hair, and she wondered if that was why cats purred when they were petted.

"It will be a soggy road for poor Dancer to traverse. Today dawn will be held at bay because the clouds darkened her sky. I am almost sorry that I insisted on meeting Bishop Henry on neutral territory, and the only neutral territory is in the middle of a very flat plain near Andover."

"Why not meet in one of the castles? It would be so much drier on a day such as this." Ella separated Matilda's hair into two sections.

"What castle is neutral? Even though we have Stephen captured, I do not trust his wife. No, the best place is in the middle of a large, flat plain where there is total safety and privacy."

"I see. Do you want your hair in plaits today, my lady?"

"Please. Today will be miserable enough without worrying about tangles."

The rain dripped off Dancer's mane and made tiny rivers down his neck. She wiped her face with the inside of her cape, but it seemed to do no good. She would never be dry again, and she imagined moss growing down her back as it did on the trees in the forests. The rain had stopped just after Matilda and Robert had left the gates of the castle, however, not before they had ridden through a cloudburst. Their tunics were soaked through and clung to them in sticky folds. Even their woolen capes did not keep the chill from them as the cold pushed through skin and muscle and buried itself deep in their bones.

Dawn had arrived, although it did not burst forth in an array of color. Instead, the sky had become lighter shades of pewter grey toward the east. The clouds criss-crossed the sky in grey-blue and white tabby-cat stripes. Moisture, in grey tones, swirled up from the ground, wrapping itself around the legs of the plodding horses as if intending to slow them even more. Dancer's feet did not make their usual tapping. Instead, all Matilda could hear was a sucking sound as the road tried to swallow each hoof.

Matilda checked on the knights who followed. It cheered her to see Brian fitzCount's pennant along with the pennants of Ranulf, Earl of Chester, Sir Corydon fitz Pyke, and Sir Griffith fitz Thomas. The azures, gules, golds, and verts that rippled at the head of each knight's unit were the only colors on this grey and windy day. Even the normally bright clothing of the knights was soggy and dull. Matilda liked the banner that belonged to Sir Thomas since it was the most complex and colorful with blue, silver, and gold. It gave her hope for her campaign.

"I do not feel as if we are about to make history. I just feel wet and miserable," Matilda said.

"It is difficult to imagine being dry after what we have been through," Robert said. "However, I see this as a bad omen for Stephen."

"Or for us. I will never trust cousin Henry, even though he is a man of the church." Matilda wrung the water from the long sleeve of her kirtle. She grimaced as a stream made its way from her up-raised wrist to her elbow.

"I have seen too many bishops forget they serve God and proceed to serve themselves instead," Robert said.

"Too many, that is true."

The wind blew fog down from the hills and held it against the ground, further obliterating the horses' legs. Matilda squinted at the trees a mile to her left. They reminded her of a story she had heard in Germany from her tutor. The trees were soldiers who had disobeyed orders and were forced to be guardians of the dark. Matilda pushed the story from her mind. It was too depressing.

"We should see our dear Bishop of Winchester soon. I hope I have not brought us into a trap. I particularly disliked following the deer trails through the woods. We could have been ambushed."

"Henry is not a warrior. He would rather have someone else do battle for him. Without Stephen, he has no one." Robert wiped rain from his forehead with his tunic sleeve without success. "I thought the forest would be safer against attack."

"You are right, of course, but I am nervous just the same. Mayhap it was the wolves that made me nervous. I saw their shadows slide in and out amongst the trees the whole time we were in the woods." Matilda looked over her shoulder at the trees in the distance, watching for the wolves. Time moved slowly and she felt they were players in a play and the soggy plain below them was the stage. She wished she knew the ending to the drama.

Dancer's ears pricked up. He snorted and shook his head. Matilda pulled on the reins and peered through the fog. As if by command, the fog parted and Matilda could see her cousin, Henry de Blois, Bishop of Winchester, riding toward her, his entourage in tow. He looked more regal than the last time Matilda had seen him. Bishop Henry sat tall and as straight as the shaft of a lance; his over tunic was tailored perfectly in crimson; a slash of blood cutting the grey mist. His body was that of an athlete rather than a clergyman.

The Bishop of Winchester raised his arm in a salute. "Hail, Cousin Matilda, our lady of England. How is my favorite cousin this terrible day?"

"Wet and chilled, but well. You look as if God has blessed you with excellent health."

"I have been so blessed. And how is my dear brother? Are you keeping Stephen in chains?"

Matilda rode closer to Bishop Henry and stopped, their horses nose to tail, and the knees of the riders close enough to share body warmth. She did not know if she should reply with seriousness or whether her cousin was joking. It was too soon to tell, so she chose to be serious.

"I have only spoken to him once, and I should have placed him in chains, but I did not."

"You are too soft-hearted, Matti. Do not trust him, for he will promise much and deliver nothing."

Matilda's eyebrows raised. "You sound bitter, Cousin."

"I am proof of his empty promises. You can tell this by virtue of my title," Henry said.

"I, too, can make the same claim by virtue of the title he took from me. You did not agree to meet me on this neutral plain to discuss titles, dear Henry. Pray, tell me why we are here?"

Bishop Henry turned his horse to face the same way as Matilda. They both moved forward, leaving their entourage a discreet distance behind them. Henry placed his hand on Matilda's arm. "I want to reiterate the proposal I made to you on our trip from Arundel to Bristol. I think you will find it beneficial to us both."

Matilda weighed Bishop Henry's apparent anger at Stephen against the possibility of a deception. She decided to play his game a little longer to see where it went. "Your proposal was intriguing. That is why I wrote to you to request this meeting, but are you not loyal to your brother?" Matilda pursed her lips to keep from smiling at Henry's frown.

"I owe no loyalty to my traitorous brother. He has broken his oath to me as well as to my uncle, your father."

"That he has," Matilda said.

"He should be put to death."

Matilda gasped. The thought had occurred to her in a fit of anger, but to hear the words spoken aloud startled her. She pulled Dancer up short and stared at Henry.

"You find my bitterness shocking? I do not mean it, naturally, for he is my brother, and I am a man of God. So, do you agree to make me your chancellor in return for my support?" Henry asked.

"You mentioned choosing the clergy for England under my rule." Matilda weighed all the known facts, including what her advisors had told her. This was her chance to continue her success if . . . She could not relinquish the opportunity.

"I agree to your proposal, Henry."

"Then let us turn our faces southward toward Winchester, and I will lead you across River Itchen and through the famous East Gate. Winchester Castle and England's treasure will be yours. You are to be our Lady of England."

Matilda was prepared for this moment, but still she felt every nerve respond to her wish. Her eyes were cast downward. She did not dare let her cousin see the joy. She kept her breathing steady, and when she felt calm once more, she raised her eyes. "How am I to trust you? You are offering to help me gain the kingdom at the expense of your brother. If you are a traitor to him, then what prevents you being a traitor to me if the mood suits you?" If she caught the Bishop off guard, he hid it well.

"It is a simple matter of need. At this moment I need you, for Stephen is not available to me. More importantly, you can not enter Winchester Castle or retrieve King Henry's treasure without me. It seems the balance of need is in my favor."

A frown flicked across Matilda's forehead. "You are so right, Cousin. I have no choice but to work with you."

"It is late in the morning and there are plans to be made. I must gather a few bishops, for you can not enter Winchester without proper ceremony. I will meet you here again tomorrow at this time, and before the sun is down you will be settled in Winchester Castle."

"Agreed. You must formally receive me in Winchester in order to show the people your change of allegiance," Matilda said.

Bishop Henry took her hand and kissed it. "Of course. Tomorrow, then."

Robert pulled back on the reins, causing the horse to lift both front feet in the air, then drop stiff-legged to the ground. The jolt, although slight, pushed Robert into Matilda.

Matilda looked around for the enemy. Seeing no one, she reined in Dancer. "Is anything wrong?"

"Nothing is wrong. Yesterday we met with Bishop Henry and a pact was made. I want you to myself before people and time take you from me. I want to remember how you look on this historical day."

"Why, Robert, I did not think of you as a poet. You sound like our story tellers about to embark on a long tale."

"Do I? It seems that the years have been a monumental struggle. The time has gone slowly, and yet it has sped past us. We stand on the threshold of history with Empress Matilda leading England through the fog of anarchy and into the sunshine of King Henry's laws. The story tellers will call this the moment of your triumph. Your coronation is the symbol of victory in the Battle at Lincoln, the turning point in our war with Stephen. The River Test is less than a mile ahead. Bishop Henry will meet us as soon as we cross over. To me, it represents your crossing from uncrowned to crowned."

"You are a poet. I find that trait refreshing in my warrior brother. I grow to love you more each day, Robert. There is nothing that I would not do for you."

Robert smiled. "Nothing except give up the crown."

Matilda whispered, so the fates could not hear her, "I would even forgo the throne of England for your safety and your life."

"Now who is the romantic? It would be a foolish thing to do, and I forbid you to harbor such thoughts. I am nothing in God's scheme."

"Dear Robert, you are everything. Without you, I would not have had a chance. You are as important to me as was our father. Come, let us see what wonders Bishop Henry has prepared for us." Matilda kissed Robert on his cheek, then kicked Dancer into motion. She felt regal, and the feeling was wonderful. She sat astride Dancer, her blue chemise exquisitely accented by a yellow kirtle embroidered at the sleeves and neckline in blue. The contrast with her black hair, which flowed down her back, was striking.

The day was sunny, but still chilly. Matilda felt a sense of freedom from the rain, the grey sky, and the general depression that had accompanied the poor weather. She was in a good mood, for sunshine seemed to be a positive omen. She looked behind her at Brian fitzCount's standard waving gaily in the breeze. Matilda noted the other standards fluttering at the head of each army. She saw Miles of Gloucester's army, Robert of Gloucester's army, and though she could not see other standards in the distance behind her, she could see the armies. She listed the supporters in her mind and was elated that so many were coming with her into Winchester to help her claim England.

There were many who were willing to follow a woman to the throne. Matilda looked skyward and wondered if King Henry could see and hear what was happening to England on this day. "I hope you are as happy, Father, as am I."

"Look ahead." Robert pointed. "I see Bishop Henry with quite a collection of the clergy in tow. You will be the center of attraction today in England."

"He has only a small army with him." Matilda squinted into the sun, which was not yet at its apex.

"He does not need an army. He is not your enemy. Bishop Henry is intelligent and knows that the tide of fortune has turned in your favor. He supports the winning side." Robert pulled back on the reins. "You are the ruler of this land. Ride forward alone to meet the conquered Bishop. He belongs to you."

Matilda relaxed and rode comfortably as Dancer picked an easy gait. The distance between Matilda and the Bishop of Winchester closed rapidly, but not fast enough for her.

"Hail, our Lady of England. You look much dryer than yesterday when last I laid eyes on you." Bishop Henry stopped his horse on Matilda's right side. The other riders stopped on Matilda's left. No proper words of greeting came to mind, so Matilda nodded to the Bishop. She was hardly ever at a loss of words. Matilda looked at the men next to her. "Who are your friends, my good Bishop?"

"Allow me to introduce them to you. Bishop Bernard of St. David's is on your left, along with Robert, the Earl of Hereford; Seffrid, the Earl of Chichester; and Robert, the Earl of Bath."

"I am pleased that you found it in your hearts to come to greet me." Matilda smiled at the men.

Bishop Henry leaned toward Matilda. "Others await us at the market place in Winchester. Shall we proceed?"

"I have waited years for this time to come. Let us not wait any longer." Matilda looked behind her. "Brother, since my husband still fights in Normandy, come forward and ride with me as my escort."

"No, my lady. It is best that you go surrounded by your new supporters. Everyone understands my feelings for you. I will be right behind you as is my place."

"As you wish, but I feel your place is at my side."

"I am there, always, in spirit." Robert saluted her.

"We will enter Winchester by the east gate, which is near my palace. From there we meet your subjects in the market place. I am sure that you remember Winchester well," Henry said.

"Before we go to the market square, I would like to visit Winchester Cathedral. I need to thank God for what has been returned to me."

"As you wish, my lady." Bishop Henry slapped the reins against his horse's neck and moved forward with Matilda keeping pace.

They rode down the gently sloping hill to the River Itchen's shallow crossing. Matilda followed Bishop Henry, letting Dancer delicately select the way across the river. Looking down through the clear water, she could see streaks of white chalk showing through the gravel like pieces of delicate lace.

Immediately after crossing the river, the retinue made its way southwards down the road past the poorer cottages built outside the protective walls of Winchester. Matilda felt like an intruder when she accidentally looked inside a windowless, one room dwelling and could see the people staring back at her. Women, old before their time, stood at the doorways with two and three children at their knees and often a baby in their arms. Kirtles were grey and hung on thin bodies of the grey mothers. Matilda looked away. The poor were in every large city, and they would never be anything but poor. It was the way of life.

The main entrance to Winchester crossed a bridge that spanned three stone arches. It represented the strength of her grandfather and her father with its heavy stones. The bridge had been built years ago and still stood as solid as the cliffs on the Channel. To her right, built across the river to take advantage of water power, was a three story grist mill. The paddle wheel cupped the water, took it to the top, then dumped it back into the River Itchen. The mill was engulfed in a fog of its own making as years of chaff seeped from every opening and floated skyward on the eddies of wind created by the man-made buildings, walls, gates, and bridges.

The noise of Dancer's hoofs on the pavement stones echoed off the outside wall of East Gate as they rode through it. Large pieces of granite had been cut and placed so that hardly a fingernail could be inserted between them. The center arch, pointed at the top, was only large enough for two riders to pass through at a time. It was better for defense, her father had told her. Smaller arches on either side of the main arch were for pedestrian traffic only. Above the twelve foot thick gate was St. Michael's Church. Small windows of clear glass imbedded in stone frames overlooked the bridge on one side and the streets of Winchester on the other side. Matilda could see faces at the windows.

Dancer's hoofs echoed off the walls as she moved under the church, followed by the thunderous noise of the army behind her. She felt contented, for she was returning to the city of her birth. Soon she would be at Winchester Cathedral, the place of worship for her family, and then on to Winchester Castle.

"When last were you here?" Henry asked.

Matilda was startled from her revery by the intrusive question. She hesitated in order to prevent irritation from creeping into her voice. "I have not been here since my father appointed you bishop."

They were on the main street of town, High Strete, and the acrid odor wafting up from the adjacent Bucche Strete reminded Matilda why she preferred the country. Down a side street she saw wide ribbons of wool hanging across racks to dry after having been dyed. Some of the shops had stacks of wool piled outside waiting to be woven into cloth. The man-made ditch carried man-made dyed water down the center, splashing miniature rainbows in all directions.

Weavers stood next to their shops, some outside, and the more timid ones in the doorways, staring at her as she passed. Matilda was surprised by the colorful streaks of dye across the tunics, worn like badges of office.

The pungent odor of leather being cured in sheep urine assaulted Matilda before the next street came into view. Her nose started to run. She sniffed to control it, but to no avail. She pulled out a handkerchief from her sleeve and quickly blew. Matilda wanted to place her sleeve across her face to block the smell, but she was afraid she would insult her subjects. She reminded herself that it would be upon this street that her shoes would be made, and she needed several pair. The thought did not help, for her nostrils stung.

The man-made ditch down the center of Tannere Strete carried yellow-brown water from the dredges of the tanning industry, and only mud-colored droplets splashed onto the grassless banks.

Matilda felt relief when Bishop Henry led her down a side street to the left away from the smells and toward Winchester Cathedral. When she saw the facade of the north transept and the choir tower rising above it, her eyes teared. She fought her emotions lest the Bishop think her weak. Within the cathedral, she would find strength as her family had done since William the Conqueror had invaded the island and claimed it for the Normans.

"Which entrance do you prefer, my lady?" Henry asked.

"I want to savor this moment of my return. I would like to enter the western end of the nave, Cousin."

"Of course. I would have it no other way for you."

It was not until Matilda had dismounted that she realized how incredible was the cathedral. Its square, Norman architecture was a reflection of her memories of her solid and dependable father. She stood between the twin towers and waved away the guards. She entered alone through carved doors that were five times as tall as she. Sunlight flowed in with her and illuminated the nave. Her shadow drifted before her across the flagstone floor. She walked down the center of the long room, her footsteps silent because of her soft leather shoes. She looked to the side where stone arches built upon arches held up the enormous roof three stories above her. The majestic beams reminded her of the canopy formed from gigantic branches of trees in a forest.

Matilda moved through the patterns of colored light that shone in through stained glass windows on either side of her, the colors rippling off her kirtle and cascading down to the floor. She felt like a ship parting the waters, only to have the water knit together as if it never had been disturbed. She wondered if her role in history would be like a ship sliding through the water. Would her presence be forgotten?

Matilda stopped before the altar, crossed herself, and knelt to pray. She did not know how much time passed before she stood, but it did not matter. She looked to her right and saw the tomb of her father's brother, William the Red. She was attracted to the grey marble and walked over to the roof shaped lid. She ran her hand across the cold stone.

"This is as cold as you are, Uncle William. My father has told me of your murder that brought you death before my birth. Your accident was strangely similar to my own; both shot by an arrow, but your destiny was to end your reign. You are the last of my family to be buried here. If you had not been shot, mayhap you would have had sons to rule. Forty years you have lain under this rock in your robes of red and gold. The good luck omen of turquoise placed about your neck was too late. My father said a golden griffin's head on an ivory staff is in your left hand to show your royal birth. You were buried, as a king and in kingly garb after your murder. Will I have the same fate? Or will I die a grey-haired crone in my bed? Only God knows."

Matilda walked around the choir section to look at the mortuary chest of the Saxon Kings that had been preserved by Bishop Henry. She stopped before a chest placed on a low wall that surrounded the choir. It held the bones of two kings, a queen, and two bishops. She felt a kinship to these rulers and men of God. Though they were not related by blood, they were related by circumstance. Matilda leaned forward to read the inscription carved on the wooden chest. Words were placed on the likeness of a ribbon, intertwined and fluttering as if there were a wind. "In this chest are the remains of Cnut and Rufus Kings, of Emma Queen, of Wina and Alwyn bishops."

Matilda blew a cobweb away from the corner of the lid. She turned from the sarcophagus and walked past the dais into the nave, past the lacy, wrought iron grill work on the Pilgrim's Gate that laid a pattern on the floor at her feet like a spider's web.

Matilda put both her hands on the handle of the massive door that she had entered before time had stood still. She hesitated not wanting to trade what could be an eternal peace for the woes of the crown. When she at last pushed against the door, the brightness of the sun startled her, and she realized that not much time had passed after all.

The guards rushed to open the door for her and she felt a quick dislike for them, not because they were Bishop Henry's men, but because they represented reality. Matilda felt guilty for disliking them and smiled. She hoped it did not seem artificial.

The market square was more than she had hoped it would be. People were crowded together, twice as many, she guessed, as the square normally held. They were all staring at her, jumping up and trying to get a glimpse of her, pointing, laughing, and shouting. The drab-colored mob was in disarray, unlike the orderliness of a stained glass window, and Matilda had a difficult time making sense of the panorama before her. She blinked rapidly to try to clear the confusion from her eyesight, but it did not help, and she ceased.

She was glad to be outside and on a platform, for she felt as if she were suffocating. There was so much for Matilda to look at that only the rustling of Bishop Henry's tunic reminded her of his presence. She wished Bernard, the Bishop of St. David's, would quit staring at her. Bishop Alexander of Lincoln had the annoying habit of clearing his throat every minute and the subsequent noise made her grit her teeth.

Matilda looked over at Nigel, Bishop of Ely. Here was an old enemy of Stephen's, but did that automatically make him a friend of hers? Her memory caught at the picture of Stephen imitating the chubby bishop's walk, and she frowned trying to erase any thought of Stephen. It was appropriate that she remember Roger, the late Bishop of Salisbury. His death was indirectly on Stephen's head. Matilda had felt sorry when she had learned of the fat bishop's death, even though she had heard rumors of his disloyalty to her.

The bishop had piled the treasures from his church on the altar to prevent Stephen from taking it. However, Stephen was not intimidated by the altar and had stolen the treasure. The shock of Stephen's blasphemy had caused the bishop's death less than three days later. Stephen's avarice had created more enemies for him and more supporters for Matilda.

The trio of Roberts was on the scaffolding with her. She still could not get her brother to stand next to her. Was he protecting her back, maybe from an arrow in between the shoulder blades? Robert of Hereford and Robert of Bath stood on either side of her sibling, names alike, but each different in temperament and looks. Her brother was handsome as were all the men in the Conqueror's family whereas the other Roberts had flaws.

Seffrid of Chichester stood on the steps to the scaffolding. He was tall, and from that vantage point, he would call up to Matilda to tell her to look at whatever seemed interesting. "My lady, see that woman over there? She holds up her baby so the child can see you. The mother will tell the baby stories of this day. The baby will grow up and tell her children of this day. History will be written by the people about you."

Matilda smiled at his excitement, catching some of his enthusiasm herself. "Thank you for being my eyes, Sir Seffrid."

"My lady! The size of the crowd is larger than any in recent times. Nay, even in my lifetime I have never seen such a crowd. The people love you. Look! The monks and the nuns make up a part of the crowd to your left."

Matilda glanced about the crowd until she saw a brown mottle of tunics. It made her happy to see the large number of monks from Hyde Abbey and nuns from St. Mary's. She felt God's presence through them and God's blessing for striving to become what few women had done before. The fleeting thought that God would be angry with a female king had entered her mind when she had remembered the ancient story of Boadicea who, as Queen, had led her army against the Roman soldiers one ill-fated day. The crowd of monks and nuns gave her comfort.

Resounding voices pushed toward Matilda like a wave from the ocean. At first, she could not hear what the crowd was saying, then, as the wave washed toward her, she heard "Give her the crown!" and, "My lady, my lady."

Bishop Henry whispered to Matilda. "Turn toward me."

Matilda turned in time to see the crown pass from Bishop Bernard of St. David's to Bishop Henry. Matilda's breathing stopped as her cousin held the crown high above her head for the crowd to see. She looked at the circlet of gold, so simple, but standing for so much. The sun shone off the metal, precious to Matilda in many ways.

Matilda listened to the words of Bishop Henry. In his deep voice, which traveled across the square so that every man, woman, and child could hear, Bishop Henry proclaimed, "Here is the crown of England above the true ruler of this land. Beneath the crown worn by William the Conqueror, William the Red, Henry the First, stands our Lady of England, Empress Matilda. Chosen by her father, chosen by the barons, chosen by me, chosen by God and now chosen by the people, long may Empress Matilda reign."

Matilda felt as if a fire burned in every inch of her body. She had to force herself to breathe for fear of fainting. The words she had longed to hear were spoken. Her thoughts were drowned out by a great shouting as the people hailed her as their ruler with screams of "Our Lady of England!" "Our King!"

Bishop Henry lowered the crown and replaced it on the cloth-covered tray that had been used to bring it from the treasury. Bishop Henry bowed.

"Arise, cousin Henry. No man of the church need bow to me."

"God may be my ruler in Heaven, but you are my ruler on Earth, and I do homage to your superiority."

Matilda placed her hand on Bishop Henry's shoulder. "Arise, for we should be equal in our representation of Heaven and Earth."

"As you command. You must be tired from the last two days. Would you like to ride through Winchester to the castle? I have made certain that it has been prepared for your use. Your own Ella has seen to the servants and the preparation of your apartment," Henry said.

"You are very kind. I do not feel tired, but I am weary of the noise. Thank you."

"Then we will be on our way. There will be many things for you to do, so today you must rest and prepare yourself for the trying times that all rulers know." Bishop Henry took her arm and steered her toward the edge of the platform.

CHAPTER
XV

HE THREE DAYS SINCE HER CROWNING had been peaceful ones for Matilda. She savored every moment, for she knew that it would not last. She stood at her apartment windows and looked out across the trees toward Winchester Cathedral. Its strength strengthened her. The choir tower, square and sturdy, rose above the nave roof. Beyond the cathedral's roof, the sun rose over wooded hills, scattering the darkness and releasing the wood colors that had been trapped. Matilda was content for the first time in years. It would be wonderful to spend spring in England, especially at the castle her grandfather had built and where she and her twin brother had been born.

"Poor twin brother. First born and first dead."

A knock on the door interrupted Matilda, and she turned to see Ella put her mending aside. "I will get the door, Ella. Do not stop." Matilda opened the door to her expected visitors.

"Sister, you are looking happy this morning." Robert kissed her cheek.

"You are acting well," Matilda said.

Robert laughed. "Here is Miles as I promised you. He has come to tell you of the meeting between those silly bishops and Stephen."

"Come in and sit by the fire. It is chilly, for March has not yet given up winter to spring." Matilda gestured toward three chairs that had been set up next to the fireplace. "There is mead on the table and though it is early morning, I think you will find it suitable." Matilda sat in the chair closest to the fireplace, arranging her woolen kirtle about her feet to cover them. She waited for the two gentlemen to seat themselves. "So, tell me about the Archbishop of Canterbury and the others."

Miles leaned forward, his elbows on his knees, and hands clasped in front of him. He looked as if he were ready to throw himself to the floor. Miles cleared his throat. "Theobald, never having been very brave or intelligent, was caught between two forces. He was afraid of both you and Bishop Henry as well as Stephen. Chosen Archbishop of Canterbury by Stephen, he was not brave enough to change his allegiance to you without permission from Stephen. He and some of the other bishops, along with other citizens, could not visit Stephen without your blessing."

"I found it laughable that they asked my permission to visit Stephen for his permission to betray him." Matilda shook her head. "I gave it to them, of course, along with a directive to the guard to allow them in to see that worm."

Robert leaned back in his chair, smoothing his hair away from his face with both hands. "We have been told that Stephen was at his best with his knightly chivalry. His high standards required him to tell his visitors that they must do whatever seemed best to them."

Matilda leaned forward in her chair. She felt the anger surge through every part of her body. She did not know whether she was angry with Stephen's stupidity or his attempt at valiancy. She spat out the words. "His knightly chivalry did not prevent him from taking the throne."

"It seems that his chivalry is selective," Miles said.

Matilda waved her hand with impatience. "Enough of Stephen. I do not want to waste time discussing him."

Miles nodded his agreement. "While we were with the barons to see Stephen, we were told that Robert d'Oilly came from Oxford castle to pay homage to you."

"He did, and I accepted his support, for I believe that Oxford is most important to us."

"There are barons every day, so I hear, that are switching to your cause," Robert said.

Matilda shrugged. "I expect them to do so, since the tide has turned to our favor. However, I have no illusions about what would happen if Stephen were to escape or be rescued."

"Mayhap it is time that Stephen be executed." Miles said.

"What!" Matilda felt her breath leave and her heart beat faster. She knew Miles was right, but she could not bear to think of it.

"Miles has a point, Matti. With Stephen alive, we are always in danger from his wife, who sits with an army in Kent. There is also danger from the barons who still support him," Robert said.

Matilda could no longer sit still. Blood raced through her veins and forced her to fairly jump from her chair. "I find it difficult to speak of such a barbaric idea."

Robert glanced over at Miles. "If we do not execute Stephen, then believe me, there will be a time of regret. As long as he lives, there is the chance that we could lose what we have gained."

"I can think of several reasons not to execute Stephen." Matilda stopped before the window and stared through the tops of the leafless trees toward Winchester Cathedral. The branches looked like skeletons. She listened for her father's voice. Mayhap he would give her advice.

"What reasons are there for keeping an enemy alive?" Miles asked.

"In battle, all is fair, but to execute Stephen as a prisoner would rile his supporters to the point of attack."

Miles slapped his hand down on the arm of his chair. The resultant crack echoed off the stone walls. "I would welcome an attack. The usurper has no right to an army of supporters. They are cowards and would soon see the wisdom of supporting the rightful heir."

"Do you think there would be a small war, then all would be peaceful once more?" Matilda asked.

"I believe that would be true," Miles said.

Robert opened his mouth to say something, then closed it.

"Go ahead, Robert. Say what you are thinking." Matilda waited while her brother collected his thoughts. He had always been careful when trying to convince her of something. She found this idiosyncrasy endearing, though sometimes nerve wracking.

"I was thinking that many mistakes have been made by people in command who did not execute their enemies."

"I was thinking of the mistake that our grandfather, William the Conqueror, made when he did execute one of his enemies. Our father told us that the execution haunted grandfather for the remainder of his life." Matilda turned back to the window. "Father told us that The Conqueror never killed a man except in battle save for Waltheof."

Miles looked toward the ceiling and rubbed his chin with fore finger and thumb. Miles had always done this when he had had to argue with King Henry.

"Say what you need to, Miles," Matilda said.

"Waltheof was an enemy of the Conqueror. His own wife told the Conqueror that he was plotting against him."

"Judith was the Conqueror's niece, and he found it convenient to believe her. She hated her husband and used his dislike for William as an excuse to rid herself of him. It was a mistake from which the Conqueror never recovered." Matilda sat on one of the stone benches that lined the window alcove. When she leaned back against the stone wall, it did not take long for the cold to seep through her kirtle and under-tunic to her skin. "The Conqueror had to order the execution at dawn so that there would be no fore-knowledge of it."

"Matti, who knew what Waltheof would have done had not our grandfather had him executed?" Robert tapped his fingers against the arm of his chair.

"I can understand killing a man in battle, but I wonder if it is it not against God's commandment to have a person beheaded." Matilda shuddered at the thought of Stephen's head rolling away from his body.

Robert continued tapping his fingers. "I wonder if your love for Stephen is not clouding your judgment."

Matilda's teeth clenched. She waited until her temper was under control. She tried to speak in a voice devoid of emotion. "Robert, there is no longer any love for Stephen. First he took my heart, and then he took the throne. I can not forgive him for either, but it is worse that he took the throne. When he broke his vows to me, I was the only one who hurt. But when he took England, many men, women, and children were hurt."

Matilda felt her face flush as her inner most thoughts were shared. She walked toward the fireplace hoping the heat would cover her embarrassment. She stared into the flames, seeing death and destruction that she could not stop. No, would not stop. She could not run back to Geoffrey; she would stay to fight Stephen's supporters if they were foolish enough to attack.

Matilda looked at Robert. "We have begun a civil war where good men will die. Stephen started a war for me to finish. I can not love such a man as that."

"If we executed Stephen quickly, before anyone found out, then the war would be extinguished and men would be saved from battle." Miles rushed on. "If we do not do something, this war could last for years."

"Is it not over, now that I am in possession of the treasury and the crown?" Matilda asked.

"There is always the chance that the other Maithilde will continue to raise an army to harass us," Robert said.

Matilda felt silence in the room become heavy as the three of them fell silent. She wondered if her advisors were grappling with their particular thoughts as was she. She was shocked at her vindictiveness, and she had to fight the urge to agree to Stephen's execution. She smiled at the thought of sending Maithilde along to Hell with Stephen. It would be much easier to keep the throne without Stephen.

Matilda shook her head. Executing Stephen would be against the laws of God. Without looking at either Miles or Robert she said, "I can not allow Stephen to be executed no matter the consequences. Do not speak of this again, for I will not change my mind."

"As you wish," Robert said.

The promise of spring had come with April flowers, which put Matilda in good spirits, but the remains of winter still blasted through the castle corridors on the rainy days. Today she felt good in spite of the grey sky. The breeze, although chilly, was not uncomfortable. Matilda had hoped the day would be pretty, for she needed everyone to be in a good mood. Mayhap she worried too much. She had agreed to Bishop Henry's audience with the Londoners and so everyone was sitting in Winchester Cathedral, waiting for Bishop Henry to begin.

The stone columns of Winchester Cathedral framed the audience of barons, bishops, abbots, nuns, and townspeople. The delegation from London had been given an excellent position in front of the dais. They were a choleric bunch of old men who were adverse to change, and she would have difficulty convincing them that Stephen was the usurper. Matilda's spies had reported that Stephen's wife, Maithilde, worked through the Londoners against her. Matilda was glad to have Bishop Henry's support.

Matilda sat in the high backed chair and watched the faces of the Londoners from her position to the left of Bishop Henry of Winchester. He presided as Papal Legate over the Legatine Council. She almost smiled as she realized how cunning her cousin was in politics. If he had not called the meeting as Papal Legate, then the Archbishop of Canterbury would have had control, and he would never have agreed to lead such a council as this. Of course, the Archbishop of Canterbury would not have had the intelligence to do it.

Matilda did not like the faces of the Londoners. They were as cold-looking as the April sky outside — grey, menacing, and clouded over. It was obvious they continued to support Stephen. The old fools were so imbued with tradition that they could not see that she was following King Henry's wishes. She had to control her anger when she saw that some of the same men who had promised King Henry their support, had obviously forgotten their promises. Bishop Henry would help convince them.

Matilda sat with her chin tilted, a dispassionate look on her face to hide her excitement. They had to convince the Londoners that she was the true ruler of England, and to ignore Maithilde's lies about her. It was too bad that she and her advisors, including Bishop Henry, had agreed that to have a reception to celebrate her crowning would be detrimental to her cause. It would underscore her weakened position in her fight with Stephen to regain the eastern lands. When the battle for the crown was over, she would have her celebration.

Bishop Henry stood before the curious crowd. When words flowed from Bishop Henry, they resounded off the thick stone walls and enveloped the crowd. Bishop Henry spoke. "We are here to confer on the state of this great country that was in grave danger and near to shipwreck because of this horrible civil war. This war, which could have been avoided had it not been for the untimely ambitions of my brother, need not continue. During the days of my uncle, King Henry, England had been the haven of peace to an extraordinary degree, for no man — not the peasants, not the barons, not the clergy — dared to cause trouble in this beautiful country. King Henry would not allow dissent. Peace had been cultivated by King Henry because he knew that peace brought prosperity and happiness to his subjects."

Bishop Henry as he paused to look over the crowd. "Some years before our king's death, he called the bishops and nobles together and made it clear that these self-same nobles should swear on oath to support Empress Matilda, his only surviving child, as the ruler of England and the Duchy of Normandy at his death."

He stared at the Londoners. "No son was born to him before his death to replace the heirs who had died. His line should continue straight and true. Empress Matilda has given him three grandsons."

Matilda glanced toward Robert who stood with Miles at the edge of the crowd near the Londoners. She could not see any passion in either of their faces, and she wondered if they noticed Bishop Henry's difficulty in justifying his move from one side to the other. She looked back at Bishop Henry, curious about how he would explain his support of his brother instead of her.

Henry cleared his throat. "It seemed that there might be a long wait before the King's daughter would arrive. She was living in Normandy and there were delays in her coming to England. The peace of the country had to be safeguarded, so that King Henry's peace would continue to reign after his death, and thus my brother was allowed to become king. I, myself, stood as guarantor between my brother and God, and Stephen promised that he would maintain those good laws of King Henry." Bishop Henry waited for the murmuring of the crowd to dissipate. "It is painful for me to remember and shameful to have to put into words the kind of king my brother showed himself to be."

The crowd stood quietly, no facial expressions betraying any of their thoughts. Matilda wondered what they must think of the Bishop who stood before them telling them what a failure his brother had been as king. He was good with words, and Matilda was glad that he had come to her side. She started when she realized that the Bishop was talking, and she had missed part of what he had said.

"The king had listened to the counsel of evil men and had treated the advice of good and wise men with little worth. You yourselves know how often I appealed to him. I gained nothing by my efforts but hatred. I, as Legate, have invited you to meet here so that the kingdom may not falter and fail. The greater part of the clergy of England has decided that King Henry was correct in his choice of England's ruler. We agree and we choose as Lady of England and Normandy the daughter of a king who was a notable peacemaker, a king glorious, rich and good, a king who has had no equal in our times. We choose Empress Matilda, and we promise her our loyalty and support."

The polite applause from the Londoners was drowned out by Robert and Miles's robust clapping. Matilda took a deep breath and let it out slowly. No matter, she said to herself. They did applaud. A movement from the crowd caught her eye and she cringed, a habit developed out of fear of assassination.

A man jumped up on the platform with Bishop Henry and held a document out to him. Matilda blinked with disbelief as she recognized Christian, a clerk for Stephen's wife, Maithilde. Bishop Henry took the parchment and read it in silence. "This document has no validity, and furthermore, the name upon this document is that of a despicable man." Bishop Henry's voice reverberated off the stone columns and rumbled across the onlookers. He stared at the crowd before him.

Matilda's ear drums rattled from the booming of the Bishop's voice. She could not take her eyes off him. She did not think it was possible, but the Bishop looked taller. The quiet in the cathedral was overwhelming. Christian took the parchment from Bishop Henry and turned toward the crowd.

In his youthful voice, high-pitched but strong, Christian said, "I want to read what our Queen Maithilde has written." Christian glared at Matilda, then at Bishop Henry.

Matilda felt her blood freeze along with her body. Had she had the ability to move, she would have jumped up and dragged Christian off the platform. He had the audacity to call Maithilde 'Queen'. She tried to shut out his voice, but he continued, "The Queen has written the following: 'I earnestly implore all the assembled clergy, and particularly the Bishop of Winchester, the brother of my lord, that he will restore my lord to his throne since Countess Matilda's own wicked men have cast him into bondage.'"

Matilda's temper flared as she caught the reference by Maithilde to her title as a countess rather than Empress or King. Matilda's eyes darted from Christian to Bishop Henry and back to Christian. Cold reality gripped her heart, for if the Bishop could not overcome this moment, then the Londoners would be lost to the other Maithilde and Stephen's cause.

Christian hardly paused before continuing. "The Queen has asked that I convey this message to you, Bishop Henry, and to those assembled here."

Matilda wanted to jump up and shove her fist into the babbling man's mouth.

"The message from the Queen is that Countess Matilda was not, in fact, crowned and thus is a traitor to King Stephen."

Matilda heard a roar from within herself fill her ears until she believed she was dying. Her heart contracted not once, but several times, and she gripped the arms of the chair to keep from tumbling to the floor. Not crowned? The Londoners did not need to have such thoughts put in their heads. Matilda barely heard the next words from Christian, even though the crowd was deathly quiet.

Christian's voice was louder than it should have been in the quiet cathedral. It bordered on a pitch not unlike a young boy's. "The crown was never placed on the head of Countess Matilda, but merely held above it. Therefore, my lady, Queen Maithilde, says that Bishop Henry did not crown a female king. He did not do so because he knew it was wrong in the eyes of God and man."

Matilda wanted to look at Christian, but she could not. She could not see anything. The crowd that was gathered in front of her were nothing more than a blur. She could not feel, could not see, and could not breathe. Everything she worked for could be taken away by this foolish young man reading the lies Maithilde had written. It was never the strong who surprised one, her father had said, but the weak.

Christian was weak and malleable, but today he appeared strong. Matilda focused on the Londoners. She saw some frown, but she could not tell if they frowned at her or at Christian's impudence. The problem was that the Londoners had been given a reason to go against her. Her adversary was more clever than she had thought. Her father had always warned her not to underestimate anyone, especially the enemy.

Matilda looked at Bishop Henry for help. He was the only one who could sway the Londoners not to follow the words of Maithilde through Christian's mouth. How would he refute the words that had just been spoken?

Bishop Henry's eyes snapped with controlled anger as he glared at Christian. "Please be advised that although I respect a wife's plea for her husband, we know that Stephen, in fact, was the usurper. He went against King Henry's wishes. That reality should not be forgotten. Before you sits the true heir to England's throne." Bishop Henry turned toward Matilda and bowed.

Matilda gasped at the impropriety of a man of God bowing before her. She guessed that Bishop Henry wanted to impress the audience of his loyalty, but it made her feel uncomfortable. What if the Londoners thought she made him bow to her? The gentlemen from London were whispering amongst themselves. She wished she had not seen the heads nodding toward her. Robert's shifting from foot to foot caught her eye, and she looked at him. His face was pale, making his hazel eyes darker by contrast.

The leader of the Londoners stepped forward and addressed Bishop Henry. "We would like to take the Council's decision of honoring King Henry's wishes back to London with us to put before our fellow citizens. We make no promises until we confer with our compatriots about this matter."

Bishop Henry eyed the speaker with almost hidden contempt. "I understand. It was good of you to hear my entreaty. I know you will abide by King Henry's wishes and the laws of God."

Bishop Henry turned toward Matilda and extended his hand to help her to rise. They exited the church through the side door with both their entourages following behind. Matilda waited while Dancer was brought to her. Bishop Henry himself helped her to mount.

She looked down at the Bishop. "I do not know how to thank you, Henry." Matilda had used the childhood name unconsciously, for she was grateful that he had stood by her during Christian's outburst. "I hope that we have silenced any doubts that may be spoken by the Londoners. You are a brilliant politician. I am glad that it is your brother I am fighting and not you." She smiled sweetly at him. Her heart was overflowing with gratitude.

"I am not certain that you will thank me if the outcome is not as we hope. I did not want to give credence to that young man by talking to him at length. Let us pray that the Londoners were not deceived by his zealous nature."

"I trust your instincts, Henry. Let us forget the Londoners for awhile." Matilda reined Dancer about and nodded to Bishop Henry as she rode away. She was anxious to get to the castle. She wanted to discuss the Legatine Council with Robert and her advisors. If she did not have the Londoners on her side, then retaining her crown would be most difficult. Matilda looked at the sky. It was still grey. Where was the sunshine of her life? She hoped it would come soon, for she did not know how long she could wait for peace.

"I can not believe our good fortune, Robert. Here we are in Westminster. We are home. Only six weeks ago we were in Winchester at Bishop Henry's Legatine Council and now, here we sit in the place from which we can rule England. May King Henry rejoice in heaven." Matilda traced the pattern of the stone that framed the alcove for the window. "It seems so long ago that Adelicia and I sat in these apartments and sewed."

"You? Sewing?" Robert grinned. "It was more like you sticking your finger and yelling a lot."

Matilda laughed. "Yes, poor Adelicia never did teach me to sew. I had no patience."

"I have no doubt of that, sister." Robert stepped into the alcove and looked through the clear section of the stained glass window toward London. "The day is bright and beautiful. It seems that summer is actually here."

"It is June, after all." Matilda picked up a small piece of vellum from the writing table and fanned herself. "Haven't you noticed the increasing heat of the days?"

"I have been so busy talking with London's leaders that I have hardly noticed the weather." Robert gestured toward the window seat. "Sit down and we will discuss the plans for the next few weeks."

Matilda sat in the window seat and looked at Robert. "I am listening. You are about to give me advice, for you have that stern look on your face. That look has been part of your repertoire since I was a child." Matilda's memory swept her into the past. "I remember how you talked to me before I left for Germany. I do not recall what you said, but I do recall that look." She folded back the sleeves of her kirtle and took a deep breath. "Please continue."

Robert took her delicate hands between his rough ones and held them as one would hold a small bird. "I have spent many days and long evenings talking with every important leader, nay even unimportant leaders, in London on your behalf. Miles of Gloucester has accompanied me, as has Brian fitzCount. We have made tenuous progress."

Matilda frowned. "What do you mean?"

"We have been able to convince many of Stephen's followers and the conservative Londoners that you were the rightful heir to King Henry's throne, not Stephen. They also see the futility of supporting a captured ruler. However, Stephen's wife, Maithilde, has been attacking you on two fronts. Brian fitzCount was able to discern that not only has Maithilde continued to raise an army, she has sent men out to the countryside and here in London to discredit you."

Matilda shrugged her shoulders. "That is to be expected from her. She wants to be queen. She will do anything to make certain that Stephen has support."

"That is not the problem. The problem is that there is a tendency to believe her stories."

"What are these stories? I can overcome them."

"I would not tell you if it were not important, for I do not want to upset you." Robert's face was serious and he chewed the corner of his upper lip, pulling it downward.

"I will not be angry with the messenger. I must know, so that I can discount her lies."

"That may be difficult, for she is telling everyone that your first born, young Henry fitzEmpress, is in reality the son of Stephen." Robert stared at the floor.

Matilda leaned back and looked at the ceiling of stone above her. She liked the window alcove. It seemed to her that as long as she stayed here, she would be safe. She tried to push what Robert had told her to the back of her mind, but his words could not be forgotten. "Good God in Heaven. She is a foul-mouthed woman. I hope her tongue turns black and falls out."

Robert almost choked as he stifled his laughter at Matilda's curse. "It would be too late for us even if her tongue did fall out. The damage is done."

"Then we shall have to turn that to our advantage. We can claim that since young Henry is twice over the heir to the throne, that gives me the more right to follow my father in ruling England than Stephen. We can also start our own rumors about Maithilde and her William of Ypes. He is not even royalty. I had been told by Stephen himself that Maithilde's second child, William, was not his, but her lover's. Her twins who died at birth were not Stephen's either."

"Are you certain you want to discuss Maithilde's indiscretion?"

Matilda shook her head. "No, of course not. It is unbecoming to spread gossip. Foremost I must consider Geoffrey's feelings. He has taken Henry as his own child. He has clothed him, fed him, taken him on hunts, and taught him more grace than Stephen could ever have. I can not publicly humiliate my husband after what he has done for my son."

"She attacks you on another front and tells everyone that you are the most arrogant person she has ever met. She has stories, distortions of the truth, to back her claim."

"Such as?"

Robert squeezed her hands. "Your treatment of the London delegation at the Legatine Council. It does not matter that it is not true. She is convincing. She has also said that you refused to allow Adelicia to accompany your father to Normandy to see your children."

"That is stupid!" Matilda exploded, jerking her hands from Robert's and pounding her fist into the cushions on the bench. "Adelicia did not come because she is terrified of the ocean. She has always had bad dreams of drowning in the sea. I would never do anything to hurt Adelicia!" Matilda sat, fuming, until she had thought the accusations through. Robert took her hands in his again. Their strength comforted her, and she became calmer. "I can not deny these stories, for then it would make them seem credible to some people. I am trapped by lies and can do nothing. To discuss them would keep the ideas before the people."

Matilda stood, pulled her hands away from Robert's, and leaned against the window frame. The sunny day turned a little greyer for her. "I will have to be careful, for most people will watch for any sign that I am arrogant. If I frown from the sun, people will say that

I am contumelious. If I disagree with someone I become contemptuous." Matilda ran her finger down the leaded outline of a rose, stopping her finger at the point of the thorn. She smiled at the irony of art imitating nature, but leaving out the hurtful parts.

Would history be as kind to her? Would the lies become facts for centuries to come? She hoped not, for if she were remembered, she hoped it would be for what she tried to do for her son and her father and not because of Maithilde's lies.

"We will counter her lies and innuendos with the truth," Robert said.

Matilda whirled around. When she spoke, her words were harsh. She felt her chin tilt upwards and she made an effort to appear less haughty. It was a habit that she would have to break, for people would misinterpret it. "I hate to say this about my fellow man, but it seems that most people want to believe the worst. I am afraid that the lies may do us more harm than arrows."

Maithilde looked down at the dirty pair who knelt before her. They had been Stephen's advisors. Although Maithilde had never been impressed with her husband's choice of advisors, she had used them because she knew they were loyal to him. What were their names? Oh, yes. Bernard de Avon and John fitzWilliam. They were such a dirty pair. Their tunics were streaked with dust and perspiration, for they had been ordered to make haste to her apartment as soon as they had arrived. She could tell from their expressions that they feared to tell her what she dreaded to hear. She had expected Matilda to refuse her request. It would have been stupid of Matilda to honor it, but Maithilde had to try.

Maithilde wanted to kick the messengers before her. She fantasized that mayhap she could have them tortured, but immediately dismissed this idea as foolish when she was trying to get the people to support her. "What news have you for me?" Maithilde fanned herself. It was a hot day, even for June.

The silence was cumbrous and hung like a tapestry in the chamber. "I wish to know what news you bring to me from my enemy who holds my dearest possession a prisoner." The words were spit out abruptly. Maithilde made no attempt to hide her displeasure. "Do stand. You annoy me with your groveling."

John fitzWilliam was the first to his feet. He stood, clasping and unclasping his hands while waiting for his companion to get up.

Maithilde grimaced as the odor of unwashed bodies wafted towards her. These simpletons were exasperating. Stephen never did have sense enough to have decent men to give him advice. "For God's sake, speak. I will not turn against those who have tried to help me. You have tried to help me, have you not?"

"Oh, yes, my lady. We have always supported our king's cause from the day he was forced to fight his way to the throne." John fitzWilliam looked away from the angry face of Maithilde and back at the floor.

"My lady, we tried to reason with the Empress." Bernard de Avon spoke more loudly than was necessary.

"I see." She rankled at the use of the title 'empress'. "Well! Go on!"

"We pleaded with her for mercy, but she would have none of our words. She scorned us," John said.

"Did she behave with her usual arrogance?"

John fitzWilliam pulled his shoulders back. His eyes shifted. He cleared his throat. "She was most arrogant. She spoke rather badly of our king."

"Did she speak of me?" Maithilde's fingers tapped the arm of her chair.

"I do not wish to repeat what she said, my lady," John fitzWilliam said. "She was rude. Bernard and I were forced to beg for our king, but to no avail. We were ridiculed."

"I hope that you will make this ill-treatment known to our supporters and the Londoners so that they can see who will rule them. If they continue to support Matilda, they will continue to be ruled by an egotistical and emotional woman as they have been for half a year. How much better to be ruled by King Stephen whom we know is generous and amiable." Maithilde leaned back in the chair. "You may go to the kitchen for supper. You must be hungry after riding to and from London all in one day."

"You are generous, my lady. There is one other thing that you should know before we go. It will comfort you," Bernard said.

"Yes?" Maithilde found his face an interesting mixture of fear and hopefulness. She almost comforted him, but decided she enjoyed watching this minor noble sweat from fear. "Can you not get your tongue moving? Has your brain died?"

"No, my lady. It will interest you to know that a delegation of Londoners is very unhappy with Empress Matilda. They went to her and asked that they be allowed to follow the laws of King Edward instead of the harsh laws of King Henry. She told them 'no' in a brusque manner. She demanded that they pay the taxes to her that were overdue. The nobles pleaded with her that because of the civil war, they were without resources. They asked that she give them more time. She agreed, but the time extended was only until the next holy day.

"When the nobles reminded her that they needed more than eight days to raise money because they had given all they had to Stephen, she forgot her manners and rose from her chair. We were told that she said to them, 'Yes, indeed. You have poured out money to the usurper. You have squandered your wealth in strengthening his cause and weakening mine. Long have you plotted with my enemies to do me harm. You have no claim whatsoever to any leniency on my part nor any right to have your tax reduced in the slightest degree. You will pay me my due.' Needless to say, the nobles were stunned. They left Westminster Palace in a very disgruntled state."

"She has done well for us. It was only a matter of time before she showed the Londoners her true personality. Now go and leave me to my plans. It seems the time has come for the tide to turn once more in Stephen's favor."

"By your leave," John fitzWilliam said.

"Yes, go. Have a hearty supper and if you desire more, please ask for it. God's speed. You have my blessing."

Maithilde leaned back in the chair and stared at the tapestry that hung across the room. "The time is right for my army to be moved toward London. I shall tell my commander immediately." She stretched her arms above her head. She felt content, for things were moving exactly as she had hoped. William of Ypes would be here this evening, and they could discuss how fast to move the army and then . . . She laughed in anticipation of a rollicking time with her lover.

King David leaned against the back of a chair and clasped his hands behind his head. He stretched his long legs in front of him and stared at Robert of Gloucester. "Does my niece know of Maithilde's latest trick?"

"Do we dare tell your sister of the army that is camped outside London?" Brian fitzCount asked.

Robert frowned. "Matilda is our leader and has to be privy to these things, for she makes the decisions, not you, not I, and not Bishop Henry." Robert glanced around. "Where is Matti?"

The plank door opened and Matilda headed a processional of servants carrying trays of food. "I am here, Robert, with subsistence for you, my dear Uncle David, and Brian. I have enough food for Bishop Henry if he and Miles care to join us. We have enough for even Maithilde's pitiful army that is camped outside London."

Brian pulled a stool away from the table and assisted Matilda in being seated. "You have heard about the army?"

"Indeed. I have more friends than are in this room." Matilda enjoyed the look of surprise on her brother's face. "I have had a glorious day. Sit down, all of you and let me tell you about it. I have never felt so at peace. A small army belonging to Maithilde does not even change my mood." Matilda patted the stool next to her. "Come on, dear Uncle David. Tell me of the beauty of your Scotland and I will tell you of the gaiety of London town and the jolly people who live here. I could almost remember the happy times I spent with my father and mother when we visited the shops in London."

King David waited for the servants to leave the table before he heaved himself from the chair and strode across the room toward Matilda. "I must be getting old, Matti. These bones do not move as they once did."

"Do not tempt the gods with such a thought," Matilda said. "Sit down and help me to re-live these last few happy days."

King David sat and put his hand on Matilda's arm. "Yes, I will help you re-live your happiness, for the happy days will be few and far between."

"Why, Uncle, how depressed you seem. What reason do you give for this countenance of foreboding?"

King David smiled. "Pay no attention to me, Matti. It is merely homesickness for my own lands. I miss the summer heather and the bogs. I miss the chirping of the spring sparrows and the brogue of my own people. The Londoners sound so harsh to me when they speak. Most of all, I miss my own son who stands guard with his army at our borders against Stephen's friends."

Matilda leaned her head against her Uncle's shoulder. "I did not realize how selfish I have been to keep you in a war and away from your family. Mayhap . . ."

"No. You need me and I need to be here. I promised my sister as she lay dying that I would take care of you. I promised your father that I would pay homage to you as King of England. I am a man who keeps his word. Enough said on this subject. You have my armies at your command and here we shall stay." King David looked across the table at a covered serving dish. "Pray, Matti, let me have some of the good English beef hidden in that dish."

Matilda laughed. "You do change the subject quickly. Come, Brian and Robert. Sit down. We will not wait for Miles and Bishop Henry. They are walking the outer curtain wall to get a glimpse of Maithilde's army. I have already sent out spies to get a closer look, for although I trust my dear friend, Miles, I do not trust my cousin, Henry."

Brian fitzCount sat on Matilda's left. "You are right about Bishop Henry. I never trust anyone who can trade sides so easily, and who has a gift of a golden tongue to sway an audience."

Matilda waited while the servants poured water from the aquamanile over the hands of her guests and dried their fingers with white linen towels. The guests being so served, Matilda held her hands up high enough for the catch bowl to be placed beneath them. The warm water was poured from the mouth of a fish-shaped pitcher, its dorsal fin deformed to make a handle. The softness of the warm towel brought back memories of the banquets she had shared with her father and Adelicia.

The servants laid out eight small loaves of bread and left quietly. Matilda handed a small loaf of bread to Robert who sat across from her. "I miss Ella. She would have enjoyed London as much as I, had she been with me."

"Where is she?" asked Robert. "Was she not supposed to join us here?"

"Yes, but she is pregnant once more and due the end of July. She can not travel well at all. This child is giving her more trouble than the first baby, but she will be all right according to the chirurgeon. I have her safe at Gloucester."

Matilda looked up as the door opened and Bishop Henry walked in with Miles of Gloucester behind him. "What news, Cousin?"

"The army is camped on the south side of the River Thames. It is a fair sized army, but in no way comparable to yours," Henry said.

"If I may contradict you, Bishop Henry, I think there are hidden troops. We must not be complacent." Miles walked over to the table.

"Sit down, Miles, and cousin Henry. I am sure you must be hungry after your nightly walk." Matilda picked up the aquamanile while the two men seated themselves. Etiquette required that she pour the water over Bishop Henry's hands first.

"You always have a good table set with good food," Bishop Henry said. "How do you manage?"

"I have spent two days roaming around London and buying everything edible I could find. London is still as exciting as it used to be. The people are the jolliest. The French seem sedate and dull compared to our Londoners." Matilda picked up a serving dish of roast pigeon and passed it to the Bishop.

"You seem happy," Bishop Henry said.

"Today was exciting. I even went to the selling fields and watched the sale of horses. I was tempted to buy several, for they were noble and elegant, healthy and shiny." Matilda wiped her mouth. "I was intrigued by the market. There were spices from Arabia, and gold for making jewelry. I saw precious stones and incense, wonderful furs from Russia and Norway. I would have bought a lovely cape, but it was so hot today I could not bear to plan for winter. I bought a beautiful piece of purple silk from China. I will have a kirtle made from it tomorrow. Of all I saw, that was more of a treasure for me than any of the vast treasures."

Matilda reached for the wine. "I bought this excellent French wine for our dinner tonight. Allow me to pour for all of you."

"The French do one thing right, do they not?" Miles said.

Robert chuckled. "We should forgive them all their other faults, for their wine is perfect."

"Some of their women are perfect, too," King David said.

Matilda gasped as she set down the wine. "Uncle David!"

King David grinned as the other men laughed. "Sorry, Matilda. I forgot your presence."

"You forgot your age about which you were complaining a few minutes ago." Matilda smiled at the pink color of her uncle's cheeks.

"I can not forget my age when I look at you and see a woman instead of a little girl. I remember I used to take you to see the boys play on the ice of the great marsh." King David leaned forward on his elbows.

Matilda stared into the past. "Oh, yes. I had almost forgotten. They tied shin bones of animals on their feet and flew like birds over the ice, pushing themselves along with poles. They were like the spirits of the night, only they were there in the daylight. Sometimes they were so fast, and there were so many of them trying to hit the same stone that they fell and broke an arm or a leg. It is odd, but they did not seem to care about broken bones. The game was too important to them." Matilda looked at her Uncle. "I have not remembered that for years."

"And here we are, that same little girl leading a strong country," Robert said.

"For how long and how successfully, I know not," Matilda said. "Henry, I wonder if the London nobles were unhappy with my imposed taxes upon them."

Henry coughed and dabbed his mouth with a napkin. "You need the taxes to support your cause."

Matilda sighed. "I was a little harsh with them. I lost my patience with their sniveling about how they had spent all their money supporting Stephen. I should have held my temper, but they are traitors in my eyes."

"They will give you their taxes when they are due," Henry said.

"I am not certain that your idea was a good one, and now I question your counsel. I could tell that the men before me had little to give what with the civil war." Matilda stared at the Bishop's narrowing eyes.

Henry frowned. "I will not take blame for your actions since you chose to berate the gentlemen. You do need the taxes in order to continue."

"Really? I wonder sometimes about . . ."

"About what?" Henry sat stiff and straight.

Matilda watched the red creep up his neck until it was invading his face. "Nothing. Let us forget that episode. I need to remember the good times. In this day and age, good times have to be made. Let us remember this dinner as a good time."

Robert raised his chalice. "Let us drink this fine red wine to that."

"And forget, for the moment, that Maithilde's army is posted outside of London," Brian fitzCount.

"I have already forgotten that." Matilda smiled at Brian. "Her army is not large enough to do us any harm."

"Unless the Londoners join her," Henry said.

King David glared at Henry. "Forget that thought. If the Londoners joined Maithilde, then we will lose a great stronghold in the east."

"Please, do not mention such things. Miles, your plate is empty." Matilda reached for a platter of venison when she hesitated, her hands resting on the handles.

"What is it?" Miles asked.

"I know not. It sounds like bells." Matilda pushed the platter away and cocked her head toward the window. "Why would there be bells this time of night?"

"A fire?" Robert asked.

Matilda pushed back her stool so quickly that it fell with a thud. Her instincts were always good, and the sound from beyond the windows frightened her. Whatever was happening was bad for her. She rushed to the stained glass window and pulled it open, ignoring the night breeze that rippled through her hair. "I do hear bells. Many bells. What is it?"

King David crossed the room to stand behind her. "It is very bad news, Matti. It is the call to arms for the Londoners."

More stools hit the floor as Brian, Miles, and Robert jumped up and joined King David and Matilda at the alcove. Matilda whirled around and screamed at Robert. She could feel the blood vessels in her neck straining. "Do not tell me! Do not tell me that they are joining Maithilde in support of Stephen. They can not. I am the ruler of England, not Stephen. He is my prisoner. Mine! How can they do this to me?"

"We have no time to discuss this now. We must flee at once." Robert grabbed Matilda and pulled her away from the window.

Matilda grabbed the wooden shutter and held onto it. "No! I will not run. We must fight. Robert, call our armies. We must fight for England."

"We are outnumbered and unprepared. Our men are not in armor. We must fly." Robert grabbed her fingers and tried to pry them from the shutter.

Matilda turned away from him and clung harder to the shutter. Over her shoulder she shouted at him. "Fight! Damn you, fight!"

Robert stopped pulling at her fingers and put his arms around her. He leaned close to her and whispered in her ear, "We can not. I wish we could. It is your life. Now, flee. If not for yourself, then for your son."

Matilda stiffened, then slumped against Robert. She did not want to believe him, and her mind raced with thoughts of how she could get the army together. She closed her eyes and thought, but nothing would come. There was no way to get their men in armor. She had to admit that Robert knew what he was talking about. She kept her face averted so that the men would not see the tears that threatened to flow down her face.

"You are right. Let us leave before we are captured. We will fight another day. How sick I am of fighting and running."

Miles stepped away from the alcove and ran across the room, calling back to Matilda. "I will get Dancer ready for you."

King David pulled on Matilda's arm. "Come, Matti. It is no great shame to run to avoid capture; the shame is in fearing to fight. God knows I have had to retreat."

Matilda shuddered, but turned and crossed the room quickly, pausing just long enough to grab her wrap from a chair. Swinging it around her shoulders, she tied it as she followed Robert down the stairway with Brian and Henry behind her. She stopped halfway down the steps, causing Brian to bump into her. "I have to go back. I forgot my rings, and I need my books."

Brian pushed her forward. "We do not have time. I do not care if every jewel you own is up there, we can not go back."

"I have them for you. I have run often enough to know what is precious to those on the run. Go quickly, " King David said.

Matilda quickened her steps to keep from falling down the stairway. She felt Brian grab her shoulders, and he propelled her down the hallway. The small band ran across the inner courtyard, the men shouting warnings to the army along the way. When they reached the stable, Miles was struggling with Dancer while the groom tried to saddle him.

Matilda could see the whites of Dancer's eyes and he pranced around, threw his head back and snorted. "Here, let me hold his harness. Saddle your own horses while I calm him. He knows when there is trouble. He senses a battle and wants to fight." Matilda was glad to see that Miles did not hesitate to follow her orders. She was an expert with horses, but with Dancer she had an affinity that was unusual. No one could have handled Dancer at this moment except Matilda.

Matilda talked quietly with Dancer, while she stroked his nose with her left hand and draped her right arm about his neck. She reached for the bridle, which was handed to her by a servant, and slipped it effortlessly into Dancer's mouth. "Now, quickly, slip a saddle on him. Make haste, for we have to fly, but make certain you do well by my mount and me." Matilda waited for the cinching, checked to make certain that it was not too tight, and then gracefully mounted, pulling her chemise and kirtle above her knees. She would forget that she was a lady for a while.

She moved toward the gate, Robert in the lead with Brian and Miles on either side of her. Henry and King David followed. They clattered out of the castle, horses' hoofs beating a poignant rhapsody on the paving stones. They headed north, away from the enemy. Matilda clung to Dancer, bending low, and letting his mane slap her face. Only with the sting could she be certain that it was not a dream, but in reality, a nightmare. Matilda pulled back on the reins, causing Dancer to rear, and she turned him around. Matilda heard Brian yell for Robert to stop, but she paid no attention to their admonishments of her behavior.

Brian reached out and pulled on Matilda's sleeve. "We are not out of danger yet. Oxford is hours away, my lady."

Matilda shook her arm free from his hand. "Leave me alone."

"We do not have time to look," Miles said.

"I have to see my beautiful London where the people were so jolly and wonderful; where each day was filled with excitement; where for nine months I ruled the world's greatest kingdom. I have to see her fate."

Brian looked toward the southeastern horizon. "Oh, God."

King David's face reflected the reddened sky and in it Matilda could see the sadness of first hand knowledge of the looting, pillaging, and destruction. She looked toward London again and shuddered. She was aware that a tear slid down her cheek and dropped onto her kirtle. Happiness was like a piece of moonlight. It only shone without clouds. Her happiness was gone and mayhap the future for her son.

"You have a right to be distressed," King David said.

"It looks so small from here. That is what makes me cry. I have cried seldom in my life, but the other time is when I watched England grow smaller and smaller."

"When was this?" King David asked.

"I was on the ship, sailing to Germany as the betrothed to the Emperor. I was only in my seventh year. England got smaller and smaller and finally disappeared. I thought, childishly, that England was gone forever. Then I cried. Even though I am an adult and I know better, seeing London getting smaller and burning, causes me to cry just as that lonely child did."

King David leaned across the space that separated them and kissed Matilda on the cheek. "That is for the lonely little girl still inside you." He took her hand and squeezed it. "That is for the grown-up Matilda who needs to be reminded it is time to force our mounts to fly toward Oxford."

"Yes, Uncle." Matilda turned Dancer toward the northeast. She looked over her shoulder. "Where is cousin Henry?"

"Do not worry about Henry. He will make his way to Winchester. I am not certain of his loyalty anyway," Brian said.

"I wondered, too, but this is no time for discussion. Follow me." Miles kicked his horse in the ribs and the mount leaped forward into the night.

The air was still. Not a leaf stirred and the sun beat down relentlessly on the Itchen River and Winchester's inhabitants. The cows and sheep stood listlessly in the fields, barely moving. The horses switched their tails to shoo the pesky flies, but without the usual vigor. Matilda leaned out the window of Winchester Castle and stared across the lifeless fields with the spiritless animals. She held her hair off her neck and wished she had taken the time to have a servant braid it. It was odd to worry about hair when only two weeks ago she had begun to worry about how she was going to rule England. All was not lost. She effectively controlled the western half of the country. However, it would certainly be more difficult to gain all of England without the support of the Londoners. She stared across the roofs of the town of Winchester. Thank goodness, Henry had supported her. Winchester was an important stronghold on the Itchen. She was safe here until it was decided what they were to do.

Matilda wondered at God's schemes. She had run from London to Oxford and now she was in Winchester, again, all in a matter of a few weeks. "I have ridden across half of England." Matilda talked to herself as she rubbed her backsides. "I have felt every bump on every road, too." She clamped her hand over her mouth. "I should not be talking aloud." She looked at the river again. Without a breeze, there was no use hanging out the window. She moved across the room, leaned against the wall, and let the cool stones soothe her. She slid down the wall and plopped on the floor, giggling as she did so. It was a most unroyal position.

Robert knocked on Matilda's open door and entered the apartment at her invitation. He laughed. "Are you comfortable, Matti?"

"Robert, it is cooler down here." Matilda pulled the skirt of her kirtle below her knees.

Robert chuckled. "You hardly look the lady down there. What's the matter? Has July's heat melted your reserve?"

"I have never felt such sticky heat in Winchester before. It is rather disconcerting." Matilda stood, fanned her face with her hand, and walked to the window alcove. Her sweat-dampened kirtle wrapped itself about her ankles. "Even this open window does us no good. There is not a leaf that is not lifeless." Her eyes traveled over the tops of the trees to the roof of Winchester Cathedral. She gathered strength from her grandfather through his favorite place of worship.

"Is it not strange that history will remember people I know, myself included, but the pages will only record deeds and not feelings or personalities. How will people know why I struggled against Stephen? How will they know me, if indeed, I am part of the pages of history? That would be worse, would it not, to have to struggle daily for a place for one's son, only to be forgotten?"

"I did not know you were a philosopher as well as a leader," Robert said.

"I am in a depressed state. I have sent for Bishop Henry — repeatedly — and he sends me notes saying that he is preparing himself. My spies tell me that his preparations are hastily built fortifications. He has turned against me."

"He was not worth your while."

"But, Robert, you know better than that. He was very necessary to my quest. How much more can I lose before I lose?"

"You still have Stephen."

"That baggage. For how long?"

Stephen held out his arms. He ignored the perspiration that trickled down his face. The heat of July was worse than usual and, coupled with his anger at Matilda, made him hot. Ten months of captivity and no end in sight. His followers were continuously hopeful, but he was not.

He hated Miles of Gloucester, but he had to keep Miles from guessing the depth of that hatred. Stephen hoped the time would come when he could do something about the offensive manner in which he had been treated by Miles. Stephen decided to play the innocent, but injured, prisoner. "I will not struggle against the chains imposed upon me by Matilda. I fail to see, however, why she ordered me harnessed like a common prisoner. Does she think I am a dog?"

Miles stood against the door to Stephen's apartment, arms folded, and a scowl on his face. "Twice you were found wondering around the castle at night. It would do our cause no good to allow you to escape. It proves that even here at Bristol Castle, there are those who can be bribed and those who can not."

"I am the King. I do not have to bribe people. I have followers who will do anything for me." Stephen winced as the bands were snapped around his wrists. He stood patiently while the ankle bracelets were clamped on. The weight made him feel like a martyr and he felt good. When he walked, the sound of the dragging chains pulling the reeds along behind him almost made him laugh. Stephen turned and looked at Miles. "Tell Matilda that I will think of her each day as the weight of these chains has taken the place of the love I had for her."

"I would not lower myself to take her that degrading message." Miles opened the door and walked out, slamming it behind him.

Matilda pushed herself away from the table. "We have been in Winchester for two weeks. We have found that Bishop Henry has spent the entire time fortifying his castle. Our spies have discovered that he has been meeting with Maithilde in secret." Matilda folded the sleeves back on her kirtle. It should have made her cooler, but it did not. She was still sweaty. "I have to attack Bishop Henry. Uncle David agrees with me, do you not?" She looked at King David who stood at the window, his hands clasped behind his back.

He nodded. "It is time we went on the offensive. Bishop Henry's fortifications are poorly done. We still have Stephen chained at Castle Bristol, far behind our own lines. If we do not strike soon, we may lose our nerve."

"An army gets lazy if it does not fight," Robert said.

"We have to be sure we are strong enough to win. A siege without a surrender is worse than no siege at all."

"We can not just sit here," Matilda said.

"Our forces are weaker than they were. Maybe we should send for the Count of Anjou to help us. Geoffrey should be here. If we can not keep England, we may lose Normandy and Anjou," Miles said.

"No!" Matilda's brow was furrowed. "He has to keep his armies across the channel. We must keep peace there." Matilda rubbed her hand across her forehead. "I wish my young Henry were older. In my heart, I know he will make a great leader. I saw my father in him even when he was just a knee-baby."

Robert poured a chalice of wine and handed it to Matilda. He waited until she took a sip, then said, "I think we should lay siege to Bishop Henry's castle. We can not let him snub you any longer without ramifications."

Matilda set the mug down. With the forefinger of her other hand, she wiped a drop of wine off the rim, then licked her finger. "Are we strong enough? Bishop Henry has an army of his own."

King David turned away from the window. "He is not a warrior. If we do not strike soon, then Maithilde may join Bishop Henry. If that happens, we will be cut to the heart."

"Brian, do you concur with the others?" Matilda studied his face. She loved to see his freckles darken when she looked at him.

Brian glanced down at the table and tapped his fingers on the mug in front of him. "I think like the others. We have no choice but to flush out the 'wolf' from Wolvesey Castle whether we are at the peak of our strength or not. We must move soon."

"Are the armies ready?" Matilda asked.

"They have been ready their entire lives," Robert said.

Matilda took a drink, watching Robert over its rim. "I suggest we choose a day to trap our wolf in his den. Get the army ready to move the next moonless night when there is no rain. That should be within a fortnight."

Miles banged his fist against the table, making the dishes jump. "Good! I am ready for a fight. We have too long been idle."

CHAPTER
XVI

WILLIAM OF YPES kicked the ground with the toe of his boot. The reins of his horse were slack in his hand, and he listened to the soft snorting of his war horse who pawed the ground.

"I am bored, too, old boy. There is nothing like combat for the likes of us. We have been playing at war, but the real battle has eluded us. Ah, for a little blood to make life worthwhile." He glanced toward Westminster Castle, but could not see it or London because of the trees. It was ironic that he liked fighting and war more than he liked the woman who ruled from that castle. Maithilde might rule in the name of her husband, Stephen, but she was the real power in that family. William could understand why. She frightened him with her temperament, and he strove to do as she asked rather than risk her wrath. Once she had angered him so much that he had slapped her, and she had laughed. William felt his face get hot at the memory.

The wind lifted William's brown hair from his forehead. The breeze felt good after the scorching day that was hotter than usual even for July. The sky was the clear blue of a perfect summer day. The sun hung straight above him, bright saffron in color. The wind was coming in from the east, and William could smell the salty ocean. That happened on rare days when the weather was clear and hot, or clear and cold. William inhaled again. He liked the smell of the Channel.

He bent down, picked up a piece of flint and rubbed it until he had removed all the dirt. Some people claimed the ancients had made weapons from this same type of rock. William rubbed the stone between his fingers. He shrugged. Maybe it was so. Men had always fought. Men had always died.

William took a last look around the quiet countryside, and patted his horse's neck. "Come on, boy. It is time to go back." He swung effortlessly into the saddle letting his horse move forward as he did so.

They reached the postern gate an hour after high noon. William dismounted and handed the reins to the groom. "Make certain that you rub him down well."

William climbed the steps to Maithilde's tower apartment. He smiled at the idea of sneaking into her apartment. It seemed hypocritical, but it was best not to flaunt their relationship at this crucial time.

He knocked on the door and waited for Queen Maithilde's command. He could judge from the tone of her voice whether or not she was in a good mood. He frowned at her command to enter, for today her voice was neutral, and he would have trouble decoding her disposition. He stepped inside, closed the door, and leaned against it, giving himself time to adjust to whatever attitude Maithilde displayed.

Maithilde looked up from the dressing table, one hand poised near her cheek, fingers laden with silvery-white cream from one of the many pots in front of her. She smiled into the mirror. Her eyes met William's. "I am so glad you came. What news of my enemies? Are they still laying siege to hapless Bishop Henry?" Maithilde laughed. "I hope he thinks he is in Hell, poor man."

William was relieved. She seemed to be in tolerable humor. "Poor, indeed. He has countered with fire brands to such an extent that almost all of Winchester has been burnt to the ground. I find it pathetic that the Bishop has ruined his own city."

"Please come and sit while I finish." Maithilde smoothed the cream into her cheek and down her throat. "This is the latest face cream from Egypt. It will stop time, and I will be young forever. It is made from the same ingredients that were used for the queens of Egypt."

William winced. Whenever Maithilde talked of her youthfulness, he found that he had to compliment her endlessly on her beauty. That was difficult for him. Complimenting women did not come naturally for him as it did for those used to the life at court. He cleared his throat. "You do not need creams to make you beautiful."

Maithilde glanced into her mirror, then turned and looked at William before wiping her hands on a cloth. "Come and sit beside me, so we can plan for Matilda's demise. First, tell me about the problems in Winchester."

William crossed the room and sat on the bench next to Maithilde. He could smell the perfume she wore, and it brought back pleasant memories. He leaned over and kissed the nape of her neck.

"If you continue to do that, we will not get any plans made." Maithilde leaned against William's shoulder. "What of Matilda's siege? Has she forced Bishop Henry from his castle?"

"Our spies tell us that Bishop Henry has destroyed St. Mary's Abbey. It was necessary since the nuns were sympathizers to Matilda's cause. Bishop Henry also destroyed the Hyde Monastery. His firebrands were so powerful that they went over the walls and outside Winchester to route the monks from their beds in the middle of the night."

Maithilde chuckled. "The clergy should have known better than to side with the weak." Maithilde leaned forward, her lips curled upward. "Tell me, how have the disloyal people of Winchester fared? Badly, I hope."

"It is difficult to describe the terrible destruction. Hardly a building is left, so I am told. The homes with their thatched roofs went up like haystacks. There are many homeless who have nothing more than the charred rags on their backs. Many lost their lives, and I am told the stench was horrible from the burned bodies. I do not think the survivors like being the center of war."

Maithilde pulled William's face toward hers and kissed him. "I find your talk of war fascinating, William. Tell me more of the piteous cowards of Winchester, the traitors."

"Then I should never want this civil war to end, for you will no longer need me." William reached behind Maithilde and untied the lacing on her kirtle.

Maithilde jerked away from William. "Stop that! I am not finished discussing our plans. Matilda still continues to fight, and we must do something to loosen her hold on the Bishop. I enjoy watching him squirm, but he has agreed to switch loyalty back to us if we get him out of his predicament. He is such a fool, for now his loyalty will always be in question."

"The city is ready to collapse. Matilda has the inhabitants nearly starved to death. It is time for the besiegers to become themselves besieged." William took Maithilde's hand and kissed her palm. "I have had a report that supplies are going to be smuggled into Winchester by the men who support Robert of Gloucester. More supplies are going to arrive from Bristol through Andover for the Empress. I have to leave before dawn to get to Andover. My men and I will burn that city to the ground and hold the area around it. No supplies will be able to get through. There will be further repercussions, for I have excellent spies who tell me every move that Matilda and her brother plan. The walls at Winchester Castle truly have ears."

"No more talk of war. Come to my bed and let us forget our problems."

"In the middle of the day?"

"The better to watch you, dear William."

Her hand felt so tiny in his, but William knew that it was not the hand of a weak woman. She would have England and she would have him. "Do you not want to hear of more of my war plans?"

"No." Maithilde stood and pulled William toward her bed.

The stone wall pressed into Matilda's back as she leaned against a merlon, but the strength of the wall did not comfort her. She turned and looked out the slit that formed the arrow loop and watched the setting September sun. The rays slid across the burned out homes of the people of Winchester, wrapping the blackened beams with false gold, obscuring the tragedy.

How much longer could she let her soldiers die and her people starve? How much could England take before Matilda had to give up what was rightfully hers? She heard her father's voice as if he were beside her. He had told her many times that war kills by necessity. A ruler could not think about the deaths, but only of the victory to come. Matilda turned away from the sight and leaned against the merlon, again. She pushed her back against the stones to force herself to feel something, anything, but it was to no avail. She felt hollow. She was so exhausted that she had to force herself to move, to walk, to get up in the mornings. She was afraid that if she stopped, she would slide into a permanent sleep.

The sun had dropped below the level of the horizon and a chilling puff of air caused Matilda to shiver. It was only two weeks to Michaelmas, and the nights were getting cooler. She walked along the wall walk to the tower with the stairway down to her apartment. An armed guard opened the door for her and she smiled her thanks and wondered how long he would live if she sent him into battle against Maithilde's forces.

The curved stairways always wound down to the left and Matilda remembered her father told her that was so a castle could be defended from intruders coming up. The enemy would be at a disadvantage, for his right arm would be next to the supporting column and confined by a narrow space. She lifted her arm, an imaginary sword in her hand, and cut through the imaginary enemy who came up the steps. She did have more room to maneuver.

She put away her imagination as she neared the apartment door. If the servants had seen her, they would have thought her possessed by evil spirits. Matilda slipped inside. She wanted to be alone, but she could see her brother standing in the center of the room. Matilda knew from the look on his face that he was about to give voice to a major concern. She hoped it was not another lecture about her health.

Robert of Gloucester put his hands on Matilda's shoulders. "Matti, you must eat. You have paced along the wall walk of the outer curtain until you have worn it down at least six inches. You have to keep up your strength. The times ahead will be difficult and you will have to be strong in mind and body."

Matilda leaned against her brother. She loved the feel of hard muscles through his tunic. Without Robert, she knew she had no future for England, for herself, or for her son. "I can not eat as long as there are people starving. There is little enough food, but even if there were, I would feel no hunger."

"You are our leader. You must remain strong. I have ordered food brought to you." Robert pushed her toward the table and made her sit down. Robert motioned for a servant to remove the lid from the soup tureen. Steam arose, but he winced when he saw that it was mostly water, pieces of fat, and one stunted carrot.

Matilda waited for the soup to be ladled into the mazers, then waved the servant away before he could perform the washing ritual. The servant stood a little ways from the table, uncertain of what to do. Matilda did not have the energy to tell him. She was glad when Robert told all the servants to leave. She could not think any more.

Robert sat opposite her. "Why do you stare at me, Robert?"

"I worry about you. I have yet to see defeat on your face, but I fear I see it now."

"Why should you not see defeat? Am I not done? Has not Bishop Henry burned Winchester and William of Ypes burned Andover? Our supplies are stopped and we starve. Have I not failed and brought about the deaths of many innocent people? I walked the wall and saw ashes where homes once stood, where families once dwelled and lived and loved.

"I smelled the flesh of the dead and dying as it wafted upwards. I saw the innocents roaming the streets looking for their mothers. I caused that, Robert. I caused generations of people to be unborn because I killed the receptacles that held their seed. I caused the deaths of nuns and monks. I will go to Hell for this, and it will still not be enough punishment for what I have done."

"Stop that!" Robert reached across the table and grabbed Matilda's wrist. "You are not to blame for what has happened. Do you not remember who usurped the throne? It was Stephen who broke a twice-sworn promise to King Henry. It was his despicable wife who forced the weakling to take what was not his. The deaths that you saw today are not on your soul, but upon his."

"That does not make the dead less dead." Matilda felt Robert release her wrist. She had never seen him so animate. "I still feel that the decision I made to fight Stephen has caused these deaths. If I had only been content to stay in Anjou. . . ."

"If you had been content to stay in Anjou, then young Henry would not have a chance to become king of England. It is his due. We do not want Stephen's issue, Eustace to rule. He has the temperament of his mother."

"I have heard of Eustace's cruelty," Matilda said.

Robert's voice softened. "Young Henry has the best temperament of his mother, his grandfather, and even the wonderful charm of his father — his real father. I can foresee him as England's greatest king. Do not deny him the chance to make England the greatest country in the world. If you do not fight for yourself, fight for young Henry. Fight for England."

Matilda picked up her spoon and stirred the soup, looking for a thread of meat clinging to the fat. There was none. She put the spoon down and watched the ripples. "The price is high."

"The price is high for the most valuable jewel, the most precious perfume, the rarest spice," Robert said.

Matilda studied his face. Of all the people she had in her entourage, Robert was the most trustworthy. His advice meant much to her. She picked up her spoon and began to eat. She stopped only after she had finished. "We can not stay here. We will have to leave by the West gate. Tell the men we will have to travel with few possessions, but in full armor. We will leave just before dawn and go to Castle Ludgershall. From there, we may have to retreat to Devizes or even Gloucester Castle."

Robert nodded. "We can make it if our plans are kept secret. I will tell the army to ready themselves, but I will not tell them until early morning, and I will not tell them where we go."

"It will not be difficult to tell where we are going. We can not go east or north or south. William of Ypes will know which way we go. We can only hope that he will not expect us to leave now." Matilda pushed up the sleeve of her chemise. Her kirtle seemed too large for her, and she felt as if she were wearing a sack. Matilda jerked at the offensive sleeve, but it did no good. She ignored the uncomfortable feeling and promptly forgot the sleeve. "It will be a long night with no sleep and a difficult day tomorrow, for there would be much riding to do. Tell Uncle David that if . . . if things go badly, he is to make his way back to Scotland. He will do us no good if he is captured."

"I will tell him. I leave now. You get some rest. I will wake you in the morning."

"I will not sleep."

Matilda sat astride Dancer and watched his hot breath push out from his nostrils. The colorless breath made her shiver. Winter was not far away and already the nights were cold. She pulled her woolen cape tighter. Tied across the saddle in front of her was a leather pouch that held her jewelry and the small, green suede book that Geoffrey had given her so many years ago. She touched the pouch to make certain the book was there. She had most of it memorized and at once a quote flashed before her. 'Oh, Achates, is there anywhere, any place left on earth unhaunted by our sorrows?'

Matilda looked over her shoulder toward the east. The sky was not yet light, but the men were ready and anxious to ride out. The war horses pawed at the ground, undoubtedly sensing the mood of their riders. She patted Dancer on the neck. "What would I do without the strength of you, boy?" She was startled that she had spoken aloud and turned to see if Brian fitzCount had heard her. He sat on his horse next to her, but was turned away from her talking with King David.

Miles of Gloucester was on her right and her brother was directly in front of her, breaking the custom of having her lead the army through the gates. That would never do. Matilda kicked Dancer in the ribs and moved forward. "Robert, may I speak to you?"

Robert leaned closer. "Yes?"

"I want to lead the army as usual. It looks as if I am afraid, and I have to ride behind you. I am a woman and your chivalry is admirable, but I am also the leader of this army, of this country."

Robert shook his head.

"Robert, if I do not lead my army, I am not fit to be king."

"You are right, but I can not take a chance on your safety."

"I can not take a chance on my losing what little support I have gained. I can not act like a woman when I am in the role of a man."

Robert frowned. "All right. I will ride to your right and slightly behind you with Miles to my right and Brian and King David on your left. Is that satisfactory, Matti?" He took her hand and kissed it.

Matilda smiled. "Thank you."

"I fear for you, mayhap too much so, but without you, Matti, I have no reason to exist. I feel that I have taken the place of our father to make certain that you keep the throne."

Matilda placed a finger against Robert's lips. "Say no more. It is time we move out, Robert. The sky gets lighter, and I am most anxious."

"I await your command," Robert said.

Matilda raised her arm toward the gatekeeper. She watched as the bars were pulled back and the inner gates were opened. She heard the wail of stretching hemp against wood as the outer gate was lifted. Before the gate was all the way up, Matilda raised her arm again and motioned her army forward. Matilda winced as they clattered out of the gate, trying to be as quiet as possible for an army of two hundred.

She set a steady pace, trying not to move too fast or too slowly. She wanted the army to ride out in good order, not as if in retreat. They rode away from the sky that was getting lighter and from Winchester Castle that was getting smaller. She looked back once, then not wanting to see the castle disappear, stared straight ahead.

Thirty minutes into the ride Dancer's ear flicked forward and he snorted. Matilda felt as if she were being watched. She looked over her right shoulder toward the eastern sky, but saw nothing except trees and small hills.

Turning in the saddle, she called back to Robert. "Do you see anything unusual?"

"No, but my instincts tell me that something is amiss. We have to ride too close to the woods for my comfort, but there is no other way."

Matilda raised her arm and stopped. The army stopped behind her. It was at that moment Matilda thought that Hell had come to earth. She saw Stephen's gules and silver banner carried, she guessed, by William of Ypes. The Flemish mercenaries swept down on them from three directions. Robert grabbed Matilda's horse and shouted for Brian. "Take her from here. Fly and save her at all cost. King David and Miles, stand with me to hold the devils away!" Robert slapped Dancer on the rump and the horse bolted forward.

Matilda leaned forward, and gave the horse his head. She was vaguely aware of Brian's presence, but it was submerged by the noise of pounding hoofs beneath her, beside her, and behind her. Riding low with Dancer's mane stinging her face, she reached into the left sleeve of her kirtle and withdrew her dagger. If she had to die, then she would take an enemy with her.

The sun made bloody streaks across the cloudless sky, and Matilda thought it ironic that such a beautiful day might be her last. She caught a movement from the corner of her eye and a hand grabbed for her. She brought the dagger up and as she caught the eye of an armored soldier, she slashed out toward his uncovered cheek. He grabbed her arm and would have unseated her had not Brian fitzCount swung his battle-axe into the soldier's back. Matilda turned away as blood splattered her cape. The only thought she had was to survive in spite of Maithilde and the damnable William of Ypes.

As she raced in front of Brian, Dancer picked up speed. Dancer's ears laid back, and he flattened into a racing stride. Matilda hoped his heart would hold out, for he was using every ounce of his strength. She was aware of the chaos around her, but she refused to believe it. Her army had tried to hold rank, but they were outnumbered and out-maneuvered by the mercenaries. Her mind saw her men fighting for her and dying for her, but part of her refused to believe it.

Once she cried out for Robert, but she could find him nowhere. Brian appeared as if from nowhere and tried to keep pace, but he could not. It seemed like an eternity until they saw Ludgershall Castle. With no standard showing, Matilda wondered if the guard would get the gates opened for them.

She ventured a look behind her, but she and Brian were alone. Dancer stumbled and her heart jumped. She pulled back on the reins and slowed down to a trot, then to a walk. It would never do to lose her horse. Not this horse, for he was a part of her.

Brian rode up next to Matilda. "My lady, do not tarry now for they could be close behind."

"I can not take a chance on Dancer's straining his heart. He stumbled. He is exhausted. I would rather die myself than have him fall from under me." Matilda looked over her shoulder. "Where are the others? Do you know?"

"I left them all in order to be with you. I fear the worst, for I saw many of our knights die at the hands of William of Ypes' men." Brian shook his head. "I fear we had a spy among us. Robert did not tell the men until a few hours before we left that we had planned to move out."

"It was a only a matter of time before Maithilde sent her Flemish lover and his mercenary army after us. I do not understand why she wants us to return Stephen to her. She seems to be doing fine without him." Matilda felt the bitterness filling up inside her. She wondered how much more she would have to endure before she gave up. If only she could have a victory. A small victory would do.

Mayhap a soft bed is the only victory that I need. Victory over sleep first, then victory over Stephen.

"I see the guards at the gate watching us closely. Without our colors showing, we may have to ride on to Devizes." Brian held up his arm and waved. "Hello! May we stand for inspection?"

Matilda and Brian stopped in front of the thick, wooden gate. From the tower above the gate, several guards looked down on them. "Who calls us?"

"It is a friend. I present to you our Lady of England, Matilda, King of England and Normandy, Holy Roman Empress, and Countess of Anjou. I, who escort her, am known as Brian fitzCount, castellan of Wallingford Castle. Please tell Count John of Ludgershall that we are here."

The guards saluted and one disappeared. Matilda sat silently, feeling the heaving sides of Dancer beneath her. She should have dismounted, but she was as exhausted as Dancer. She was afraid that she could not get back on. It would never do for people to see her in a weakened state. She looked down at her wasted and thin body and decided that it would not matter much whether she got off Dancer or not. He probably would not be able to tell the difference.

It seemed a short time and a long time before the gates were opened, and they were allowed in. Time was a peculiar thing Matilda thought. It was not so long ago that she had had strength and hope that England would be hers entirely. Now, she was on the losing side again, and time favored her enemies.

Matilda rode slowly through the gates into the inner courtyard. Count John was there to help her from her mount. He said nothing, but half carried her to the great hall where he deposited her in a chair.

"Take care of Dancer." Matilda's voice sounded harsh to her, and she smiled to offset the curtness of her request.

Count John nodded, his curly, brown hair falling across his forehead and tangling with his bushy eyebrows. "I have already ordered that brave horse cared for. My best groom is with him. Dancer's worth to you, my lady, is legendary."

"Where is Brian fitzCount?"

"He is seeing to the possibility of traveling on to Devizes immediately. Please excuse me while I see to some nourishment for you. I have to be less than mannerly, but it is an unusual time."

Count John pointed toward the doorway to the kitchen. "Amelia is coming with a tray for you. Brian will be in soon."

Matilda nodded, watched Amelia come toward her with a tray filled with slabs of bread, meat, cheese, and two mugs of ale. The food was placed on the table before her, but she had no appetite. Instead, she put her head down on her arms. The last thing she remembered was the sound of crackling reeds as Amelia left her to sleep.

It seemed only a minute before Matilda felt hands on her shoulders shaking her. She tried to shrug the hands away, but to no avail.

"Matilda, you must hurry and eat. This is no time to sleep. I know you are tired, but we have to leave. We are not safe here." Brian shook her shoulders again. "Please, my lady. I have arranged for fresh horses."

Matilda felt as if she were coming back from the dead. Her arms felt so heavy that she could not lift them, and her eyes refused to open.

Brian pulled Matilda into an upright position. Her head fell against his arm. "Please. England needs you. Your son needs you."

Matilda pushed Brian away and laid her head on the table. "I need sleep."

"You can sleep when we get to safety." Brian pulled her up and held a mug of soup to her lips. "Drink this, my lady. Be strong."

Matilda took a sip and opened her eyes. She held Brian's hands that were around the mug. When the soup had been drained, Brian handed her a piece of venison. She took it like a starving animal, jerking off the strips of stringy meat and nearly swallowing them whole. She did not wait for Brian to hand her a piece of bread, but tore a chunk from the loaf and crammed it into her mouth. She washed down the bread with ale.

"You are not eating, Brian. Please, eat while you can. We have a hard ride." Matilda held a chunk of bread toward him. "Eat this while I wrap some food in a cloth."

Brian took the bread and tore off a bite.

"Did you say that we would have fresh horses?"

"It is time to go," Brian said.

Matilda's knees were weak and her legs were shaking. She held onto Brian's arm, took a deep breath, and walked with him across the great hall. They stepped into the courtyard and the sun hurt Matilda's eyes. She heard a familiar snort. Dancer was being rubbed down with a wet cloth. She walked toward him and stopped in front of the horse to let him nuzzle her. She liked the feeling of his hot, wet breath. He was confirmation that there was life in her world of new death. Matilda rubbed his forehead. "How is he doing?" She looked at the groom, who worked to get the sweat-soaked mud off his coat.

The old man straightened his arthritic body slowly. His grizzled face had seen many years. He looked directly into Matilda's eyes for a long time before he spoke. "If you ride this horse one more step, he will collapse. He must care for you a great deal, for he would die for you. He is a king among horses."

"I can not leave Dancer! Could I not lead him to Devizes?" Matilda rubbed Dancer's velvety nose.

The old man tapped Dancer's front leg and the horse lifted his leg. "His frogs are bloody from the ride. His right front foot is the worst, for he has thrown a shoe. I will keep him here and care for him. When he is well, I will find you and make my grandson bring him to you. I promise that he will get the best of treatment." The old man rubbed Dancer's leg. "He deserves the best that I can give him."

Matilda bent over and looked at the bottom of Dancer's foot. She stood and wrapped her arms around Dancer's neck. "I will have to leave you, my friend." Matilda turned to the groom. "He has saved my life several times. I . . . I love this animal as one might love a true friend."

"I promise that I will take good care of him." The groom patted Dancer's rump. "I have saddled a good horse for you. He is an excellent steed. The best we have." The groom pointed to a brown horse in the courtyard, ready for riding.

Matilda rubbed Dancer's forehead, turned quickly, and walked over to the other horse. She waited for a servant to hold the brown horse, then mounted him astride. She adjusted her kirtle, checked to see that the leather pouch with her book and jewelry had been attached to the saddle, and looked around for Brian. He rode across the courtyard toward her.

"My lady, we must hurry. We have spent too much time here." Brian kicked his horse and moved toward the gate.

Matilda fell in beside him, pulling the horse to the right, then the left to check his response. He was good, but not as smooth as

Dancer. She looked back once when Dancer neighed at her. She had to turn away from him quickly lest she cry.

"When we leave the gate, run as fast as the horse will take you. We will have to ride without stopping the eighteen miles to Devizes." Brian signaled the guards at the gate to open it.

Matilda kicked her horse and he started forward. She watched two men turn the capstan to lift the gate. Before it was fully opened, she rode under it aware of the spikes just inches above her head. She felt like ducking, but it would be unseemly for an Empress to do so, especially when she was running for her life as it was.

The two outer gates were pulled open, and Matilda kicked her horse hard. He vaulted forward. She loosened the reins and gave the horse his head. He ran, the ground sliding under them at a dizzying rate. Matilda could not hear Brian's horse because of the wind in her ears and she glanced out of the corner of her eye. He was there, as always, keeping pace and protecting her. Still, she felt vulnerable. They had decided against the use of the army from Ludgershall. The army might have given them some protection, but Matilda had pointed out that the dust raised by an army would attract too much attention.

As if sensing her emotions, the horse lunged forward at a faster speed. Matilda leaned forward; tears streamed down her face formed by the wind in her eyes. She let the horse run full speed for only five minutes. She pulled back on the reins and forced him to a trot, then a walk. Matilda looked back and realized that Brian's horse could not keep up. She stopped the horse, patted him on the neck, and looked around the horizon. Nothing moved, but that did not calm her. She felt tired, tired enough that she knew she could go to sleep and never awaken. It was a comforting thought, but Matilda forced it from her mind. She had sons who needed her. She missed young Geoffrey and young Henry, and little William.

"Please do not run so far in front of me. This poor old horse can not keep up with the one given you," Brian said.

"I am sorry. I am too tired to think properly." Matilda slapped the reins against the horse's neck and both she and Brian moved out at a slow pace. "Do you think we will be safe at Devizes?"

Brian looked back over his shoulder, then at Matilda. "We will not be safe until we are at Gloucester Castle."

Matilda shuddered and increased the pace of her horse. Brian's horse trotted beside hers, keeping pace. "I am so tired, Brian."

"I can tell. You have not been eating well. Of course, there was little to eat while we were under siege. We will be at Devizes late this afternoon. We have to get you to Gloucester Castle without being seen."

"I worry about King David and Robert. I have not seen them since our enemies surrounded us." Matilda pushed her hair away from her face.

"I am afraid for them."

It was said so simply and with so much conviction that Matilda gasped. "Brian, no."

They rode in silence the rest of the way to Devizes Castle. Matilda's energy, what little was left, had dissipated with Brian's confession. She was in such a depleted condition that when the castle towers appeared on the horizon, she almost failed to comprehend that they had made it this far. She saw four tall towers rise above the hill inside the inner courtyard and surrounded by a wall, then wide steps that led to the lower castle. She thought that she saw people on the steps, watching their arrival. The turrets were farther back, rising above the wall-walk that rose from the main level of the castle. The vine-covered outer castle wall surrounded the entire complex with two octagon-shaped gate towers guarding this approach.

Matilda glanced behind her to make certain the enemy was not in sight. She was shocked to see that she had crossed the bridge over the moat and had ridden through the gates of Devizes Castle without knowing she had done so. She rubbed her eyes. She had to maintain her senses. Even this stone fortress did not seem safe to her, but she was relieved to be here. She was aware that hands reached up to catch her as she almost fell from the horse.

Matilda allowed someone else to completely control her for the first time in her adult life, and she let them carry her into the stable and lay her on a linen sheet atop a pile of hay. She drifted in and out of consciousness. The thudding of the horses' hoofs against the stable floor became part of her torturous dreams.

"I can not awaken her." Brian shook Matilda. "See, she seems nearly dead, but she still breaths at a regular pace." Brian turned toward the physician. "Can you not give her something to revive her?"

"Not without endangering her heart. The medicines I have are too strong for such a delicate body."

"We can not stay here. I have to get her to Gloucester Castle or she will be captured for certain." Brian closed his eyes. Her fate and the fate of England was in his care. He wanted to be able to carry out his mission, but he worried about his ability. "I can not let anything happen to my lady."

The physician shook his head. "She can not ride. She is still enough to appear dead."

Brian snapped his fingers. "That is it. Who would bother a poor husband taking his wife back to her people for burial? Get me a death shroud and a litter. It does not suit my lady, but it will be safe. Do not stare at me so! I can not think of the appropriateness of the action when I have to think of her safety first. Go, sir, we must make haste."

The physician smiled. "It is a remarkable plan. I will get a new shroud right away."

Matilda felt as if she were suffocating. She pushed against the rough woven material that nearly covered her face. Her arms were crossed over her breasts, and were held in place by the tight wrap. She cried out and the bouncing stopped.

"My lady, you are awake." Brian laid his hand on her shoulder. "You are still very weak."

"I do not understand why I am trussed up like a Christmas goose." Matilda gazed up at Brian. He seemed farther away than he should be.

Brian loosened the laces on Matilda's shroud. "You are in disguise as a corpse. I am sorry to say, but your exhaustion gave me the idea. I know the litter makes the ride rough, but I have ridden past two men who looked like they were from William of Ypes' army. They paid us no heed." Brian looked around. "I hope that no superstitious peasants see me talking to a dead person."

Matilda chuckled. "I hope no superstitious peasants see the dead person talking back. You are very ingenious, Brian. I salute you. How far to Gloucester Castle?" Matilda tried to flex her stiff legs.

"Less than a mile. You have been asleep the entire way. If you will allow me, we will ride the rest of the way in this charade," Brian said.

"It is a good idea, but go carefully over the rocks."

"Gloucester Castle is ready to receive us, my lady."

The knocking on the door to her apartment in Gloucester Castle interrupted Matilda's thoughts. How long had she been here? Oh, yes, Ella had told her that it was less than two days. Matilda heard the door open and Brian's voice drove away some of the clouds in her mind.

"It is good to see you again, Ella. Have you and your family fared well?" Brian asked.

Ella curtsied. "It is good to be with my lady once more. My husband and family have fared better than my poor lady."

"In spite of our problems, my lady refuses to quit. Has she rested well?"

"She has slept from sundown to sundown and then to sunrise. She has risen, but sits as if dead in the window alcove, save for letting silver coins drop from hand to hand." Ella shook her head. "I worry more that she speaks so little and does not shed one tear."

"May I see her?"

Ella opened the door wider and stepped aside. "Of course. She needs you."

Matilda held up a piece of silver. "See the coin Robert had minted with my likeness?"

Brian sat next to Matilda in the alcove. "You are more beautiful than the coin's representation."

Matilda rolled a coin back and forth between her thumb and forefinger. "I find it ironic that this silver will survive me, mayhap by hundreds of years. Will the person not yet born who holds this coin know me? Or will my deeds be forgotten? See? The likeness wears a crown. Is that not a counterfeit image of a counterfeit king?"

Brian frowned. "I will not honor such talk with a reply."

"How soft is the flesh that holds the coin? Softness that decays."

"Matti, we may decay, but what you are doing for England will not die. Believe that with all your heart."

"My heart is too full of worry. I watch for Robert, King David, and Miles of Gloucester, but I see no one. I am afraid for them all."

"We can do nothing but wait, Matti. It is far too dangerous to send any of our army, given what is left of that army, to spy. If, perchance, Robert, King David, or Miles of Gloucester survived, it is only a matter of time before they will ride to us here."

"The waiting is so difficult, Brian. I feel as if I have been consigned to eternal damnation. I can not imagine Hell being any worse than the pain I am going through now." Matilda stood and leaned against the stone frame of the window. She saw a figure riding slowly toward the castle. She could not make out the person through the bubbled and rippled glass, so she pulled the window back, nearly stepping on Brian in her haste.

"What is it?" Brian leaned out the window with Matilda.

"Can you tell who rides? He looks exhausted," Matilda said.

"There is no banner and he is quite alone." Brian shaded his eyes with his hand against the morning sun. "I can not see who rides toward us."

Matilda lifting her skirt and ran across the room with energy she did not know she had. "Let us go meet him. Mayhap it is good news."

"Wait! It may be something you should not see." Brian hurried after her.

Matilda raced down the long hall, her feet barely touching the reeds. "I have seen the death of my quest for the throne. What worse thing is there?"

"Nothing, I suppose." Brian followed her down the stone steps that led to the inner courtyard. They crossed the courtyard, past the garden that was no longer green. Most of the plants were edged with brown and past the bearing stage. A gold and black cat sat sunning herself, licking her front paw. Matilda was prepared to leap over the cat, but the cat ran through the garden and disappeared behind a small bush.

"Open the gates! Open the gates!" Brian shouted as he approached the guards.

The men leaped into action. The gates swung inward. The outer lattice gates were raised just as the rider reached them. Matilda was astonished to see that the only clothing the man had on were linen braies. He was bare-chested, bare-footed, but worse, he had no armor or weapons. The horse he was riding could hardly walk. Its head was down, matching its rider's posture.

Matilda gasped when she recognized Miles of Gloucester. She ran toward him, but Brian was faster and caught Miles as he fell from his horse.

The wearied man whispered, "My lady, I have failed you."

"No, Miles, you could never fail me. You are as faithful as the castle dog." Matilda knelt down next to him on the dusty ground. "What news of my brother and my uncle?"

Miles pushed himself up on his elbow. "The news is not good for Robert."

The world crashed for Matilda. She closed her eyes to steady herself, for the ground was threatening to heave itself upwards. All was lost if Robert were lost. She whispered, "Is he dead?"

"No, but he was captured by that Flemish warrior, William of Warenne. He is no doubt in the hands of Maithilde by now." Miles closed his eyes. "I feel the traitor for bearing this news."

"Do not think such things. If anyone is to blame, it is I." Matilda snapped her fingers at the guards who stood near, overcome with curiosity. "Get a litter and take him to my apartment. See to him, Brian. I will order broth and bread from the kitchen."

Matilda paced back and forth in the hallway outside her apartment, waiting for the chirurgeon to check Miles' condition. She would not allow herself to think that Robert could be executed as a traitor, for when she did, chills coursed down her spine and made her stomach churn. She cursed Maithilde with every step she took.

The door finally opened and Brian motioned her inside. She did not like the frown on Brian's face. "Has he eaten? Is Miles all right? He is much too old for this."

Brian stepped aside as Matilda entered. "He is exhausted, half starved, and dehydrated. He is in worse condition than we were."

Matilda watched as the chirurgeon closed his chest of medicines. "Is there anything that he needs that you do not have? I will send for it."

"Nothing, my lady. Although he is past life's prime, he is strong, thus healthy in spite of his ordeal. There are no injuries either to his outside or his inside." The grey-haired doctor wrapped his gnarled fingers around the handle of the medicine chest and picked it up.

"Only his soul is injured, for he feels he has failed Robert and you, my lady."

Matilda moved next to the bed and picked up Miles' hand. She was shocked to see that the hair on his arms had turned white. She wondered when that had happened. It shone in the light from the window and Matilda looked at the hair on his head. It, too, was whiter than she remembered. He was of her father's generation and so she should not have been surprised, but she was. Time seemed warped for her, but she pushed the thought to the back of her mind to think about later.

Matilda squeezed the bony hand that she held. "You have been a faithful friend to my father and to me. How can you think that you have failed? You are like family. You were always there whenever any of us needed you. I remember when I was just a child barely able to walk, you were by my father's side daily. If anyone has failed, Miles, I have."

Miles squeezed her hand. "Thank you for your words of comfort, but in my heart I will always wonder if I could not have saved Robert from our enemies."

"No, Miles. I have no doubt that if you could have, you would have." Matilda was silent, then she said, "Tell me of my uncle, King David. How goes it with him? Do you know?"

"He is one of the bravest knights I have ever seen. Three times he was captured, and three times he fought as a bear protecting her cub. Three times he swung his battle-axe with such ferocity that even though surrounded by the enemy, Robert was able to drive them back. Blows from his axe made blood fly, and he made many widows and orphans that fateful day. He has made his way back to Scotland, so I was told, to strengthen his army."

"I will never be able to repay such loyalty." Matilda turned to the chirurgeon who stood patiently beside her. She wanted no audience with an outsider when she asked about her brother, Robert, for she feared her reaction. "Would you check on this gentlemen tomorrow? Until then, *adieu*."

"I will do so. By your leave, my lady." The chirurgeon bowed and left the apartment.

Brian placed a stool next to the bed for Matilda and she sat, arranging her kirtle with great care, delaying what she knew was the inevitable. She did not want more pain, but there would be more pain. Could she be strong? Could she get up once more when knocked down by fate? She plunged forward with no further procrastination. "Miles, tell me of Robert."

Miles closed his eyes and turned his face away from Matilda. "His last words to me were of you, my lady. Robert and I stood between you and Maithilde's army. I fought until I was unseated, then with no enemy near-by, I watched as Robert fought like a possessed man. He killed men on his left and on his right. When his sword broke, he rode past one of William's men, pushed him from his horse and grabbed his battle-axe.

"He rode back into the thick of the fighting and killed two more men. Robert had ridden into the waters of the River Test at Stockbridge when Maithilde's army suddenly swarmed him like bees. The water turned crimson with blood as Robert fought furiously. Men fell and drowned, held under by their armor. Others were lucky enough to loosen their armor and let it fall, and thus with the burden lightened, made speed in front of the chasers.

"Alas, poor Robert was captured by more than a dozen men. I ran toward him. His voice boomed across the few feet that separated us."

Matilda swallowed, trying to rid herself of the lump in her throat. "What did he say?"

"He asked if you were safe. I shouted that you were. He told me to forget about him, that I had to fight my way free to be with you. I obeyed him, though my heart did not want to leave him. I picked up a dropped sword and slashed my way to freedom. My mail was discarded, but my padded leather under tunic was still intact, however, not for long. I thank God that the only thing cut to shreds was that. It hindered me so, I had to discard it as I ran. I was fortunate and found a horse. You know the rest." Miles groaned. "We live in wicked times when God helps the likes of Maithilde."

Matilda's eyes flashed. "It is the devil that helps Maithilde."

Brian fitzCount turned from the fireplace where a small fire blazed. His face was red from the heat. "I agree. It seems the devil possesses Maithilde and William of Ypes."

Matilda touched the dagger she wore hanging from her belt. She had worn it for so many weeks that it seemed a part of her.

There were spies and enemies everywhere. Matilda liked the feel of the solid handle in her hand. "If Maithilde causes even slight harm to befall my brother, I will search her out and murder her with my own hands. It would pleasure me to see her life's blood flow out of her body like the River Avon flows out to sea."

Brian let out a sigh. "Where is Robert being held?"

"Possibly Rochester Castle, but it was a peasant who told me this. He heard it from his neighbor, a shepherd, and thus we do not know of its worth." Miles opened his eyes and looked at Brian. "Do we have enough men to ride to the coast and rescue him?"

Matilda answered in Brian's stead. "No. We have an army scattered by a force stronger than they are — fear. If we ever gather our men again, they will be fewer in number, for some barons will switch sides having perceived me as the weaker leader of the two."

"A mistake for them to think that," Brian said.

Matilda waved the suggestion away. "Nevertheless, true. We can not rescue Robert with force, so there is only one thing to do. I will hold Stephen so long as I can, but if we must, then a trade for Robert will have to be made."

Miles pushed onto his elbows. He looked at her for the first time since he had begun. "But, my lady, that would mean the end of your quest for the crown. Without Stephen, you have nothing."

"Without Stephen, I have no brother."

"Forgive me, but would Robert want you to give up England for him?" Brian asked.

Matilda's smile was wry. "I ask not what Robert wants, for he is not at liberty to say at this moment." Matilda smoothed a wrinkle from the linen covering on the bed. "I have no campaign without my closest advisor and my closest friend. It would be a hollow quest without him."

Brian looked at Miles and nodded. "We will wait to see what Maithilde proposes, but we should not give in too soon or too easily. It was a calamitous day when Robert was taken."

"That it was." Matilda looked at the flames consuming the log on the grating and wished the log were Maithilde.

Robert stood quietly, watching as Maithilde stared at him from a brocaded chair, cat-like. He imagined that he was the cream.

She tucked a strand of hair behind her ear. "Well, Robert, you have been treated properly these past few weeks, I assume. Does

Rochester agree with you? I had you placed near the coast for the fresh sea air."

"Quite nice, but not as agreeable as Gloucester Castle." Robert felt like squirming under her gaze, but he did not want her to think he was nervous. She merely disgusted him.

Maithilde laughed. "You always did amuse me."

"You have managed very well in spite of your husband's captive status. I find your military strategies well-planned and executed." Robert bowed, watching Maithilde's eyes.

"Do sit, Cousin." Maithilde motioned toward the brocaded chair opposite hers. "I am most anxious to talk with you of matters of some importance."

Robert did not like the sound of her voice. It was too sweet, and he suspected her motives were not honorable. She was intelligent and manipulative. "Would it offend you if I stood?"

Maithilde glared at him. "Yes, it would offend me. Sit."

Robert sat, watching as Maithilde twisted a gold ring set with a blue stone around her forefinger. He recognized the ring as one that had been given to Matilda by their father, and he gripped the arms of the chair to suppress his anger.

"I understand that, as brother to Matilda, it was only fitting for you to promise to help her, and I admire that. However, now that all is lost. . . ."

"Forgive me, but all is not lost. Though we are seemingly at the nadir of our quest, I believe that God will see us through." Robert's eyes narrowed as Maithilde's face contorted in anger. Until normal color was restored to her face, she was silent.

"Such a brave man as you should help our king restore order to this kingdom. Too long have we laid waste to the good people of this land, and too long have we laid open the bodies of good men to let their souls escape Heaven ward. It is time to heal the wounds of England. To do that, I need your help."

Robert was silent, studying the individual stones that made up the fireplace next to him. He felt the muscles in his jaws tighten as he maintained silence, for silence was the only way he could assure himself that he would not lash out at the enemy he faced. It was difficult to remember he was a gentleman.

Maithilde leaned forward, letting her unplaited hair fall over her shoulders and across the bodice of her gown. "I know you are a gentleman, for William of Ypes has told me so, though I am not certain he would recognize the finer points of chivalry. You have been treated very well, at my command, for I feel that together we could restore England to its greatness."

"I believe that it is in my power to restore England to what it was under my father, King Henry. That is why, when I swore to him to support his daughter, my sister, I have done so faithfully." Robert leaned back in his chair, again watching Maithilde's eyes. He liked to see them flash in anger. She was easy to bait. There was a secret, inner joy to the winning of these small battles for his sister.

"Let me try to convince you, again, Cousin. I am not offering you mere freedom. I am offering you something you can never have with Matilda. I am offering you power over the whole land. You would be second only to the king in that power. You would be his advisor, for we both know that although King Stephen is loved by his people, he is in need of someone to help him with the decisions in running this land." Maithilde placed her hand on Robert's. "I do not want to see you imprisoned. I am taken with your . . . manner, and your loyalty to your sister, but the time has come to review the situation without emotion. You could become powerful and wealthy, more so than Bishop Henry who changes direction as does the wind."

Robert disliked the heat of his jailer's hand on his. She was so close he could smell her spicy perfume, and he felt as if he were suffocating. He wanted to withdraw his hand from under hers, but it was not the genteel thing to do. This was an arduous time, and he had to be careful. He did not speak.

"My dear cousin, do you not want power and riches?"

"I have power in the love of Matilda. I have riches in knowing that I have kept my oath to King Henry."

Maithilde took her hand from Robert's, and sat back. She tapped her bejeweled finger on the wooden arm of the chair. "If I did not believe in your knightly vows of valor, I would think you unchival-rous. Again, I ask you to join us in re-uniting England."

"I am not a free man. I am in the power of others. When I am once more my own master, I will decide what seems best with regard to your proposal. That is my answer. I will speak no more of this until times change and Matilda no longer holds my oath in her heart."

Maithilde sighed. "Then, can we not talk of an exchange? Surely that would not break any oath that Matilda holds in her heart."

"That is true. We may talk of an exchange, for although I am being well-treated, I do not like being unable to ride as I choose."

"At least we did not put you in chains, as was my poor Stephen."

Robert smiled. "Chains are of different sorts. Castle walls and castle gates are enough chains for me. Stephen was seen wandering outside his apartment. He needed chains to prevent his escape."

"You agree to an exchange? You for Stephen?"

"I am unworthy of such an exchange, and firmly opposed to it. The king is a much more valuable commodity than am I. He is a king, I a mere knight, unworthy, at best." Robert flicked a piece of lint from his sleeve.

Maithilde stared at him, her eyes glittering. "What do you think a worthy exchange would be?"

Robert looked up. "It would only be a fair exchange if all the men captured with me were freed at the same time."

"Impossible." Maithilde stood. "This interview is over. I am not a fool. If you persist in these ideas, you will be sent to Boulogne forever."

Robert had jumped up when Maithilde stood and looked down at her. "If I go to Boulogne, then Stephen will be sent to a monastery in Ireland where the only thing he would see would be his jailer, and mayhap a glimpse of heather now and then. The Irish are not fond of us Englishmen, and they would welcome a chance to harass an English king."

"I remind you that, without your help, the Countess will have no one to guide her." Maithilde's cheeks flamed. "The defeat by my army at Winchester was decisive, and a disaster for your sister. We will continue to seize all her castles, one by one. It is conceivable that we will capture Matilda herself. The degradation for her would be enormous. Need I go on?"

"No. Your point has been made." Robert forced himself to relax his clenched hands.

Maithilde sat again. "Sit," she commanded. "Let us talk of this exchange. Only you, is that clear?"

Robert sat slowly and leaned back. He waited a full count of ten before he answered. "It is very clear." His words were short and hot like tallow flying from a fire.

"You will be released after Stephen is freed from Bristol Castle." Maithilde smiled.

"Matilda will not allow Stephen to be released without some protection from you for me, and your word that I will be allowed my freedom."

"Would my son, Eustace, and I be ransom enough?"

What game was Maithilde playing? Did she imagine they were pieces on a chess board? Robert looked into her eyes for signs of jest. There were none he could see. "I believe that would be satisfactory. I fear that Matilda would not want to be in the same castle with you, however, so I would prefer that you arrange to be housed at Wallingford, under the tutelage of Brian fitzCount. I would prefer not to be so deep in your territory. Mayhap I could be held at Castle Wallingford, as well."

Maithilde smiled. "I did not get and hold the territories I have by being naive, dear Robert. I think we will hold you at Winchester under the auspices of the good Bishop Henry in Winchester Castle. I am told it was not completely destroyed by Bishop Henry's forces and, in fact, is in good repair. When Stephen is released, I will have him go to you and set you free. To insure that my son and I are released, someone of value to you must be left at Winchester. Who might that be?"

Robert saw faces flash through his mind. "My wife would be a suitable hostage."

Maithilde laughed. "Your wife? No, I think not. She is of no value. It is your son, William, named for your grandfather, the Conqueror, who will serve. He is of value, or you would not have named thus."

"You are an astute observer of human nature and difficult to fool. I agree that William will be sent to Winchester until you are free. This is a most complicated plan. It involves much traveling. Mayhap you will allow me a pen, ink, and vellum to write of these plans. My lady has to approve before it is carried out." Robert enjoyed watching Maithilde start at his use of 'my lady'. He did not want her to think that he believed her to be queen or that Stephen was king, even though he had to discuss his cousin in those terms with her.

Maithilde's lips were white from being pressed together. Her eyes narrowed. "It will be done. As soon as you have written the letter, I will have it delivered. We will transport you to Winchester upon receiving a reply. Good day, Sir Robert."

Robert rose, bowed, and backed toward the door. He placed his hand behind him to pull the latch upwards, bowed again and stepped into the hallway. Two guards escorted him down the hall to a small apartment with no windows. He missed not seeing the October leaves turn from green to their painted colors, but his captivity would be over soon.

Robert lay on the bed staring out the window at the smooth, pearl-grey sky that seemed a reflection of his mood. He had been here from All Saints Day through Martinmas, almost two weeks. He had refused to celebrate the feast of the plowman by returning the traditional frumenty to the kitchen. He did not want the boiled wheat, even if it did have raisins. November had never been his favorite time of year. He felt as close to being a non-entity as he ever had in his life. It was if he were an orb that existed, but had no end, no beginning, and no color. He thought it ironic that the last time he had been in Winchester Castle, nay, this very room, it had been the beginning of a Matilda's reign and the beginning of the end.

He sighed, for it was nearly time for Stephen, who had arrived the night before, to visit. He did not want to see his cousin. Robert felt too weak. Inactivity and imprisonment were poisonous to him.

A dull knock prompted Robert to leap from the bed. He brushed his hair into place with his hands, crossed the room, and opened the door. Stephen stood straight, looking directly into Robert's eyes.

"Good day, Robert. How do you fare?"

"I am fine. Come into my humble quarters. You are looking well. I trust that imprisonment was not difficult for your health." Robert stepped aside and waited until Stephen entered before closing the door behind him. "Be seated."

Stephen sat on a bench at a trestle table. "Please join me, for I have a matter to discuss with you."

Robert sat on the bench opposite Stephen. He put his elbows on the table and folded his fingers together, index fingers upward. He focused on his hands. "Do you know, that every time I find my hands in this position, it reminds me of a game my mother taught me when I was just a knee-baby. My mother used to say that hands folded thus represented a cathedral and its tower. Is it not odd what we remember from childhood?"

"I found myself remembering many childhood things while I was imprisoned. Mayhap it is because we have much time on our hands," Stephen said.

Robert nodded. "We have no future while in prison, so we have to live in the past."

Stephen leaned forward, placing his arms on the table close to Robert. "I have come, not to talk of the past, but of the future."

Robert leaned back. "What future?"

"If you would join me in support of a unified England, the bloodshed could end at this moment."

Robert held his temper with difficulty. Stephen knew nothing of loyalty; it was obvious from his actions, but to be approached so easily by Stephen was abrasive to Robert's sense of chivalry. He had to summon all his control to reply in an even tone of voice.

"You said you were in love with Matilda. You gave her a son, the sunlight of her life, but you lied to her. With your proposition to me, you not only do her an injustice, but an injustice is done to me, as well. I never pretended to love her, but have truly loved her with all my heart. As her brother, I have protected her all her life. I will continue to protect her unto death. I refuse your request on the grounds that it would dishonor me." Robert dropped his hands to his lap and waited for the wrath he knew would come.

Stephen's left eyebrow was raised and his dark eyes were overshadowed by his frown. "Your stubbornness has cost England her peace."

Robert stood, leaned across the table, and spat out his acrimonious words one by one. "Your broken vows, twice told to King Henry, have cost England her peace. Do not lay the blame for bloodshed with Matilda. Do not lay this civil war in her lap, for you bowed to the wishes of your wife. May your nightly dreams be your Hell."

Stephen leaped from the bench, knocking it over with a crash. He leaned on the table, hands fisted, knuckles white. "Go! Your son waits in the stables. I wish to see you only on the battlefield as we take down your castles one by one!"

"I go only when you promise safe passage for my son after your own son arrives here."

Stephen exhaled. "So be it."

Robert stared at him, the hatred growing minute by minute. "How can I be sure? Is it easier to break more vows after once done?"

Stephen's face was red. He bellowed, "Go! Go before I have you executed for the traitor you are. Never will we be cousins again, you bastard son of King Henry."

"Illegitimate I may be, but I walk with honor." Robert bowed. "By your leave."

Stephen motioned toward the door, turned his back, and crossed to the window. "Leave. May our paths cross on the battlefield. Then we shall know whom God favors."

Matilda ran across the courtyard, oblivious to the spittle of snow that dropped from the grey sky. Robert was not yet off his horse when she threw herself at him and entwined her arms about him.

"Robert, I have dreamt of this moment every night and prayed for it every day. May God hear the thanks that comes from my heart." She kissed his hands, his neck, and his bearded cheek. "Robert, these weeks have been years to me. Time seemed like the garden snail. Did they feed you well? Have you returned to me as healthy as when you left? Are you ill?"

Robert held tightly to the diminutive woman who had dragged him from his horse. "I am well, and I have returned, but at a great cost to your cause, Matti. You should not have traded Stephen for me. I am afraid I cost you your kingdom, and I shall live with the disgrace the rest of my days."

"Never will I allow you to say, nay, to think such thoughts again. I gave something of no value for a priceless soul. Without you, Brother, there is no hope."

"Still, I should have . . ."

Matilda placed her hand across Robert's mouth. "Shhhh. I am alive and free because of your bravery. Now, listen, for my husband, Geoffrey, has written me. He can not come to me unless you and your men travel to Anjou to help put down the Normandy rebellion. It still rages because the barons think that I am weakened and will not be able to help Geoffrey. You must go to him."

"Oh, Matti, I can not leave you during this time of stress. There is danger still." Robert brushed her hair away from her face.

Matilda's eyes opened wide in surprise. "You must! When we have strengthened ourselves in Normandy, between Geoffrey's troops and mine, we can squeeze Stephen's forces like a vise.

"The vise is strong only as long as both its sides apply pressure evenly. Our side is weak," Robert said.

"Weak? Why stop for mere weakness?"

"Think how difficult it will be to bring Geoffrey's army here. Our army is small."

"It is true that we have a small army, but if you went to help Geoffrey, the men who left us would see that we could become strong again. They would join us once more, and victory would be ours. I can feel the hope. I know the price of victory, but I also know the taste of it. I want to savor that dish once again."

"If you insist, then we must spend the next months preparing for my departure. I will strengthen Oxford Castle and you must go there. The source of water is much better at Oxford in case of siege, for Stephen has no love for us at this hour." Robert shrugged. "It is not wise to leave you, but it is what you wish, therefore it is my will."

Matilda hugged Robert. "There is one other thing. We must send an envoy to Bishop Henry, who will hold a council at Westminster on December seventh. He is bound to support Stephen again, and we should try to stop him."

"I think that we could send Brian fitzCount to speak on your behalf. He would do an admirable job. Tonight we will make plans. Now I would like a hearty dinner with my friends, and then, mayhap, a walk with my sister." Robert put his arm around Matilda's shoulder. "Let us get out of this miserable weather."

Matilda leaned against Robert and matched his stride. "I have a fine dinner for you, Robert. I went hunting myself."

"Ah, Matti, I can not live on air."

Matilda swung a fist at him, connecting with his stomach. "Air, is it? I will have you know that I brought down four hares and a small hart. You will eat well because of me, not in spite of me."

"Then I shall thank you for a bountiful feast."

CHAPTER
XVII

ECEMBER SEVENTH had come quickly. Brian fitzCount had had barely enough time with the newly released Robert to prepare for the council called by Bishop Henry. It would be interesting to see how the good bishop would explain his change of loyalty from Stephen to Matilda and back to Stephen. He traced the pattern of lines on the table with a forefinger and avoided the eyes of the other knights.

A stirring in the crowd caused Brian fitzCount to look up. He watched Bishop Henry enter the chamber, followed by King Stephen. The Bishop sat at the head of the huge oak council table, King Stephen on his right. Although both men were many feet away, Brian had to acknowledge the power of their combined presence. It dominated the room. The other men who were standing at the table turned toward the Bishop of Winchester. Brian's curiosity was fraught with dislike for the twice turned bishop. The appearance of King Stephen confirmed what had been rumored— that the Bishop had not remained true to Matilda.

Bishop Henry motioned for all to sit and waited until the scraping of chairs subsided. Brian laid his hand in his lap to feign calmness.

Bishop Henry placed a tri-folded sheet of vellum on the table, rested his eyes on Brian fitzCount, and opened the flap of the letter. "I would like to make it known to all of you that this letter is from the Pope." Bishop Henry looked at each person again, pausing to watch Brian fitzCount's reaction.

Holding the letter aloft, Bishop Henry said, "In this letter, I have been reprimanded by our Pope for shirking the duty of releasing my brother, King Stephen, from captivity. Because of this order from the Pope, I did what I could to make certain that King Stephen was released. As you can see, I was successful."

The bishop gestured toward his brother. "I would like to explain why it was necessary for me to recognize Matilda, Countess of Anjou, rather than my own brother and rightful heir to the throne. I had no choice but to appear to concur, since King Stephen was captured and in a position of danger. It was an intelligent move to seem to be in agreement with the change of rulers so that a way could be found to save the rightful king. I could not depend on any of the barons to continue in their support of the king. They had asked him for permission to betray him while he was imprisoned by Countess Matilda. I found this lack of loyalty to the king difficult to fathom.

"I was under siege from Matilda, the Countess of Anjou; the sound and fury of arms about Winchester was deafening. The Countess had broken all pledges made about the rights of the Church, and I had it on good authority that she intended to have me murdered." The Bishop scanned his audience. No sound was made by any of those present, so he continued. "Still I counterfeited acceptance of her leadership, all the while plotting to get King Stephen released from bondage.

"Under the guidance of God, to Whom I prayed hourly for King Stephen, it came to pass that events were turned in favor of the rightful heir. The rest of the story you know. I have called you here to ask you to assist the King in every way possible. He is blessed by the good will of the people. We must help end this civil war that tears the thin fabric of our country."

He held the vellum aloft. "This reprimand from the Pope means nothing to me." Bishop Henry tore the sheet of vellum in half. The gasp from the crowd echoed off the stone walls. Silence enshrouded everyone. All eyes were on the bishop. Time seemed not to move; the main players held in tableau.

Brian fitzCount sprang to his feet. The stillness of the chamber was torn by the crack of his fist. Brian struck the table with such force that it sounded like thunder, reverberating throughout the stone room, vibrating his breastbone. He saw heads snap toward him. He knew his face was drained of color, save for freckles. His brows were drawn together. When he lashed out at Bishop Henry, it was with no concern for his own safety.

"You traitor!" Brian pointed a finger at the Bishop. "You, who claim to be a man of God, are no more than a liar, no better than a thief of justice. You were the one who invited, nay, begged the Empress Matilda to come to England to save it from Stephen. Many letters came to her, from you, each the same in content. Each asked that she, as the true heir to the throne, come to save England. It was you, Bishop Henry, who helped in the capture of your own brother. You supplied the arms, the money, and the men in secret. It was you who helped us at the Battle of Lincoln."

Brian stopped to stare at King Stephen. "You, sir, are sitting next to a traitor called brother." Brian felt spent. He picked up the chair and sat as suddenly as he had stood. He barely heard the murmuring amongst the others at the table since the blood was rushing about his head and through his ears like a stormy sea. He did not care about the reaction of Bishop Henry or Stephen. He was not certain whether he would live beyond this day or even this hour. He may die, but it was no matter, for the anger boiling inside him pushed all survival instincts and reason aside.

Brian fitzCount's awareness resurfaced slowly, and he was cognizant of the Bishop watching him with cool detachment. Brian's jaw was tight from his teeth being clenched together, but he did not want to relax. He had spoken the truth. He knew the truth, the Bishop knew truth, and Stephen knew the truth. He hoped the nobles who stared at him knew the truth. If it cost him his life to tell Matilda's story as it should be told, then so be it. He would gladly die for her.

The Bishop cleared his throat. "The matter at hand has been resolved to my satisfaction. I see no further need to continue this meeting. It is adjourned. You may all leave, except for Sir Brian fitzCount."

Brian felt his heart skip, but nodded his assent. He watched the others leave in order to keep unpleasant thoughts from spurting through his brain. He was surprised when Bishop Henry arose and came toward him instead of ordering him to go to the bishop. The man had used this act as an effective tool to feign camaraderie before, but Brian was not fooled. Brian sat calmly, not standing when the Bishop sat near him, for the Bishop deserved no deference.

"I understand your feelings. Your protective behavior toward your empress is impressive. You, too, have been traitorous."

"If you mean to Stephen, I never swore an oath to uphold him." Brian looked at the head of the table where Stephen still sat.

"I mean that you were traitorous to me."

"To you? That is difficult to fathom." Brian's anger turned to curiosity.

"Do you not remember I asked that your men not interfere with the travelers to the Bishop's fair of St. Giles? You sent no letter refusing to do so. I took it to mean that my people would travel in safety. Yet, your men attacked those poor pilgrims, who needed a diversion from war, and took their possessions. You made the roads into Winchester quite dangerous. You seized my possessions and supplies meant for the hospitals that I personally had built. I have to number you amongst the faithless of England."

Brian could not help his quick laughter, and he saw that he had startled the Bishop. "I am sorry. I have not gone mad, but your arguments are sophomoric. Nephew to King Henry, cousin to Empress Matilda, and a priest of the Holy Church, you enjoined me to be faithful to the daughter of your uncle, to help her win her rights that had been taken from her by force, and to help her hold all she already had. You amuse me, oh great Bishop. I have followed the orders of the Holy Church through you. What did I get for my troubles? I have the respect and love of Empress Matilda. That is worth all the lands that were taken from me because I obeyed your command. In these times of greatest need, my family, my army, and my servants go hungry because I am not reaping one acre of corn from the property King Henry gave to me. Yes, I do have to scavenge and take what I can to keep my men alive. I should have no need to take the goods of other people, save that I may carry out your commands. You should know that neither I, nor my men, do this for money, or fief, or lands, either promised or given, but we do it solely out of obedience to your command, and out of regard for what is right." Brian no longer feared for his life, for he had discovered the bishop was inept in this game. He wondered why the man, who was intelligent, could not see how stupid he looked.

"I fear you misunderstand me," Bishop Henry said.

"I fear I do understand you. Let all the faithful of the Holy Mother Church know that I, Brian fitzCount, whom good King Henry trusted, who received from him arms and honor, am ready to prove, either by battle or ordeal, all these things of which I accuse you, Henry, Bishop of Winchester, nephew of King Henry, and Legate of the Apostolic See. I am not one upon whom a price can be set."

"A most admirable quality, albeit a foolish one, if too tenacious." Bishop Henry answered calmly, in spite of the whiteness of his knuckles that gripped the arms of the chair.

Brian looked into Bishop Henry's eyes. He knew he could challenge the bishop and win. "My guess is that now I am to be imprisoned for crimes against the Church." He enjoyed baiting Bishop Henry.

The Bishop shook his head. "No, for it would only bring Matilda and her pitiful forces down upon Winchester once more, and although we could easily defeat her, it would not be worth the effort for my war-weary city. I guarantee your safe passage back to Gloucester Castle with my blessing. You will not trust me, so I shall make no further protestations of my honesty. Just be gone immediately so I may not regret my generosity."

Brian's eyes narrowed. He considered a reply, but decided against rebuttal. He was tired, and he wanted to leave for Gloucester where he did not have to worry about a knife finding its way into his back.

The Bishop rose and left the chamber, Stephen preceding him. Brian heard Stephen say, "We have some matters to discuss, dear brother."

Brian waited until he could no longer hear footsteps, then stood and walked calmly from the room, still expecting an ambush. Outside, he took the reins from the groom and mounted his horse. His fellow knights followed suit, and the retinue rode out the gates and toward Gloucester Castle. Brian was anxious to re-join Matilda. He worried about her safety now that Stephen had been freed. Brian glanced back. His army looked pitifully small, for a third of his men had been captured by William of Ypes in the flight from Winchester. It would be a difficult winter for all of them, and especially for Matilda, who was more depressed than he had seen her since Robert's capture. Maybe the Christmas holiday would help raise Matilda's spirits. What could he do to make her smile? He had fallen in love with Matilda for many reasons, but her smile was first on the list.

The noise and laughter startled Matilda. She stopped her pacing and stood with her back to the fireplace and looked across the great hall toward the main entrance. Brian burst through the door, brushing snow from his hair and stamping snow from his boots. Miles followed close behind, hooting with laughter. He carried an arm load of holly and pine cones. He dragged pine branches across the floor, scattering the reeds. Dogs barked and jumped about the men, adding to the confusion.

Matilda was perplexed. Why were they acting like children? She watched as more knights, followed by servants, entered the hall carrying half the forest with them. When the last, Robert and Edward, Ella's husband, entered the great hall, they carried a giant trunk of a tree. They groaned as they struggled to carry it to the main fireplace.

"Brian and Miles, what madness is this? Robert and Edward, what have you there?" Matilda had her hands on her hips. She tapped her foot. "Did I not say that we would have no celebration this year, other than Mass, for we had nothing to celebrate?"

Miles stood before Matilda and tried to bow, but the branches he carried prevented it. He looked baffled, then dropped the bundle of greenery before Matilda and bowed again. "My lady, I would never disobey an order of yours. We are not celebrating. These branches were cut only to make this smelly castle smell better." Miles inhaled deeply. "I find the change remarkable."

Brian stepped beside Miles and bowed. "I, too, have found the castle smelling like the garderobe of late. The boughs of pine and holly will make our stale, smoky air fresh. It is a long time until spring."

Matilda tried to keep from laughing at the silly expressions on the faces of the two knights. She looked around the room at the faces of the servants. She caught a look of hope from both Robert and Edward. What had Brian and Miles been doing behind her back? Had Robert coerced them into something? All of them acted like naughty children who had been caught. "Look at the mess you made. You have destroyed the fresh reeds that I had the servants put down only yesterday. Do you think my housekeeping skills are inadequate? Are you telling me that the castle stinks because I have not kept the servants busy?"

"Oh, no, my lady!" Miles bowed once more. "It is the stink from all of us gentlemen that foul the air."

Matilda gestured toward Robert and Edward. They had dropped the giant log in front of the fireplace, scattering bark across the floor. She pointed toward the log. "Are you going to tell me that tree trunk is not a yule log?"

Brian's freckles darkened and the corners of his mouth twitched. "There are no small trees left in the forest. We have to have firewood."

"That is a yule log, Brian. I know a yule log when I see one." Matilda crossed her arms and tried to pretend to be angry with him.

Brian grinned. "Describe a yule log, Matti. Tell me how it is different from a big, old, tree trunk."

"A yule log burns in the fireplace from Christmas Eve through the Epiphany," Matilda said.

Brian turned to Miles and rolled his eyes. "She has discovered our secret. We can no longer sneak in here with Christmas decorations and yule logs. We will have to confess."

"May I be the first to confess my sin, my lady?" Miles bowed so low that his head almost touched the floor.

Matilda could not help herself and she laughed. "Stop, you two. How can I maintain my sanity when surrounded by crazy friends?"

"Does this mean that we will be allowed to decorate the castle for Christmas? May we burn that old tree trunk and call it a yule log? May we have good food to eat?" Brian folded his hands in prayer.

"You have infected me with your gaiety. I was wrong to try to prevent a Christmas celebration. I say 'yes' to all that you ask. We need some happiness. Robert, since you and Edward are in charge of the 'old, tree trunk,' you can make certain that the 'old tree trunk's' bark is cleaned up. We can not have a gay Christmas with a dirty floor."

Robert bowed low enough to start picking bark off the floor. "Yes, my lady." He motioned for Edward to join him.

"When you finish groveling, Robert, you may help decorate the great hall. I will decorate my apartment. I am sure Ella would like that. She has been hinting all week. Do you want to help us, Edward? Ella would like to have you near."

Matilda waved her hand toward the people who watched her. "We will celebrate Christmas. I will talk with the cooks, for I was wrong. We are alive, we are healthy, and we have hope for the future."

Matilda walked toward the kitchen. The cook and his helpers would have a lot to do. Christmas dinner would have to be ready in three days. Matilda made a vow to never forget to celebrate the small victories along with the large ones.

Robert groaned, making Matilda laugh. She leaned against the stone wall of the window alcove and put her feet on the opposite bench. She was glad they were away from the noisy crowd and in the relative quiet of her apartment. "You ate far too much, Robert. I thought you were afraid you would never get to eat again."

"I may never want to eat again. I could not pass the trays of cakes without trying to sample each one."

Ella giggled. "I thought for certain that you would get the bean hidden in the cake."

"He should be King of the Bean. You ate more cake than any-one, Robert. I think the sin of gluttony is yours," Edward said.

"If there is a crown for that, then Robert should be wearing it." Brian stretched his arms above his head. "I think our Christmas dinner was perfect. You can still hear the servants and towns people celebrating downstairs. Who was the burly man that found the bean? He is still dancing and drinking with every woman around."

Miles raised himself up on his elbows. The light from the fire created a halo around him. "That is the blacksmith and armorer. He can shoe a horse while making three sets of chain mail at the same time. He is most valuable to us."

"He is acting like a king and ordering all the women to dance with him. I am glad we escaped up here," Ella said.

Matilda yawned. "I have not felt so relaxed since . . . since I know not when." She went to the window and opened it a crack. The setting sun on the light covering of snow made it sparkle like droplets of silver mixed with saffron and rose colors. It looked as if the sun had fallen to earth. She shivered and closed the window.

Turning to her companions, she said, "I wish we could sit here and rest, mayhap forever."

"I am not certain we can stay forever, but once we get to Oxford, Matti, we can rest for awhile. The fortifications will be completed before Easter," Robert said.

"Let us not talk of moving right now, Robert. Let us just think about the pleasures of this day." Matilda sat on the alcove bench.

"We will have more fun when the mummers arrive. They should be here tomorrow or the day after," Ella said.

"That should be a rollicking success. I have always loved the mummers. They make me laugh until I cry," Brian said.

Matilda leaned against the wall. Her thoughts drifted away from the conversation of her friends and to the Christmases she had spent in Germany. She had few worries then. Her husband, the Emperor, had celebrated Christmas, but it was more formal. She believed that this Christmas was more satisfying than any she had had before. Maybe when things were going badly, it made the special times more meaningful. She vowed to make the most of Christmas and Epiphany. If she never had another Christmas, then that would be all right.

Miles was asleep by the fireplace. Robert had thrown himself across the bottom of her bed and was also asleep. Ella and Edward were sitting arm in arm on the bench in the window alcove across the room from her. Only Brian remained awake. He stared at her. She smiled, then noticed he blushed. She was lucky to have these people. The only person missing was her son, Henry. He should be with her, but she had been afraid. Matilda clenched her fist and glanced toward heaven. She would never quit until she was king or Henry was king, even if it took decades.

The day of the move to Oxford Castle was alternately bright and grey, threatening to rain every fifteen minutes as only April can. Mixed in with the winter wind, were gusts of warm air, tantalizing and teasing Matilda with promises of summer. She loosened the ties on her woolen cape, which was too warm right now, but would feel good if she were caught in a downpour. Matilda scanned the sky. Grey clouds rolled across the sky, blotting out the sun, then cleared, allowing warmth to penetrate the chilled travelers.

Dancer tossed his head, his mane rippling. Matilda leaned forward and patted his neck. "We are lucky to be out of that dreary castle, even if it is temporary." The thought of temporary freedom sobered Matilda until she remembered that she was free. Had she been captured in her escape from Winchester, she would have been imprisoned for life or executed. She never again would have been able to see her brother, her friends, or her sons. Matilda's hand went to her throat. More than likely, Maithilde would have her beheaded. So, a self-exile in Oxford Castle was not as bad as it could be. Even though Oxford was closer to Stephen's headquarters in Westminster, she was protected by Brian fitzCount's castle at Wallingford. It was only twenty-two miles to the south. Devizes Castle, Ludgershall Castle, and Bristol Castle were farther away to the south and southwest, but they, too, were a protection. Adelicia and her husband still held Arundel Castle to the southeast. With Gloucester behind her to the west, she had only to worry about being attacked from the north.

Matilda leaned forward and whispered to Dancer, "If ever I am about to be captured, I will fight to the death. I will not give Maithilde, or Stephen, the satisfaction of seeing me in chains."

Matilda rode quickly, keeping pace with the knights who surrounded her. As usual, Brian fitzCount, Robert, and Miles of Gloucester were next to her. Ella and her husband rode directly behind them. Ella's children were farther back in a wagon with the nurse and some household goods. The wagons would be a day behind by the time they reached Oxford Castle. The remainder of the army was scattered along the road in front and behind them. If any spies had reported their movements, they could be attacked by Stephen.

Matilda looked at the horizon. There seemed to be no activity. Matilda was surprised at her relief. There had been days in Gloucester Castle when she was ready for a battle. Mayhap it was because she knew that without Geoffrey's help, she had no hope.

Matilda turned to Robert. "When will you leave for Normandy to help Geoffrey?"

"As soon as I have you settled in Oxford." Robert hesitated. "I also have to meet with the barons' sons who will be going with me."

"Why are their sons joining you? Will they fight with Geoffrey?" Matilda did not understand Robert's rationale.

"Matti, I am worried about your safety while I am so far away. As you know, Stephen was taken ill during the Epiphany and almost died. I have heard rumors that he was poisoned, mayhap by his son, Eustace. He has recovered, but I worry about something happening to you. To prevent such attempts, I have forced those barons, of whom we are unsure, to send their sons with me. If any harm comes to you, then I have a means to bargain." Robert pushed a lock of hair away from his forehead. "I am taking hostages with me, so to speak. They had better fight with Geoffrey and me, or they will wish they had. I am losing patience with the barons who teeter on the brink of supporting us."

Matilda did not speak. The scowl on her brother's face precluded conversation. She was trying to think of another subject to discuss with him when a shout arose. She thought first of an ambush, but quickly realized the shouts were joyous. The towers of Oxford Castle were ahead. She would be glad to be inside so that the chilling feeling that slithered up and down her back would go away, at least for awhile. She did not feel like a coward, but she knew life was erratic, and she wanted to preserve hers. She hoped the wagon with her best bed would arrive early tomorrow. It made her feel safe.

She wanted her own tapestries hanging in her apartment, too. It had always been important to her to have familiar furnishings. She urged Dancer forward and looked around one last time at the world from outside. It would be a long time before she could ride free with the wind blowing her hair and the sun on her face.

The bronze pen bounced across the table where it rolled to a stop next to the ink pot after having been dropped by Matilda. She pushed back her chair and stood. "I can not write another word." She felt that she could no longer sit, so she began walking back and forth across the room passing Ella as she sewed.

"My lady, why do you pace about the room like a caged animal?" Ella laid aside her sewing. "You have not been content since we came five months ago. One would think that you were imprisoned. Are we not safe here?"

"I do not feel safe without Robert." Matilda pointed to the vellum that was spread open on the table. "I have sent several communiques telling him that since Stephen recovered from his mysterious illness, he has hit us with renewed vigor like a man re-born. Thus re-born, he has the energy of youth in his body and soul. Many of my supporters have lost their castles, and I sit like a lonesome island in the midst of a stormy sea. Even the legendary strength of John Fitz Gilbert le Marechal, named by Stephen as our 'limb of Hell and the root of all evil,' was grievously wounded because of Stephen."

"Was it true, Matti, that Sir Marechal survived a fire? Mayhap he is enchanted, after all," Ella said.

"Sir John had helped foil Stephen's army by leading them away from our retreat here in Oxford Castle. Sir John hid in a church, but the church was set afire by Stephen's men. Sir John climbed to the bell tower and hid while the fire raged below him. The flames came closer and closer and the fire scorched his skin. Still, Sir John refused to come down. The lead roof was so hot from the fire that it melted and a piece dripped onto Sir John blinding him in one eye. Yet, he ignored the fire and pain and refused to surrender. Stephen assumed that Sir John could not have survived the fire and he left. Sir John climbed down and rode back to his own castle to heal. Later, he rode out again and again, fighting Stephen for us."

"He has been a wonderful supporter, but sometimes his deeds make me think that he is the devil." Ella wrinkled her nose. "He frightens me. I could never tell Stephen to go ahead and kill my son like Sir John did. What did Sir John really say to Stephen?"

"Sir John knew Stephen's weakness. When Stephen took Sir John's young son, William, as a hostage to prevent Sir John from joining us again, it did not deter Sir John at all. Stephen, in his anger, told Sir John that his son was to be catapulted over the fortified castle wall and would land in pieces at his feet unless he gave up that stronghold. Sir John knew Stephen could not do anything of the sort. I have laughed along with the rest of England at Sir John's reply. To have told Stephen that, 'It was all right for the boy to be sent over the wall, for he, Sir John, had the anvil and hammer with which to forge still better sons,' was both brave and humorous. I am glad to have Sir John on my side. He would be a formidable enemy."

Matilda paced again. "I feel trapped."

"We can do nothing but wait for Robert to arrive with an army to carve us a path to freedom, so you may as well save your energy and the reeds upon the floor. Come sit next to me, and I will show you the new kirtle for my baby daughter. I have trimmed it with the tiny flowers that your second mother, Adelicia, taught me so long ago."

Matilda leaned over and inspected the embroidery. "I could never do such fine work. How you and Adelicia have the forbearance to sit there and make art of threads, I will never understand. I fear the angels forgot to give me that virtue."

"Matilda, you have a different forbearance that I envy. Would I be able to fight for years, as you have, to give my son a kingdom? No, I would not. Yours is the greatest sacrifice, for not only have you given young Henry the gift of life, but you have given him a reason for life. He will rule this land, someday, and he will be like your father reborn. I have had the astrologer do his chart." Ella reached into her sewing box for a different color thread.

"I do not believe in reading the stars to chart our future." Matilda watched as Ella threaded the needle with bright red wool.

Ella looked up at her. "But you do believe in young Henry's greatness, do you not?"

"Yes, but only because I have observed his intelligence, his perseverance, and his uncanny understanding of people. I miss my sons so much. I miss William with his bright smile and little Geoffrey with his winning charm.

"I miss Robert as well, and I worry about his safety. Even if Robert returns to England, he can not land at his son's castle. Stephen has captured Wareham."

Ella put her sewing aside. "Let us forget this talk of war and go for a walk about the castle walls. Even if we do not dare go into Oxford village, we can still get a breath of fresh air. We should make use of the sun after so much rain. I thought that the world was being flooded, and we would have forty days of rain."

"A walk is a good idea. These stones close in on me after awhile. I would find it difficult to be imprisoned." Matilda took Ella's hand and pulled her from the stool. "Come on, little turtle. I feel a renewed vigor from your suggestion."

Ella laughed. Together they left the apartment and walked down the long hallway to the closest tower. They scampered up the curved stairway without talking, for it echoed too much for decent conversation. When they reached the top of the steps, they stepped out into the fall sunshine and, giggling like children, strolled down the top of the inner curtain wall as if they were on a Sunday walk to mass. The shadows of the merlons made consistent patterns, and soon Matilda and Ella were jumping across the shadows pretending they were ditches. They laughed at the astonished looks on the faces of the guards, and chattered like youngsters at a party.

"Ella, this was a great idea. Oh, look at the forest over there." Matilda put her hands on Ella's shoulders and turned her toward the east. "See the steam rising from all the rain we had? The leaves are just starting to turn the pretty colors of a tapestry. If winter did not follow so closely behind, I would like the fall."

"It is September already. Soon it will be Michaelmas. How difficult it is to believe that time has flown." Ella frowned and stepped closer to the merlon. "Look at the River Thames. It is swollen and overflows its bank. The ford of Oxford has disappeared swallowed up by the river goddess."

"You sound like the court poets who used to come to entertain us in King Henry's day. Do not fall, Ella, or you could drown, it is so close." Matilda leaned over and watched the swirling water rush by the castle walls. "I have always found it fascinating that these castles could be built so close to the river without falling in. I do not know what keeps the water from wearing away the stone. The river and the castle will be here long after I am gone. How peculiar that man-made and nature-made things persevere, but we can not. Is anything fair?"

"Matti, whatever is that cloud of silver just beyond the river? Is it a magical storm?"

Matilda shaded her eyes with her hands. "I know not."

"It is peculiar."

"Oh, God in heaven! It is an army!" Matilda hiked her kirtle up to her knees and ran to the nearest guard. She grabbed him and turned him toward the east. "Sound the alarm. The largest army I have ever seen is coming this way."

Ella ran up behind her. "How do you know it is not Robert?"

"I can see the gules and silver of the standard. It belongs to Stephen. We are doomed to a siege. Alas, poor Oxford. The people will suffer. They always have to suffer."

"We can run, Matti! Let us fly. Dancer can get you to Gloucester. Run, Matti!"

"No. I will never run again. Death is preferable. Thank goodness Robert fortified the castle and laid in provisions before he left. We have a good well, but we will not be able to leave until we are rescued."

Ella bit her lip. "How many are there?"

Matilda put her arm around Ella's shoulders and squeezed her. "There are more than we need to count, at least a thousand men marching toward us. That makes me very valuable to Stephen, I suppose." Matilda shuddered. "I would not want to be captured."

"Are you afraid of Stephen?"

"No, but Maithilde would like to see me dead or, better yet, imprisoned for life so she could taunt me every day." Matilda was quiet. "That would be more difficult for me than death. I shall never let her know."

"What are we to do, my lady?"

"We have plans in case of a siege, and they are being carried out. There is nothing to do but wait for the disaster that comes." Matilda looked down at the inner courtyard that was a flurry of color as people ran back and forth in an excited frenzy of preparation. "There had better not be any of the barons who have sons with Robert here to fight on Stephen's side. If there are, I hope Robert cuts out their sons' hearts."

The sky was split with the sound of bells as the various churches rang out the warning to the people of Oxford. Matilda held her hands to her ears, not because the sound was hurting her, but because bells brought back bad memories of her escape from Westminster Castle in London. She shook her head to clear away the memories. Would she never be rid of the opposition?

"Matti, look at the town's people. They act so fearful and with good reason. The army is nearly on us. Oh, God, Matti. I have never seen so many in one place. The sun shining off their armor is a fearful sight. Maybe they can not cross the river."

"Too late. I think that Stephen is leading them into the water. I hope he drowns." Matilda chewed her lower lip as knight after knight splashed into the water after Stephen. Their silver armor blended with the silver water until the knights looked as if they were being born of the river. They were close enough, and there were enough of them that Matilda could hear the shouts. She pointed toward the marching foot soldiers. "The army has split and is surrounding the town. See the machines being brought to the front? Those are for throwing the firebrands that will burn Oxford to the ground. I cause the very war I hate."

"It is not you who caused this. Stephen is the culprit."

"Ella, would it matter to you who caused it if your home burned?" Matilda walked to the next merlon. "You may not want to watch, but I have to see. Mayhap I am making my own Hell."

Ella pulled at Matilda's sleeve. "Be careful of stray arrows, my lady."

"Do not fret. We are too far away for any weapon to touch us. We are safe from injury, but not from starvation."

Ella patted her stomach. "I could lose a few pounds of baby fat."

"I wish you could give it to me. I feel like a walking skeleton. I have had no appetite for months, and now I fear that with a ration on food, I will feel forever hungry. My stomach fights me, too," Matilda said.

An arch of red swished below them and Ella gasped. The fire brand struck the butcher's shop and the thatched roof was eaten in one bite by the hungry flames.

"By God's blood, that was fast!" Ella leaned over the wall and looked down. "It burns the walls. And the next shop is on fire. I can not see what is happening along the outer curtain wall."

"Fire is unforgiving and will take anything from anyone. Even kings and queens can die." Matilda cried out as the army pushed through her troops, killing them in great numbers. "Oh, brave men and braver boys. How I wish history could record your deeds name by name instead of as if you were one. Today will be black in the pages of my history."

"The gates have opened and people are struggling to get inside. Let us not watch any more, Matilda. The drawbridge is red with blood. I will never like that color again and nothing I sew will have a single stitch of red thread." Ella turned and ran from the scene, crying.

Matilda followed Ella to the apartment. When she got inside, Ella was closing the shutters on the windows, blocking out the sun, the smoke, and the screams.

Ella turned to Matilda and leaned against the shutters. "I want my children. I want them here with us."

"I will send for the nurse. They will stay here for as long as you want."

"I am glad that my Edward went with Robert. I would fear for him, if he were here."

"I shall return, Ella, with the children. Please calm yourself. The siege has just begun."

The air in the room was bitterly cold and Matilda pulled her arm back under the covers. She tried to go back to sleep to extend the night. She wanted to avoid another hour of siege, but it was too late. The cold had awakened her. She opened one eye, but could not tell what time it was since the shutters were closed. The siege had lasted through Michaelmas, All Hollows Day, Martinmas, and it was almost Christmas, again.

How much longer could they withstand the siege before Robert would be able to gather enough men together? There was a way out of this mess, but it was risky.

Matilda threw back the covers, gasping for breath as the cold air engulfed her. She grabbed one of the blankets from the bed and wrapped it around herself as she trotted to the window. She threw back a shutter, not caring about safety. She wished that she were a bird, free to fly away. The day had dawned white on white as snow and frozen rain mixed to whitewash all animate and inanimate objects. The snow had fallen throughout the morning and afternoon.

The small hills, usually greys and greens, as light struck them became cloudy and mystical. A streak of pale pink sunrise edged with smoke grey fought to add color to the world, but lost the battle as a snowstorm marched across the horizon and obliterated all traces of warmth and what little color was left, creating a rainbowless world. Matilda closed the shutters.

The weather was bitterly cold — colder than it had been in years. The River Thames was frozen solid, and with the thick snow on top of it, was nearly indiscernible. The conditions were right, and she could hardly contain her excitement.

"Ella! Wake up!" Matilda was impatient with her sleepy lady-in-waiting. "Arise, for it has been a perfect day for our plan to be carried out."

Ella sat up, rubbed her eyes and looked across the room at her sleeping children. "What is it?"

"Send for Miles, Brian, and John of Ludgershall! The day has come for our escape!" Matilda danced up and down with excitement.

Ella jumped from her bed and grabbed a kirtle. "I will get them myself and return quickly with the gentlemen." She pulled the kirtle over her sleeping chemise, bent down and pulled on shoes before exiting the room in a hurry.

Matilda ran to the window and pulled a shutter open. The snow was coming down harder. It was going to be a wonderful storm. It was too bad that Miles, Brian, and Count John of Ludgershall had been under siege with her. It seemed to be a God send now. "I have never been so happy to see snow!" She chuckled to herself for talking aloud, then hurried to get dressed.

Ella returned in less time than it took for Matilda to finish changing clothes. Matilda grabbed her by the arm. "Did you find all three of them?"

"Yes, Matti. They will be here very quickly." Tears came to Ella's eyes and she bit her lower lip. "I am afraid for you."

Matilda looked up from her position on the floor where she was dragging her boots out from under the bed. "You should know better than to worry about me. I have always escaped before. Here, help me get these things on. I have so much trouble with the laces."

"I shall wonder about you until I get word that you are safe. Send me word immediately." Ella knelt in front of Matilda.

"You shall know I am safe when Oxford is no longer under siege. Tie that one tighter. I can not lose a boot now. My feet will perspire from all the sheep's wool lining until I get outside."

Ella jumped when a loud rapping was heard. She hurried to open the door and stepped aside as the three men entered. "Do you have the robes ready, Ella?" Brian asked.

She nodded and pointed toward the bed where Matilda stood.

Matilda held up a white linen robe with a hood. She slipped it over her head, and it draped itself down the length of her body, covering her feet. She flipped up the hood to cover her hair. "Let me stand against the grey stone of this room and you will have some idea of the disguise." Matilda stepped back and turned away from her friends.

"The costume is very good, but I still do not like the idea," Brian said.

Matilda turned back around. "I am going to escape. If I stay here, Stephen will starve us all. If I try to escape and do not make it, then the siege will end, for the prize will be captured. If I try to escape and do make it, then the results will be the same. I have to do this to save the people. I have to do this to save the children."

Miles shook his head. "It is too great a risk."

"No human is worth all this suffering, least of all me. Where does it say that I should be the cause of the burning, the looting, the starvation? I would rather be dead. If I am suicidal, at least let it benefit others." Matilda looked from one man to another. "Who will join me in my escape?"

"I will, of course." Brian stepped forward and took a white robe into his hands.

"And I can not be left behind," Miles said.

Count John took a robe from the bed. "I have supported you from the beginning. I will not stop now."

"I thank you. Meet me in a few minutes at the west tower closest to the river. Be certain to dress warmly, for the storm rages outside. I need a moment to say good-bye to Ella."

"As you wish." Brian kissed Matilda on the cheek and followed the other two knights out the door, closing it softly behind him.

"Ella, you are not to worry about me. I will make this escape work. At any rate, I must go, so that your babies can live."

Ella fell into Matilda's arms, sobbing. "I am so frightened. I have been afraid since that day three months ago when we first saw Stephen's army. I do not understand why I was able to exist before without fear."

Matilda held Ella close. "It is because you have reason to live — two reasons, nay, three if we count the father of your children."

"I fear for you, too."

"I can not be in worse trouble than I am right now, even if I am captured. I have no future here." Matilda patted Ella's shoulder. Matilda felt very calm. The decision had been made, the plan was set, and it was time for action. "Now get the woolen kirtle you made for me, and the cape of fur. I will need them under that thin, white robe."

Pieces of frozen snow stung her face as did the rope that rubbed her raw under the arms, even through her clothing. She looked at the guards who lowered her slowly down the side of the stone tower on the western side of the castle. She watched the stones one by one as she was let down because it made her dizzy to look at the swirling, white snow against the grey wall.

She forgot to push herself away from the wall, and her boots scraped against the stones. She slammed against the rock before she had a chance to recover and her descent stopped. She was irritated with her stupidity and jerked on the rope above her to signal that the descent was to continue. She looked down. Miles and John were closer than the last time she had looked. She promised God that she would never again watch a bird glide through the sky and wish to be one.

Hands on her legs and about her waist signaled that she was near the ground. It was not until the rope was untied that she felt relief. Without speaking, she walked between Miles and John toward the frozen river. Brian was to catch up with them as soon as he was lowered from the tower.

Matilda stumbled in the snow, slipped on the frozen pieces of ice, and finally fell. She pushed herself up before her companions had a chance to help her. The heels of her hands were rubbed raw. The only gloves she could find were not suitable for this adventure. Both gloves and skin had been torn when she fell.

The wind blowing across the river seemed colder as the trio crossed to the frozen Thames, and Matilda pulled the white hood tighter about her face. It did no good. She heard the wind whistling through the branches of the trees in the forest across the river, a sound from Hell itself. She looked back once. Brian was close behind.

"Wait for Brian," Matilda whispered.

"We are not supposed to," Miles said.

"I do care not. We wait." Matilda looked at the castle that was disappearing in the swirling snow. She felt exhilarated at being free.

She looked for Brian, but could not see him. At least the disguise was working, mayhap too well, and she was concerned that Brian would not be able to find them. She squinted, trying to see through the snow that was falling harder than before.

"My lady, we can wait no longer. It is too dangerous for you." Miles placed his hand on Matilda's arm and tried to get her to move westward. "Wait, I see movement." Matilda stared through the spinning snow, but shook her head. "I fear not, after all."

Brian appeared next to Matilda and touched her arm, causing her to jump. "Your voice carries, Matilda. That is how I found you. Be silent, and let us make haste. We are in grave danger. You should not have waited."

"I could not go without you by my side to give me courage," Matilda whispered.

"You need not get your courage from me, for you have more than enough. Let us go in silence, my lady." Brian took hold of Matilda's elbow and guided her across the river.

Matilda perspired and froze simultaneously. She found the combination of heat and cold disconcerting. Her feet throbbed from the cold, and her skin itched from perspiration. The wind made her eyes tear until the whiteness floated around her, and she felt dizzy. She had to reach down and touch her legs in order to tell which foot was down. She stumbled in knee-deep snow and, for a few terrifying minutes, could not find her companions nor could they find her. She was certain she would not be found until spring.

With neither a person, nor a body for Stephen to see, the castle would continue to be under siege. By spring, all the people inside would be dead. Death could not be in her plans.

Strong hands pulled her to her knees, then to her feet. Matilda brushed the hard snow from her face, but she could feel neither nose nor fingers except for a burning sensation. She took a shallow breath, for she had learned that breathing deeply of the cold air scalded her lungs. Matilda plunged through the snow that hid the frozen river, her cloak wet and clinging to her soaked kirtle, making it even more difficult to walk. She crossed the river by counting each step she took. Each step was for young Henry and against Stephen. She counted and counted, not wanting to think because it was too difficult.

When the far side was reached, the bank was steeper than anticipated. The four hooded figures clawed and crawled up the bank like animals. No one spoke, but each held out hands to pull the others along. At last they clambered over the top, and Matilda made a mental note to celebrate the feat later. She looked at the grey shadows in front of her and was glad for the forest at the same time fear wrapped itself around her throat.

She could hear the enemy as the fugitives came nearer their front lines. Once, when the snow stopped, she saw the tents next to the forest, and it appeared the soldiers were looking straight at her. Matilda pulled the hood down, and lowered her head, more to shut out the vision of the enemy rather than to protect herself. She walked faster toward the comparative safety of the forest. She preferred the wolves.

The sounds of the trumpets made her skin prickle. She scarcely breathed while the call for the changing of the watch sounded. They were on twenty-four hour watch, so Stephen must suspect that Robert would arrive. That was good, for then Stephen would not be thinking about a possible escape. Matilda relaxed and allowed herself to breathe.

Matilda leaned against a tree and rested. It was a long trek to Abingdon Abbey, made longer by the weather and the chance of discovery. She thought it could be the most difficult six miles she would ever have to travel.

Matilda brushed away the snow that clung to the bark of a giant oak tree. She wanted to see color — any color but white. It cheered her to see the dark brown wood. She traced nature's pattern in the bark. At last, something of substance. She was so tired of soft snow. Matilda looked toward the sky. The branches of the leafless trees criss-crossed the sky like cracks in an old pane of glass.

Brian pulled on her sleeve and she had to leave her tree. The quartet walked silently through the forest. Although the snow was not as deep, they were in more danger from Stephen's army camped nearby. Matilda could easily see her compatriots as they moved past the huge trees. Matilda stopped, cupping her hand behind her ear, listening.

"What is wrong?" John whispered.

"I thought I heard a twig crack."

John raised his hand and signaled the others to stop. The four white figures stood like Biblical salt pillars, listening to the sounds of trumpets, shouts from the army, and the branches squeaking as they rubbed against each other in the wind. Finally, Miles motioned them to continue.

Matilda felt uneasy, but she tried to suppress her instincts by telling herself that nerves were making her imagine things. It took all her will power not to scream when a man stepped from behind a tree into her path. She knew by his colors that he was with Stephen. Brian, Miles, and John stopped beside her. The only sound was the wind as the five weary people stared at each other. Matilda had her dagger, but it would be useless against an armored knight.

The others were not in armor, and they carried no weapons save daggers like hers. She was afraid to move, for fear the sound would carry to other soldiers who were close. Apparently, the others had thought the same thing.

The knight bowed to Matilda. "My lady. I am blessed by your presence. How glad I am that you escaped. I was in court the day you proved a crippled man could not have made an attempt against your life. I was impressed by your abilities. If it were not for my loyalty to my father, I would have been with your army." The knight took Matilda's gloved hand and kissed it. "Go quickly and God bless you."

The knight stepped aside and waited for Matilda to pass. He turned to Miles. "If you are traveling south, stay away from the river, for the army is camped near it for its water. Go quickly before Stephen's hunting party finds you."

Matilda swallowed the lump in her throat and saluted the knight before moving more quickly through the forest. It would be good to get to Abingdon where horses would be waiting for them. It would be even better to arrive at Brian's Castle Wallingford, recaptured from Stephen's forces. They would be safe for the first time in months. Matilda watched a trail of frosted breath leave her mouth, and she hated the whiteness of it because it was without warmth.

Stephen's mouth dropped open. He waved a parchment above his head; the four seals that were attached by strips of skin to the parchment danced like court clowns. "What is the meaning of this communique?" His bellowing voice hurt his own ears. "I sit here in a freezing tent waiting for the Empress to give herself up, and I discover that she has escaped. I find that ludicrous. How long has she been gone? One hour, one day? No more than two days, I imagine. What does this mean?" Stephen held the vellum above his head and shook it.

"I do not know, sire. I was told by another messenger that it is from Empress Matilda and was to be given to you and to you alone."

"When I find out which incompetent fools let her escape, the price they pay will be high. The war was almost over, but now, without the prize, it will rage on." Stephen threw the parchment to the ground. He turned to William of Ypes. "See to it that the people in the castle are given the chance to leave if they wish, but take Oxford. We will get that much, at least." He waved his visitors away.

"Yes, your majesty." William of Ypes followed the messenger out the tent flap, letting it drop behind him.

Stephen stood at the door of the tent, holding back the flap. He wished he could hate Matilda, but if the truth were told, he loved her. He had betrayed her, and it was the worst mistake he had made. He had wanted to capture her, to bring her down. At first, he had wanted to treat her like he had been treated by her. Now, he wanted to have her caged so he could make her love him. He had spurned the wrong woman. If he had captured Matilda, he might have found a way for them to rule together. Maithilde could have met with an unfortunate accident.

Stephen looked to the south and laughed. "When we meet again, I must compliment you on a daring and clever escape, Matti. Alas, all of England will suffer for your ingenuity. How sad that fate could not have made us a match. We would have been excellent together." Stephen saluted toward the south. "May your Christmas be merry. Enjoy the gift of freedom." Stephen let the tent flap drop, shutting out the sunshine that shone off silver-colored snow. He was alone.

CHAPTER
XVIII

ORE HOT WATER, PLEASE." Matilda slid further down into the tub, letting the steam wet her forehead. She watched her hair swirl, making ebony bracelets around the bubbles as more water was poured into the bath. "I never want to be cold again."

"Yes, my lady." The servant added more cloves to the water and stepped back to await her lady's commands.

Matilda held up an arm and smiled at its pinkness. She would hate anything white from this day forth. The white robe had already been burned in the fireplace, although, because it was so wet, it steamed for more than an hour before the flames finally overcame it. She laid her head against the edge of the tub, resting it on a folded cloth, and closed her eyes. The sounds of the servant's footsteps faded as she fell asleep. Dreams of summer floated through Matilda's mind, and she was a young girl again running after her brothers, Richard, William and Robert, laughing as they teased her. The colors of summer faded, and she was running through a white fog trying to find someone, anyone, even Stephen. Matilda felt she had been running for years and yet she could not tell how far away the beginning was from the end. She was on the inside of a colorless world and could find no way out. The world began to shake and at last she heard a voice.

The servant shook Matilda's shoulder. "My lady, you must awaken. Sir Brian fitzCount has news for you."

Matilda's eyes opened, and she was confused. She sat up and reached for a linen drying cloth. "What did you say?"

"Sir Brian wants to meet with you immediately. He has news for you."

Matilda stood and wrapped the linen cloth around her. As the servant dried her back, she squeezed the water from her hair. "What has happened?"

"I know nothing, my lady."

"All right." Matilda stepped from the tub onto the folded, white cloth that covered the floor reeds. She looked down at the cloth. "From now on, make certain that every piece of material that comes into my chamber has been dyed a color — any color will do."

The servant looked at Matilda and seeing that she was serious, said, "Yes, my lady."

Matilda walked across the great hall to one of the three fireplaces. She had told Brian to meet with her here because she was anxious to see the decorations for Christmas that was only two days away. The boughs of greenery were draped above the stone hoods of each fireplace. Circles of pine boughs were hung on the walls at regular intervals, and bright ribbons had been tied to them. The great hall smelled like the woods. Even the floor had been covered with pine boughs. Matilda liked the effect although the boughs were rougher to walk on than the reeds. The aromas that came from the nearby kitchen whetted Matilda's appetite, much to her surprise. She was about to check with the cook on the preparations for the Christmas banquet, when she saw Brian coming toward her. She noted that his step was light and he was smiling. "Good news, Brian?"

"The best, Matti. As you know, after Robert's difficult crossing to Normandy last June, he and your husband were able to take more than ten castles from the enemy these last six months. Having completed that mission, Robert was on his way back to England to rescue you from Oxford Castle. He has recently landed with fifty-four ships at Wareham, which, as you remember, had been taken from his son by Stephen. Robert has re-captured that castle. He also has captured Lulworth and Portland castles. Miles of Gloucester was able to intercept Robert to tell him that you are here." Brian took her hands. "The best is yet to come."

"Is Robert here?"

Brian turned and pointed toward the archway behind him. "Of course."

Robert came through the doorway. "He looks more like my father every time I see him," Matilda said.

Robert's black hair was streaked with silver at the temples, and there were tiny lines around his eyes. She watched a young boy step from behind him, a miniature version of Robert, with broad shoulders, and a long stride, but with auburn hair. She stared at the youth and let out a cry.

Gathering her skirts, she ran across the great hall. "Henry! Oh, my son. Is it you or merely a mother's dream that I see?"

Henry opened his arms and ran toward his mother. "It is I, mother. I have come to help you."

Matilda wrapped her arms around Henry, surprised at how hard his muscles felt. She loved the smell of his skin and hair, and she kissed the top of his head. She held him tightly, but was not able to hold enough of him. "How I have missed you these last two years. I have an ache in my heart for you and your brothers." She felt his arms about her and she could not stop crying. The only person missing from this joyous occasion was Geoffrey. Matilda said a silent thank you to her husband who seemed to have understood her needs perfectly.

"Mother, my hair is getting wet from your tears. I have been told that you never cry." Henry patted her awkwardly on the shoulder.

Matilda pulled away from her son and looked at him. "I seldom cry. I can not remember the last time I cried, but to see you in front of me is more than my heart can bear. You are the reason for my existence. What mother would not cry for a son she has not seen for two years? Show me a mother who could not cry, and I will show you a mother with no heart."

"Are we winning?" Henry asked.

Matilda smiled. "Sometimes we are and sometimes we are not. It is difficult to decide. Come, let us go to the apartment so that we may catch up on the news. You must tell me of your brothers."

Matilda turned to Robert and took his hand. "Thank you seems not enough to say, but I am at a loss."

Robert put his arm around her waist. Matilda, in turn, put one arm around Robert's waist and one around Henry's waist. Matilda squeezed Henry. "You are getting tall. I can barely see over your head."

"I am also strong, mother. I am going to be a good warrior."

Robert looked around Matilda toward Henry. "He tells the truth, Matti. He is already an expert with the bow. His strategies in war games are quite good, too."

Brian walked beside Henry. "If he is anything like his ancestors, then he will be a fine king for England."

Matilda smiled. "He will be wonderful. I can feel it in my heart."

"Is that why you fight so hard?" Brian asked.

"That is one reason."

Brian and Robert dropped behind Matilda and her son as they climbed the narrow stone steps to the rooms above. "And the other reasons?" Brian asked.

Matilda walked in silence down the corridor. At the door she turned and looked at the trio. "I think that I fight because of the oaths to my father that were broken. He was too great a king to have that disgrace follow him after death."

"What about you, Mother?"

Matilda waited until Robert opened the door and they had passed through it. She motioned toward the chairs by the fireplace. "You ask a good question, my son." She sat in the one closest to the fireplace and waited for Robert and Brian to seat themselves. She laughed when Henry threw himself onto the sheepskin in front of the fireplace and lay on his stomach with his chin resting on his folded arms.

"I also fight for myself because I was betrayed by Stephen. He will pay for that deception." Matilda turned to Robert. "Enough of this. Tell me of Geoffrey. Is he well?"

Robert thought before he answered. "Geoffrey is well. Still, his concern for Normandy makes him unable to sleep at times. He misses your company — more so, I think, for your fighting ability than anything else."

Matilda's eyebrow raised. "I am not certain that is a compliment. A lady would prefer to be remembered by her husband for reasons other than how well she kills the enemy."

Brian laughed. "You are not an ordinary woman, and you do not behave in an ordinary manner."

"You are right, I suppose," Matilda said. "I would like to have an ordinary Christmas. In two days we will celebrate the birth of the Christ child. Do you think it possible that we could forget the war for a few days and celebrate as we did last Christmas?"

Henry tugged at his mother's kirtle. "Mother, does that mean that I would get a gift in the name of the Child?"

"If you plan to give a gift in the name of the Child, then you will get a gift." Matilda pushed a lock of hair out of Henry's eyes. "You need to see about a hair cut."

"Oh, Mother. I hate to sit still while a servant drops pieces of hair down my back. It sticks and itches worse than the nettles that grow in the fields."

The three adults laughed in chorus. Robert reached down and tousled Henry's hair.

Brian leaned toward Matilda and took her hand. "This is a happier Christmas than last year's, so I will order the entire castle decorated, not just the great hall."

"Your castle is lovely, Brian, but more so with Christmas decorations," Matilda said.

"We will have a wonderful feast. Can you not smell the roasted lamb, the venison, the freshly cured ham? We will have good wine and the best story tellers. We will get the jugglers to come and the dancers. This Christmas will be a good one, Matti, for you."

"Thank you. I have already received an unexpected gift from Robert — my son. The two of you will make this a memorable Christmas."

"Thank not me, but thank Geoffrey, for he felt that Henry would be the best gift he could give you. Geoffrey sent Henry to you as a living reminder to the barons of King Henry's lineage."

Matilda looked at her son who was pushing his finger through the ashes along the edge of the fireplace. She could not believe he was actually at her feet. He had grown and his legs were gangly, sticking out from under his too-short tunic. She smiled as she imagined the difficulty the keeper of the wardrobe must have in clothing Henry properly. Matilda sat back and thought about all the daily tasks that she had missed the last two years. It was the mundane things that kept a mother aware of a child's development, and Matilda was saddened. Had it been worth it?

"Tell me Henry of your brothers. How goes William's studies?"

"He studies more than I, but can not learn as quickly. I help him with Latin, but he is good with geometry and helps me. He sometimes cries for you at night, but I tell him that you will come riding to our castle on Dancer."

"He cries?" Matilda felt like crying, too.

"Not for long. I tell him stories of your battles. I do not let him sleep until he laughs."

"You are a good brother and a wonderful son," Matilda said.

"Sometimes little Geoffrey begs to sleep with us so that he can hear stories of you. He clings to William and the nurse does not like it, but she does nothing. Father allows Geoffrey to sleep with us."

"You watch your brothers well, for I can not." Matilda leaned forward to see what Henry had scratched in the ashes. "What do you write?"

"I am practicing my Latin, for when I return to Anjou, I must please the abbot who instructs me. He says that I have a gift for languages. Do I have a gift?"

"I think you have many gifts. The gift of language is just one. I hope you still remember the German I taught you." Matilda smiled.

"I remember it very well. One of the monks speaks to me nearly every day, telling me German stories that make me laugh. I speak the language of our court, though I find the French pronunciations different from what is written. I find that English is not so difficult." Henry pushed himself onto his elbows and squirmed into a sitting position, crossing his legs in the fashion of ancient scribes. "I do wish I did not have to spend so many hours listening to my teachers. I would rather be hunting and fishing."

Brian and Robert laughed. Robert leaned over and tweaked Henry's ear. "It was the same with me, Henry. Never did the hours crawl more slowly than when the teacher talked of wars long gone, or of men who were but piles of dust in their coffins."

"We survived, as you can see," Brian said.

"I have days when the voice of the teacher puts me to sleep, and my head falls forward on my chest. I have to pretend rather quickly that I am studying the parchment in front of me." Henry tugged on his mother's skirts. "Is it necessary for me to return to Anjou?"

Matilda looked down at her son. "I do not believe so. I think your Uncle Robert would like a companion for his son, who is your age. His name is Roger. Since you will stay, you will have teachers and be taught as much as possible because you will be England's king one day, and a king has to be learned."

Henry sighed. "Is there school everywhere?"

"I am afraid so," Matilda said.

Robert chuckled. "When you get older, you will wish for the simpler days of school. Roger is studying with Master Matthew at Bristol Castle, safe from Stephen's army. Roger likes Master Matthew a great deal. He is a very educated person, a master teacher."

"Will I study the same things?" Henry asked.

Robert nodded. "You have already been taught the manners of the French court, so I am certain that will suffice. However, Roger is studying French, Latin, grammar rhetoric, dialectic, geometry and astronomy."

Henry wrinkled his nose. "All that? Is there time for anything else?"

Brian leaned over and patted Henry on the shoulder. "In the winter in England, there is not much else to do, anyway."

Matilda leaned back in her chair and stretched. She was more content than she had been in months. "Tell me, Robert, where are Miles and John? Are they not to be here for Christmas?"

"They are spying on Stephen's army. I expect them late tonight or tomorrow. I heard from them yesterday. I was told by their messenger that Stephen is to attack my son, Phillip, at Wareham Castle once again. We will not let that happen. We are going to beat Stephen soundly this time," Robert said.

Henry stood and with hands on hips said, "I will help you fight Stephen. I want an army of my own, as well. When may I have one?"

"I know not, Henry." Matilda looked at her young son. "I would think that a few years more of growth would be necessary. I would not mind that in the future you lead an army into a safe battle. Robert, what banner should young Henry carry?"

"Why, Mother, I should carry yours."

Matilda shook her head. "I think not. We should arrange to have you knighted and a banner designed for you. Mayhap you might carry a banner that has the lions of Anjou and the fleur de lis. You will be king and must have your own banner." Matilda turned to Robert. "I wonder what banner our father would have carried had we had them then?"

Robert shrugged. "One that would signify his holdings across the Channel, I suppose."

Matilda stretched her arms above her head. "I feel like the kitchen cats who purr at a touch. As soon as John and Miles get here, this will truly be a good Christmas."

As she walked across the great hall, Matilda looked at the boughs of pine that had been so cheerfully placed about the castle just a week ago. They seemed to droop as did her spirit. She nodded at the servant who opened the door to the outside. She pulled her cloak tightly about her and hurried across the courtyard to the small chapel, anxious to get out of the snow, but not anxious to enter the place of worship. She hesitated at the door, then pushed her way inside, flinching as the wooden door slammed shut.

The chapel was quiet compared to the outside where the banging of a hammer against the anvil had reminded Matilda that life continues, no matter who has died. The thick, stone walls closed out life, but held in death.

Matilda walked slowly up the aisle as she had done countless times in the last few days. She had to force herself to believe what she saw. The bier had been placed in front of the altar. The castle chaplain was lighting fresh candles that had been placed at either end of the altar. Matilda had instructed him to not let the flames be extinguished. When he saw Matilda, he bowed to her. She nodded in acknowledgment, then dropped her gaze to the body on the bier.

Miles of Gloucester was dressed in shiny armor, complete with a new sword. She had had the armorer re-condition an old suit of chain mail, and she had given it to Miles on Christmas Day. She stepped closer to the bier. She imagined she could smell the vinegar in which the chain mail had been soaked to clean it. She reached out and touched the armor. Matilda sobbed at the irony of the lifeless limbs had had held life just a few days ago. Why must all her happiness be destroyed? Had she done so many wrongs in her life that God had chosen to punish her? Was she not allowed joy in her life?

She laid her hand on the cold chest of the body of Miles of Gloucester. His eyes, that had been full of wisdom, were closed. "How could you survive so many wars, help me so much, then die so tragically in a hunting accident? How can God take you from me when I need you most, when England needs you most? You were one of the pillars that supported my father before me, and then me. Here you lie, life's warmth void from your limbs. No longer will you guide and protect me."

Matilda heard a sound behind her. She did not turn. Robert put his hand on the arm that Matilda had placed on Miles. "Let him go, Matilda. You have kept him on this bier for three days. All your prayers will not bring back our dear friend. You have lived with death for many years, so why the refusal to accept this one?"

"Robert, I can accept the death of a father who has lived a long and wonderful life, and I can accept death on the battlefield, but I find it difficult to allow a hunting accident to take one of my best supporters. Miles was one of the cornerstones of my fight for the throne."

"He can no longer help you. For the sake of his soul, allow him to be buried. You know he will not go to Heaven unless he is buried. Put his soul to rest." Robert pulled Matilda away from Miles. "Let us plan an honorable burial for an honorable knight. Come, you have said enough farewells."

"I am afraid he will not go to Heaven, Robert. Will God accept an excommunicated soul? Bishop Henry has done more to harm Miles by damning his soul than the arrow from Miles' own man." Matilda shuddered.

"Can you believe that a good man would be kept from Heaven because of a false bishop's actions?" Robert put his forefinger under Matilda's chin, tilted it upwards, and looked into her eyes. "Do not you think that God will see the goodness within Miles?"

Matilda blinked. "I have to agree with you. Why would God keep Miles out of Heaven just because the Bishop said a few words and wrote an edict?" She frowned. "I feel blasphemous for thinking such thoughts."

"Do not worry. I have given this much thought. Just because Bishop Henry is our enemy and we are his, does not make us an enemy of God. I am certain God knows this as well. Let us leave Miles to the angels."

Matilda allowed Robert to guide her away from the bier. She looked over her shoulder at the form that had once held life. No more would Miles advise her. Who would be next?

"Matti, the loss of Miles will affect us greatly. I will talk to his men and see if they will join my army to continue our fight."

"I had not thought of the loss of the army." Matilda leaned against Robert as they left the chapel.

Winter was slow in leaving this year, much like the end of the civil war that refused to be resolved. Stephen threw another log in the fireplace to remove the chill from his room. He watched the sparks fly up the chimney, making certain that none flew out onto the floor. He waited, enjoying the warmth and sat down at the table to finish signing another treaty. It was too bad that he had lost Normandy. If Robert had not helped Geoffrey, Normandy would still be his.

Stephen rubbed a pumice stone across the mistake he had made, erasing it from the vellum. He wished he could erase his enemies as easily. He picked up the pen, dipped it into the ink pot, and re-wrote the word. The scratching of the pen was interrupted by a knock at the door. He did not glance up as a servant opened it. The blast of cool air from the hallway rippled the bottom of Stephen's tunic, and he looked up to see who had interrupted him. He was not happy to see William of Ypes with his customary smirk as he brought bad news.

Stephen tapped the bronze pen against the palm of his hand. "Yes?"

William of Ypes rocked to and fro on the tips of his toes. "I came to report on the army from Anjou that is under the leadership of Prince Henry. It appears the Count of Anjou believed fifty men were enough for his son to lead into battle."

Stephen threw back his head and laughed until tears came to his eyes. "So the huge army that supposedly was coming over from Anjou with Henry fitzEmpress in the lead is no more than fifty?" Stephen wiped the tears away with the back of his hand. "Tell me, William, how old is Henry now?"

William of Ypes frowned. "I do not know, your majesty, but he can not be yet fourteen. I only know that he spent Christmas with Empress Matilda and Robert of Gloucester. We learned Henry was asking for money, none of which was given him, for neither the Empress nor Robert have any funds to spare."

Stephen moved away from the frosted window and, shivering, sat in the chair closest to the fireplace. He stretched his long legs and placed his feet so that the soles of his shoes would get the warmth of the fire. "He amuses me. I must say that he has the determination of his mother. Whoever could have guessed that he would be allowed to 'invade' this land? We must be careful and watch this young wolf as he grows."

"I find his attacks upon Cricklade and Burtuna irritating even if he did no more than cursory damage," William said.

Stephen tapped the arm of his chair and stared at the tapestry that hung above the fireplace. It was the one that he had given Matilda when she left England to be with Geoffrey so many years ago. She had apparently carried it with her until the time she had to leave London with nothing but the clothes she wore. In spite of all she had done to him, he knew that he still loved her. The years would not erase the memories of stolen moments when he and Matilda could exist without the outside world. If things had been different . . .

Stephen looked back at William. If he had not valued William's expertise, he would have sent him back to Flanders long ago, more to irritate his wife than for any other reason. Stephen hated to have to rely on the man who cuckolded him. Stephen had one thing in which he could take pride. He and Matilda had produced an heir worthy of both of them.

"William, do you not find young Henry fascinating? I do."

"Then you will be interested to know that Henry has requested an audience with you. He stands in the corridor, scowling. Of course, you do not wish to waste your time talking with Henry."

"But I do. I wish very much to talk with the lad, and in private. Send him in on your way out." Stephen smiled at the ease in which he had put William in a servant's position.

"I do not think it is a . . ."

"I did not ask you what you thought, did I?" Stephen dismissed William of Ypes with a frown. William bowed and backed toward the door. He opened the door and called out, "Henry, you may enter."

Stephen's left eyebrow raised as Henry advanced too close to him for comfort. For one moment, he thought that mayhap the young man had been sent to assassinate him, and he was sorry he had sent William away. He watched the boy study him.

Stephen was taken by Henry's bright blue eyes. "You have the eyes of your mother and your grandfather."

Henry stared at Stephen, his eyes never wavering. "And you have the heart of the devil."

Stephen's mouth dropped open. He shut it quickly to hide his shock, then, as anger gripped him, he felt the heat move up his neck. He fought his anger, one that he seldom allowed anyone to see, and said, "You are just a cub. You have promise, yet you behave as an untrained colt. You act foolish."

Henry folded his arms across his chest. "We will see how foolish I am when I sit on the throne, for I will be on the throne, as my mother should be, instead of you."

"How do you propose to do this? You could not even take two relatively easy castles away from me."

"Unfortunately, the men who followed me insisted on money. I have none," Henry said.

"I see. Yes, money does seem to have replaced loyalty. Loyalty has always been easier to finance, but much more difficult to maintain." Stephen motioned toward the chair opposite him. "Sit down. You must be chilled. I am sure you do not fare well in this cold, spring weather. It is much warmer in Anjou."

"I fare fine, but I will sit."

"Do you know who your father is?" Stephen was startled to hear the question voiced aloud. He had not meant to say the thought that had been buried in his memories.

"Mother says it matters not who the birth father is. The real father is the one who has fed and clothed and trained the son."

Stephen winced. Matilda had taken that away from him as well. He took a deep breath and asked, "Who is your birth father, then?"

"I know that you are, but I choose to forget my mother's indiscretion."

"Ah." Stephen was relieved that Henry had been told, but he wondered why. Mayhap it was because, being somewhat egotistical, he wanted a son who would obviously make him proud. Lord knew that the son, Eustace, would never be a credit to him. The son

Stephen was allowed to claim in public, William, was despicable, somewhat stupid, and too much like his mother and his real father, William of Ypes. Seated in front of him was the boy who would make history, and history would never know Henry's parentage. A piece of glory would be lost to Stephen, but worse, immortality.

Stephen brought himself back to the present. "Do you find it that unpleasant to be the son of a king?"

"To be the son of an usurper is shameful, but to be the great-grandson twice over of William the Conqueror is most pleasing."

"Really? Why is that?" Stephen leaned forward. This boy was interesting.

"First of all, even though you are an usurper, you do control the treasury and thus the country. My parentage allows me to claim the throne in both my mother's name and your name. I find that delightfully distasteful."

Stephen chuckled. "I have to admire your straight-forward answers. You have a pragmatic view of life. You must tell me the purpose of your visit, however, for I can not guess what it might be."

Henry sat as straight as a lance, his hands folded loosely in his lap. "Since I have come to England against Geoffrey of Anjou's wishes, and because I can not gather one penny from mother or Uncle Robert, I have come to you."

"You what?" Stephen nearly lurched from his chair at Henry's statement. Curiosity forced him to refrain from doing so.

"I believe that the money due me was through my mother, and my grandfather, King Henry the First. Since you have squandered the treasury and have taken what is not yours, then you are obliged to give me part of my due. I want money."

"I hardly believe what I hear. You are the son of your mother, after all. May I ask for what you want the money?"

"I need it to take your castles. I mean to fight you until I have wrested the throne from you. I intend to be king."

Stephen wanted to laugh, but could not. This boy seemed to be more of a threat than he had thought possible. "You do not have the army or the experience to take my castles."

"Give me the money and I will gain both. You can not be afraid of me. I am just a 'cub,' as you say."

Stephen chewed on his lower lip. "My other sons have experience as soldiers. Mayhap they would be upset at having you take the throne from me."

Henry's smile was devious. "I understand that Eustace has so many enemies, he most likely will be murdered, and William most likely harkens from the loins of that heathen from Flanders. Would you not prefer me on the throne? I have double the claim of William and am more honorable than Eustace.

Stephen flinched. "You and your mother have had many conversations, it appears." He folded his hands with his index fingers extended, and tapped them against his lower lip. "I shall give you the money to try to take my castles. I do so because I want to see how well you direct a battle, for one should know one's enemies. I do this to see if my son will make a proud father of me."

"I do not see how my expertise in battle can make you proud, since all that I have learned has come from my mother, my uncles, and my other father."

Stephen shook his head. "Mayhap when you are older you will understand the need for sons. Come back in two days and I will have the money for you. In the meantime, might you not join me for a meal?"

"No, thank you. I travel to Gloucester to see my mother. I trust that you will not set up an ambush for me."

"You have the king's protection."

"I fear on two counts, then. Firstly, the king is an usurper, and secondly, the king's protection has been broken at least twice that I have heard. Forgive me if I trust you no further than I could throw a castle stone."

Stephen stood and took Henry by the arm, leading him toward the door. "Do not mistake natural intelligence for experience. You are not yet seasoned. If you were, you would not talk thusly to someone older and wiser than you. Give my fondest regards to your mother."

Stephen opened the door and watched Henry leave. He could not help but feel pride at Henry's straight back and strong legs. His carriage was that of a king, and Stephen knew that the best of Henry's ancestors had culminated in this one person. He should be king, not Eustace. Eustace did not deserve a place on England's throne, but Matilda's son did. Stephen smiled. That time would come, mayhap.

When Henry disappeared down the stone steps, Stephen went back to his apartment. He shut the door and sat by the fireplace. Looking at the tapestry that had belonged to Matilda, he smiled at his memories.

The winter of Miles' death had passed without Matilda's remembering it. She walked across the courtyard and looked at the apple trees. She wondered when the leaves had yellowed and dropped from the branches. In fact, she wondered when the flowers had burst from the leafless branches, or when they had turned to apples. She felt as if she were coming out of a long sleep. There had been small battles won and lost, but nothing significant on either side. There had been nothing to cheer her. Maybe she would be melancholy the rest of her life. It was a tremendous blow to her campaign to have lost Miles, but she felt the blow on a personal level even more. Miles had been her father's advisor. With the death of Miles, she had lost the last person of her father's generation, and thus, she had lost the last vestige of King Henry's time.

Likewise, when her son had worried her to death with his forays against Stephen, she had emerged from her stupor for only short periods of time. She remembered laughing once, when Henry recounted his meeting with Stephen. The remainder of the time had been spent simply existing.

Matilda found herself at the chapel door. She opened the door slowly, watching the sunlight split the shadows before her. A few dried leaves tripped through the sunshine into the darkness of the chapel. Matilda entered, glad to be alone. At least here, she would be left with her thoughts. There would be no interruptions save for an assault from Stephen. There had been no direct attacks for many months. Mayhap Stephen had run out of energy, too.

The softness of Matilda's step did not alert a field mouse, and she was almost on it before they saw each other. Matilda laughed at its surprised squeak before it ran under the altar, and she pondered whether or not it was proper to laugh in God's house.

She knelt before the altar, prayed for all who had died for her, then rose. Like the last ten months, her prayers had been the same each day, and she had no memory of them. She hoped God would understand.

The noise of the courtyard was deafening as Matilda came out of the chapel. The hunters were getting ready to ride out for an afternoon hunt, and the knights had just returned from a ride around the perimeter checking security. The geese were squawking, goats were bleating, and dogs were barking while there were shouts from the servants to each other. The noise seemed to be worse than usual, but Matilda thought that she should be glad she was aware of her surroundings.

She was at the door to her apartment when she heard Ella's voice. Matilda waited, her hand on the latch, while Ella caught up with her.

"My lady, you must come quickly to Robert's apartment. Remember that he said he felt ill only two days ago? You had him stay in. He has become much worse. You must go to him."

Ella held up the chest of medicines that Matilda always used. "I was on my way to Robert to ready the medicines for you. It is fortunate that I found you."

Matilda grabbed Ella's arm. She did not like the look of anguish on her lady-in-waiting's face. "What are his symptoms?" She did not wait for an answer, but ran down the hall to the apartment next to hers.

When Matilda opened the door to Robert's chambers, she was unprepared for the smell of sickness coming from the room. She hurried across the room and stood next to Robert. His breathing was ragged and shallow. Sweat-soaked hair was plastered against sallow skin. When Matilda glanced at his prone body under the sheet, she was astonished at his frailness. He had been all right a week ago.

Matilda pulled a stool close to the bed and sat down. She motioned for Ella to place the medicine chest at her feet. For the next hour, she tried everything to bring down Robert's fever, but she failed. Twice, he called out as if he were in battle, and she grimaced at his painful dreams. If she could not break the fever within the next few minutes, she would have to get the chirurgeon. More often than not, the chirurgeon presided over a death bed rather than a recovering patient.

Matilda waited as long as she dared, then gave up. She had to admit that she needed help. "Ella, send for the court chirurgeon, and hurry! I have nursed many a soldier, but none as ill as Robert."

Matilda wrung out a linen cloth in cool water and placed it across Robert's forehead and pulled the soaked sheets down to his waist. She squeezed a second cloth until the water no longer dripped. Matilda bathed Robert's chest, stopping only when a wracking cough shook his body. She bathed his arms, the smell of medicine so strong that it stung her nose and eyes. With a feeling of hopelessness, she sat back on the stool. She laid her head on the bed next to him, longing to hear his voice.

A hand on her head caused her to lift her face, and she let out a cry. "Robert, you have awakened. How glad the sight of your eyes makes my heart."

Robert's hand dropped next to his body and lay there, without strength. "Matti, I can not live. I have already seen Heaven, and I have only returned to tell you farewell."

Matilda grabbed Robert's hand and held it to her cheek. It felt hot and dry, like the hidden, ancient dust that she had found in the corners of the chapels when she was a child. "Do not talk thus. I forbid it."

"You can not forbid Death to enter this chamber and take my soul."

Matilda turned to the trio of servants who hovered near the end of the bed. She did not know they had entered. They irritated her, hovering over Robert like vultures. She snapped at them, seeing the surprise in their eyes at her anger. All she wanted to do was be rid of them. "Where is that chirurgeon? Go forth and find him or I will have you whipped. Do not come back without him. Go!"

The servants, shock in their eyes, scurried out of the apartment. Matilda watched them go. She would be nicer to them later. Matilda dipped her hand into the cool water and squeezed water out of another cloth. "Robert, without you I have no one to help me. Henry will not be able to become king without you. Please, do not leave us."

Robert winced when the cloth was applied to his head. "You want Henry to be king. What happened to Matilda being king?"

"I was king for almost a year, but time has taken Miles, and time has taken my strength. I fight for Henry."

"He will be king. The angels told me so." Robert closed his eyes.

Matilda lifted Robert's head from the pile of pillows to wipe the back of his neck. The pillows were soaked with fevered sweat. "Robert?" she whispered.

"I am still here."

"I have sent for the chirurgeon."

"You are better than any chirurgeon I have ever seen." Robert's voice cracked, and he suffered a spasm of coughing.

Matilda helped him to sit, but could do nothing else. While she was holding him, the door opened and the court chirurgeon walked quickly across the room to the bed. He put his chest of medicines on the floor and took out a jar of salve. Opening the lid, he dipped in his fingers, took the smelly, dark ointment, and smeared it on Robert's chest and throat.

"What is wrong with him?" Matilda asked.

"I fear it is what many have died of already this month." The chirurgeon looked into Matilda's eyes. "I must tell you that none have lived. If the coughing does not fill up their insides and drown them, then the fever kills them. I can do nothing, but smear this salve about and pray. I feel worthless."

Matilda closed her eyes and shook her head. "I can not lose my brother. He has been my protector since I was born."

Robert opened his eyes. "Matti, do not ride so fast or you will cause the horse to become winded and die. There, that is better, child. Watch out! If you jerk the reins, then the horse's mouth becomes raw. You must be more patient."

"Why does he talk from the past?" Matilda asked, but she knew the answer. She leaned closer to Robert. His eyes were open, but unseeing. She pushed his hair back from his face and saw the small scar she had caused. She smiled at the memory of the game of chase in which she had scurried beneath the bushes only to have Robert crawl in after her and run into a broken branch. He was her first patient. How odd to remember that now. She smiled at him.

Robert's eyes closed and he coughed. The last rattle escaped from his lungs, and Robert of Gloucester was dead.

Matilda laid down her head, and holding Robert's hand, cried and prayed for his soul.

The sun was setting and the streaks of orange and pink across the sky were cut by slashes of black from the branches of the barren trees as Matilda walked along the top of the outer curtain wall. Robert had died the last day of October, his favorite month, and had been buried in November, the month that always depressed him, so he had told Matilda. There had been better falls, but none worse. Robert's death left Matilda with a gaping hole in her heart, her life, and her quest for the throne. The void was bottomless.

"My lady, come quickly." Ella ran along the top of the wall. She stopped when she got to Matilda, took one great breath and gasped, "It is a second time within a week I have had to come to you with distressing news. We need you in Brian's apartments."

"Has Stephen dared attack us now? Does he think that without Robert I shall be weak?" Matilda turned and walked back toward Brian's quarters.

"It is not that. The chirurgeon has sent for you. He is with Brian fitzCount." Ella's face was white with fear, but her cheeks were flushed from running.

"No! Do not tell me Brian has the same illness as Robert." Matilda ran along the top of the wall, ignoring the stones that pushed through her thin shoes and bruised her feet. She did not stop running until she had flung open the door to Brian's apartment and was kneeling next to him on the bed. She looked first at the chirurgeon, who shook his head, sadness brimming from his eyes, then she looked at Brian.

"The man of medicine has told me that I have what killed Robert. There is not much hope. It is a matter of hours, for I have not the stamina of your brother."

"Has God no mercy? How can one, two, then three of my dearest friends and strongest supporters be taken from me?" Matilda leaned over and kissed Brian's cheek. She knew he was going to die. Everyone else had died. She saw a pit in her life that threatened to get larger until it swallowed everything she loved and needed.

"We have done what was necessary for England. We will be vindicated." Brian's next words were interrupted by spasms as coughing shook his entire frame. It was then that Matilda noticed he had lost much weight. He looked just like Robert had.

"How could I have not known you were sick, Brian?" Matilda felt the guilt surge through her.

"You were grieving over Robert, as I was. How could your mind know about anything else?" Brian looked at the chirurgeon.

"You can do nothing for me. Please leave us alone. Take Ella and the servants with you."

The chirurgeon nodded, closed his medicine chest, and led the entourage out of the apartment.

"My mind refuses to believe that you are in danger of losing your life." Matilda noticed Brian's skin was pale and his freckles were more red than brown. His hair was lifeless as if a prelude to death.

"I wanted to confess something to you that I have kept secret for many years." Brian coughed again, then gasped for air.

Matilda placed her fingers on his lips. "Do not talk."

"Listen to me." Brian turned his eyes toward Matilda. "I have loved you from the moment I saw you at King Henry's Christmas court the first year you returned from Germany. I have sworn an allegiance to you based on passion."

"You, Brian? You never let me know. Why did you wait until now to tell me?" Matilda whispered.

"You loved Stephen. I could see it in your eyes. I could tell that Stephen loved you. I could not interfere with a force so strong. Even after all these years, I think you still love Stephen." Brian closed his eyes from exhaustion.

"How wrong I was. I do not love Stephen as I thought. I only loved what might have been." Matilda took Brian's hand. "I have been unlucky in love because of my ignorance. When a good man like you, Brian, came along, I did not recognize his love, only his generous spirit. How lucky your late wife was and how stupid I have been."

"No, you were not stupid, Matti. You had a purpose in life and that was for the one love in your life."

"Who?"

"Your son, Prince Henry."

"Ah, yes. My son, my life, my heir in all things." Matilda looked out the window. The sky was stone grey and colorless, the sun having set and night not quite settled in. When she looked back at Brian, he was lifeless.

The cold wind ruffled Prince Henry's hair, but he did not care. He sat astride his horse, staring at history. His mother had agreed to his meeting with King Stephen, but she was not happy about it. Stephen was an old man now. Prince Henry was twenty, in the best years of his life, and he meant to be king. His mother had sacrificed for years to this end. He was old enough to finish the task that she had begun. In her quest for the throne, first for herself, then for him, she had watched Miles, Robert, and Brian die. She had suffered loss, victory, more loss. He would take up where she had left off. He would be king — for his mother, King Matilda.

Prince Henry, Duke of Normandy through his mother's lineage, and the Count of Anjou through Geoffrey's lineage, looked across the River Test at the walls that surrounded his ancestral castle. The plainly cut, but powerful stones that formed the towers rose above the outer curtain walls. His mother had always told him how the Norman architecture had given her strength, and now he understood why. He patted his horse, a gift from his mother. She had insisted that it would be good luck to call him 'Dancer' after another powerful war horse that had served her well.

Henry shivered and pulled his sable-lined cape tighter about his shoulders. The dull, grey rain had changed to dull, white spittle of snow. The ground was beginning to hide under the snowy droplets. Henry was not certain that Stephen would answer his messenger. He smiled at the memory of their last meeting more than six years ago when he had been an arrogant child of thirteen. If the recollection had not been so amusing to Henry, it would have been embarrassing. Henry had done what he had promised. So far he had taken back Castles Bristol and Gloucester, the latter being particularly sweet to him for both his mother's sake and for his Uncle Robert's memory.

Crowmarsh was under his siege and would fall within a month. Henry had followed his mother's advice and crossed the Channel in the dead of winter because such a move would be unexpected by Stephen and his forces. What Henry had accomplished had been done with fewer than twelve hundred knights and foot soldiers. He would take Stephen's castles one by one.

Dancer's ears pricked forward and he pawed the ground. Henry looked toward the gates to Winchester City and watched them open. Stephen rode out of the gates, but stopped at the bridge. He raised his arm. "Hail, my son. I have come in person to invite you to my humble castle."

Henry raised his own arm in salute. "I come, but not alone. I have a few of my men with me."

"They are welcome. Enter my city, and we shall discuss that which is most important to you. I have prepared a small meal for us. Do me the honor of dining with me now."

"It will be my pleasure." Henry motioned for the five men who accompanied him to move forward. They rode across the bridge, the hoofs of their horses dictating a joyful cadence as they moved toward Winchester's gate. Silently they rode through the snowy streets still scarred from the war waged between his mother and cousin Henry, the Bishop of Winchester.

Henry was escorted by King Stephen on his right. Occasionally, Henry saw a shopkeeper looking out a door, but for the most part, the streets were empty. Henry smiled, for he knew that his reputation had come before him, and when he and his men had appeared on the horizon, the good citizens had expected the worst.

Dinner was excellent. Henry felt fuller than he had for many weeks. He leaned back against the wall behind him, the rough stones cool against his back. He searched Stephen's face for a clue as to his thoughts. Seeing no hint, Henry waited. He was used to waiting and had endless patience. The talk at dinner was of ordinary things and had done nothing to reveal Stephen's intentions.

Stephen put down his knife and folded his arms that he rested on the table. "How is your mother?"

Henry was startled at the question. It seemed to be delivered with more than merely politeness. He recovered and answered, "She is a remarkable woman, and is quite well. She has been one of my most astute advisors, and I find her counsel invaluable."

Stephen looked down at his plate. "Does she speak of me?"

Henry smiled. "In terms that I am too much a gentleman to repeat."

Stephen coughed. "Am I to understand that time has not healed any wounds?"

"My mother is much too stubborn to change her mind about anything, especially you, who took so much from her." Henry saw that Stephen had aged more than his mother in the last few years. Stephen was still a handsome man, however, and a formidable foe. It would be best for war-weary England to negotiate. Matilda had told him what to expect, what to ask for, and what to insist upon. Henry knew he would enjoy taking from his natural father what had been his mother's by birth right. It would be a most pleasant encounter.

Stephen sighed. "Let us begin our negotiations in private. Then, when we have decided what each of us will accept, we will meet before the council and have the scribes write it. I know what you demand."

Henry leaned forward, placing his arms on the table, putting him close to Stephen. "That which is rightfully mine is all that I demand."

Stephen held his ground. "You still speak the same as you did at thirteen."

Henry laughed. "The difference is that now I have the men and experience to back up my threats."

"True." Stephen paused. "I am tired of the fighting. I am tired of Eustace raging around England on a personal quest, tormenting my people. I am tired of living. I never thought I would wish for my wife to return to the living, but since her death, I have no reason to fight. I am ready to discuss your proposition."

"It is a simple one. I want the throne."

"I do not wish to be deposed. I like power."

"Obviously."

"I wish to rule until my death, which is not far off," Stephen said.

"You look healthy to me, and I do not plan to have you assassinated. Are you expecting to lead your men into battle?" Henry picked up a pewter chalice and took a drink of warm mead, the thick sweetness of it giving him energy.

"No, my body seems old."

"What is there to discuss? I am following the dictate of Empress Matilda, once king of England. I will concede that you may remain king for life, then I shall inherit the throne."

Stephen lifted his chalice. "Shall we toast to our agreement? May you rule with power, kindness, and in health."

Henry raised his chalice. "May you rule in peace and health."

Stephen looked down at the linen table covering. "I have agreed to this for Matilda, to undo the wrong that I have done her and to you, my own son."

Henry said, "Why do you not have feelings for Eustace? He has lived in your castles, clambered about your knees as a baby. Have you not taught him to hunt, and the manners of court? How could you go against your own son?"

"It is difficult to have respect for a man who is so selfish that he would kill his best friend, nay, even his own mother, if it would benefit him. With Eustace on the throne, England would drop further downward into a pit of inequity. No matter what you believe about me, just remember that I have nurtured England. She is the land of my birth, and I love her dearly. I have fought for her, and I took the crown for her. I can not let Eustace tear her asunder."

"I can fight Eustace. I suppose I will have to do so, although I do not relish the idea. I, too, love England and do not wish to see it torn in further civil war."

"Do not worry about Eustace. He will not live past the summer, for he has too many enemies. I, for one, await the news of his death each day. My other son, William, is not interested in the throne. He fears for his life, but for no reason. He is a coward and will most likely hide behind the robes of a priest."

Henry studied the face of his host for a hint of what he meant, but he saw only the face of a statue.

The great hall was cheerful in spite of the snow that fell outside. Henry had slept surprisingly well, and he had bounded out of bed because of his excitement. In just a few minutes, England would be his to inherit by Stephen's decree. He thought of his mother and wished that she could be here, but she had moved to Rouen where he planned to join her and his brothers until Stephen's death. Without her years of struggle, this moment would not have been possible. The war was over.

The trumpeters announced the King's arrival, and Henry stood, showing allegiance to Stephen for the first time in his life.

King Stephen sat at the head of the council table with Henry on his right. A parchment was placed before him. Stephen held it up, one hand holding the unrolled top, the other holding the unfurled bottom. "Stephen, King of England, to the archbishops, bishops, abbots, earls, justiciars, sheriffs, barons, and to all his liegemen of England, greeting."

Henry looked around the table at Stephen's glowering brother, the Bishop of Winchester, and William of Ypes and the other knights and barons who had supported Stephen against Matilda. Other than Stephen's brother, all seemed congenial.

Stephen continued reading the charter he had had prepared late the night before. "Know that I, King Stephen, have established Henry, Duke of Normandy, Prince Henry fitzEmpress, Count of Anjou as my successor in the kingdom of England and have recognized him as my heir by hereditary right." Henry heard the muttering from the onlookers and suppressed a smile. They had always heard rumors of his parentage and now they knew with certainty.

The voice of the king boomed. "Thus I have given and confirmed to him and his heirs the kingdom of England. The Prince, in return for this honor and gift and confirmation that I have made to him, has done homage to me. I have also given an oath of surety to the Prince, that I will guard his life and honor by every means in my power, and that I will maintain him as my son and heir in all things."

EPILOGUE

MATILDA LEANED BACK and let her eyes follow a column from bottom to top where it fanned out against the ceiling like a flower in bloom. With Henry as king, England would bloom, too, after nearly two decades of lying dormant through the fighting.

Ella leaned forward and placed her hand upon Matilda's arm. "Is not Westminster Abbey most beautiful during the season of our Savior's birth?"

"Yes, and more so since it is the coronation of Prince Henry, henceforth to be known as Henry the Second, King of England. He will be the greatest king England will ever have. I know this to be true, for I feel it in my heart."

"Is not his queen, Eleanor of Aquitane, most beautiful? Do you like her?"

"I find her fascinating. She cares not for formality or tradition. She will lead Henry on a merry chase." Matilda looked at her daughter-in-law and mother to her first grandchild, also named Henry, ironically born the same day that Stephen's son, Eustace, had died.

"She has had practice at being queen," Ella said.

Matilda suppressed a laugh. "As Queen of France she horrified people by going with her husband on a crusade and in armor. I think that I like her very much. We shall know each other better, now."

"You shall have an interesting life as advisor to King Henry and as Eleanor's mother-in-law," Ella said.

"I wish that Adelicia could have been here. It saddens me to think that with her last child she drew her last breath. The deaths that I do not care about, nay, even celebrated, were Maithilde's and that of Eustace. I am glad that someone poisoned him; he was himself so poisonous. He plundered the innocent and helped England to ruin. Peace has come at last."

Matilda looked upward at the vaulted ceiling, and her eyes moved to the stained glass windows that towered above them. From the windows she let her eyes wander to the south side of the high altar. Her mother was buried there. Matilda's mother had told her that she was destined for greatness and that she would have to make sacrifices. Her mother had been right, but what she had not told her was that all the heartache, all the fighting, and all the bloodshed would be worth it, not only for her personally, but for England.

Matilda was glad that her son had chosen this place to be crowned. She closed her eyes to stop the tears that threatened to flow down her cheeks. All the years of fighting, the deaths, the starving, had culminated into this one moment.

"Why, Matilda, I see a tear upon your cheek. I rarely have memory of tears from you, except when the men who supported you died. You cried for days when Geoffrey died."

"Yes, for I learned too late he was my truest love," Matilda said.

Ella looked at her hands clasped together in her lap. "And again when Stephen died," she whispered.

Matilda opened her eyes and patted Ella on her hand. "The tears for Stephen were for a love that never was. These tears are for what is to be. These tears have been waiting for years to make their appearance. I shan't keep them waiting any longer."